THE SERPENT'S GIFT

HELEN ELAINE LEE

SCRIBNER PAPERBACK FICTION
Published by Simon & Schuster
NEW YORK LONDON TORONTO SYDNEY TOKYO SINGAPORE

SCRIBNER PAPERPACK FICTION
Simon & Schuster Inc.
Rockefeller Center
1230 Avenue of the Americas
New York, NY 10020

First Scribner Paperback Fiction Edition 1995

Manufactured in the United States of America

1 3 5 7 9 10 8 6 4 2

Library of Congress Cataloging-in-Publication Data
Lee, Helen Elaine.
The serpent's gift/by Helen Elaine Lee.
p. cm.
I. Title.
PS3562.E3535S47 1994
813'.54—dc20 93-27450
CIP
ISBN 0-689-12193-8
ISBN 0-684-80160-4 (Pbk)

For my ancestors, who passed down the spirit of the quest and gave me their stories as guides.

And especially for my mother, who, like our cherished errant knight, knows who she is and who she may be if she chooses.

ACKNOWLEDGMENTS

I would like to thank *Callaloo*, in which parts of this book appeared as the story, "Silences," in the Spring of 1990.

I would also like to thank the Corporation of Yaddo, the D.C. Commission on the Arts and Humanities, the MacDowell Colony, and Blue Mountain Center, for their support.

For the various gifts they gave, I thank: Dorothy H. Lee and George E. Lee; George V. Lee; Renée Raymond; Carla R. Du Pree; E. Ethelbert Miller; Henry Louis Gates, Jr.; Claude Summers; Ted-Larry Pebworth; Maria Perez; Paul Butler; Verna Williams; Sharon Malone; Terri Hill; Randy Hertz; Rowan Wilson; Lori Green; Patrick Gerdes; Conrad Duncan; Donna Masini; Teek McNeil; Kathy Elaine Anderson; Jenice View; Odeana Neal; Kamili Anderson; James Williams; Sheila Vaden-Williams; Carolyn Daniels; Jenny Pizer; Doreena Wong; Jennifer Divine; Ebenezer Adewunmi; Freda Guttman; Lisa Tate Jenkins; Jack Stein; Kim Taylor; Linda Gray, Gretchen Franklin and many more of the PDS tribe; Fred Olive; Reggie Allen; Karen Freeman-Wilson; Monica Weed; Sophia Davis; Martha Hoefer; Jill Nelson; Alan Alden Thomas; Mary Joan Woods, Luba Berton and Suzanne Rose of "The Mafia" book club; the D.C. girls; Marilyn Buck, for the incomparable experience of reading at the D.C. Jail; Jay Cooper; Josephine H. Love; Grace Poore; Debra Katz; Debbie Morris; Mary Farmer and Lammas Women's Books & More; the Washington Project for the Arts; Assata Wright; Walter Mosley; Thomas Sayers Ellis and the Dark Room Collective; Faith Hampton Childs; and Lee Goerner.

For their stories, whose echoes they have no doubt heard, I thank: the Lee family; Renée Raymond, Diane Chapman, Lisa Chapman, Danny Chapman and Angelle Chapman Ivy; Teek McNeil; Mary Ella McNeil; Lois Jones; Tom Mason; Sara Anderson; Clara Seley; Alice Norris; Pat Gorman; and Ralph Gardner.

And my deepest thanks to Andrew, who listened, trusted, and provided.

I have slept the dreams of the stone that never dreams
and deep among the dreams of years like stones
have heard the singing of my imprisoned blood,
with a premonition of light the sea sang,
and one by one the barriers give way,
all of the gates have fallen to decay,
the sun has forced an entrance through my forehead,
has opened my eyelids at last that were kept closed,
unfastened my being of its swaddling clothes,
has rooted me out of my self, and separated
me from my animal sleep   centuries of stone
and the magic of reflections resurrects
willow of crystal, a poplar of water,
a pillar of fountain by the wind drawn over,
tree that is firmly-rooted and that dances,
turning course of a river that goes curving,
advances and retreats, goes roundabout,
arriving forever:

From Sun Stone, *Octavio Paz*

I

He wanted Sonny to leave the shoreline
and strike out for deep water.
He was Sonny's witness that deep water
and drowning were not the same
thing—he had been there and he knew.

From "Sonny's Blues," James Baldwin

1

It was the single misstep that Vesta Smalls believed in. That slight lapse in judgment or balance that could send you hurtling through the air.

Her father had given her this, and she held on to it, sensing that it gave her a certain edge on things, understanding the power of the small deed to rip the sky apart, and return it to seamless blue.

Ontario Smalls had risen from sitting to squatting, untucking one leg and raising it up, and then the other, balancing with his arms and hands, and reached for a grimy corner of glass. He had widened the distance between his feet a fraction of an inch, redistributing his weight on the wooden planks of his scaffold, and stretched to wipe away the last bit of dirt along the window's edge.

And then, somehow, his feet had gotten reckless, and the scaffold swayed. As he tried to steady himself, he lost his footing and in a blur, an arc of blue, he was hanging over the street, upside-down, his foot tangled in the side rope.

The people below stopped and looked up at the curious figure of a colored man dangling, feet in the air, five stories up, and for a stretched-out instant, everything froze. Sound and motion were suspended as shoppers and office clerks looked up.

Ontario heard only the creaking of the rope that held him and saw a cloudless sky spread out above. He looked over at his window-washing partner, Ross T. Ross, who sat on his scaffold staring, his mouth O-shaped, and then Ontario swung his body forward, reaching for the rope. And he almost caught it. Almost. As the wooden seat crashed into the window, scattering broken glass, his foot pulled free and he ripped the silence open with a cry.

The spectators followed him to earth, their heads moving downward in unison. But as soon as he had fallen, things resumed, and the onlookers, each on his way somewhere or other, each with his own destination and task, moved on.

2

Vesta reached for the bottle of aged brandy, armed against excess with two firm rules. She never had a drink without a reason, and she drank only the best.

Today, she had one excellent reason and one that, if less compelling, was often invoked. It was her seventy-first birthday. And she needed something to soothe her aching joints.

She measured an inch of liquor into the hand-cut crystal glass which she felt lent the activity dignity, and straightening the tatted dresser scarf on her coffee table, she leaned back against the damask-covered couch that had been sealed for decades in plastic.

She smoothed out her white skirt and put the brandy on a coaster, reaching for an orange from the glass bowl on the end table. Resting her head against the back of the couch, eyes closed, she turned the fruit in her hands, reading its glossy pocked skin. "It feels like the color orange," she thought.

As the little twisted button fell off the end and dropped in her lap, she could smell, again, in its sweetness with an edge, that night when she was eight, that night of running, and an open door.

She sank her nails into the springy pulp, piercing the thin lacquer, and remembered waking to the sound of breaking glass, fetching LaRue from his crib and tucking him into the curve of her body to anchor herself with the rhythm of his breathing. She could hear, again, the splintering of each shard.

"No, Ontario. Please." She heard her mother's voice. "Not those . . . Not those."

Vesta knew from the flowery smells that her father was smashing the perfume bottles that he had brought as gifts, that had appeared in his hands like fragile birds. He had saved for the tiny creations of blown colored glass, little by little, from his window-washing and carpentry jobs. Vesta lay curled around LaRue and imagined the breaking of tiny wings.

A few months before, she had stood with her mother at the sink, reciting the verse she had learned that day in school, "Twinkle twinkle little star . . ." and stopped suddenly to stare at the purplish finger-shaped marks on the arms that disappeared again and again into the soapy water. Her mother looked over at her and then straight ahead, scraping hard at a burned pan.

After a long silence, she offered the only thing she had. "He didn't mean it, Vesta. He's crazy when he's drunk."

Vesta stared up at her while she continued. "Your father's a good man," she said. "Now go on the stoop and play." As Vesta walked toward the door, Eula added, "And please don't soil your dress."

With her jacks in the hollow her dress made between her legs, she sat and wondered if her mother had been "bad," and what that meant for parents. She thought about that label on her own little lies . . . back talk . . . and forbidden reachings, and thought that maybe it was like when her mother sent her outside to pick a switch, and she knew she had been wrong and felt ashamed.

Vesta shared her mother's shame, and noticed the tightening that had been taking place around her mouth. And to keep her from an open sense of smallness, they devised a language for what went on.

"Is this a good morning, Mama?"

"Can I get you anything?"

She tried to help by never naming it, by never asking her why. And when he wasn't looking, she watched her father for some clue that he might betray.

He sometimes let her choose the colors for his carved decoys, and bits of cherry or oak for the inlaid landscapes he made on Sundays. He let her sit and watch him as he shaped and painted the pieces of wood with long thin hands that were calloused, yet deft. And Eula would find her staring at the detailed bits of artistry that she was forbidden to touch, which spoke of gentle patience and distilled care. The little things he had taken such effort to reproduce: the curve of a beginning wave or a hint of shadow behind a tree. She stood looking at his work on the decoys with their individual feathers painted on, and longed to touch them. To feel the polished grain of the wood.

She studied her father for a clue, and even though she had never seen him hit her mother, when she closed her eyes at night she saw an entire landscape the color of her mother's bruised arms.

Learning the sounds of nascent violence, Vesta could hear anger in his footsteps . . . the scraping of a chair . . . a falling fork. Her body tightened when she heard him at the door and relaxed only when he slept, and on the nights when there wasn't sleep, she lay awake and heard the little bits of killing that were delivered from his long graceful hands.

"No, Ontario. Please . . ." She tightened her hands around the orange as she heard it again.

The thud against the wall. The perfume. And the sound of her mother swallowing her cries.

Again and again she heard the thud, and then a cry that started to escape but was sucked back in, as her mother ran in and pulled her and LaRue from the room, trailing the covers behind her down the stairs in one hand. As they ran past the bedroom door in stockinged feet Vesta saw him, doubled over on the floor, clutching his crotch. She could see her mother's breasts moving beneath her nightgown as she fumbled with the door. Her hair stood out in clumps, matted with blood.

"Don't you even think about trying to leave me," he called out. "Woman, I'll kill you before I let you go."

They ran down the porch steps in their stockinged feet and turned toward a lighted window of the block they had just integrated. Each sound was a signal that he was close behind. LaRue had begun to cry, and Vesta stumbled as she tried to look back while her mother pulled her along by the arm.

They came to a lighted porch and Eula lifted the iron knocker and slammed it down. The door opened and a sliver of light shone through.

"Please my babies he's after me." A telegraphed message for help, where each word costs. But the gray-skinned woman shook her head and said quietly, "I'm sorry, but I can't," pushing the door closed with firm, flat palms.

They stood on the porch for a moment, stunned. Ashamed in some way for the stranger who had just turned them away. And then they moved on to the next light, where Vesta's mother stood, knocking and pleading as the curtain was lifted and lowered.

Looking frantically back the way they had come and then ahead, searching for lighted windows, Eula turned back and forth and then moved on.

They saw the lights go out at one house as they reached the porch, and at the next house and the next, "I'm sorry, but I can't," and there was the image of her mother leaning, leaning, into their closing doors.

None of them could help her as she ran with matted, bleeding hair, holding one wailing child on her hip and pulling the other by the hand, toward their lighted homes.

They ran, then, with no end in mind, moving in order to get somewhere else, and came to a house several blocks away where Eula stood whispering "Please." She looked at the house, trying to remember if she had seen colored over that way.

As they approached, a head peered beneath the yellowed shade, and a woman with golden-brown skin opened the door. "Please," Vesta's mother repeated in a whisper, as the woman motioned for them to enter. "Ruby Staples," she said as she took LaRue from Eula, and she noticed that a wedge-shaped part of one of his eyes was a lighter brown than the rest. Vesta sat on the couch where Ruby had led her, her feet not quite reaching the floor, and looked around at the braided rag rugs and the rich dark wood around the windows. She stared up at the half-moon panel of stained glass at the top and stared at the ceramic bowl of ripe shiny oranges that sat in front of her.

Ruby put her arm around Eula and supported her as she guided her upstairs to wash the blood from her hair and dress her wound, and Vesta heard the baby's crying stop and the sound of running water and quiet voices. She looked at the oranges, mesmerized by their luster and their sharp sweet smell. She knew better than to touch.

When she had gotten Eula to bed, Ruby returned to the living room and Vesta looked up at her face with its strong cheekbones, broad nose, and narrow, slanting eyes, which were the same color as her skin. And then Ruby took a piece of fruit from the bowl, and after pulling apart Vesta's locked fingers with palms so dry and lined they seemed like maps, she placed an orange in Vesta's hands.

Vesta sat in that spot holding her orange while Ruby brought blankets and tucked her in on the couch. She drifted in and out of sleep most of the night, listening for footsteps, and awakened to the biting perfume of her orange, cradled against her chest, then, as it was sixty-three years later.

It visited her often, the memory of that night, triggered by the smell of citrus . . . the finality of a closing door . . .the sound of breaking glass. That night of oranges, where loss and receiving had met. Lined unknown hands and a gift of fruit. Running, and an open door.

When Eula had opened her eyes the next morning, she didn't know where she was. The only thing that existed was the pain that encircled her head. As the overlapping images of the previous night entered the present, her stomach began to burn, and she closed her eyes and was ashamed.

Ashamed for being someone on whom doors closed, and for strangers knowing the underneath part of her life. Ashamed for being the kind of person that violence visits. She slipped her hands under the blanket and covered her breasts.

Ashamed for this unknown, unrecognized, sought-for thing that she didn't quite manage to do right, but that she knew was there.

And ashamed, too, for Ontario, whose actions, through the bond of their marriage, were somehow hers.

She lay on the bed holding herself until Vesta pushed the door open and came over to the bed. Neither one of them spoke, and then

Eula pulled Vesta to her and hid her face from the something resigned that she saw in Vesta's eyes, the something closed. Although she hugged her, Vesta's arms hung limp at her sides. When Eula relaxed her arms, Vesta turned and left, pausing at the door to say, "This is not a good morning." Eula sank back into her pillows and pulled Ruby's quilt around her.

The next morning she struggled to a chair by the window that looked out on the street, and mumbled "What to do . . . I must think of what to do."

Vesta came in and found Eula sitting at the window in Ruby's white cotton nightgown, looking out as if she was studying something. When she came back in the afternoon Eula was in the same spot, and at dusk, she found her still there.

Eula spent that day and the next at that window, asking herself, "What to do," watching the closing of the light. Vesta played with Ruby's daughter, Ouida, and Ruby came and looked in on her during breaks in her work as a seamstress and her washing chores to check the bandage on her head.

Ontario Smalls showed up, three days later, shaved and sober, and Eula refused to see him for nine days running.

He had walked the streets looking for signs of them, watching for colored faces. He had narrowed it down to the Staples house, where he saw Ruby's girl, Ouida, coming and going.

Each time he came, he stood on the stoop with his hat in his hand and his "water hair" brushed down straight with a soaked stiff brush. Each time he asked Ruby, through the glass door, "Is my wife here?"

Ruby Staples stood with her arms folded and replied, each time, as she had been instructed, "Why no, Mr. Smalls. I don't believe she is."

He said, "Thank you," and returned the next day, asking the same question.

Each time Ontario approached the house, Eula sat at the upstairs window and watched him climb the stairs to the stoop and down again, as though she were looking at someone else's life. The tenth time he came, Eula descended from the second floor and brushed past Ruby, touching her forearm. "It's okay, Ruby. I can't stay here forever . . . I have to go home."

She would tell him to come the next day, refusing to hear his explanation because there wasn't one, and then turn and go back upstairs. And they would give back their borrowed clothes, say good-bye to Ruby and Ouida, and follow him down the five blocks to their house.

Ontario reached for a pillow and slipped it behind Eula's back as she sat down, and offered to get her something from the kitchen. He had brought a few groceries and had made tea. And although he was attentive all day, helping her put her feet up and asking what he could do, when dinnertime approached, he sat and read the paper as she got to her feet.

That night would go unspoken, pushed down into memory space with her disgrace, put away in order to move into the opening and not the closing light.

Vesta would have trouble meeting his eyes, but when he called her to sit with him while he worked on a decoy, she found a way to seal off something, to put that part of herself that couldn't sit with him away. She pulled up a stool.

"What do you think, girl? What color should I make the wings?"

She stared at the paints and said softly, "They're all pretty. I'm not sure." She looked at the array of colored oil paints spread out along the back of his worktable, but saw only the whole of them. None by itself.

He bent his head to the side so he could see her face and asked her again, "Which color, girl? I'm letting you choose."

She stared at the table, wanting to say, "Purple. Paint the wings purple and the body pink," but she knew that birds didn't really come in those colors, and so she looked down and said nothing.

Finally, Ontario said, "Well, if you can't choose one, like I'm giving you the chance, we'll just paint it gray. And if you don't want to help me, you don't have to. You can just go on outside and play." She climbed off her stool and went to the Staples house to find Ouida.

Over the next few months, Ontario's vigilant kindness faded into the restrained violence of words, until one day when he came home to a supper pulled together with what was left of the money Eula had stretched thin across the week, figuring in necessary shoe repairs and cleaning supplies. Vesta was on the stoop playing with her jacks, her hands darting under the red ball like brown birds, capturing the metal as it chinked against stone. She stopped and her body tensed as Ontario climbed the stairs and touched her head lightly before going in the front door.

Ontario came through the living room and stood in the kitchen doorway as Eula put a plate of eggs on the table and glanced his way. And he looked and saw not the eggs and cheese and butter that they had, but only the meat that wasn't there. He spread his feet apart and lowered his shoulders, unconsciously, into a fighting stance.

"Hard as I work to provide for you," he said, his face getting red and the vein at his temple distended and throbbing, "is this the best you can goddamn do?" He swept the glass butter dish off the table and across the room as he glared at Eula with his hand raised.

As Vesta tossed the tiny red ball and went to scoop the jacks, she heard the crash of glass inside, and looked up at the closed front door, the sharp points of her tiny jacks cutting into her hand. When she looked back to the street, she saw the red ball bouncing beneath the wheels of a passing car. She stood up to stare at its crushed gray guts, and then pushed the door open and ran toward the kitchen.

Ontario and Eula looked at each other silently for a long time, and then he noticed Vesta standing in the doorway, the little metal stars scattered across the floor. The fear he saw in his daughter's face and in the way she held her small arms tight around herself, the fear he saw of him, made Ontario turn away, snatch a coat from the hook by the door, and leave.

Late that night, Vesta lay facing the wall, her socks on and her shoes arranged just by the bed, when she heard a voice downstairs. She held herself still and listened. Unable to make out the voice, she crept out of bed to her mother's door and pushed it open with her finger just wide enough to see that Eula was in bed, and then she went to the landing of the stairs.

"Green . . ." she thought she heard. "Green . . . Green . . . Green . . ."

She crept midway down the stairs and looked through the railing at her father.

He sat in his overcoat in the middle of the couch with her mother's sewing scissors in one hand and a cooking pot between his legs. There was a nearly empty bottle of cheap scotch on the coffee table in front of him. Vesta held the dowels of the banister and sat still, watching to see what he would do.

First, he drained the last bit of scotch from the bottle, holding it upside down to his mouth even after it was empty, licking the threaded glass rim. And then he slammed it on the table and wiped his face with the back of his sleeve.

Vesta stared, amazed at how hunched over and small he looked. And then she noticed that his face was wet with tears.

He held the scissors up in the air as the tears fell, and then he grabbed a button with his left hand and held it out from his coat.

With his right hand, he hacked at the button, moaning, "Green . . . Green . . . Green," until it fell into the pot at his feet.

Vesta tightened her hands around the bars of the railing. She didn't know what it meant, this "Green," but she knew that she was watching something private, something that was his. Rising quietly, she went back up the stairs to her room.

The next morning, she got up early and straightened his mess. She threw away the empty scotch bottle and put her father's coat and his buttons away, and she helped him off the couch and into bed.

When she got home from school, her father had left for work, and Vesta tried to help her mother around the house, putting things back into the cupboard and icebox behind her, peeling and dicing potatoes for supper. And she checked on LaRue, making sure he wasn't wet or hungry.

She had just finished helping with the dusting when Ross T. Ross knocked. He had stood at the door for several minutes, raising his hand and putting it back into his pocket again and again. When he finally got up the resolve to knock, and gave Eula Smalls the news of

Ontario's death, she sat down right where she was, on the tiled vestibule floor, while he stood in the doorway, stuck between inside and outside, hiding the hands that had knocked and brought the bad news in his pockets as if they were guilty, while he shifted his weight from foot to foot.

Vesta had stood beside her mother and watched her sink to the floor with the news, the news that Ontario Smalls had fallen, undoing the sky for an instant, like a zipper that is opened and closed.

Vesta looked up at Ross T. Ross, waiting for him to either explain what he had said or take it back. When she decided that that was all, that he had nothing else to give, she stepped forward and took hold of the door handle. Ross T. Ross backed slowly through the door, as Vesta said, in her eight-year-old voice, what she imagined her mother would say:

"Thank you, Mr. Ross T. Ross, and do come again."

She put her hand on her mother's back and said, "Mama . . . Mama, come on inside," but unable to get Eula to move or speak, she ran the several blocks to get Ruby Staples, crying, "Come quick. Papa fell and Mama's on the floor." When they got back to Eula, Vesta went to check on LaRue, whom she heard crying upstairs.

As she came downstairs, she remembered going with her mother to ease others into death, delivering macaroni and cheese and baked ham studded with cloves and pineapple chunks. She remembered the house full of people who cried and hugged each other, and brought all kinds of food, and she went into the kitchen, opened the icebox and cupboard, and got out the bread, butter, and strawberry preserves.

Standing at the kitchen table cutting and buttering hunks of bread, she returned again and again to the few words Ross T. Ross had said. "He slipped . . . he slipped and fell . . . there wasn't nothin' else to do for him . . . neck broken . . . broken . . . broken." She buttered furiously, until she had done the whole loaf. Bread slices and crumbs were everywhere. There was butter on the front of her dress and all over her hands. "He slipped and fell," she said to herself. "Mr. Ross T. Ross said he slipped and fell."

Ruby came through the kitchen door as Vesta was adding jam to the bread slices and putting them on a platter. Chunks of wax were mixed in with the jam from where she had broken through the paraffin seal and kept going. Ruby gently took the knife and preserves jar from her and pulled her close as she began to cry. And then she took Vesta into the living room and sat her down next to Eula, whom she had managed to coax onto the couch.

Ruby called the Winters Brothers' Funeral Home and Father Johnson. She called the few family members whom she knew about. And she called the Episcopal church ladies' club, which she asked to pass the information along. The entire time, she stroked Eula's hair.

When she hung up the phone, Ruby moved them upstairs to shield them from the body that she knew would be arriving soon, and began to straighten up.

Vesta took care of her mother, as Ruby had instructed. She sat and patted her as she began to rock back and forth. "He slipped and fell . . . slipped."

To Vesta it just didn't fit. It just didn't. She had seen her father at work with his hands and had once gone along when he had to do a weekend window-washing job. She had watched him move around on his scaffold with grace and control, knowing exactly what his body could and couldn't do. And that's how she knew that he had not been careful. Or at least not careful enough.

"I promise you, my dear Mrs. Smalls, that I will be well and able to dignify your dear husband, positrively, as he was among those gracioused by the pleasures of the living." Leverett Winters took Eula's hand and glided, in long-stretched-out steps, across the room where the coffins were displayed.

He had begun by reciting the Winters Brothers' motto, which everyone knew from the colored newspaper: "Why Not Pass with Class?" And then, with a voice that was measured and sedate, he went on to quote her prices, lowering his voice each time he did so to a gentle caress as he patted her hand.

Ruby had taken her through it all beforehand, imitating Leverett

Winters's elaborate speech and rehearsing Eula's responses with her. And yet, when he paused and looked at her with a subtle expectation of devotion, she made a choice that she wanted to snatch back as it left her mouth. Once it was out, there was no way of stopping what she had set in motion, of saying "No," that she thought she wanted a cheaper model for her dear departed. They had come to the last coffin, and Leverett Winters had stood with his long tapered hands clasped before him, bowing ever so slightly from the waist . . . waiting.

Eula had looked into his eyes and thought she saw glimpses of the night when she had had to run from Ontario. She saw herself fleeing, beaten and bleeding, and the doors that held out slivers of light closing and closing and closing. And for a moment she asked herself "Does he know?" but it didn't really matter, because for Eula, there was no one who didn't know, as she brought the memories, instantaneous flashes of her open shame, to every exchange.

She raised her eyes and declared with them that she had loved Ontario Smalls. That they had been happy. And as she opened her mouth to tell him that she would like the shiny black casket with the elegant satin cushioning and pillow, her gloved hand flew to the scar on her forehead.

As she descended the steps of the funeral home, she couldn't believe she had spent all of her money. "Keep it simple. Remember, *simple,*" Ruby had said. And she had gone and picked, not the most expensive coffin, but a luxury model, nonetheless. At least, she thought, she had gotten everything for the price: flowers, "rich, but quite tasteful," the coffin, and the plot. And people had already started bringing food the night before. The only thing she hadn't figured in was the bill for broken window glass, which was already in the mail, headed her way.

Eula put on her black dress with deliberate care, pushing away all thoughts about her loss and the slim gain that came with it. She focused on the next step of the mourning process, canceling time with the swallowing of each cloth-covered button by each tiny buttonhole.

In the next room, Vesta stood in front of the mirror. Her face seemed to get darker the longer she looked, darker than anyone else in her family, darker even than LaRue. She was used to people looking from her light-skinned mother and reddish father to her and back again, thrown off. They settled, in the end, on her thin nose and lips, wrapping up their sentences with, ". . . but she does have nice features . . ." She was darker than just about everyone she saw at school, church, and visits to her house. Darker. Every now and then, she stopped by a mirror to verify it.

The night before, Vashti Martin had come by the house to drop off a dish of smothered chicken, and had stood talking to Ruby and Eula when Vesta walked in. She had stopped, looking from Vesta to her mother, and asked, "And whose little brown one is this?"

Eula had reached out and smoothed Vesta's hair. "Why this is my Vesta, Vashti. Vesta, sweetheart, say hello."

Vashti had stood silent for a moment and then laughed thinly as she straightened her gloves. "Hello, child . . . But . . . you sure are a grown-up girl."

As Vesta left the room, she heard Vashti lower her voice to say, "Now I know you aren't going to dress that child in black. It would be so serious and well . . . unbecoming. All right, I've said it . . . it would be positively unbecoming. You know they say black people should never wear black."

Vesta stood at the mirror, looking at her face and the high rigid collar of her light blue dress. "I am darker," she said. "I'm even darker than LaRue. She told the truth, I am." She thought about her mother's aquiline nose and fair skin as she reached up and touched her cheek and her short thick braids, then turned her face from the mirror.

After peeking in on LaRue, who was sleeping, she went into her mother's room and helped her with the buttons she couldn't reach.

By the time people began arriving, Eula and Vesta were seated downstairs next to the casket, and Ruby was answering the door.

The house slowly filled, each visitor pausing to talk to Ruby and then entering the living room, where Ontario Smalls was laid out. The first one moved toward the casket, stopping to hug Eula and Vesta. "He lived a good life, honey, and he's with the good Lord now."

She stood at the casket for a moment and shook her head. And then she moved into the dining room and helped herself to little cakes and sandwiches.

The line that passed by Eula, Vesta, and Ontario began to fill the dining room. People stood around talking, "like a party," Vesta thought, and she had never even seen some of them before. She caught snatches of conversation from her seat: "Lost my cousin Franklin Lee last spring . . . pulled right into the printing press, beginning with the arm. Poor man was so destroyed, they had to have a closed casket."

". . . windows . . . dangerous business . . . crippled last April . . . never walk right again . . ."

"Good solid pay, though . . . good and solid."

Vesta could see one woman parked at the dining room table, shoving one sandwich after another into her mouth. Every now and then, she went for coffee or tea, but she kept returning to the food. Two ladies in big broad hats walked by the doorway where she sat:

"It was the fifth story, you say? The fifth story up?" Vesta heard.

"Yes, honey. The fifth story up. Not so far to fall, but 'twas the *way* he come down . . . Neck snapped right in two."

The lace around Vesta's neck felt itchy and stiff. Her house was full of strange people who looked at her as if she didn't belong there. She forced herself to remain seated, focusing on following the swirls of wood grain in the oak floor, and when someone came up and hugged her, she looked past them at their tucks and ruffles, the fabrics they wore, their hair.

She glanced up and saw Leverett Winters coming through the door, bowing and gliding in his lunging steps, and then nodding in satisfaction at the bier and the coffin it held, nodding to Eula as he caught her eye. And then he went for the food table, where he stood eating and patting his vest-covered paunch between delicacies. As Ruby came up to him and asked him if she could get him anything else, he patted his waist:

"Oh noooo, Mrs. Staples. My goodness no. My sufficiency is quite suffonsified."

Ruby stood staring at him and then forced herself to close her mouth and walk away. Hurrying over to Eula in between condolences, she told her what he had said and they laughed, knowing they would be repeating it for years to come. Ruby saw someone coming and slipped away.

Vesta saw Vashti Martin at the door, hugging Ruby. She glanced at her mother, and suddenly felt an itchy spasm from her collar lace. But instead of letting it pass, letting that be the end of it, she gave in, reaching her small hand inside of her collar to scratch. She had no sooner returned her hand to her lap when a stinging itch along her shoulder blade made her jump. And when she twisted her torso, lifting up and then lowering her shoulder, it was all over. It was as if all the itching in her rose up and caught her in a tight hug that sent her shifting desperately in her seat, aiming for the slight rearrangement of a seam that might set it straight.

Eula heard Vesta's shoes knocking against the chair rungs, and turned from a consoling pair of hands to shoot her a disciplinary look.

Vesta stilled herself in mid-itch, one arm wrapped almost around her back, as her eyes met her mother's, and when Eula looked back at the face that belonged to the hands that were holding hers, Vesta slipped from the chair and stood at the coffin.

She looked at her father first from a distance, her fingers locked behind her back, and then stepped closer and stood on her toes to see over the rim, pressing her hands against the polished finish of the wood for a better look. She concentrated for a clue, for something that would make him and his fall make sense to her.

The skin looked thick and stiff, and the hair had been greased down flat, but was pulling away and springing up in places. He lay there in his one suit, all pressed and starched. Altogether, he seemed flatter, she thought, "Ironed. They have ironed my father."

Just as this thought came to her, Eula pulled Vesta's hands from the coffin and caught them in both of hers:

"Look, don't touch," she whispered, squeezing a little bit too tight. "You must remember to look, not touch."

Vesta went to the corner of the room and stood, watching Eula wipe her fingerprints away with her lace handkerchief and return to her seat to arrange herself at an angle, just to one side, her skirts spread out around her. She watched the last light of the afternoon as it came through the front window and fell across her mother, and could see the little bits of dust and lint that were caught in its stream.

Vesta saw that between hugs and handshakes, Eula's hand strayed again and again to her forehead to touch the scar, which seemed to creep out of the hairline like a small snake, working a jagged path toward her left eyebrow. Eula lifted her fingers to her delicate face and played along the raised and knotted scar.

Vesta remembered that night, that night and the days that followed. Ruby bathing and dressing her mother's head, and her father's determined visits . . . turning him away until they could stay no longer and had nowhere else to go . . . returning borrowed clothes, and taking leave. And Ruby removing the dressing, seeing how it would scar, and saying, "Eula, you've got angry healing flesh."

3

Descent and flight haunted them. Bound them. They could not be released. Eula and Vesta saw themselves run from Ontario, saw him fall again and again, and they didn't know any more which had happened first. Broken glass, a drop to earth, and crevices of light. Blood and an offering of fruit, protected in the bend of an arm.

On waking, Eula forced a hollow into the middle of herself to replace the terror of her barren nights. In her dreams there was coming fury and a bitter emptiness, for Ontario was with her, in the threat of return, and in what he had taken from her with his fall.

He was with her, like the serpent on her brow, raised and troubled skin that bound her to the memories she managed to keep away, mostly, in the light.

In Vesta's dreams Ontario had wings that grew, fleshy, from his work-clothed shoulder blades and saved him from his fall as they unfolded, easing him to the ground. But his gentle landing sometimes turned to anger and he cried out savagely for green. Wounded, wounding, with his cry.

Ontario with opened wings and doorways of every color filled her dreams. Entryways with small openings she had to crawl through and guarded portals with handles she couldn't reach. Some were closed and some opened to safety, and some were thresholds to sky so endless she couldn't place herself beneath its dome. Through those she could fall without warning, and she couldn't tell which was which before the crossing. They disappeared on waking, the doorways and the wings, and Vesta could never recapture the brilliant colors of her unremembered dreams.

Ontario visited his wife and daughter with all that he had been and not been, but the blood and the fruit, the single misstep, had all happened before memory for LaRue. His father didn't push the colors from his waking world, nor yet disturb his sleep.

The day after Eula had buried Ontario Smalls, a letter had come from the company whose windows he had been washing when he fell, and Eula had put it aside with the other sympathy cards. A few days later, she had returned to it and was shocked to find that, inside, was a bill for broken glass.

After stuffing the letter into her pocketbook, she began to straighten the hall table, returning the vase and bowl that always sat there to their proper places, touching the flowers to rearrange them just a bit. She brushed the polished wood with her hand to sweep away traces of dust.

She called up to Vesta from the foot of the stairs to watch LaRue while she ran an errand and walked the blocks to Ruby's house in torment. Once she arrived, she couldn't find the words to say what was wrong and sat for an hour drinking tea, unable to tell Ruby why she was there, and unable to leave. Ruby, who could tell that there was trouble, but was trying to let her take her time with saying it, finally asked, "What is it, Eula? You're in a downright state."

Eula took the letter out of her pocketbook and handed it across the kitchen table to Ruby, who read it, gave it back, and then set in, straightaway, to help her clear a path.

By the time Eula went home that evening, she had worked out a plan for how to start the next day. She would begin packing, and by the end of the week, she and her children would move to the basement floor of Ruby's house. Ruby's husband, Polaris, was a Pullman porter who was gone a good bit of the time, and he would be happy for Ruby to have someone there with her. Although there was a door that separated the downstairs from the rest of the house for privacy, they left it open, after all.

The two women agreed that Ruby would help her pay for the broken glass, and Eula would reimburse her in small amounts, as she was able. And they had worked out a manageable, symbolic rent, which would leave Eula's pride intact until she got back on her feet.

That night, after returning home and putting the children to bed, Eula stood in the middle of the living room floor and slowly looked around. She lifted the picture of inlaid wood from the wall and laid it face down on a table. And then she moved across the room, touching the things that made up her living room display.

She picked up the crystal bell she had received as a wedding present, wrapped it carefully in a piece of cloth, and put it aside. And then she looked around for a place for the bill, and settled on the jar that held dried rose petals given her, early on, by Ontario, and saved as a testament to early tenderness. She folded the letter and lifted the lid of the jar, pausing to absorb the memory flashes that the muted scent of flowers brought, feeling a whirl of color that was wide and light-filled. Gripping the table's edge to steady herself, she slipped the letter down into the jar where she would keep it always, and replaced the top.

When they went to Ruby's a week later, they moved light. Eula had cleared out most of the things collected over the years, scraping away the residue of the past. In order to bring in a little money and avoid sorting out the things to be taken and things to be left, Eula decided to sell or hock most of her things. She boxed up ornaments and furniture and sold them to the secondhand dealer and the pawnshop down the street.

When the boxes had been moved to Ruby's flat, Eula assembled the things she had saved. She rubbed the dark cherry wood of her bureau with a soft cloth, and instead of covering its nicks and scratches with the customary dresser scarf, she left it bare. Closing her eyes, she stroked the nicks and grain that told the story of the wood and unpacked the potpourri jar that held the letter. After placing it in the center, she stood back and looked at it, then unwrapped the crystal bell and put it down.

She added a few small things that had meaning for her, alone: a lock of her mother's hair, the wool cap her father had always worn, Vesta's first tooth, and a button from LaRue's christening gown. And she finished with a pine cone, a shell with tiny spots spiraling out from its base, and a smooth stone that she had found as a girl, with which Vesta was never allowed to play.

When she was done, she went upstairs to see Ruby, to offer thanks, again, for opening her door.

Next, Ruby helped her focus on what she could do to earn a living. She remembered that an affluent white woman for whom she had done some sewing had mentioned that she needed someone to come in and wash her hair regularly, and Ruby suggested Eula. This woman gave her name to her friends, and soon Eula had a regular clientele. She and Ruby made special soaps and hair oils on weekends, and Eula took them to her clients' homes when she went to do their hair.

Eula's clients loved their sessions with her, spaces in the week when they admitted to being the centers of their own worlds, when form, for them, was abandoned, and it didn't matter that they paid for it. They didn't have to ask how someone else's day was, or present themselves to be tolerated or ignored.

At first, Eula was shocked at how different they were when alone with her, their talk crude and their limbs open and loose as she ornamented and perfumed them, displaying each curl and twist for maximum pleasure, transforming them for their evening performances. As she prepared them for the parties and the meals made, according to their husbands' pleasures, by someone else, they revealed to Eula their hidden, backstage personas.

And she didn't just do their hair, she listened to them, often with the feeling that once they had started they would go on talking, whether it was her, or a coat rack, standing there, ". . . and I just told her, 'Rebecca, I won't have you ruining my party with all of your chitchat about negative things, going on about everything that's wrong and whatnot . . .' Don't you think that that took nerve? . . . Don't you think it was just . . . just . . . inappropriate?"

Her periodic "Mmn hmmn"s were sufficient to satisfy them, and she soon stopped paying attention altogether, injecting an exclamation whenever she heard a pause. She disconnected, fulfilling her role, and then came home and tried to find some peace.

* * *

The first time Ruby had opened her door to Eula and her children, Polaris had been on a railroad run. When he returned, he agreed that they should let the Smalls family move into the downstairs flat. Ruby couldn't fully explain why it was necessary that she accept this family into their home, and Polaris didn't ask. He knew there was something Ruby carried alone, something that moved her in ways he couldn't comprehend. He knew, from the silence she kept, that it involved some wound, passed from her father on to her.

Although they came to live together like one family in a single house, Eula spent most of her evenings in her flat, alone. She did household chores and offered to take care of extra things so that she wouldn't feel as if she was abusing the kindness of Ruby and Polaris, but after dinner, she retreated to her sitting room while the children played upstairs, and if Vesta sought her out, she leaned her head on the back of her chair and whispered, "Please, I'm resting my eyes."

Despite her initial fascination with the details of privilege, she returned home exhausted from standing all day acting her role, and wanted only to be outside of time and place. Some days it took all her energy not to yank them by the hair, these women who sat before her chattering, chattering on in mock sisterhood, and ask them if they thought she cared about what menus they were planning, or the things they planned to buy.

In the evenings, she sat in the darkness and tried to shed her resentment and fatigue without casualty. Sensing the explosion that slept just beneath her surface calm, she was afraid to release any feelings at all. With nothing left for her children, or at least nothing she thought was good, she sat with her eyes closed and tried to undo her day.

Most of the time she tried not to think of Ontario Smalls, and he began to fade from her waking life. But sometimes she felt lost without him. With him living, she had been someone's wife, and now she was just her, and who was that? She was trying to forget how he had turned his rage on her, while holding on, at the same time, to that piece of the past. Holding on to the proof it gave her that she had been loved hard, that it had had depth, the thing Ontario had felt for her. It seemed better, in the end, than indifference.

She tried to let go of Ontario, mostly, she tried. But he appeared now and again, uninvited, cleaving her peace, and when he did, he was leaving her and he was trapping her, once again.

She fantasized about landscapes, concentrating one day on sand, and the comfort of its vast uninterrupted tone. Or she thought of pale, empty skies and smooth blue ones with stretched-out streaky clouds. Sometimes it was wide water, oceans with no end in sight, and she thought about how she had heard that up in Chicago, the lake was so big you couldn't see the other side. She didn't see herself in her landscapes, just the broad, peaceful expanses of her own making.

Sometimes she crocheted an endless series of scarves that no one ever wore, or read and reread a few Bible passages. If she couldn't escape her memories of Ontario, she went upstairs to be with the rest of her family, and sometimes Ruby came down and they sat together. Ruby, who knew all about the underneath part, to whom she didn't have to speak at all. She went to bed early most nights, not to sleep, but to the privacy of the night.

Vesta and LaRue knew that Eula loved them, but they weren't sure when her love was safe. They might find treats in their lunch bags, or feel her gentle hands tuck them in at night, turning and smoothing their covers and whispering prayers for safety. She might smile at them spontaneously as they came to tell her what they learned in school.

But never knowing when or why, they might strike a vein of bitter, angry ore that ran within her.

When LaRue had reached up and touched her forehead once, Eula had pulled his hand away as if her scar were a fresh wound, painful to the touch. She gripped his hand and slapped him sharply, whispering, "Don't touch!" and then pushed him from her lap, the flash of anger her weapon against remembering.

And there was the time, etched forever in Vesta's mind, when Eula had had to take them with her to a steady client's house. The whole way there she had told Vesta she would have to behave for herself and for LaRue, and make sure he didn't get into any mischief crawling around and putting who knows what in his mouth. When they got to the porch, Eula leaned her face close to Vesta's to say, "Just don't touch anything," and then delivered her final warning, "These are white folks now . . . Don't you go embarrassing me."

A brown-skinned maid had opened the door and showed them to a playroom where Eula could change into the housedress she wore at work and leave her kids. Once Vesta and LaRue had been settled on a blanket spread across the floor, Eula had left the room to get started on her client's hair.

Vesta had played with LaRue quietly until he was asleep and then had gotten up slowly, watching him from the corner of her eye as she looked around the room. She turned in a circle from her place on the blanket, staring at the ornaments and toys. "So this is a white house," she thought, as she examined each thing from the blanket's boundary, her hands out of danger, clasped behind her back. As she looked about the room it had caught her eye: a stereoscope resting on the mantelpiece.

She stepped off the blanket to cross the room, planning only to look, and stood before the strange and wonderful object that seemed as if it belonged to another world. She extended her hand and touched it quickly, withdrawing her fingers as though it might be hot. After staring at it some more, her hand went out again as she gave in to her curiosity and closed her fingers around the forbidden thing.

As she held it up and the slide inside magically became three-dimensional, she gasped, and then she saw Eula across the room, and her mother's fingers closed on her wrist in what seemed like an instant. She could feel the fingernails about to pierce her skin, skin that burned, burned from her grip. Her mouth open and mute, she looked at her mother's eyes and her lips twisted with anger, and it was what she saw there that she could not forget.

She saw that her mother was balanced, with Vesta in her grip, that they stood together at the yawning edge of chaos, known and unknown, and Vesta didn't say a word. There it was, that edge, that edge, and she was going to take her there with her, going to cross it, her mother was, pull her over it, and Vesta didn't say a word. "What did I tell you?" her mother said, with strangulated words, pulling her back to the blanket, "What did I tell you to do?"

"'Look don't touch,'" Vesta whispered. "You told me 'look don't touch.'"

When Eula caught a glimpse of herself in the beveled mirror above the hearth, she dropped Vesta's hand and straightened her body, trying to get control of her breathing. She smoothed the unruly flowers on the front of her housedress and left the room, her fingers on her scar. Vesta stood next to LaRue, her mouth still open and her hands hanging at her sides.

The next day Eula had come into Vesta's room in the morning to kiss her, and Vesta had flinched. Eula stopped short and registered her daughter's fear, and then Vesta tried to make up for it by putting her arms around her mother and kissing her special. But the only thing Eula knew to do with her feelings was to turn her back on them. She removed Vesta's arms and left the room. After that, Vesta tried to read her mother's moods, and learned to keep a distance that was safe.

In the mornings, after Eula left on her appointments, and Ouida and Vesta were at school, Ruby started in on her washing and ironing, and the sewing that she took in. On Mondays she put on her good clothes and went to the dress shop downtown that served wealthy white women, to collect the things she would work on for the rest of the week.

She played word and spelling games with LaRue while she sorted clothes and took them in batches to the washing tub and wringer on the back porch. She would give him a letter and its sound, and he would come up with a word that began with it. She would tell him about the animals and plants she had seen growing up in the country, while he listened, in awe of nature's feats, his rocker stilling so he could catch the details about night owls, camouflaged moths, snakes shedding their skins.

LaRue loved the smell of her homemade soap, and he followed behind her as she transferred the clothes from tub to line, and moved on to iron yesterday's wash. As she sewed, he took his nap next to her on the couch.

When it was time to start the evening meal she pulled up his rocking chair and taught him about the different moods that herbs and spices gave to foods. And he helped by measuring things out for her, sifting flour, fetching things. She let him taste as they went along, consulting him about seasonings, and about anything else that came up.

She told him all kinds of stories, but his favorite ones, which he asked to hear over and over again, were about the Dustman, who came softly upstairs and threw dust in children's eyes to make them sleep, waving a painted cloth over those who had been good to make them dream, and over others, a white one that brought blank and heavy sleep. The Dustman told a story, one for each day, perched on the sleeping children's beds in a patchwork coat of silk that was green and red and blue.

On Monday, the Dustman decorated a sleeping child's room by making potted flowers grow into big trees, until the bedroom looked like an arbor full of branches, heavy with flowers and fruit. On Tuesday, the Dustman touched the furniture with his magic wand and made it dance and talk. When he touched the landscape painting on the wall, it came to life, its birds singing and the boughs of trees swaying, and the Dustman helped the child step into the picture frame and take a sailing journey through woods where plants and animals told him tales. And on Thursday, the Dustman shrank the child small and helped him borrow a doll's clothing in order to attend a mouse wedding.

LaRue's favorite day for the Dustman was Saturday, when an antique portrait on the sleeping child's wall spoke up and told the Dustman not to misinform the child that stars could be taken down from the sky and brightened. The Dustman prevailed, saying that he was older still than the man in the portrait, and on Sunday, the child turned the portrait to the wall.

Ruby tried to temper LaRue's delight at this story by adding, whenever she told it, that "Even though we've got to do our own thinking, it's important," and she paused for emphasis, "to respect our elders." LaRue always nodded and said, "Yes, Mama Ruby," and smiled.

As far back as anyone could remember, LaRue was telling stories, tales that were his, and seemed to flow as naturally as tears or sweat. Ruby listened as LaRue tried out his storytelling skills, and said to herself, "Boy, you are a little bit of somethin'." As a child, his favorite place to tell a story was in his rocking chair next to the stove, and the antics of his jaywalking parrot friend were invented and took shape in that spot.

She enjoyed the laughter he brought to her working days, his imagination, his wonder at everything. And the way his eyes sparkled when he was happy, with a chink of light shining through the center of one iris. She knew he was a gift, and she remembered how it had been broken glass that had brought him to her.

She really couldn't remember him not being able to talk and he entertained her with the antics of his parrot friend who was always getting in trouble for jaywalking when he came to town.

"There goes LaRue, tellin' his lies again," Vesta said as she passed through the kitchen.

Ruby smiled at them and returned to the stove. LaRue sat next to her in his little green rocking chair and told her about his parrot friend, "And then the parrot went to Pill-addle-pie-a . . ."

Ruby stopped stirring and turned to face him, "To *where*? Where did the parrot go?"

"Pill-addle-pie-a. The parrot went to Pill-addle-pie-a and sat on a blue mountain while it rained and . . ."

Ruby wrote the letters in the air with her spoon and smiled.

"You mean Philadelphia, LaRue. Fill-a-del-fee-a. It's in the state of Pennsylvania, on the East Coast, between . . . well, it's a state that's a good ways away."

He stopped rocking and looked at her for a long time. Looking back at him, she could see Ontario's full lips taking shape in his brown face. LaRue leaned back, his feet lifting off the floor, and began again. "The parrot sat on the mountain and talked to the flowers . . ."

"Un hunh. And what kinds of flowers did the parrot talk to?"

"Red ones. He talked to the red flowers. And then . . . and then . . . when he told them things, they started to grow. And some of them got bigger than me, even," he said, stretching his hand over his head, "and then the parrot said . . ."

She interrupted him. "Did he only talk to red flowers, LaRue?"

"Yes. Only to red ones."

"And why was that? Why only red flowers?"

"Because that's what they have in Pill-addle-pie-a."

LaRue would pronounce it that way, with obstinate pleasure, all his life. Cooking next to him under the stamped-tin ceiling whose squares LaRue liked to count, Ruby heard about the parrot's trips, and about other animals, too, as he rocked in the chair carved along the back with flowers and vines. Within those vines, almost hidden, but visible if you looked with care, were letters: an "A," a "B," and a "C." LaRue held onto the arms as he rocked, tapping his feet along with the squeaking of the caned seat, as they traded stories.

She told him the tale of a slave girl, Lilly, whose father sneaked at night through fields to learn the forbidden alphabet. Together, Ruby and LaRue imagined the father's moonlit sojourns, the risks he took in order to make the world bigger. Ruby told how he had passed down what he learned, once he could read himself, by meeting other slaves in darkened cotton rows to give them the simple gifts he had received: a "T" or an "S," claimed by courage and stealth. And they decided, LaRue and Ruby, that Lilly's father had brought those cherished letters home and carved them into the rocking chair he made for his own little girl.

There was Lilly, and LaRue's parrot. And there was Miss Snake, who got in and out of fixes each time she appeared. She started out with purple spots, but changed each time she shed her skin, and over the years, she would be adorned with many patterns, even plaid, as LaRue saw fit. Each new adventure would bring new markings and a tale to go with them. LaRue wrapped up his tales with Miss Snake sidling up to a big rock and rubbing herself against it to pull off her old skin and leave it behind, excited to see what she would look like next.

4

Ruby stirred and felt Polaris's bare feet against hers. She pushed closer to him for a moment, taking in the smell of his neck, and then pulled back the covers and swung her legs over the side of the bed.

Her feet met the cool, smooth floorboards and she sat on the edge of the mattress absorbing the breaking blue morning light. It was the quiet that got her at this time of day. The distilling quiet, making room for each sound, each color and feeling to be new again.

It was Sunday, when she rose before the rest of the family and set aside a few hours for herself, when each morning thing felt pure. The water she splashed on her face with cupped hands. The grain of the wood floor picked up by her toes. The smell of the fresh towel against her face.

She listened to the sound of her shoes on the stairs, worn down in the middle from use. She descended, entering the light that moved from blue into gold as it slanted down through the transom window, and paused for praise. It felt like the first moment.

There was the rushing, blooming sound of the blue flame that came alive under the coffeepot, and the scratched kitchen table wood where she set her favorite chipped cup and rested her palms, waiting for the water to boil. She inhaled the dark smell of the coffee as it dripped, and touched the beaded mist collecting at the rim of her cup with her fingertips. She heard her spoon against the cup against the still background of the unformed, opening day, and she heard the door unlocking as she went to sit on the porch. She heard the sound of her own breathing.

In warm seasons she watched the light pale from the front stoop, while in winter she saw it from her kitchen window, where she leaned her folded arms, savoring her coffee and enjoying an hour that was completely free of tasks, a time she called her "recognizable moment of the week."

As she sat out front, other folks in the neighborhood started the day, and Ruby liked imagining what was going on in the homes around her. She smelled baking ham and corn bread through the open windows of women who did their cooking before they dressed to go to church, and heard the voices of little girls who were getting their hair done, and humming, and families saying "Mornin'" to each other. Ruby liked to feel the Sunday rhythms as the people all around her got ready to worship in their own ways.

She liked this little bit of time for not thinking, for just being, and afterward she gradually joined the day, and the past and present that it held. She caught something sometimes, the heavy pipe tobacco smell of her father's clothes or the sound of a wagon's wheels, that brought with it memory, triggering where she had come from, where she had been. That little town she had finally been able to leave, that didn't feel big enough to hold her and the incident she had carried in bitterness and shame.

When the neighborhood really started stirring people began to come outside, drifting by Ruby's stoop, and found themselves telling her things about their lives, things they had not been able to free up.

Ruby didn't offer advice, but was the kind of listener who allowed people to give up their burdens. When they paused at her house she greeted them and chatted about their Sunday plans, and soon they were sitting with her, speaking about their lives. Some of them fumbled as they worked their ways to revelation, and others were more direct. Sometimes they didn't even know what it was they meant to say, but were just drawn to Ruby, and often they merely sat with her and never got things said.

Crenshaw Wells, whom Ruby had taken in once when he was out of work and hope, came around to see her every few months for years and never did let go of what was on his mind. He sat with her and circled the subject of his father again and again, and Ruby waited, because she could see something broken in his eyes. They sat and talked and she waited, but Crenshaw never could tell her his recessed pain, and each time he realized he couldn't do it, he clasped and rubbed his knees and then rose from the stoop to say good-bye.

Ruby knew about the power of secrets, their growth heavy like tumors, and the way they fed from you. She had carried hers alone and she wasn't sure which part of it was more difficult to bear. There was the punishment, like a closed face, renewed again and again. And there was the question it raised about what to claim, the open side, that was harder to resolve.

Although Crenshaw never got it said, most of her visitors were like Frosty, who lived in the next block. She came by wiping her hands on her flowered apron, and began with what she was cooking that day. Eventually, she launched from cooking into something else. ". . . but you know, Miss Ruby, cookin's one thing . . . and love's another."

"Mmn hmmn, Frosty," Ruby answered, "I sure do know the truth of that. I sure do. But how do you find it so?"

Frosty went on with her observations about the power of love and then she said, "Now love is one thing. And trust is something else again."

When Ruby knew that Frosty had arrived at the point of telling, she shifted her eyes away, snapping beans into a pot to give her the room she needed to get her thing said.

Frosty touched the flowers on her apron and finally told her that she was sure, not because of lipstick or discovered notes, but just in the way you come to know these things, that her husband had an outside woman. What she didn't know was what to do about it.

Seeking merely someone who could listen, she told her story about love and trust, and once she had finished Ruby said, "Mmn hmmn. I sure do know what you mean," and put her hand on Frosty's with an understanding grace as she moved back into talking about her garden or the neighborhood goings-on, so that when Frosty was ready, she could go.

Another neighbor came by to talk, and when she was finished, Ruby began to hear movement in the house, as Eula was getting Vesta, and then Ouida, settled on the floor between her knees while she oiled and wrapped their hair around her wooden curling stick. After another visitor or two, Ruby stood up, stretching, and went inside.

Eula was at the hall mirror adjusting her hat and gloves. In the five years since Ontario's death she had developed a Sunday routine of her own. She never missed church, and she often took all three of the children with her. She would come upstairs decked out in hat and gloves and smelling of perfume, which made LaRue grit his teeth and turn away, complaining, "Mama, I hate that stuff!" She ignored him and went about preparing to leave. He wasn't sure why, but he couldn't bear the flowery smell, and asked her not to wear it. "Ladies wear perfume, LaRue," she answered, "and when you grow up and get married your wife will wear it, too."

Although Ruby had joined the Episcopal church to which Polaris's family belonged when she had married him, she didn't attend regularly. She felt she needed her Sunday mornings at home, but she often worked on community service projects and helped organize celebrations and bazaars. Eula periodically tried to get her to come to Sunday services with her, but Ruby usually told her that her flowers and her puttering around by herself gave her her own kind of peace.

She finished up the preparations for supper that Eula had gotten underway before she left for church and did some reading while Polaris looked at the paper and slept late in their room. They ate an early supper after church and then they spent time alone on their own pursuits.

When Eula got home she retreated to the dim light of her rooms, took off her corset, and tried to rest. She worked on her crocheting or embroidered the edges of her pillow cases and tatted doilies to protect the backs and arms of their chairs. And she tried not to surrender to the closed-in feeling that came with thinking about returning to her white ladies and their hair the next morning. She wished she could think of a better way to bring money in, but she couldn't imagine anything she could do that didn't involve servicing white folks. So she tried to accept, and not dwell on it. The arrangement between the races was past her understanding anyway, and she didn't let her anger get out of control, because she couldn't see that fury helped. In fact, she wasn't so sure she had a right to the rage she felt flare up at times.

She knew that your feelings would consume you if you let them, the way they had Ontario, and then who knew what would happen. In those evenings of lace-making, she tried to dilute it, her rage at the unfairness, to move it from the riot of color flaring within to something pale that she could afford to have in her life. She tatted her edges, moving the anger in, under control.

What could she do about any of it? White folks ran things and her husband had been what he was, and now he was just gone. Her fingers turned out spiderwebs of lace.

What could she do? She could go to her ladies the next day and work hard and try to be good. She could be a positive example and show them there were dependable colored folks worth something in the world. And then she could come home and try to be good to her children and do her share.

Sometimes on Sundays she got to feeling guilty about her failure to do motherly things, and she put down her handwork and made a batch of cookies or mended something for LaRue or Vesta. She called Vesta downstairs and tried to ask her what she was working on in school, but there was no easy communication between the two of them. Vesta answered her inquiries completely and courteously, as if she was waiting to be told that she could go back upstairs.

Vesta hated the stretch of Sunday afternoon because she could never figure out how to occupy herself. She didn't like to be alone unless she had a task, and she always tried to arrange an activity before Sunday afternoon arrived. She asked Ruby what things needed doing, and Ruby tried to encourage her to develop an interest that was hers, alone. Because she knew how hard it was for Vesta, Ruby gave her books and showed her how to make things, but she seemed at a loss, and started fidgeting and itching whenever she didn't have another person to do things with, to do things for.

Ruby taught both girls to sew, giving them a marketable skill, and Vesta enjoyed darning and mending. Ruby helped her with this while Ouida and LaRue were stretched out on the multicolored rag rug reading. Vesta fought giving in to books, afraid of where her unbridled imagination might take her, and she couldn't really imagine lying on the floor or sneaking on the light at night to find out what happened at the end of a book. To her, reading felt like work, and she got started on something and then realized she wasn't even sure what she had just read.

When LaRue was really little he had begged for stories, and even wanted the same ones read to him over and over, until he knew the words by heart. He loved poems and nursery rhymes, too, and Vesta didn't really understand this. If there was one thing she really didn't get, it was poetry, especially the kind that didn't rhyme. She just didn't think that way, and she didn't see why the meaning of something would purposely be hidden. The things in books seemed way in the distance, and she never quite understood what they had to do with her.

It seemed to Vesta that Ouida stepped into the lives of the characters in the poems and stories she loved. She started talking like them and feeling their feelings, and it amazed and frightened Vesta. She had seen Ouida lying in bed crying because of the plight of someone she was reading about. "Miss Drama," Ruby called her, laughing, as Ouida recited something from a table or a chair, crying out as if her heart would break, "To strive, to seek, to find . . ."

"What on earth!" Eula would exclaim if she saw her. "What on earth are you doing on that chair? . . . Ruby? . . . Don't you see that? . . . She's up on your good chair . . . If I were you I'd put covers over those chairs with these children all over everything like wild animals . . ." She looked from Ruby to Ouida and then sucked her teeth at the lack of response. Ouida jumped down and, undaunted, continued her recitation prostrate, from the floor.

Even though there was something about Ouida's immersion that Vesta envied, it disturbed her, too. When there were no chores to be done, Vesta sometimes put together jigsaw puzzles while Ouida made toys for LaRue out of scraps and discarded things or worked on one of her ongoing collages assembled from pictures cut from the Sears, Roebuck catalogs and other scraps of paper, fabrics, and dried flowers she found. Often the three of them lay stretched out on the braided rag rugs of the living room floor, the afternoon light streaming through the tall narrow bay windows, little bits of green and blue through the crescent of stained glass at the top making a dancing pattern on the wall that moved around the room in its daily cycle.

While the children entertained themselves, Polaris and Ruby spent some part of the afternoon together. He cherished the days when he wasn't on the road, which were few and far between, and he loved to unpin her full springy hair and put his thick fingers in it while they talked, loved the smell of skin he caught when he kissed her at the temples. He was a quiet man and even with Ruby he didn't talk much, but she tried to pull him out of his silences as they lay touching, by asking about the things he had seen on the train, about why people were traveling and what they were like.

Polaris struggled to tell her how he felt about his good steady job as a Pullman porter. He felt kind of proud to be better off than most folks, to have the prestige the job carried for colored folks in those days, and he thought he could even work his way up to be a conductor someday. But the other side of that was the role he had to play for the white passengers, and the things he witnessed about his people's lot.

LaRue had been pleading to go on a train trip with him, and it had Polaris looking at himself in a different kind of way. He had been trying to tell Ruby about his feelings, but he had such a hard time sorting them out and explaining them. One day it just poured out. "I feel trapped sometimes," he told her, "between two spots." She looked at him and said, "Yes . . . well how do you mean?" and waited for him to go on.

"On the one hand, there's no question where I fit in. They don't even let colored folks porter for freight service . . . only for the passenger trains. The unions sure don't want us, and do everything they can to keep us out, and here I am passing on *The Defender* in secret whenever I can. And sure as I'm sittin' here, if I'm a passenger on one of those trains, you know where I am. I sit in the colored car. I sit in back.

"And here I am in this uniform, lifting these white ladies' bags, and turning their sheets down, which is the thing I hate the most, the going all into their lives . . . touching their sheets, Ruby, but being, still and yet, like some kind of a thing. On the edge. And if they feel bad about it, there's the kind of distance they make between themselves and me, so that they can stand to have someone all up in their lives, waiting on them, like they're better, because it's the order of things. Sometimes I hate those white people as they give me their tips and treat me like I'm a camel . . . or an ox. Like all I live for is their use."

Ruby rubbed his neck as he talked, and she realized as she saw his eyebrows rise and fall and his nostrils flare, how she loved this stocky, dignified man who held his passion in. He tried to tell her the thing that was harder, still, to tell, looking at her a long time until he got the courage to face what he felt and say it. "Sometimes, Ruby, I hate my own, for being all cramped up in the little dirty colored car with their boxes of chicken and their one set of good clothes that aren't even as nice as the worst thing the white lady's got in that leather bag of hers I just lifted to her berth. All wrinkled and dirty-faced after a night with no face bowl, the hems of their clothes grass-stained and damp from morning dew where they have squatted by the tracks. Sometimes I hate my own."

They were both silent and she took his hands. "And sometimes, Ruby, I stand there between those two places and I'm absolutely nobody, and I just plain hate myself."

He was afraid LaRue had romantic notions of what he did, and afraid of all the things having his adopted son as a witness would raise in him. Because he knew he couldn't explain his feelings, he asked Ruby to help him make the boy understand. "Eula's always talking about how lucky I am to have this fine job . . . but you know, those chain gang men, those men who built so many of the railroads, they haunt me, and sometimes I can hear them at work when I'm standing on the platform. I can hear their hammers fall and their voices, chanting to survive. To survive here"—he touched his chest—"here, inside."

"I know Eula's right . . . I am lucky I've got this job, but tell the boy, Ruby, tell him because I can't. Tell him what it isn't and what it is.

"You see . . . LaRue's pleading with me to go somewhere," he said to his wife, "to travel on a train, you know . . . and sometimes I feel like here I am, running in place, as these folks travel back and forth. Seems like I'm not even moving. Just on a long trip, keeping still."

Ruby agreed to talk to LaRue about Polaris's job, but she felt as though he shouldn't worry about the boy glorifying it all. She knew he was a perceptive, sensitive child who wanted to know things, and he would be able to see the whole of it, she told him, if not now, in times to come, and she didn't believe in shielding children from the world, anyway. Finally, Polaris worked it out to take him on a short run north the upcoming autumn.

As summer came to a close LaRue grew more and more excited. He watched fall arrive, and as the trees began to rage with color and drop their leaves, he knew he would be going on his very first trip.

Ouida had been helping him make a book of the leaves he had collected, affixing each one to a large thick piece of paper and writing underneath what kind of leaf it was and where he had found it. They were spread out on the living room floor with the project, and Vesta was looking the leaves up in a book for their proper names. LaRue was asking what kinds of leaves were found in other places. When they got finished with the pages, Ouida guided LaRue as he sewed the edges of the pages together with yarn to make a binding for the book. When they were finished they looked through it, page by page, as if seeing it for the first time, and he loved the rustling sound of the book as he opened the pages and was delighted at the rediscovery of each red and gold leaf.

"I'll bring back something for my book from my trip," he shouted. "And from everywhere I ever go . . . and my leaf book will grow and grow, and never be finished." He danced around the living room "like a falling leaf," he said, and when he came to rest Ouida tickled him until he was tired. Vesta laughed, but kept her distance because she hated to be tickled, and never would have subjected anyone to the spasms and squeals it produced.

As they sat down to dinner that night, LaRue chattering on to his parrot friend about leaves and trains, he was given a nickname that would stick for the rest of his life.

LaRue talked while the family sat around the table waiting for Ruby to bring in the turkey one of her neighbors had brought her as a gift. As she came through the doorway with a huge platter, everyone exclaimed at the golden bird. Polaris stood up and began to carve, and everyone remarked, as they always did, that it looked like the biggest turkey ever.

LaRue chattered on about his parrot friend having stowed away on the streetcar in order to get home. "There he goes again . . ." Ruby laughed her full, deep laugh. "So young, and such a liar."

As Polaris carved, he came upon the wishbone and held it up, announcing ceremoniously, "The wishbone, I've got it. Now whose turn is it to wish?"

Everyone agreed that it was LaRue's and Vesta's turns to wish, but Vesta shook her head and told Ouida to wish in her place. "Come on, sweetheart, it's all in fun. Make your wish," Ruby coaxed, but Vesta looked down at her lap. Eula was silent, and then said, "Come on, Vesta dear. It's okay, make a wish." Vesta said she didn't really believe in that kind of thing, but Ouida and Polaris joined in urging her on, and all eyes were on her. She looked around the table at each member of her family . . . at Ruby's hand holding out the bone to her . . . and at LaRue by her side, ready to compete, and she said, "Okay, okay. I'll do it, but it really doesn't mean a thing to me . . ."

Ruby told them it was time for each of them to make a wish, "for anything at all you like," and looking at them both, she said, "Okay, now you each take a side," and placed LaRue's small fingers around the archway of bone.

Vesta reached out and took the other side, and they closed their eyes. Vesta thought about what to wish for . . . whether it should be something big that she didn't even know the shape of, like happiness . . . or long life, or a small, tangible thing that she could really use, like extra money, a new pair of shoes, or an "A" in Latin. She looked up and saw her mother's fingertips on her scar, and closed her eyes again, recalling in a flash that she had awakened that morning with a feeling of intense color, but whatever she had been dreaming had slipped away. She had closed her eyes, then, and tried to recapture it, but as always, it was lost, and she had wanted to know it, wanted to know what that feeling of color had been about. As she held onto her side of the wishbone, she wanted to remember her dream.

Ruby's voice pierced the darkness. "Are you ready? Have you settled on something?" and Vesta chose, abandoning her wish to know the colors of her dreams and going for a little extra money, so Eula wouldn't have to work so hard.

She felt LaRue pulling against her and she opened her eyes and held her hand firm, pushing with her thumb, until she felt the bone split. As she heard him squeal wildly and opened her eyes to see him hopping around, she thought he must have won, until she looked down and found the big end of the wishbone in her own hand. She had won, after all, and everyone, including LaRue, was clapping and saying, "Go 'head, Vesta. You've got your wish."

LaRue was dancing around the table, doing the cake walk, and he hadn't even won. He had the smaller end.

Ouida leaned over and put her arm through Vesta's. "Tell me, what did you wish for?"

As Vesta opened her mouth to say that if she told her wish it wouldn't come true, LaRue's voice exploded with excitement. "I wished for the world, Ouida! I wished for everything!"

They all laughed and Eula and Ruby looked at each other and shook their heads. Ruby said, "What a mess this child is," and turning to LaRue she added, "I guess we'll have to call you Wishbone . . . the one who wishes for everything."

On the morning of the train trip Polaris and LaRue left before the rest of the family got up. The night before, too excited to sleep, LaRue had come into Ouida's and Vesta's room and convinced them to push the beds together to make room for him. He climbed in between them and talked on and on about what the train would be like and the people he would meet. He asked them what they knew about each town the train would be traveling through, and where they would go if they could travel anywhere.

Ouida talked about all the places she had read about and imagined and Vesta chimed in that she, too, would like to see the world, but in truth she wasn't sure about the idea of sitting up against people she didn't know, their skin and their sweat and their smells right next to you, their breathing perceptible, with them maybe even coughing in your face. If she took a trip, she thought, she would have to know exactly where she was going, have it all mapped out beforehand. She had boarded the wrong streetcar once and had ended up way out of her way, in a rich white part of town reminiscent of where her mother worked. When she realized that nothing around her was familiar, she panicked, but was afraid to approach the conductor and ask him how to get home from there. That's why she always preferred to travel on foot, so that she knew just what she knew and what she didn't know, knew what was what, and had the feel of the ground underneath her.

She listened without voicing her skepticism, and when she fell asleep Ouida and LaRue were still talking. Vesta hadn't slept next to LaRue since the night they first came to Ruby's, and she turned toward his voice and shaped herself around him in an unconscious gesture of protection. When it was almost dawn Polaris roused LaRue without disturbing the others and they woke, later, to a house that seemed empty without him.

Polaris held LaRue's hand as they crossed the station to approach the train, and imprinted in LaRue's memory were the shiny buttons of his uniform. There was the pride he felt as he looked up at Polaris, and the fatherly hand on his shoulder that guided him, and the building feeling inside that signaled the beginning of an adventure. As Polaris had helped him up the heavy iron steps to the train LaRue had crossed, without knowing it, into another part of his life.

That evening, when they got home, Polaris carried LaRue through the front door and put him to bed. And then he slipped off his shoes and stretched out on the bed with Ruby, too tired to undress.

The next morning, Ouida and Vesta were sitting on the edge of LaRue's bed when he awakened, full of questions about his trip. He sat up, rubbing his eyes, and his impressions spilled from him as he tried to tell his sisters what it had been like.

He told them about the rocking of the train and its high screech as it came to a stop. Its whistle, and the blur of green as they passed a thicket of trees, and a little brown girl in a lavender hat waving as the train went by, and how he had waved back at her and wondered had she seen him, that little girl. Did they think so, he asked, did they think that girl in the lavender hat had seen his wave?

He told them that when he had unwrapped the sandwich Ruby had packed for him it had made him miss them all, and then he had heard talk of white people and "The Other Side," and wondered, as he did whenever he heard that phrase, what went on where they lived. He heard people talking about "boll weevils" and "the five-dollar day," and he asked Ouida and Vesta if days counted for money.

The train had moved forward and trees had leaped toward him in a rush of orange and green and red, and then he had been transfixed by the fleeting image of a lake, striated with reflections of the turning trees.

Ouida asked him what leaves he had found to add to his book and he realized he hadn't brought any back, for when they had left the train he had lost all thought of collecting leaves, overwhelmed by something else. This he didn't tell, but recalled in a flash, how he had known something was wrong without understanding it.

He hadn't been told that only the white passengers had bathrooms on board, but he saw that it was people like him who left the train for the field, and Polaris had come to get him, had taken him by the hand and led him outside, where he reassured him that it was okay to relieve himself. "Go on, son," he had said, when LaRue didn't seem to get it, "this is where you have to pee." And LaRue had looked at the others who were out there with their makeshift strategies of seclusion, shielding their private acts while their faces showed. He had not understood it, and only later would he have a context for the thing he had seen in their expressions that he knew was wrong.

He had unbuttoned his pants and went to the bathroom in the knee-high weeds, Polaris by his side. And he remembered that the tips of his shoes had gotten wet, and that they had climbed back on the train and he had sat looking through the window at the people who were still outside. He had watched the clustered figures knowing, feeling something was amiss, and wanting to ask Polaris to explain. And because it hurt him, though he didn't know why, he looked beyond the squatting figures who were turned away from the train, and out in that field just claimed by winter he saw yellow flowers, blooming against the shame. The blossoms caught his eye and he focused on them until everyone was back on board and the train was moving, tunneling into evening.

LaRue would remember the faces of the other people on the train. The old woman who shared her corn bread and nectarines with him, her eyes looking gently at him from folds of mottled, light brown skin, her hands bony and big-knuckled and loose with wrinkles. The talk of the races, and of opportunity waiting somewhere else, and the rhythm of the train and discovery from the window glass. But of all the things that would stay with him from that first time leaving home, LaRue would remember most those defiant flowers by the road.

5

Ouida looked across the room at Vesta sleeping in the early amethyst light. She studied her face and imagined what was going on behind her closed eyes, what things Vesta dreamed about that she could never share.

Ouida turned on her back and stared at the hairline cracks in the ceiling plaster as she scolded herself for what had happened the day before. She felt bad for worrying everyone, and she wondered how she had lost track of things like that, over a little bit of blue. It was something Vesta would never have done.

"Where is that girl?" Ruby had said as she returned to the window and pulled the curtain aside. Ouida was almost two hours late, but Ruby was trying not to think of the dangers that might be out there waiting for her child, and she knew if Ouida was in trouble she couldn't count on help. "She was supposed to be home a long time ago," she whispered. "Where could she be?"

The family, collected in the living room, offered suggestions for why Ouida was late. Maybe she was somewhere climbing trees, LaRue ventured, knowing that the two of them had lost all track of time engaged in that pursuit before.

"I don't know, Ruby, but . . . I'm sure she's all right," Eula said. "She probably forgot to tell you where she'd be. You know how Ouida is, half the time all caught up in a book, or dreaming she's somewhere else, wrapped up in her own little world."

"Maybe she got tied up at school," Vesta said quietly from her place on the couch. She had seen Ouida near the end of the day in one of the many classes they shared. "Or she stopped at a friend's house on the way home, and the time . . . the time just got away from her, that's all."

Ruby moved back and forth from the front window to the kitchen, where she was trying to keep the dinner warm. They heard the slam of the oven, and snatches of her voice. ". . . she knows we always eat together . . . I know she's just messin' with me . . . testing my tolerance . . . pushing my limits, that girl."

And Eula sat on the couch between Vesta and LaRue, making optimistic comments as she wrung her hands and silently expected the worst. "Oh, Ruby. I'm just sure she's all right."

Nobody spoke for a while and then LaRue burst in, "I bet she's in a real fix now, and she better be talking her way out of it mighty fast, 'cause the same thing happened to my parrot friend once, as he crossed against the light, but I just know Ouida can get out of it, you know, she thinks *and* talks real fast . . . I bet the police are probably talking to her right now, downtow . . ."

Eula grabbed LaRue's arm and squeezed it. "I ought to just snatch you, Bone, carrying on so. Can't you just sit quiet for a minute?" Vesta had to turn away and swallow her smile before she got snatched too. She couldn't believe the things that came out of LaRue's mouth, and if she wanted to see some trouble without starting it, she just waited for him to make it happen, all on his own. His wildness both amused and frightened her.

They heard Ruby muttering in the kitchen. ". . . sweet and agreeable, and just does exactly what she feels like doing, nodding at you all the while."

"Don't worry, Ruby," Eula called into the kitchen as she glanced at the clock and got up to help her, "there's absolutely nothing to worry about. I just know she's all right."

They both came back into the front room and sat down, and the ticking of the clock seemed to get louder and more insistent. Ruby got up again and went to the kitchen, and Ouida burst through the door.

Her face was dirty and her plaits had come loose, but she was flushed with excitement as she said, looking from face to face,

"There was this lot, and these little bits of a . . . a kind of aquamarine blue, you see, behind and under things, and I saw them and oh, I just couldn't . . ."

Ruby stood in the living room archway with her hands on her hips, while the others sat staring at Ouida. Suddenly, in mid-stream, Ouida realized that something was wrong. "Oh . . ." she said as she stopped her story and looked at the clock. "I'm late." And while they waited for her explanation, LaRue reached out to catch a flower that fell from her arms.

She tried to explain that she had lost track of time, as she went home from school a different way past the vacant lot, and a touch of blue among the weeds had arrested her, the small bit of color that was almost hidden by a pile of bricks and rubbish.

She had peered at it first from the sidewalk, and then entered the lot, fearless, climbing over discarded machinery, pushing past refuse. She ranged the whole four-block lot, looking behind and under other growth for the bits of color in the small water-blue heads of wildflowers most people called weeds. As her armful grew, she stepped outside of time, swept up, enchanted, as she pulled them up like treasure and filled the jacket she had taken off and made into a sling-like basket.

They sat looking at the mound of ragged flowers spilling from her dirty, misshapen jacket, until she looked where they were looking, at her arms, and smiled despite the judgment in their eyes. "Survivors," she said. "Can you believe it, growing this time of year in a corner lot?"

In her excitement she stumbled, spilling them at the foot of the couch, her blooms of delicate blue mixed in with weeds and clumps of dirt with the roots attached. She had grasses in her hair, and her right cuff had separated from the sleeve of her dress, but unconcerned, she knelt and gathered the flowers to her. "Vases, Mama. We need vases, lots of vases . . ."

Ruby shook her head and pulled Ouida by the arm into the kitchen, gathering the trail of flowers as she went. She meant to scold her but instead caught her in her arms and held her hard, a reprimand hidden somewhere in the hug. "Child, you gave me a scare.

Didn't you think we'd be worried? You mustn't act so, child. You mustn't act so."

Ouida squeezed her and said into Ruby's breast, "I didn't mean to scare you . . . I just thought we should have flowers, Mama, lots of flowers."

As she lay in bed the next morning feeling the fresh air come through the cracked window that she argued with Vesta each night to keep open, Ouida shook her head at her own behavior. Then she looked again at Vesta, curled on her side, who always held her arms the same way in sleep: the top one bent at the elbow with the hand turned in as if cradling something, and the one underneath stretched out, her fingers touching the spooled wooden bars of the headboard. To Ouida, it looked uncomfortable, but for as long as she had known her, Vesta had slept that way. In fact, she thought, that's how she had looked the first time she had seen her on the living room couch, only then there had been an orange tucked in the hollow made by her wrist and arm.

That morning, five years before, Ouida had stood at the foot of the couch assessing the stranger who seemed close to her age, until Vesta had opened her eyes and stared at the light brown girl with plaited ropes of wild hair coming loose at the ends. Ouida had heard voices and crying in the night, and she could tell from looking at Vesta that something bad had happened. She blurted out, "My name's Ouida. Who are you?"

Her directness struck them both as funny and after they laughed, Vesta said, "My name is Vesta Smalls." Ouida stared at her for a while, and seeing something hurt, something that needed befriending, Ouida walked over to the couch and made a place to sit down. "Is that your mama upstairs?" she asked quietly, and when Vesta nodded with tears in her eyes, Ouida nodded, too. Then she took Vesta's hand and said, "Come on, let me show you around," and her narrow brown eyes disappeared when she smiled.

She took her from room to room, identifying each one at the doorway: "This is the kitchen. We cook in here . . . and this, here, is the dining room, where we eat what we've cooked." When they got to her room, Ouida showed her the games and books and toys she had, and they knelt on the bed, arms propped on the windowsill, as they looked out and talked.

They were together all day, watching and playing with LaRue, talking and giggling, and helping Ruby with the household chores. Ouida whispered long after Ruby came to turn off the light and tuck them in, and for both of them it was like being given the sister their own age for whom they longed.

When Polaris had returned from his cross-state railroad run the next day, Ruby had told him about their arrival, and she had spoken to him about the Smalls family staying with them for a while. She knew she had to have a talk with Ouida, and in the afternoon, while their visitors were napping, Ruby asked Ouida to come to the back porch with her and help ready a bowl of fruit for making pies. She said to Ouida, "You do it better than anyone else I know . . . Want to help?" and Ouida nodded and sat down.

"Sometimes," Ruby began as she dipped an apple in the big green bowl between them, and rubbed its skin, "people need help." Ouida looked up at her and waited for the rest as she copied her with an apple of her own. "Sometimes, sweet Ouida," Ruby said, "people's hurt doesn't let them be kind."

"Mama," Ouida answered, "I know that someone hurt Mrs. Smalls."

Ruby was dipping another apple into the water now, baptizing the fruit, it seemed. "Yes, it's true. Eula and Vesta and the baby, LaRue, have known some unkindness that you and I may not really be able to understand the reasons for." She dried the apple and then spoke again. "And we maybe, after all, wouldn't even act the same way if someone's hurt made them unkind to us."

She began to peel the apple with her knife and when Ouida looked up at her as though she understood, Ruby continued. "I don't expect this all to make sense to you today, sweetheart, but in times to come this talk of ours may have some meaning for you."

The skin of the fruit was coming off now in a long red spiral. "The main thing for you to know," she said, finishing with the apple and taking Ouida's head to her breast with wet hands lined and rough from work, "is that now, while they're with us, even if you don't understand it . . . and I don't know how long it will be . . . they need for our hearts to be big. They need to be a part of us for a little while, and maybe for longer. If that's okay with you." She looked at Ouida's face now and saw that it was okay. "You never know, Ouida," she said, submerging another piece of fruit and lifting it, dripping, from the bowl, "one day, you too may need an open door."

Ouida went back inside and found Vesta awake, but sitting completely still, as if frozen into place. She didn't intrude, but watched her from a distance, and when Vesta moved again, she came to her and put her arm around her and entwined her fingers in hers. She thought Vesta might want to tell her about what had happened, but she never spoke about it and Ouida didn't want to push.

Before Ontario Smalls came that last time and Eula, Vesta, and LaRue followed him home, the two girls had sworn their sisterhood and sealed it with an exchange of vows and magic words. Ouida had hugged Vesta and told her she was the sister she had wished for, and that until she came she had had only her imaginary friends to talk to. They had sneaked into the attic to play, and made rings for their fingers from twisted dandelion stalks, weaving the flower heads of yellow-slivered petals into their hair, and Ouida remembered the acrid smell of the broken stems and the milky blood they leaked.

Ouida caught a glimpse of the mass of blue-dotted weeds in the water-filled canning jar over on the washstand and returned to the present. She thought about how different she and Vesta were. "Nope," she thought, "Vesta would never be late over picking some flowers . . ."

She reached over and nudged Vesta's leg. "Get up, girl. It's time to get vertical . . . past time, in fact," and Vesta opened her eyes suddenly, alarmed. "Hunh! What is it?" waking, as she always did, as if to disaster.

"Time to get up, Morning Glory," Ouida said, "or we'll be late for school."

They got out of bed and started to get ready, Vesta following her usual routine of smoothing the bedspread carefully and tucking it around the pillows three times before she went to the bathroom. In the same order she followed each morning, she brushed her teeth, washed up, and confined her hair in plaits with ribbons on the ends. When she returned to the bedroom, she dressed and, last of all, she pulled her shoes from the edge of the bed and put them on.

Although Vesta had liked school when she was younger, she had recently come to dread weekday mornings. She had to make herself go through the door into sixth-grade English grammar without Ouida, who was a year ahead of her, by biting the inside of her mouth to steel herself. Her classmates had begun to treat her like an outcast. They teased her about Ontario, conjugating the verb "to fall" whenever she was around.

Though they, too, were all colored, her classmates made fun of Vesta's dark skin and she tried to make light of their jokes and toss their insults off, but once her tormentors discovered they had the power to get to her, she became the perfect target for abuse. She didn't understand why they had chosen her to pick on, and was puzzled by the fact that one of the instigators was a girl as dark as she was, who seemed to have convinced herself otherwise. The exclusion overwhelmed her, made things tumble and swim, until she turned inward and settled it with the understanding that there was something about her that was different.

A separate place inside was what Vesta tried to make. She focused on doing her schoolwork and getting through each day by making lists that included everything from completing an assignment to walking, a certain number of paces, down the hall. She never talked about it, even to Ouida, who probed her about her growing withdrawal. It was too hard for her to expose herself to Ouida, who didn't seem to be troubled by what others thought about her and was absorbed in daydreams and creative projects.

Vesta loved Ouida's and LaRue's quirkiness and she looked up to the two of them, sometimes jealously. But she knew that they connected in a way that didn't have anything to do with her. She and Ouida were "sissers," as they liked to say. Family. And she knew that people didn't necessarily understand the folks who were their relatives. But with Ouida and LaRue it was a different kind of thing, and it had always been that way. They made up rhymes and songs together, and expanded on the storybooks they read. And when LaRue told those lies about his snake and his parrot friend Ouida acted as if she thought that they were true.

Ouida liked to lie in bed and talk into the night, asking Vesta what she thought and felt about things. She tried to get Vesta to imagine what kinds of lives they wanted when they grew up, the sensations animals felt, what it was like to fly or breathe water. She wanted to talk about what love was like, and what someone's mouth would feel like against yours. Ouida asked her questions, but Vesta never did open up, and Ouida called her "Morning Glory," for the flower that unfolds its petals in the morning, and shuts them tight at night.

Ouida was full of so many dreams, Vesta thought, most of them unattainable. Vesta fantasized, privately, of a warm and secure married life, and she fantasized often, without telling Ouida, of a man who would come for her and love her. She couldn't express her feelings, so she mostly listened to Ouida, who was able to say she was scared, she was hopeful, she was unsure. Sometimes after they were in bed, in the distilling quiet of the night, Vesta called out, "Ouida, are you asleep?" and she would raise up on her elbow and face her. "No, I'm awake."

Vesta wanted to be able to express herself to Ouida, and she didn't even know what it was she wanted, needed to say. She wanted to be able to unlock herself and say something essential in the silence of the night, to make a bridge with another person, but she was afraid to try, because she didn't know what she would be left with if she failed. She imagined Ouida looking at her blankly, or turning to her to say, "No, Vesta, I don't know what you mean." It was that misstep, that misstep again that haunted her. Ouida lay across the room, perched on her elbow, waiting for Vesta to speak. Waiting, until Vesta said, "Nothing, just sleep tight, that's all." She wanted to speak, to speak out across the darkness of the night. She wanted to say something to Ouida, and she didn't even know what.

She tried to work everything out alone because she knew it was safest to depend on no one. She threw herself into making sure the things on her dresser were exactly in place, that there was no dust or disarray, that the spines of her books created an unbroken line. At night she got out of bed and checked her closet door to make sure her things were arranged just right, and reached down from her bed to make sure her shoes were within grasp, their toes against the side of the bed.

She let no one in on her safety measures, but a few times Ouida noticed her whispering to herself, and asked her what was up. Vesta said angrily, "Don't you worry about me. I'm just fine," resentful of Ouida's intrusion into the world of her making, which she felt she had the right to protect in any way she could. Ouida told her mother about Vesta's strange behavior and Ruby spoke with Eula about reassuring her child, but Eula didn't seem to know how to do that. Because Ruby couldn't get Vesta to open up to her either, she tried to be a constant in her life, while Vesta vowed to master her behavior so no one would rob her of her private world.

After Sunday dinner one night they were gathered in the kitchen. Eula had just showed Ruby the latest hand-me-down dresses her client, Mrs. Franklin, had given her for Vesta and Ouida. She was doing the dinner dishes and going on and on with all kinds of details about the houses and parties of the ladies she worked for and the ladies at church.

"Now I think it was at three o'clock . . . was it three or three-fifteen?" She paused to consider. ". . . I think it was three-fifteen . . . and she told me she was going to next Sunday's service. And what I don't understand is how she could be planning to go to next Sunday's service when she said she had an appointment to see the plumber . . . or was it the plasterer . . . I think it was the plasterer, because it was two weeks ago that she had that leak . . . well she said they had arranged that appointment for either three or three-fifteen that very afternoon . . ."

Ruby had been trying to tell her about a story in verse that LaRue would be reciting at school, and she hadn't been able to get it out without Eula stopping to ask her when, exactly, he had written it, and how long it was, and whether it rhymed or not. When Ruby had mentioned the time of the performance, Eula had gone off on a tangent about her friend Margarella Wilson's schedule and whether they had made arrangements to go to church together that day. Ruby thought she would scream if she didn't leave the room.

She went into the front room for a break from Eula and tried to think through how to talk to her about the habit that was becoming an obsession. Her focus on nailing down the minute details of what everyone else was doing had grown over the past few months until it had become almost unbearable. If Ruby was telling a story Eula interrupted every few sentences to clarify when and where and in what order something had happened. As she did it, Ruby imagined her placing obstacles in the path between the two of them, forestalling any communication that was too personal, that would reveal too much.

Ruby never got the chance to tell Eula the details of LaRue's recitation, or to raise a topic that was even harder to discuss. She waited until dinner and the evening activities were over, and then went down to Eula's flat to talk. When she knocked Eula was getting out of her corset and opened the door looking so haggard it made Ruby tired, too. She sat down and decided to plunge right in, before they got enmeshed in a series of details that would keep her from telling Eula what she needed to say.

It had happened at school, without Eula having prepared the way. Vesta had heard girls mention "the curse" and say suggestively, "My friend is visiting." She had watched them sit out of gym class for reasons that had remained mysterious to her, but she had never been told that she would bleed. Hearing her cry of alarm from behind the bathroom stall door, Ouida asked her what was wrong. Vesta said nothing was wrong, she had just lost her balance for a moment, and she waited until everyone left the bathroom to remove her underclothes and scrub them in the sink. Her hands shook as she scrubbed her panties. She didn't know what to think.

"I'm hurt," she repeated to herself as she tried desperately to get rid of the stain and its dark, heavy smell. "I'm hurt . . . I'm hurt on the inside."

Worried, Ouida excused herself from class and returned to the bathroom to find Vesta at the sink, and when she saw her she knew. She knew what had happened, and knew that Vesta's mother hadn't told her that it would.

Ouida approached Vesta, who took a step backward and hid her underclothes behind her back, but she couldn't conceal the tears in her eyes. When Ouida hugged her, Vesta's arms went limp at her sides and Ouida could feel her heart pounding. Ouida drew her closer and whispered, "It's all right. Vesta, it's all right."

She explained, then, what her mother had told her, and when she was finished Vesta sobbed as she held her, saying over and over again into Ouida's neck, "I was afraid . . . I was afraid I was hurt inside."

Ouida told her it was "her womanhood," and that instead of feeling bad about it, they should celebrate. She helped her finish washing out her things and then they went home for Ruby to help get her prepared. On the way Ouida told her she had been waiting to start and was jealous, and asked her if she felt any different, if she felt more grown up.

Ruby was surprised to see them home so early from school, and when Ouida announced, "Vesta started, Mama. She's a woman now," Ruby smiled and asked her where the things were that her mother had given her for when she was ready. When Vesta looked away in shame, letting Ruby know something was wrong, Ouida shook her head to tell her mother what had happened without saying anything, and Ruby understood.

Ouida offered to watch the food that was on the stove and Ruby took Vesta upstairs and explained how to use the folded pieces of cloth and pins she gave her, and while she sat and waited for Vesta to return from the bathroom where she had insisted on going to put it on, Ruby remembered the onset of her own bleeding, and how cold and matter-of-fact her mother had been. "Don't ever let your brothers, or any other man or boy, see them," she had warned her as she gave instructions on washing and disposing of the cloths, "and take extra care so no one can pick up on your smell." And then came the biggest admonition of all, not to let boys "have their way," unless she wanted a "handful of pickaninnies" all her own.

Ruby tried to give Vesta something besides fear and shame by explaining, as she had to Ouida, the beauty of the thing that was happening to her. She told her of the cushion building in her each month as a place for life to grow, so that when she was ready she could have children. And then Ruby talked about the seriousness of the transition, and added, hearing her mother speak through her, that it was best to wait until marriage for sex. Vesta held her tightly clasped hands on her lap and looked up at her with a mixture of relief and terror, as Ruby told her she had entered womanhood.

As they went downstairs, Vesta walking stiffly with the new thickness between her legs, Ruby thought of all that this entrance meant. This girl who descended the staircase in front of her, whose hair was still in plaits and a few hours earlier had been ignorant of this beginning, this end, was moving from girl into woman before her eyes it seemed, and so young she was, so in need of protecting. They went in the kitchen and Ruby poured a glass of sherry for the three of them, knowing that she needed a drink.

"God help her," she said to herself as she thought of what Eula had been through as a woman. She wished she could shield Vesta from the things her mother had faced and thought, "Now that I can't protect her is when she'll need it most."

As the three of them raised their glasses Ruby said, "To the moon," and Vesta tried to smile.

Ruby knew that Eula had been so self-absorbed that she just hadn't thought of talking to Vesta, but had she not even seen her daughter growing taller and fuller, she wondered? Had she missed the swell of her breasts and the hips beginning to define themselves? She felt sad for Eula, and angry, too, when she imagined Vesta's panic at the sight of her own iron-red blood. As soon as Eula sat down Ruby plunged right in to tell her what had happened that day, and tears collected in Eula's eyes as she realized what she had failed to do. Ruby placed her lined hand on Eula's forearm and said, "That's done . . . it's happened now. But talk to her, Eula . . . let her know it's all right."

After Ruby left Eula cried, her fingertips, wet with tears, straying to the scar that crept across her brow. Tears for her own lapse, and for the things her daughter would face.

The next day, after school, Eula went to Vesta's room to talk to her and Vesta sat quiet and still as her mother tried to lead up to the topic at hand with details about school, and the weather, and what they were having for dinner. Vesta knew why she had come and was dreading the discussion of a subject of which she would prefer never to speak again. Finally, after a time of silence that felt like years, Eula said "Mama Ruby told me . . ." and found herself unable to finish the sentence.

Finding Eula's discomfort unbearable, Vesta helped her out. When she said, "Ruby told me . . ." a second time, Vesta jumped in with "It's all right." They looked at each other and then looked away, and Eula managed to get out two more words. ". . . your monthly . . ." she mumbled, and Vesta said, "Yes."

She ached for what they both recognized as her mother's failure, and so she tried to fix it by saying, "It's all right, Mama. Don't worry . . . I promise, it's all right."

6

When LaRue first told Vesta about Miss Snake she informed him firmly of the colors available to serpents. She warned him that he must be careful not to make things up, to keep clear the difference between lies and truth. She didn't understand why LaRue would pick something unsettling like a snake about which to make up tales, and when she heard Ruby listening to his stories and asking questions about them, she got angry, but held her tongue. Although she didn't understand why Ruby indulged such nonsense, she knew not to question an adult.

Sensing her discomfort, Ruby took her aside to offer a cryptic bit of wisdom. "Vesta, honey, you don't know trouble till trouble finds you. Now stop worrying about LaRue and his tales. I don't care what people say," she went on, "you might find out that it's better signifyin' than dyin'." These words also troubled Vesta, who had little use for language that wasn't plain. She held her tongue and tried to keep her irritation to herself. But in truth, if LaRue was telling a story, any story at all, she usually found something nearby to keep her busy until he was through, as if, in spite of herself, that believing part of her fought to stay alive.

Some people found LaRue's presence disquieting. It was how he looked at them, penetrating, in a way that wasn't quite polite. And then he had that weird right eye. They were usually won over by the way he made them laugh, but he tended to throw people off balance with his manner and with his lies.

Over the eight years that their families had lived together, Ouida and LaRue had developed a special bond. They sat on the floor for hours while she taught him the poetry that she had to memorize for school, even before he knew what it meant. Or they stretched out on the floor in front of the fire after dinner and worked on making things while they exchanged stories, as Ouida tried to match LaRue's tales with ones about flowers and plants.

She loved to collect discarded objects and find innovative ways to use them, calling their new applications "afterlives." Ouida saved flowers and dried them to make potpourri, or pressed them and left them in books as surprises for the next person who turned to a passage she had loved, and sometimes she forgot where she had hidden them and delighted herself. She decorated old tins and boxes and cans with buttons and twine, with pebbles and twigs and discarded bits of things she found, and Ruby put the things she made in the curio cabinet that sat in the corner of the living room, along with her porcelain trinkets and odd china and glass knickknacks.

The whole family was involved in conserving things that had been made scarce by the Great War. Ruby grew vegetables out back and worked on recipes she could make without much sugar or flour, and Vesta collected savings stamps. Everyone mended and darned, and Ruby encouraged the girls to do needlework, as well. Ouida didn't like needlepoint or embroidery, but Ruby helped her start a rag rug and she had one going for so long that it was too big for any floor space in the house. She liked to turn scraps of cloth and sewing notions into tapestries with fringed edges and hanging buttons and threads that she put on the walls and draped over the bedroom furniture.

Vesta had tried the different types of needlework Ruby had showed them and found that she liked cross-stitched samplers the best. Ruby showed her how to plan out her pattern by counting the right number of spaces in the checked weave of white fabric and helped her select her surrounding design and little homily. She thought it over for a long time, settling, finally, on "Home Is Where the Heart Is," and became obsessed with it, doing all of one color before she allowed herself to begin another. She sat on the living room couch for hours, absorbed in making her perfect little X's.

She worked her way along the border one evening, completing the last blue X's before she moved on to yellow, while Ouida captured the textures of a group of leaves with colored pencil rubbings. LaRue started a story as he helped her choose the colors for her leaves. "Well, there was this time that Miss Snake really got into trouble." LaRue began. "It was *some trouble* she came up against this time," he said, lying on his back with his hands clasped beneath his head.

"I bet it wasn't anything . . . anything," Ouida said, "like the fix that Foxglove found herself in."

"Well, I wouldn't know about all that, but what I do know is what happened to Miss Snake . . ."

"Then I guess you might as well tell me what happened to her, LaRue, so I can show you how it didn't even compare to Foxglove's predicament. One thing's for sure," she said, tilting her head on her long, graceful neck, "I won't get a word in edgewise till you're done."

"Girl, you ain't heard nothin yet," LaRue chuckled as he flipped over on his stomach. "It all started like this, on the sunniest day of the year . . ."

"Wait, LaRue," Ouida interrupted, "you didn't say what color Miss Snake was, and you can't start without telling that."

"Oh yeah," he said. "This day, she was a startling yellow, practically chartreuse. And she was ambling on down a dusty country road, doin' the fox trot, puffing up clouds of dirt as she went. And she was so into getting the dance rhythm and the footwork right that she didn't even notice the clouds gathering overhead. She had just about got it right, and was enjoying herself something fierce, when she felt a raindrop go 'plunk' right on her head. She looked up and frowned, just in time to see the sky darken completely and the rain begin to cover the ground."

As usual, when he got engaged in telling a story LaRue's hands darted around gracefully, illustrating his words. "Miss Snake slithered up the trunk of a tree quick, quick, and was wiping her brow with a big shiny green leaf, when she glimpsed, from the corner of her eye, something wide and furry and gold. She froze, her leaf in mid-wipe, and looked at it straight on, and to her great dismay, she found herself looking into a smiling pair of lion eyes." LaRue's body was frozen like Miss Snake's and his eyes were open wide.

"Miss Snake looked from the pair of lion eyes to the gathering water below and then back again, and said, 'Mmn. Well, ain't this somethin'. Can't take a dance in the country these days.'

"Mr. Lion whispered . . . and even his whispers sounded like roars . . . that she better stay put, 'cause everyone knows that snakes can't swim. She listened to him, watching his big pointy teeth from the corners of her eyes, and even though she didn't know whether what he said was true, she knew that *she* had never been swimming. 'I hear your life flashes before your eyes,' Lion said, 'just like that, you have it, set out before you, like a magic lantern.' And as Lion told her about the hungry creatures below, and the agony of drowning, he crept closer and closer on the branch.

"Miss Snake looked at his huge approaching teeth and decided, in a flash, to jump. And, believe it or not . . . 'cause this *is* a true story . . . as she hit the water, she found she could swim. Even though she'd never done it, it came to her, naturally, just like that. And that's not all, Ouida, for as she whipped her bright, bright yellow body through the water, all the other animals stayed away, convinced that she was, in fact, a lightning flash."

Ouida laughed at his ingenuity, as he finished the story, his hands now quiet and his palms upturned, with Miss Snake swimming home and finding a high dry rock to rub up against, renewing herself for her next adventure. Ouida teased him. "Well, that was pretty good . . . pretty good . . . but Miss Snake has seen neither trouble, nor the power of wit, till she's heard the story of what happened to Foxglove.

"You see, it wasn't always true that the foxglove plant was poisonous. There was a time when it was sweet. Sweeter than sweet. Some said it tasted like strawberry jam, and smelled even better. And its purple fringy flowers, little tubelike horns, were sold around the corner at Mr. and Mrs. Ike's, along with the penny candy."

"Where did people come from for it, Ouida? And how did they get here?" asked LaRue, who liked to help a story along.

"They came from as far as it took. By boat, by car, by train. But most just plain walked, LaRue, from however far away they were.

"Well," she continued, "Foxglove was so coveted . . . that means loved, or wanted . . . that it had to find a way to keep from being just wanted all away, because sometimes, you know, you can be desired up. Strange, hunh, that sometimes a thing needs protection from too much loving . . . or at least from some kinds . . . So Foxglove thought about what to do. She watched her surroundings, and noticed the different ways plants and animals developed for protecting themselves. She saw Lizard change colors in order to be able to hide, and Skunk spray its funky smell to keep people away. She consulted with much of the plant and animal kingdoms to arrive at her strategy.

"Finally, Foxglove decided to make herself poisonous, in order to keep from being picked. And the next person who picked her and gobbled and gobbled fell over dead with a heart attack. Foxglove decided that she'd better do something about looking and tasting so good, so that people wouldn't keep eating, despite the terrible effects. So she painted herself with strange little spots inside her funnel-like flowers . . . markings that would act something like a warning . . . and she fixed it so she no longer tastes like Mama Ruby's strawberry preserves.

"But you know something, LaRue, the most amazing thing is, if you take just a little bit of Foxglove, it can help mend a sick heart. Too much, and you're finished. It's used now to make a medicine which stimulates the heart. I read as much.

"So people keep their distance now, and it makes Foxglove kind of sad." She saw LaRue smiling, and said, "She told me so, LaRue. And she just wonders, now and again, about that line, between being wanted so bad that it's just dangerous, and being lonely and safe."

"That's a pretty good tale, Ouida. Pretty good."

Ouida leaned toward LaRue to tickle him and said, "Tell your friends. I done told mine."

Ruby liked to work in her full, colorful garden at the end of the day and talk to the young folk about their days at school when they got home. LaRue sat on the stoop answering Vesta's questions on the details of his day while Ruby worked with her flowers, tying down the leaves of her tulips and crocuses once they had bloomed and explaining how the leaves fed the bulbs so they could come back the next year. Ouida loved to help in the garden, to feel her hands in the cool damp earth and to have Ruby tell her about the plants.

Ruby wanted to be out front so she could watch folks coming home. In the years since Eula and her children had moved in, the nearby blocks had turned completely colored as the expansion of wartime jobs pulled people North. Ruby had sat on the stoop and watched the white population flee west, after they had tried to keep them out with bloodletting and sky-high rents. They renamed their street as the counterpart of affluent White Oak Street in the Caucasian part of town. At LaRue's instigation, their street became "Black Oak Street" and eventually, the colored part of town was known as Black Oak.

As the residents changed, so did the rhythms of Black Oak. The tension eased up, and people talked across their fences as they tended their flowers and their small city lawns. If Ruby had to go out, there was someone she could ask to look after things, and she returned the favor. She saw people pass by whom she had helped out with meals or a place to sleep who would have done the same for her. If Miss Etta, next door, went shopping, she was apt to pick up items for Ruby or someone else on the block, and if folks ran short of some ingredient, it was available for borrowing. It had become more and more of a neighborhood.

In the next block there was a man who was a Pullman porter with Polaris, and they often had a drink together on the way home, or sat around on the rare weekend when Polaris wasn't on the road and talked trash. Ouida and Vesta and LaRue went off to school with kids who lived nearby, and Eula had a group of friends from church who made up a foursome for bridge.

A few doors down, Delta Simms, round and barely five feet tall, rocked on the edge of her stoop, her toes lifting off the iron porch as she leaned back. In the lap of her skirts, which were a quilted medley of place and time, she cradled fruit from the tree out front that was heavy almost year-round, a tree that seemed happy to unburden itself to city children as she watched their sneaking from the corner of her good eye, giving the scoldings they expected. As soon as March settled into April, she was out on the stoop chewing on the clay dug and sent by Southern hands back home, which her neighbors came to buy.

Folks who were hinkty felt ashamed of Delta Simms and the other recent arrivals from further south who were changing the shape of the neighborhood. "They're not back home anymore," they said, angrily. "Things are different up here." Embarrassed by their "country" ways, by their work clothes on the streetcar and their shouting through open doors and across fences, they organized to school these recent arrivals about city decorum. But Ruby was friendly with just about everyone on the block, and knew many residents of Black Oak from the Sisters of Charity, which worked to fill the gaps caused by lost work and short meals. Ruby used to stop at Delta Simms's porch and share herbs or flowers with her as they chatted about back home.

Her neighbors spoke as they passed. "Evenin', Miss Ruby," Mr. Wilson, the tailor, called out to her. "Those rosebushes sure are comin' along." He stopped to admire the flowers that grew in the small square of earth in front of her house. "Got a good crop of sunflowers this spring, Miss Ruby," said the printer as he passed her house. "I swear I don't know how you do it, but there's some magic in that little piece of earth."

People stopped by to tell the latest news about their sons coming home from the war that had just ended, or gathered to argue their views on politics. A group of men were singing as they assembled at the corner for an after-work drink, or went to the "Alabama Club" and the "Mississippi Club" to link up with others from home.

Ruby liked to spend this time of day outside and feel the rhythms of her people coming home.

There were those who had spent the long day canning beans, tomatoes, jams, and others who had mopped or swept the local plants clean. The elevator operators and bellboys and window-washers downtown made their treks home carrying their dinner buckets, and there was the woman who was struggling to start her own dress shop, and the neighborhood's first lawyer, too.

She watched men drag down Black Oak Street after hours of dangerous and dirty work, their slow steady gaits telling the story of their days. She watched women who had cooked and cleaned for others as they climbed to their front doors and turned their attention to their own homes as evening fell, and children who took the steps of their stoops two and three at a time and opened their front doors to the smells of food and voices they knew.

At the height of the summer, when the heat drove the neighborhood outdoors after dinner, people started telling tales. LaRue liked to sit with the folks down at the corner who collected in a circle and talked trash. Soon Brer Rabbit and Brer Fox were in the neighborhood, and there was trouble going on. Laughter and accusations of outright lying could be heard into the evening and to Eula's dismay, LaRue was right in the middle of it, listening for the way people talked and the things that moved them. If someone didn't call him in, he would spend the night down at the corner. Sometimes, in the stagnant August air, heavy with the possibility of violence, merriment crossed into anger and a switchblade came out. Sometimes, laughter was the bridge back to peace.

One midsummer evening, Ruby finished with her flowers and then sat on the steps waiting to see Polaris's figure round the corner. She saw Eula and the kids coming up the street, and before they got there, Leverett Winters's wife, Rhea, stopped at Ruby's walk and muttered, "Common . . . alley niggers, that's all . . . outside and all on the corner . . . shoes off and work clothes on . . . and laughing all loud and whatnot . . ." and then moved on. Stunned by the amount of energy Rhea spent disapproving of the things other folks did, Ruby never knew what to say to her. She seemed to arrive on a dark cloud, and just as suddenly disappear.

When Eula reached the house she went inside, and they all stayed on the stoop until Polaris arrived and everyone was ready to eat the supper Ruby had fixed earlier that day. LaRue was standing out front talking to a neighbor and a woman came running by. He watched her fly past him, catching a glimpse of something desperate in her face that he recognized, without knowing why, and he tripped on the bottom step and dropped his books.

"Bone," Ouida said as she grabbed his arm. "What on earth is it? You look like you've seen a ghost."

LaRue looked at Ouida and then turned to watch the running woman, feeling something move within him. A stirring, and with it a kind of hurt. Like the slow and painful creaking of something that had long been asleep, the feeling scared him and he held it off.

He looked up and the sky seemed to shift from blue to white in an instant. Ouida and LaRue turned toward the house and saw Vesta looking out of the window at them without seeing them. She was staring out, so constricted by her own loneliness, that she hadn't even seen him trip.

Ruby had noticed how increasingly distracted Vesta was, and knowing some of the things that had scarred her, she tried to pull her out of it. They were the things that had first brought their families together. She knew some of the origins of her suffering, but she didn't know how locked up Vesta was inside, how she sometimes felt so tight it was hard to breathe. Exiled and self-absorbed, the longing to make a crossing grew, while she became less and less able to take a step.

Ruby tried to talk to her one evening about what she was learning in English. She coaxed her to practice reciting a poem, which Ouida had told her was so painful for Vesta to do in front of the class that she got physically sick beforehand. Ruby sat with her on the couch as they read the poem together and talked about what it meant to them, and Ruby offered encouragement and then asked Vesta to read it alone. Three times Vesta got to the second stanza and had to start over, and then finally, her eyes filled with tears, she said she couldn't do it, and fled upstairs. Ruby followed her, but by the time she got to her room Vesta had locked the bedroom door.

While she got dinner ready Ruby thought about a way to ease Vesta's anxiety and make things easier for her, but she had never really been able to reach her. The entire time she had known her she had been a closed, wary child whose hurt was clear. As Ruby thought about it, she could picture Vesta that very first night, hesitating to take that orange from her, and then clinging to it once she had.

Eula came upstairs and asked if she could help with dinner, and Ruby told her she could frost the cake that was cooling on the table. Eula sat down and got started, and as Ruby heard the knife scraping against the crockery bowl she could feel a tension in Eula. She realized that, like Vesta, Eula wanted to talk about something, but could not begin. In between the scrapings of the knife there was dead silence, as she felt Eula's desperate concentration on icing the cake.

Ruby turned, wiping her hands on her apron, and decided that what she was doing could wait. She sat down at the table with Eula and after a time of silence she asked her how things were. It took a while for them to move through small talk and details about Eula's clients, past hair oil ingredients and church news and the appetizers white folks served, but finally, looking away from Ruby as she focused on joining up the icing on the sides of the cake smoothly with the top part, Eula said, "We would have been married sixteen years today. Seems like it couldn't be true."

Once she had made an opening, Eula began to talk about how she felt, and Ruby listened as she revisited the past that had held Ontario, and the past that had not. Ruby asked her about something she had wanted to bring up: whether she thought she could love again, whether she could try to allow for it, and Eula answered, looking across the worn kitchen table at Ruby with her hands opened wide.

"Oh, Ruby, people say go out, go out with people and find a companion, find a fine gentleman who will treat you nice. But before you go out . . ." She paused and looked, finally, into Ruby's eyes as she reached up and touched her scar, smearing frosting on her forehead. ". . . someone's got to call." Neither one of them spoke for a while, and then Eula said, "It's not that I'm looking for it, you see, and I'm not dead set against it either. But no one calls for me, Ruby. No one calls."

Ruby knew that no one called and she had some idea why. She knew what kind of work it was to get past the small inconsequential facts Eula placed between herself and the rest of the world. And she knew that no one called because no one could get beyond the brittle exterior in which Eula encased herself, that when Eula's fine gentleman companion looked at her he saw the lines she had drawn, and knew the cost of crossing them would be great. He saw the burden of children who would become his, and the bitterness in the way her mouth had come to set. He saw the way her fingers never left her scar for long, and he wondered at the price.

Eula's anniversary had come and gone eight times since Ontario had died, and even though she was only thirty-five, even though she was cleaved by her loneliness sometimes, she couldn't envision herself married again, and marriage was the only arrangement she could conceive of having with a man. She couldn't imagine that that part of her life wasn't over. Solitude and acceptance, she had decided, were the facts of her life.

Each anniversary she mourned her husband, even though he had hurt her beyond measuring and the whole thing had been over so long ago. She had actually managed to forget the ugly specifics of her past with Ontario Smalls, as long as no one brought them up, and even if someone had, she wouldn't have been able to recall exactly what about it had been bad. Although a vague animosity survived for what he had taken from her while alive, she resented more what he had taken when he died.

She would never be young again, and that had been true for a long time. But what was harder, there was no one left who would remember her that way. No one would ever look at her and see not merely the mother, the churchgoer, the hairdresser . . . the middle-aged woman she was now, but also the girl she had been. She had stretch marks and her breasts sagged. She was tired and her joints ached. There was half a lifetime on her body. There was caution in her eyes.

With Ontario's death so much else had passed. The image of Eula, standing in her father's barbershop the day they had met, fresh and beautiful and believing, as she listened to him talk about the green place he had left for the city, had been preserved somewhere in her husband's memory, along with whatever else he had come to see, and when that scaffold had swayed and he had fallen, he had taken with him the memory of her youth.

That anniversary she again mourned her losses, adding to the layers of bitterness she had built around her over the years.

That anniversary and another came and went and things remained the same for Eula, but with the anticipation of the transition she and Ouida were about to make to high school, Vesta seemed to be able to see a little past her own unhappiness. LaRue was excited for them, and jealous that his "bestest girlfriends," as he called them, were going into the ninth grade.

The summer before high school began both girls got jobs downtown. Doing finishing work on lingerie, Vesta spent her days in windowless rooms filled with worktables and dull walls, absorbed in the details of muted undergarments of ecru and pale pink. She sewed stays and hooks and eyes, tatting, and metal grommets through which laces and ribbons would pass, things that would shape and adorn those who could afford them in the hidden layers of garments that on many would never be seen.

She emerged from the beige world of the workroom at the end of the late summer days to a light of deep gold that struck everything around it and shot the trees through with its glow. It made the green rich, as if the light burned outward, through the leaves. There was the green-gold, and the quieting-down heat of summer's close.

Vesta stepped into the light and blinked as she went to meet Ouida, who worked for a furrier at the seasonal job of repairing and cleaning coats and wraps that had been stored for the summer. She hated the musty, closed-in work space and she hated the days spent among stoles with pointed faces frozen into anger, glass-eyed, ready to snap; and tiny, sharp-clawed feet that haunted her even at home. She said she felt as though she, too, had been stored for the summer, and when she met Vesta at a downtown corner she was relieved and energetic, as if she had been uncaged.

On the way home she told Vesta about the wealthy white patrons and together they imagined their lives of fur-wearing and traveling and soirees. She told Vesta, too, about the white men she saw look at her as if she were an ornament from a foreign world they wanted to examine and possess.

That summer they also talked about the coming year at the colored high school, and in Ouida's infectious excitement at the summer heat and light, Vesta felt as though things could maybe happen for her, too. A new school, a new situation might give her a better chance of belonging somewhere. She had always restricted herself to the present tense, had always kept to what was, but she had to admit to herself, in the long, gold days of August, that she wanted more.

Ouida talked about what school would bring, about getting new books and tablets and pens and pencils and of going to new classes and meeting people. She imagined grown-up parties and after-school events, talking about the future they would have as if it was vivid and wide, and Vesta was swept up as she listened to Ouida go on and on about the college preparatory courses she was planning to take and what the fall might bring, and how one day they would be graduated, together, and be women with jobs and families of their own. Ouida talked all the way home about the things they would do and the people they would meet, and she answered "Yes, and maybe . . . this fall . . . maybe we'll dance."

Vesta saw the future, spreading, alive and colorful in her head. She could see it opening, and she let herself want it. Let herself hope for more.

7

Vesta let herself want more, and then settled for less. She let herself imagine, for a brief time, a life that was vibrant and uncertain, and then, from the age of seventeen, she wore white. Finished with color, she disposed of all the clothes she had that were patterned and tinted, and bargained for the blankness of white.

She opted to be caretaker. Witness. She opted never to tear the sky.

From then on she would live in a secondhand world, whose hues, by the time they reached her, had already begun to fade. Her last episode with color involved a risk of loving, and began with her exclusion from a dance.

Approaching Ouida during recess, Vesta caught the end of a conversation that wasn't meant for her. "She's like my sister," she heard Ouida whisper, "and if she's not welcome, neither am I." Ouida turned around just as Vesta came up, and pulled her down the hall by the arm, distracting her with a funny story. "Do you know what Maudine did in English?" she said, looking for signs that Vesta had overheard. Vesta was quiet as Ouida's words echoed in her head until they slid into place and fit with other things she had noticed over the past week.

As they stopped in the washroom, Vesta considered the other comments she had picked up as she passed through the hallways or walked by the clustered girls in gym class, their light-skinned faces strung together like links in a chain, growing quiet as she passed. She looked at her brown fingers with their bitten-down nails through the stream of water from the faucet, while Ouida chattered on, still watching for a sign that she had overheard. Vesta lifted what seemed like someone else's hands through the water and shook them, scattering droplets across the white porcelain sink.

As she dried her hands and grabbed her books to leave, a burning crept around her middle like a tightening belt. If she had known there would be a dance, she thought, she would have guarded against disappointment, she would have been prepared. She was angry at Ouida for not warning her, for letting her be exposed. She would keep what she had heard to herself, she repeated, silently, and felt, at once, a sense of disbelief that she had been excluded from the very first dance the girls her age would attend, and a recognition that she would have been surprised if it had happened any other way.

It always seemed to be like that for Vesta, and by her expectations, she helped to make it so. Despite her wanting the new school to be different, to be a new start, it hadn't been. Seeing herself as whatever Ouida wasn't, she brought her history of exile with her and remained a stranger, whose presence, at seventeen, disturbed.

Knowing that people responded to her, Ouida worked her charm. She knew that her pull involved her tall full figure and light skin, but she didn't have the proportionate Anglo-Saxon features that were equated with beauty, and she thought her long, prominent nose and narrow eyes, which people called "tight," were strange-looking, but different enough to make her exotic and distinct.

She was learning about the power of what is considered attractive as she grew into a woman, and focused her energy there, instead of on her gifts for knowing and understanding things. She found the fact of her own magnetism fascinating, and the language, the gestures of the *femme fatale,* so easy to master, that she became consumed by the rush of playing it to a house full of applause. Her female peers measured themselves against her, and young men wanted to have her for their own.

The thing that drew people most was the way Ouida carried herself, as if something wonderful might happen to her. She walked into a room like it belonged to her, and she was always reminding Vesta not to rearrange her clothes and hair after she got somewhere: "Vesta, finish all your adjusting before you leave the house," she would say, "and then, knowing you are beautiful, enter every room that way."

But Vesta couldn't help fidgeting, and something about the gravity and the wariness in her face prevented people from ever noticing her beauty, her smooth, deep brown skin and lovely almond-shaped eyes, which were so dark that iris and pupil were indistinguishable. She seldom showed the smile that made her broad, full face radiant.

She looked at people carefully, distantly, half-expecting them to turn away, and punctuating everything she said with "kind of" and "sort of," it took her a long time to get to the point. Her tenth-grade teacher had said, "Spit it out, Miss Smalls! Don't give me a dissertation; tell me what you mean." She did for her schoolwork exactly what was asked, nothing more, nothing less, and she always followed the rules. She never decided to take a step without planning it, she took the same sure route into and out of each day, and because it seemed to her that when she walked up conversation died, she kept to herself. Radiating her sense of herself as an outsider, she distanced herself further and further from those to whom she wanted, deeply, secretly, to belong.

Ouida's public persona struggled against the one her family knew, and the things instilled by Ruby were eclipsed by the intoxication of being wanted. And although she told herself she was just finding out how things worked, the bigger part of her felt that what she was doing was wrong. She didn't tell Ruby what was going on with the dance, but waited to see if her threat would get Vesta invited. She knew her mother would ask her why she wanted to associate with small-minded people, but Ouida told herself that what she had worked out was a compromise, and the stand she had taken made it okay. She told herself that the way she had handled it, Vesta would get to go.

A few days after her ultimatum, Ouida was told that Vesta was welcome. When Ouida was sure Vesta didn't know what had been going on, she told her about the dance, and Vesta pretended it was news. They told the rest of the family about it, and Ruby took the money out of her canning jar at the back of the kitchen cabinet to buy fabric for their dresses. Ouida chose peach linen while Vesta picked a rich ocean blue and the two mothers stayed up into the night sewing for two weeks straight, while Vesta, Ouida, and LaRue helped with the finishing. Wanting to make her daughter's first dance special for her, Eula secretly took a handful of seed pearls from a secondhand dress one of her clients had given her, and sewed them to the front of Vesta's dress.

On the night of the dance, they got ready with their mothers' help. Eula washed and oiled their hair, and fixed it for them. She had seen something doubtful and afraid in Vesta's eyes each time the subject of the dance was raised, but she didn't know how to address it directly. As she put the finishing touches on Vesta's hair, which she swept up and fixed with tortoise shell combs, Eula lifted her chin and tried to smile reassurance into her face.

When Ouida had her dress on, she twirled around the room, enchanted at the way her skirt lifted as she turned. She imagined herself dancing each dance, and chatting with her suitors. She imagined that no one would ever know it was her first dance from the way she handled herself. Eula had to pull her aside to finish doing her hair. "Ouida, come on over here. We haven't got all night, and at the rate you're going, you'll never get there." She made her sit still, and wrapped her thick braid around her head like a crown.

When Eula was finished with Vesta and Ruby had put touches of makeup on their faces, Ouida jumped up and exclaimed, "Vesta . . . Vesta . . . you are sooo beautiful!" but Vesta looked away, thinking Ouida was merely overcompensating for what she knew.

Ruby let them wear her nice jewelry and Eula reminisced about her first date, making them laugh at how strict her father had been, how he had made her escort write down his address and sign a piece of paper stating that he wouldn't harm her, and looked him straight in the eye as he said he knew just where to find him should that be necessary.

LaRue objected to the smell of their perfume, but when they laughed at him he gave up and begged them to show him how to dance. He made them promise to "pay attention to everything," presented them with flowers that Eula suspected he had cut from a neighboring garden.

When they were all ready, Ouida pulled Vesta before the mirror that hung on the wall, and what Vesta saw left her speechless. Ouida was to her an incantation. With her wavy hair plaited around her long, thin, light-skinned face, she looked to Vesta like a queen, full-figured and statuesque, her peach dress simple and elegant. She looked at herself and saw everything that Ouida wasn't, saw a dark figure, stunted and plain, in a garish dress. She didn't see anything beautiful, only Ouida's negative, the border from her cut-out silhouette. She was still the dark misfit Vashti Martin and countless others had snubbed. Her arms hung at her sides while Ouida hugged her in excitement, and the tiny seed pearls danced down the front of her bodice like falling tears.

As soon as they arrived at the party, Ouida was swept up by a group of girls, and Vesta stood by her side for a while, and then wandered to a haven of purple velvet-seated chairs in the corner of the room, where she sat for most of the evening. Ouida brought her punch or shared a secret in between dances, or tried to coax her into enjoyment, but Vesta sat on the edge of the party, touching her hair over and over to make sure it wasn't coming loose, straightening the sleeves and front of her dress, as she tried to forget that she hadn't really been invited. Whenever Ouida came and sat by her, someone arrived with an offer to dance, leaving Vesta alone, again. If Vesta detected someone glancing in her direction, she avoided his eyes and protected herself with a disinterested look, praying for the evening's end. She didn't notice the man who stood watching from across the room.

She didn't see Shag Wilson appraising the party from the sidelines as he tapped his foot with an expression of detached amusement, the bored slant of his shoulders saying he had already experienced everything he saw. He turned his jaded eyes on Vesta and watched her sit through song after song, reading the fear and the need in her eyes.

Near the end of the evening, he crossed the room and stood before her, his hand outstretched. Vesta didn't move. She looked up and saw the face of a commanding man, and then hesitated and glanced away as he stood there and compelled her with his waiting hand. To be that sure of yourself that you didn't even conceive of the possibility that you would be turned down—it took Vesta's breath away. He stood before her, waiting, certain, and she rose to take his hand, as if powerless to refuse. He drew her close, and as she extended her foot, pinched in its hard, narrow evening shoe, to follow his lead, she thought she felt off balance. She didn't trust her feet. She didn't. It took so little to fall.

Shag came calling, as he said he would, bearing flowers and candy, along with just the right amount of detachment. He did the things he thought women expected and wanted, and he believed that most of all they wanted what they might not be able to have.

He chatted politely with Ruby and Eula, and when LaRue came in talking about Miss Snake, Shag's reaction told him what he wanted to know. He looked at LaRue as though he was silly, and told Vesta later that he didn't understand that kind of fooling around in a young man. Polaris lowered his paper to look him over and state a curfew time, but he never told Vesta what he thought of him. He just didn't talk about those kinds of things.

Shag's smooth demeanor made them worry about Vesta, but when Ouida asked gently if he was really her type, Vesta responded, "Because he could have anyone, Ouida? Because he could have you?" Taken aback by the resentment in Vesta's voice, Ouida withdrew her comment with, "Vesta, that's not what I meant . . . he just seems . . . worldly, that's all." Vesta blocked out their reactions, needing to believe he cared.

He moved slowly with her, graduating from hand-holding, to kissing, to touching, and he asked her all about herself, like no one, she thought, ever had. And as he gained her trust, Vesta revealed herself to him. She told him, bit by bit, about her father's violence, and his fall from the sky. She told him about the danger she sometimes saw in her mother's eyes, and even that she hadn't been invited, after all, to the dance. She showed him the seams of herself, ragged and distressed.

And finally, when it came down to whether she would move from kissing and touching to the final deed, it was "Don't you love me? . . . Don't you love me enough?" She wanted to show him she could love him, to answer that it might, it might be. His mouth bruised hers at the sweet conquering, the feeling of her underneath him in a moment when he seemed to be at the center of everything. She might as well have reached inside, pulled her heart out, and placed it, beating, in his hands.

Afterward, lying in his bed, they began to talk. Shy and overwhelmed, Vesta lay there, open to him, and started talking about a few good small things she remembered from growing up. And then somehow, against his will, he would think, looking back on it, he told her a part of him he had never exposed.

He didn't know how they got there, or what would make him show himself like that to a woman. He knew women weren't really for talking to; they were for something else. But he was lying with her and he was saying, "You remember warm cookies and tall tales. Well, try this one on for size. The thing I remember most from being a boy is this . . ." and she was nodding as she took his head on her breast. And maybe it was the dark, and the way she had opened herself, and maybe it was her pain, but he found himself back there, in a time he had chosen to forget.

He found himself in his boyhood, waiting for the father who had long since gone. There had been a promise, a promise to take him to the traveling circus, and he had waited for his father on the front porch, dressed in his best clothes, dreaming about the magic to come, imagining what his papa would look like, would be like, when he turned the corner and came his way. Imagining that he would know him, know him even in a crowd. He was, again, that expectant boy, waiting as the hours passed and he grew more and more tense, waiting for the father who never came. And he told Vesta, so many years later, about the shame and disappointment he had felt that day, pushed back among the memories that can't be looked at in the light.

She held him closer once he was finished and told him it would be all right. But he tightened his body against her touch and began to pull away inside. Then he lost himself in her body again, gripping her in the darkness, taking what she gave, and as Vesta lay beneath him, she felt herself tearing into blue.

* * *

What was to her a beginning was for Shag complete. He appeared a few more times to make his withdrawal less embarrassing for others and himself, but he had already begun his retreat. A few more living room visits, and then he disappeared. For three weeks Vesta waited in the front room where she would be able to see him approach the house, and worked on a cross-stitch sampler. She made up her face with powder and rouge, and arranged her hair for the visit that had to come. She waited, and when she had almost finished the sampler, she pulled out the glossy little X's and began again. She bit her nails in between stitches and scratched her itching skin while awaiting his return.

But her hunger, pulling him to her, was the thing he couldn't stand. Something in him wanted to punish her for what she needed him to be, and he didn't have a place in his life for the way Vesta had opened up to him, and for what he, too, had staked.

Three weeks she waited, stationary, yet with the sense that she was tumbling, tumbling with no recourse, and then she got up and left her front room post. She cursed herself for her misstep, praying that she would never see Shag again. She lay in bed, curling her body inward, and let the night come, as it must, the promise of morning far off. She wanted to raise her hands against all of the isn'ts of her life, to grieve, to rage, to rage against what she had been dealt.

Instead, she tightened her arms around herself and compressed her devastation to a manageable size, vowing, in the future, to be careful enough.

Her fear and mistrust had built up, layer upon layer, until she chose a path that would never bend back and meet itself, and something in her folded like a fan, collapsing the entire spectrum into white.

White, like a refuge. Shelter from purple, from blue.

White, like a quiet resolution. Like a treaty for peace.

From the wages she had earned in summer work at the Foundations Department of the store downtown, Vesta bought herself a wardrobe of white clothes. She had them made, and paid in advance, believing that it was better to own a few really good, timeless things, than to have lots of mediocre ones. She had them fitted specially to her small frame, "Tailor-made" she said, and her other clothes she donated to the less fortunate.

The first few days she appeared at the breakfast table dressed completely in white, LaRue asked her whether she had "gone into nursing, or joined the corner church." They all watched her for clues as to what was going on, but they figured it was a momentary thing. When it continued, Ouida tried to ask her gently what she was doing, and to say that Shag was a rake and had treated lots of others that way. She put her arms around Vesta and said, "He doesn't deserve you, honey. You'll find someone who does." But Vesta wouldn't discuss Shag or her new white clothes, and Ouida waited until Vesta left the house to slide open her dresser drawers, stunned to find each one filled with starched white clothes.

Eula didn't have the strength to confront her about it and even if she could have, she didn't know what to say. Ruby asked Polaris to say something to her, as a man, and after dinner one night he fumbled his way toward telling her that there were other men out there who would treat her with respect. Touched by his effort, all Vesta could do in response was nod. It didn't really change anything. Nothing did.

When Ouida told Ruby about the dresser drawers, she went to Vesta for answers. Ruby found Vesta folding and arranging her new clothes in careful piles within her drawers. Vesta at first answered, "All one color is easier. It's just less fuss." When Ruby continued to look at her, waiting for the real reason, she looked at Ruby directly with tears in her eyes. "There's no history to white, Mama Ruby. It just is."

Ruby reached out to her, but Vesta turned away and resumed her smoothing and folding. Ruby sat still for a while, and then went back downstairs and told the others. "It's a kind of mourning, I think. What with that Shag Wilson and all." They figured it would pass and besides, nobody knew what else there was to say.

LaRue tried to talk to her about it, engaging her with anecdotes. He told her he thought she was beautiful, that she would find someone who deserved her in time. He tried to get her to share her feelings, but she was closed off to talking, and to hearing what he had to say. LaRue and Ouida kept asking her about it, but Vesta made clear that the subject was off limits and, eventually, they gave up.

The neighbors hinted about for her reasons, which she never gave, and their curiosity gradually waned. They kept their speculations among themselves and, in time, her white became an eccentricity. Something that was hers.

It seemed like the rest of Black Oak burst into color to make up for what was absent in Vesta's life. A wave of heat came in October, as if summer just wouldn't let go, and the trees held onto their vibrant leaves through November that year. It was a tenacious fall, the yellows seeming yellower and the reds redder before autumn surrendered to winter.

People dressed with greater drama in that season and invented more outrageous stories than ever, as if they were fighting White Oak's hostility, which was growing in response to the greater numbers of colored folks moving north. LaRue sat on neighboring stoops and listened to returning soldiers tell about what they had seen overseas, and heard whispered news of more and more dark bodies found hanging from Southern trees.

On Sunday mornings Ruby saw lots of faces she didn't know on the street, and she tried to take people in or provide advice and food when she could. She saw the hostile glances and overheard more and more comments about "field niggers" and "country folk" from colored neighbors who wanted to distance themselves from the newly arrived. And they tried to deal with the message from White Oak that while a few black faces had been tolerated, there were lines to be drawn. As colored folks swelled the city, challenging the way things had been, White Oak sought to drive them back, and even to punish them for reaching after something else. Eula overheard fragments of heated conversation at the houses she visited doing hair, heard it again and again: "Less . . . there will be less for us."

Polaris came home talking about how rents had gone up all over town, and how, wherever colored moved in, whites left, passing on buildings in need of repairs that could never be afforded. New laws were put in place to keep things in the hands of those who had owned them all along. There had always been some places that were segregated, and even where it wasn't formal, everyone knew where the worlds of the races diverged. But now, stores and barbershops and drinking fountains turned to potential battlegrounds, and as much as possible, folks kept to known territory.

For those in Black Oak it was too familiar. Ruby couldn't stop thinking of what had driven her from the town where she had grown up, and Polaris was so upset he had trouble talking about what was going on. They were afraid, and they were pressed. As colored families moved in, calling on names they had been given at churches and asking for places to stay, a hostility that had been sleeping below the surface rose. Unspoken threats hung in the air and parents warned their children of the silent rules that were becoming more important.

When they talked about it later, people would say it was something they could sense around them, a tight, restive feeling in the air. Resentment, bloated and building to erupt. Ruby came home one day and said a white girl had spit at her as she headed for the dressmaking shop in downtown White Oak. LaRue said there was violence in the way a group of boys had fingered a pile of stones as he passed.

Against these things the residents of Black Oak dressed in bold colors and patterns and told their stories for passing down, and although White Oak might not have noticed it, there was resistance in the air. Resistance, along with taking care. The men held lying bouts and the women started a quilt, sewing their stories and their colors in. They prayed, drawing on things long forgotten, but held as a group. They lied and they stitched and they called on their gods, pulling on what they carried beneath memory, on the spirits they had known.

And then it happened, as the trees finally let go their redder reds and their yellower yellows. LaRue saw it, as he listened to the elders weave their tales: a pair of stones was released, in the event that became the everything, shifting forces just enough to split through fear and snap the boundaries that had kept things running and in place, igniting a rage and resentment that was generations old. A pair of stones thrown at a black boy and a policeman who failed to act.

Before anyone could stop to think, it had begun, and then there was burning, and black people, somebody's loved ones, dying. And two who fell were white and the others, fifteen and then twenty black folks fallen. And fewer left to tell the tale.

In the end, there were fewer left, and one of those gone was Crenshaw Wells, who never would get to tell Ruby what he had to say. He had stepped from a building into flying metal and fists to join the fallen.

After the burning and the dying, things settled down, but they didn't return to what they had been. People were changed by where they had seen things go and what they had witnessed themselves feeling and saying. It was as if they didn't quite recognize themselves, as if they couldn't believe their own unexpressed anger and the fact that they had stepped right into risk in an instant, when they had spent their lives up until then taking care. Now they asked themselves, "Was that . . . is this, me?"

They talked about what had occurred indirectly and their accounts of what had exploded above the surface were expressed in all kinds of ways. Folks recounted what had happened in the lies they told and spoke of it in metaphor, and it became part of what they knew about, part of the life of Black Oak. They prayed on it at church and shared news about those who were recovering, and they found small things in it to laugh about: how fast someone had moved through a crowd or the way a punch had been dodged.

The open violence passed, but it had become a part of them, and LaRue listened to it come out on the street corner, at school, and in his own home, just as he felt his own hidden past building, building for release.

8

Nobody could remember exactly when Tennessee Coal & Iron Company Jones came into their lives, but one day, LaRue had returned from school and mentioned casually, as he removed his coat and hung it in the hall, "I saw Tennessee Coal & Iron Company Jones today. He's doing just fine."

Vesta stopped setting the table and stared at him. Ruby stopped stirring her pot. After putting down the spoons, Vesta's hand went directly to her hip.

"Tennessee *who*?" she challenged. "You tellin' your lies again, LaRue?"

"What are you talking about? I told you about Tennessee." He smiled. "I met him in the park. Isn't it something how colored folk will name their kids anything? That one sure beats all, though, doesn't it?"

She watched him silently.

"You see, his daddy was a blacksmith down in Memphis. Memphis, Tennessee. And he was only a little baby. And his daddy was clean out of work. And just as they were scratching onions and potatoes that had barely got a start in life out of the ground for food, his daddy found a job at the Tennessee Coal & Iron Company. His mama was so thankful, she named him after the one piece of good fortune she had had.

"Something else, isn't it?" he continued. "Tennessee Coal & Iron Company Jones. It just about beats all." He chuckled as he left the room, swinging his book bag.

Vesta and Ruby looked at each other, shaking their heads, and went back to their tasks. And each of them wondered, secretly, if it was really true.

Some of LaRue's stories were sagas, his characters fixed marks that returned like the seasons. He would entertain his family and friends with the antics and cross-country travels of Tennessee Jones for the rest of his life, and they never knew when he was coming. He arrived, unannounced, and departed just as abruptly, leaving them, in some way, changed.

People would say of LaRue that he wasn't the *biggest* liar they knew, but without question, the most *casual* one. They would gather in the living room around the new radio, waiting for their favorite show to come on, and LaRue would say, half to himself, something like, "Did I ever tell you all about the time that Tennessee Jones went west?"

Eula looked up from her darning, Polaris lowered his paper a little bit, and Ouida and Vesta paused from their reading and embroidery. Earlier that day Ouida had explained to LaRue that the tendency of vines to climb up was due to a desire to avoid being stepped on by big feet like his. He had been working on his own story all afternoon, and he was ready to introduce it.

"It all had to do with two things: adventure and big feet."

They soon surrendered, and the radio never did get turned on. Polaris's newspaper got folded and put down, while Eula slipped the smooth darning egg into her basket and laid down her half-sewn sock. Ouida gently closed her book, forgetting to insert a bookmark, and Vesta slowed her cross-stitching down.

"Well, it just so happened that he was poring over a magazine that his mother brought from the white folks' home where she cleaned, once they got finished reading them, 'cause even though they were throwing them out, they didn't want her to have them. She used to slip them, a few at a time, into her bag, and bring them home for Tennessee. She read to him from those discarded magazines at night, struggling with the words she didn't know. You see, they had no money for books, and no colored were allowed to join their local library. Well, Tennessee used to sit on the back steps and study those magazines.

"Some of them were about other places, and about animals and nature, things like that. And some of them gave him a funny feeling of anger and shame, the ones that talked about what to do about the 'problem' of colored folks, and the 'dilemma' of Indians trying to get their land back from the white man. These weren't things he felt he could consult with his teachers at school, or anyone else, about.

"Well, Tennessee was sitting there one day, twisting the toe of his shoe in a hollow knot on the bottom step, 'cause you see, he had bigger feet than mine. In fact, he wore a size sixteen, and he was always busting the seams of his shoes and wearing them out, when he came across an article about Indians. He knew his mother had told him they were part Indian, that that's where his grandmother got her nose and cheekbones from. But he didn't really know if it was fact or fiction, seeing as every colored person he knew had at one time or another bragged on their Indian blood.

"The drawings fascinated him, and he studied the clothing of leather and feathers and beads, and the different kinds of houses they lived in, and such. And although he saw that their hair was long and straight, more like Eula's, the skin of the people in the drawings was brown, like his. Moreover, there was something in their faces, a kind of feeling of loss or pain. There was something that was kin about them, Tennessee felt.

"Much of what was in the article Tennessee didn't understand, like why these people were called a 'problem,' too, or what a 'reservation' was. He wanted to know why these stories said they were 'savages' who needed the white man, and he didn't know what 'civilization' meant. But he pored over and over the pictures and asked his mother to look for more books and magazines about them.

"It was a long time before she came back with another story about Indians. This one was about their customs and beliefs, and Tennessee Jones wanted to know about these people's gods, and was more interested than ever. They didn't worship in churches, with rows of seats or pews, he found out, but had different ways of getting in contact with heaven, and they thought about God in a different kind of way too, not up there," LaRue said, pointing to the sky, "but all around. Tennessee read on about these things, trying to grasp them on his own. And somehow, they made sense.

"Now the thing that struck him most was the way the article talked about changing the way these people, the Indians, thought about things. People who called themselves 'missionaries,' and went out West to make the Indians sit in churches and fold their hands in prayer. Tennessee knew how he felt about church, and it didn't make him feel better or more in touch with God to dress up and go on Sunday and have to be quiet and careful not to move. It made him feel more uncomfortable, as a matter of fact, and he went to church because his mama made him. It didn't really have much to do with him.

"The best times Tennessee could think of were when he leaned against his mother's knees in front of her on the floor, and when he was in the woods, or some nights when he got up and went to the window to look at the stars, and everything was quiet. Those very times felt holy to him. And so he made a vow that he would meet some of these Indian people and find out for himself about their beliefs, that he would go to where they lived and see what that was like.

"Tennessee talked to his big thick feet, busting already through his shoes, and he told them that they would have to take him other places, that they would have to get him to a corn dance and show him how to move in a circle to drums, and teach him other ways to pray. Tennessee talked to his feet of the coming adventures to which they would carry him. 'I'm dependin' on the two of yous,' he used to say, 'to get me goin' elsewhere in this world.'

"So you see, Miss Ouida," he finished up, "big flat feet like mine and Tennessee's can be a blessing, after all. They took him lots of places, and mine will carry me out into the world, too. I know just where I've been and where I am, and where I'm headed will be an adventure, and my feet will carry me there. I've got big understandings, Ouida, and they suit me just fine."

"LaRue," Ouida said, shaking her head and laughing, "I could never keep up with you, really, even if I tried. You are just a liar through and through. And the funny thing is, the way you tell your stories, I believe you anyhow."

LaRue never admitted that a single story he told wasn't true, but the fact was that for him, they were. Vesta never failed to ask him, when he was finished with a tale, if it was factual or not. "Now, LaRue," she would say, "I know that's a lie. It couldn't possibly be true. It is a lie, isn't it . . . you made that up?"

He always laughed. "Why of course it's the truth. Have you ever known me to lie?" And then he began to wrap up his stories with a coda: "I swear on high, this tale is true; if not for me, for sure for you." He was certain that nothing that was altogether false could reach people the way his stories did.

As he developed more and more finesse and ingenuity in his lying, the story of his own past was building in him, pushing into the present. The small recollections that spoke of so much more had begun to rush forward, rending his sleep with flight and breaking glass so that he woke, breathless and running, though from what to what he wasn't sure.

He woke suddenly, pulling in his breath, to the smells of perfume and blood. It seemed like everything around him splintered and the darkness broke apart.

LaRue thought he wanted to know whatever there was to know, wanted, as in that evening when he pulled the wishbone against his sister's careful hand, everything. But as it came to him, this shapeless and violent truth, he realized that he wasn't sure. In an effort to accept what was happening to him he began to tell a story that took shape gradually, over the course of a week, as if it only revealed itself to him little by little.

The first day he said, "You know, it might surprise you, but Miss Snake didn't come from a family as colorful and dramatic as she was."

He said no more and Ouida asked, "What else, LaRue? What else?" He looked at them blankly and said, "I don't know yet. I'll tell you when I do," and after staring at him for a moment they went back to what they had been doing. Vesta picked up her cross-stitch and Ouida resumed daydreaming about the perfect romance she knew would come her way. Polaris turned on the radio and sat with Ruby and Eula quietly, listening to another drama take shape.

The next day LaRue added to his beginning. "Miss Snake's mother was a lovely emerald green, but she remained the same color all her life. And Miss Snake came into the world that same basic green and wanted to stay that way. She wanted to be like everyone else, to fit in, and when she first found out something else was available to her, she refused it." LaRue stopped talking, looked around, and said quietly, "That's all for now."

Vesta hated unfinished things, and she announced that she would not listen to the rest of the story unless he was going to wrap it up for them. She stuck around for the next installment nonetheless.

"She refused it," he said a day or two later, with no further introduction, and when everyone realized he was picking up his tale where he had left off, they stopped what they were doing and listened. "She even hoped it would go away. If she didn't wish for anything else, Miss Snake figured, she could stay green, because, you see, continuity was a refuge. But then the other possibilities were whispered to her, by the forest, it seemed, and they built up, calling to her until she wasn't clear about her refusal. It would be harder to know, and in knowing, not to be sure what lay ahead."

LaRue was finishing the story of Miss Snake's dilemma for a long time, recounting her debate on the merits of a risky, colorful life and how she made her way from refusal to a decision to know. And to his own past he woke as he was able, bit by bit.

He felt the weight of his father without knowing what it meant, in the understanding pressing within, and he knew, without perceiving how or why, or even what, that there had been wrongs. He wondered about the wrongs and he wondered about their reasons, and whether they brought with them absolution of any kind. LaRue considered his place in the imagined transgressions of his line, and he thought he wanted to know. He thought he wanted to know, but was, in truth, afraid, sensing that whatever was his father's was in some way his.

His father, unknown and unchosen, from whom he came. He had heard next to nothing about him. No one spoke his name. But LaRue didn't know how he could reject what he was being offered, even if it was bitter truth. There must be something else to know about him, he thought, some other, better side, and he wondered how he could find out about that one if he closed his eyes to this.

9

Three years after Vesta's fold into white, LaRue was on his way home from an errand downtown. As he thought about his family, and the things that were worrying him started forming a list, he fought the temptation to leap from that list into even bigger things. He thought about how tired Mama Ruby and his mother seemed sometimes, and the way Polaris was gone so much. He wondered about Ouida, who seemed to be consumed with social events, and about Vesta's response to her experience with Shag. LaRue muttered to himself that it was beyond him how a man who acted like that could get up and face himself day to day. He was worried about his family. "I just don't know what trials lie ahead, Miss Snake," he whispered, "but I hope we're up to them . . ."

He was so preoccupied that he wasn't watching where he was going and turned down a side street where he was overtaken by the past. It rose up from silence, coming to claim him: the instant of his father's fall, and that night when he was carried through the darkness, in search of Ruby's door.

For Vesta and Eula, the past was a weight to be lifted and pushed away. They had kept the night of running from him, speaking not of the bruises that preceded their flight, nor of the controlled anger that followed. Most of the questions that preoccupied him had gone unanswered.

The first time he asked her where his family came from and what their stories were, Eula had talked about the place where she was born, about her mother's daily crossings into the white section of their little town. Her leaving food for her own family in covered dishes on the stove, to go and cook someone else's evening meal, and returning to their colored share of things to begin it again. She told how her father had farmed their small plot of land and worked as a barber, too, dreaming of being independent and prosperous enough to have his own shop.

Eula had started talking, forgetting for a time that LaRue was sitting at her feet, and her remembering had flowed. She grew excited as she talked, and she punctuated her story with her hands as her son tended to do, recalling how her family had moved to the city and her father had worked to start his shop, and she talked about how different city life had seemed to her from the place of trees and earth where she had lived the first ten years of her life.

She smiled as she told him about learning her alphabet on a slate at the kitchen table while her mother made candles, returning as she spoke to the smells of bayberry and vanilla, and the row of hanging wicks and metal candle molds. Simple plain ones to be sold, and a few in each batch that had other colors or delicate twists, which she gave as gifts or kept for use at home. Eula laughed as she recalled how her mother let her make free-form candles anchored by bases of sand, or poured into containers that she found. She revisited the feel of wood planks on her bare feet as she woke in the night and went to the toilet out back. The view from handmade bottle-bottom window glass. Leaving her perch in the tree out back as her mother called her inside to wash for dinner.

When they moved to the city, she told LaRue, she had missed the law of seasons and animals, the rich colors and smells of outdoors, the honking voices of tall trees as they bent in the wind. She had been scared, at first, to venture out in the new hard place where the rules were unknown and friction seemed to drive things, and she had never lost her yearning to go back. But her father had loved the feeling of possibility the city gave him, the sense that things could be done and redone, and she told LaRue about the moment when her father had decided to leave their small town.

She remembered it out loud for LaRue, the day, the instant when it was enough, when Eula and her parents went to town and the white man laughed as her father came through the doorway of the store and Eula and her mother were waiting for him and there they were, waiting too: the white man and his laugh.

It had happened in an instant, the eyes meeting and the laugh, not so different from many things that had gone before, that somehow finished it, made it enough. Eula tried to name what that laugh had held, what quiet cancellation before the erupting malice of the laugh; and it was funny, she told LaRue, how things sometimes built, little by little, until one single thing, not so very different from those that came before, is just as tall as it can grow, is just enough. "Maybe . . ." she said, ". . . maybe it was lifetimes of that laugh."

After Eula spoke of this, she sat silently, her hands stilled, and she was done remembering, as if the only way she could keep on living was to tunnel through the present. She rose from her chair and started cleaning and straightening, afraid that if she stopped too long to examine what was pressing on her, heavy . . . what had come before . . . she would never start moving again. She cut her recollecting short, and never told LaRue the other things she had to tell.

When LaRue asked how she had met Ontario, Eula looked away and mumbled, "So long ago." Although she couldn't share it with LaRue, she thought about the unpolished boy she had met at her father's barbershop, and how her father's stern skepticism had seemed an inspiration for Ontario to prove himself. Eula saw a flash of Ontario's face as it had greeted her that day, and she recalled his manner, rough and genuine. She had watched him talk about where he was from and how he had just come to the city to look for work, and then watched him turn to say to everyone in the shop, his neck moving as punctuation, "I'm goin' back."

Yet somehow Ontario had seemed to lose hold of the dream to leave the city behind that had bound them from the first. Beneath the burdens of his window-washing, carpentry, lifting, moving, cleaning jobs, it gave way, surviving only in his decoys and wooden landscapes. He slept little and went from one job to another, consumed with fighting to survive, and lost a way of reaching their dream at all, reacting, finally, in anger at the mere mention of country life.

After a few years of marriage, he had stopped talking to Eula about his feelings, or about what happened away from home, but when they had first married, and the future was still something he believed in, he had been able to come home and unfold himself to her, to tell her about the contempt in white men's eyes, revealed sometimes in a momentary glance. About their voices filled with orders and reductions, and conversations carried on as if he weren't there. At first, he had been able to tell her about the insults encroaching, encroaching on his power to return to green.

He kept these things in silence while Eula tried to figure out just when he had closed himself to her. It must have taken place gradually, she thought, without her even noticing, but it seemed as if it had happened all at once. Although she would never be able to single out the specific events around which things changed, she knew he had come to hate her for the things she had witnessed, that he turned his violence against her for the things she knew.

LaRue asked Eula for her stories again and again, hungry to know, but it seemed she had buried most of the past along with the fine black casket she had chosen for Ontario Smalls, trusting the few talismans on her dresser to ward off the rest.

LaRue tried to fill in his mother's silences by asking elsewhere, but Vesta couldn't look back at the things that had brought them to Ruby's, because they weren't within her reach. She thought LaRue should have a father he could believe in and said to Ruby and Ouida, "Let him be proud." When LaRue asked Ouida what she recalled, she didn't know how to express the patches of memory of that time, and she told him that the thing that mattered was the fact that since he, and Vesta, and Eula, had come to their house, they had been one family.

When he asked Ruby about Ontario Smalls, she said, "Grown folks' lives are complicated," and explained that there were things he didn't understand now, but would come to know. Although she didn't believe in hiding his past from him, Ruby had agreed to protect LaRue, as Vesta and Eula had asked, believing that a time for his accepting those truths would come. Until then, she offered her own memories to LaRue, and told him stories about the ways that animals and flowers and trees survived, about the perfect balance of living things. She gave him the past that was her own.

LaRue knew that his father had fallen while washing windows, but Eula and Vesta referred to it as "the accident," and never discussed the details, nor the ways it had affected their lives. His whole childhood he had watched Eula touch her scar and wondered where it came from and what it meant. And although they never spoke about these things, LaRue felt, somehow, that he would learn about what had come before.

The pieces of memory had built slowly over the years: the haunting sound of breaking glass . . . the smell of perfume that he couldn't bear . . . the terrifying sight of a closing door. He knew he had been carried through the night, and that his memories were building, layer upon layer, until he could receive them whole.

As he made his way from an errand downtown to the streetcar stop, he happened to look up and see a man balanced on a scaffold of twisted rope as he scrubbed a pane of glass. LaRue stood still and stared at him, as though mesmerized by the figure swinging gently back and forth as he wiped.

When a hurried pedestrian bumped into him, LaRue looked away from the window-washer and continued toward the streetcar. When his car came he boarded it and moved to the back, but when he got off, he varied his usual route home by going a different way through the maze of city streets.

He had been down the street before, but he stopped halfway down the block and, somehow, it felt like the first time. He turned slowly in a circle, shivering, the colors and shapes around him a blur, his feet unsteady, and all things met and rearranged, up becoming down and down up, a building uprooting a tree and branches appearing where space had been. The bits of memory that had visited him one by one cohered, and he staggered to the steps of a stranger's house and let it come.

There was perfume, and the splintering of glass, and he could feel his father's tall anger and his small pathetic strikes, and he was being carried, carried in the arms of his mother, and of the past that couldn't be denied.

There were wedges of light and closing doors, and faces emptied of color and emptied of love. And blood, and desperate hands that clutched him as they moved him through the night, seeking shelter, seeking the promise of light, seeking a door that wouldn't close.

He sat on the bottom step of stone and received it. He took the past, its blood and its irate flesh, its unknown hands and its fruit, for it had come to claim him, to push him back and forward, to say, "Take this. This, too, is yours."

LaRue sat on the steps and wept, shaken by his widening understanding of the pairs that make the whole, the pain whose partner is joy. He wept for himself, and for his mother and his father, and he wept, also, for the daughter he felt he would one day have. The bricks beneath his feet absorbed the tears that fell from his opened eyes as he sat on the steps of stone and wept for the barrier that had fallen away from him like innocent skin.

His vision of the night of oranges gave him a new way of looking at Eula. At the dinner table that evening, he watched her touch her scar, and the gesture he had witnessed daily had new meaning, and he realized that he knew something more about the woman she was.

He knew better why her hand flew to her scar when she was tense or flustered, and why she had to conquer things. He remembered the time she was using the mixer in the kitchen, and the beaters kept getting stuck, snapping her patience until she placed the mixer in the sink, its metal loops dripping trails of cake batter, and abandoned the dessert she was in the middle of. The time he had walked up behind her and saw her straightening and restraightening the scant decorations in her room which were never allowed to get out of place, muttering the names of trees and flowers to herself. And how, like Vesta, she always took the same route home because, that way, she could be sure of where she was going. All of her cautious mothering, her restraint, her "Look, don't touch" meant something more to him.

He glanced at Ruby, also his mother and so known to him, and then back at Eula, realizing that the two women understood each other, despite their differences, and he knew something of what they had shared. Lined hands and cleansing water. The truth and the scarring that bind people in the dark of night.

He looked at Polaris, so steady, so different from the father who was his own by blood. This man, sitting across the table from him like a smooth rock, was part of what he came from, too. He had taken them in and provided for them and held LaRue's hand to ride that train years ago, this gentle, quiet man. He was known and unknown to LaRue, who wondered in what ways he might be torn and wounded, as Ontario was.

He looked back at Eula, whom he couldn't recall reading to them or telling bedtime stories, as Ruby had done. She said she couldn't focus enough to enjoy reading, which she had liked when she was younger, and even when she tried to return to a book that had been a favorite, she would realize she had been reading the same sentence over and over again. The radio, with its funny programs, its imaginary characters and adventures, took her out of herself. And she liked music, if it was in the background, and as long as it wasn't the blues, which she considered too raw. LaRue had always felt as though the uncut nature of the blues was too close for her liking, and he used to tease her that she was really afraid it would tell her who she was.

She went to work doing hair on the weekdays, and sometimes Saturdays, too, and to church once a week and on holidays. And she was ladylike, always in a hat and gloves, and clothes that might have been old or reworked by her and Ruby from some other outfit, but were put together with perfect taste. People who had known her in her youth said Eula had been a beauty, and LaRue could see some of that in her, but there was something shut off and flat about her face that never made him think of her that way. He could never remember her having had a caller, but he was sure there must have been some who had tried.

How lonely his mother's years must have been, he thought. Safe and lonely. He looked over at Vesta, in her starched white, finishing one type of food on her plate before she moved on to the next in her ritual of eating, wiping her mouth with her napkin between almost every bite, making sure she hadn't spilled or left some undignified trace of food. She covered her mouth with the edge of her hand while she chewed, as if there was something shameful about things tasting good. He glanced from daughter to mother and thought that it was Vesta's inheritance, this lonely safety that made a kind of prison for them both.

The atmosphere was joyless that night. Polaris worried about making ends meet, and Ruby's overripe body was heavy with child. The landscape, gray and damp, tried to free itself from the hold of winter, and LaRue looked around the table and said, "Maybe what we need is a 'Good List.'"

Everyone turned to look at him. "A Good List," he said. "Maybe, at times like these, we need to praise the gifts. We need to make a list of everything we can think of that's good, and things that aren't altogether bad. Come on, I'll start it: Mama Ruby's sweet potato pie, that belongs at the top of the list. And the eagle flies tomorrow, and the whole neighborhood will be buying spirits on the sly. Underground bourbon and wine."

They looked at each other tentatively, suspicious of LaRue's latest scheme. "Come on, Ouida," he urged, "I know you can think of something good."

Ouida thought for a minute and then said, a smile creeping across her face, "Spring is only a little ways away."

"Yes, yes, yes. Now someone else," LaRue prodded, but got no response. "Okay, I'll go again. Music. No matter how blue things might get, there is music . . . matter of fact, there is music that's blue, and it belongs on the Good List."

Ruby spoke up next. "Soft shell crabs. Can they go on the list? I've only had 'em once in my life, but my mouth will never be content again!"

"Oh, that's perfect, Mama Ruby. Now someone else. There's lots more that can go on the Good List. Anything at all can go on, you just have to dig a little, so I'll add that it's not raining, or snowing, while I'm at it."

Everyone was laughing by this time, and they all started contributing to the list. Ruby added, "Polaris is here, instead of somewhere between South and North," and he reached across the table and took her hand.

"Yup," LaRue added, "and that means we'll get that step out front fixed this weekend. Put that on the list."

"And put on Mama Ruby's flower garden," Ouida said. "Even though it's not up yet, those bulbs of hers are stirring in the ground, just about waking up. They're down there, under the dirt and leaves and snow, and whether you believe in them or not, they'll be up again this year. That's my contribution to the list, thanks to Mama Ruby."

"Sister . . . do you have something for the list?" asked LaRue.

"Yes, I have something for the Good List. We're gonna have a baby soon." Mama Ruby patted her belly and smiled at Vesta, while the others clapped.

Next Polaris chimed in. "Well, my item everyone might not consider good news, but it isn't rightly bad: "I only have one corn on my foot these days."

At that, everyone laughed and tried to top each other's Good List ingenuity. Finally, LaRue leaned back in his chair and said, "You know, this Good List stuff, well, it sure does remind me that I saw Miss Snake today . . ." There was a collective "Aaaaw no, here we go!" and Vesta said that it was all a ruse; the Good List was just a way for Bone to sneak a story in. "We've been tricked!" she declared, and settled in for a tale.

"Miss Snake didn't believe in the Good List either, at first," LaRue began, "until she was shown its importance. It happened in the worst of times, when life was hardest for her, for she had become known for her distinctive appearance. The uniqueness of her coloring, of her patterns, was both a blessing and a curse. There was a twoness about it all, as with most things in life. Well, one day, Miss Snake learned about the blessing side, which she would lean on in the thick of the curse.

"One evening she was coming from a party, and she came upon a cluster of animals by the side of the road. They were hangin' around, talkin' trash, and among them was her worst enemy, Lion. She saw him from a ways off, and that day she happened to be a blue and green and yellow pattern, like a piece of handwoven African cloth. And, wouldn't you know, Lion saw her and stood up straight. 'Well well,' he said, 'looks like I'm about to have some dinner, and my favorite meal at that. There's Miss Snake comin' right up the road.'

"He couldn't miss those markings she had on that night, and she surely couldn't hide. 'I'll be damned!' she said to herself. 'This is wearing me out. Other snakes get to look like their surroundings, green if they live on a tree, and brown to match the dust. And some got diamond-shaped colors like warnings, that folks get acquainted with and know to stay away from. But I got to be changing all the time into some wild stuff like this.' She had to think fast, before she became someone's dinner and someone else's show.

"Well, as you all know, fast and clever thinking is what Miss Snake had been developing for generations, for as long as people had been trying to put her down for her free and mighty ways. So she came up with a plan, right there on the spot. She outsmarted Lion so bad she left him scratching his head, wondering what happened.

"When Miss Snake got out of that scrape, she stretched herself out along a tree branch and took stock. 'That one was close,' she said, and then she thought about her many run-ins with Lion, and she really had to chuckle. That outrageous skin of hers had landed her in a good bit of trouble in her life, but it had been plenty rich, and nobody would ever forget her. She laughed and laughed that night, thinking about all the adventures she would have to share with her children. In fact, she went to sleep laughing, and woke up laughing, too, at the unbelievable stories she had to tell.

"And now Miss Snake gives thanks daily for her spots and her stripes. They are God-given, she believes, for she can look back on all the colors and patterns she has known herself to be. Why, she thinks of the rainbow as a kind of personal history.

"Miss Snake has got plaid, and herringbone, and purple and blue on her Good List, and I swear on high that she knows, as she works her way across the spectrum, that she's a bona fide survivor after all."

The Good List would survive and become a tradition that LaRue would spread wherever he went. It usually got people laughing so hard that, at least for a moment, they forgot their troubles and, at best, made them praise a few of the gifts that were surely theirs to share. He liked to think he was spreading it, that the folks to whom he passed it on went home and made Good Lists with their families and focused, in some small, momentary way, on joy.

10

The year LaRue's eyes were opened and he came to know more fully his own and his father's pasts, Ouida and Vesta graduated from secondary school and moved on to the next phases of their lives.

Vesta took a full-time job in the Foundations Department where she had found summer work before, and she felt lucky to be the only colored woman hired. Her school life had been so painful socially that its conclusion brought relief. She looked forward to the routine of a job and a steady income that would be her own, not minding the long windowless hours at her sewing bench, where she was able to handle delicate fabrics and ribbons and lace and lose herself in the intricacies of her work, as she had in previous summers. Compared to the intimate service her mother performed, standing and attending to an endless string of women who talked on and on about their own lives, she felt blessed. At least she wouldn't have to play a role in the realm of someone else's home, a world where she could observe and not touch.

Because it seemed like an extension of the path she was on, the next logical step, Ouida enrolled in normal school. Teaching primary school was a choice that had been beyond Ruby and Eula, and when people talked about the expanded options for women who were coming along they seemed to end up there. Ouida was instructed on how to be ladylike and on exactly what should be memorized and recited. On how to teach handwriting that conformed exactly to the accepted model. As much effort seemed to be directed toward instruction in manners as to the subjects they would be teaching.

Ouida spent a great deal of energy on love: on who was doing what with whom and which man now wanted her for his own, and among those competing for her attention was one of her white rhetoric instructors. She went to class dutifully, but found it hard to focus, and in the evenings she was bored by her lessons and fell asleep over her books. She fantasized more and more about marrying, and she didn't know what she would do about the rule that required teachers to stay single, when she decided it was time.

Ouida never confronted the question of what she really wanted. People said how lucky she was to continue her schooling and knowing it was so, she pushed ahead to play the role of teacher. Always busy with school or part-time sewing work or dates, she didn't talk to Ruby much about how she felt, and even if she had been able to seek advice, Ouida wouldn't have even known the questions to ask. She couldn't afford to indulge or examine her sense of constraint when she didn't know what her options were. She continued what she had begun.

Just after graduation a conflict had arisen that, months later, was still unresolved. Eula had asked both Vesta and Ouida to make personal visits to her main client, Mrs. Franklin, to thank her for the hand-me-down clothes she had given them over the years and although Eula continued to press her, Ouida had not agreed to go.

"Vesta's going Saturday," Eula said. "Are you sure you won't change your mind?"

Vesta had agreed to go and thank Mrs. Franklin, even though she was dreading it, because it seemed like the appropriate thing to do, while Ouida said she would write a note of appreciation, but could not bring herself to call in person. It wasn't that she didn't feel grateful for the clothes, she explained to Eula, but she just couldn't bring herself to go to that woman's house, "no doubt through the back door," Ouida said, and thank her for letting her have the cast-off things she was never going to wear again anyway.

"I've decided not to go, Mama Eula, and besides, you've complained about how that Mrs. Franklin works you to death and demands your energy like you don't have a family and a life of your own."

But Eula would not relent, even though she herself resented Mrs. Franklin. She asked Ruby if she would tell Ouida to go, but Ruby reminded her that she couldn't make Ouida do what she wanted her to do. It simply wasn't her decision to impose upon her, Ruby said, and pointed out that Ouida was capable of making her own decisions by the age of eighteen.

But the conflict between Eula and Ouida escalated, until Vesta pleaded with her to just go on and see Mrs. Franklin in order to keep the peace. While Ouida couldn't confront the bigger questions about her life, she channeled her energy into small efforts at resistance. She spoke out brashly and cursed, and she made outrageous comments at the dinner table. She challenged conventions in dress by abandoning her hat and gloves and took to arriving late for social engagements, as if she was testing that limit, too. The battle over "The Dress Lady," as they had called her in earlier days, was symbolic to Ouida, who was trying to keep a fighting spirit alive in little ways.

As Ouida and Vesta were moving on into other worlds, LaRue was entering the ninth grade. Eula had shared her distress with Ruby over the years about LaRue's refusal to obey the rules at school. Because his grades were excellent, she could only get so provoked with him, but she never forgot how he had colored as a little child without regard to the thick black outlines in his picture books and had come home later with his own variations on art assignments, pictures drawn wildly, messily, giving people purple hair and scarlet feet, even after he knew better. She didn't like to know he was playing pranks and she worried that he would never learn to just go along, but Ruby knew he would never color within the lines.

He had always been a loner at school, for different reasons from Vesta's. His classmates liked to be around him and enjoyed his entertaining stories and pranks, but they held something back, and might not have even realized it. The way he looked right into things and said what he truly thought set him apart and he knew it. They teased LaRue about his big lips and his "mismatch eyes" and he came home roughed up more than once, punished by the tougher boys for being "sensitive" and "strange."

He seemed to take his isolation from the main group of boys in stride, and at the beginning of high school, LaRue found someone who was as different as he was, and they became friends for life. LaRue saw Church Newman sitting alone outside, sketching with charcoal and a pad after school one day. LaRue noticed that he had a deep purple-blue scarf woven round and round his neck. After watching him for a while LaRue walked up and asked him what he was working on and he showed him.

"My name's Church."

"Church?"

"Yeah. Church Newman."

"How'd you get a name like that?"

"How'd any of us get our names? Guess my mama hoped if she called me that I'd go."

"Well I'll tell you what. My mama and my sister will be mighty glad I met someone with your name, and they'll be hoping some of it'll rub off on me. My name's LaRue Smalls. Wishbone for short. Bone for shorter."

LaRue saw right away that Church didn't judge him as strange, and didn't pull away from him. He was fascinated with LaRue's eye and he tried again and again to capture it on paper.

Church told LaRue how he dreamed of one day being a painter and LaRue said his deep purple-blue scarf reminded him of an adventure Miss Snake had once had, and entertained him with wild descriptions of funny things he had seen. He and LaRue set out on adventures together and talked about being traveling companions one day. While LaRue told Church all about Tennessee Jones, Church drew LaRue's characters the way he imagined them looking, and they planned to collaborate on books in which Church would illustrate LaRue's stories.

Because he wasn't close to his own family, Church became like part of LaRue's, often there for meals and for evening radio programs. Their home was wide open to him and Ruby took him under her wing, treating him as if he were just another one of her children.

As they sat down to eat at night, Vesta began her "interrogations" as LaRue called them, about what had happened to him that day. She had become even more insistent in her questioning since finishing school herself.

"Tell us what happened in school today, LaRue."

She followed this up with a question and another after that: "Well, what did you learn, then? What happened? What did you do?"

His anger flaring, LaRue had warned her that it wasn't fair to draw his experience from him. He had tried to tell her a story Ouida had told him once about bracket toadstools which live on trees, growing threadlike tendrils into the trunks, feeding on the wood and turning it into crumbling powder until the trees, hollowed out, either die or collapse in a storm. But it had appeared to go right past her, and she couldn't seem to help herself, so that when she got going with her questions at the dinner table the dining room seemed to shrink and shrink, until none of them could freely breathe. Sometimes, if LaRue didn't respond, Vesta set in to questioning Church.

Ruby had tried to get to the root of it, to find out why Vesta's inquisitions were growing, but she was, as usual, closed. Ruby offered to take her chores for her and encouraged her to get out of the house and make her own fun, but Vesta continued to come straight home from work and either do household tasks or focus on her cross-stitching.

She was knocking off samplers at a phenomenal rate, and the borders of her pictures seemed to be getting wider and wider. Amazed at her level of production, LaRue asked her why she didn't start a little side business with some of Eula's and Ruby's clients, but she placed them aside in her bureau drawer as she finished them. "For safekeeping," she said, "where they won't get dirty. Until I decide where they should hang."

Ouida, Vesta, and LaRue sat on the stoop one afternoon while Ruby worked in her garden, weeding and folding peat moss into the soil. Ouida whispered to Vesta that although she liked Ruby's flowers, which took time and attention and had fancy names next to their pictures in books, she preferred the weeds and wildflowers that stuck around in spite of the odds, the ones that "grew and grew and grew" unchecked, and surprised the world with their exclamations of color. The "in-spite-of" flowers, she called them.

"It's those rough wild ladies over there that I like, the ones with the big wide-brimmed white hats," she said, laughing, pointing to the Queen Anne's lace next door. "That's why I love Easter, Vesta, all the hats.

"You know how on Easter everyone stands out front and talks, and it's starting to look like spring, so people feel kinda relieved . . . about winter letting up. And there's the organ music and the singing, and the dress-up clothes and all. I love all of that stuff about Easter.

"But then there are the hats." She was gesturing with her hands now. "Hats that speak. Hats that shake. Hats that have lived. Hats." They were both laughing as she continued. "Wide-brimmed straws with defiant flowers. Pastel domes molded out of that delicate mesh. Black ones with beaded bands, and narrow brims tilted up, just so, insouciant. Smooth feathered felts that have known danger for themselves. Hats. Hats and more hats. Hats nodding in affirmation as the singing begins, nodding 'Yes, yes,' it is this that we have come for. It is this that we need."

"I swear, Ouida, your imagination is something else."

"Well, the hats and the flowers are the best things about Easter, and they almost make up for those terrible bands that hold your Easter bonnet on, and the hard dress-up shoes that cut into your feet. Those lovely long graceful white Easter lilies, and all the other bulbs that come up in the spring, whole wild patches of daffodils and crocuses I'm gonna have one day, can't you just see it?"

Vesta and Ouida had an ongoing debate about which plants were the most beautiful, and which way Ruby should trim her shrubs. "Mama Ruby," Vesta said one day as she came out front with a book that had pictures of wedges cut in geometric cones and squares, "you could have a garden like this." Ouida hated Ruby to cut the bushes at all, begging her, if she did so, to clip them into natural free-form shapes. "They're alive, Vesta," she cried, "they're not cast iron. Why do you like 'em better like that?"

"I don't know, I just do. I like 'em all arranged in these patterns." She closed the book, thinking about Ouida's freeness. Although order was her refuge, she longed for what Ouida had, for someone to look at her the way she had seen boys look at other girls. Ouida and LaRue practically had their own language, and even though Vesta laughed at the teasing and storytelling that went on in her house, she could never really be a participant. Her isolation was building, and with it her mute longing. She got up and went inside.

When she heard the others' laughter, Vesta returned to the door to ask them if they wanted to go to the corner store for candy. She was putting out the milk bottles for pickup on Monday, and she dropped one on the stone steps. LaRue started as he heard the glass shatter and, trembling, reached for the iron railing, somehow in the present, and in some other moment that had risen up from the past. The breaking glass was all he heard and it sounded stretched out.

Ouida looked at him strangely. "Are you with me, Bone, or am I talking to myself?"

"I . . . I'm with you."

"You okay, Bone?" Ouida asked him as she took his hand. Unable to say anything, he looked at her and nodded. Ouida told Vesta she wanted to go to the corner store for candy, and went inside to put together her pennies. LaRue said he would wait on the stoop.

While they were gone, Church came up the walk and sat down next to LaRue. He tried to get a conversation going, but he realized something was going on with LaRue and didn't push him to speak. Neither one of them said a thing for a long time, and when Ouida and Vesta returned, LaRue shook off his strange feeling and tried to talk them into sharing their candy with him.

He didn't have to ask what Ouida got. She had an eternal weakness for breakup chocolate, which she said was religion to her. "What about you, Vesta?" Church asked. "Whatcha got good?" She said she had bought black licorice, and LaRue said he didn't know she liked licorice. "I don't," she answered, as she pulled a long candy rope from her bag, "but for a nickel I got all this."

They teased Vesta for her practical approach to a thing like penny candy, and Ouida said, "That sure does remind me of a story I once heard about collard greens. It went like this. One holiday, the goddess of the whole plant world was feeling mighty generous, and she came and visited all the plants on earth. She gathered them together and when they were listening, she said she was offering them a one-time chance to have any single thing they desired.

"They could have flowers where there had been none . . . petals of special shapes . . . more leaves or less leaves . . . certain colors they cherished . . . different kinds or lengths of stalks . . . anything they wanted. Anything at all. The catch was that if it was beauty they opted for, it would have to be balanced by a weakness. Well, she went around to each one and they chose the single thing they longed for most. The day lily chose flowers of the most unbelievable hues, the colors of sunsets and cloudless midnights, which would bloom for only one glorious day. And the rose chose its perfume, to balance out the sharpness of its thorns.

"Now when the plant goddess came to ask the collard green plant what it wanted to have in life, it stated matter-of-factly, 'Just give me as many big sturdy leaves as you can spare.' It didn't even allow itself to dream of some amazing magenta petals, some center extravagantly fluted like a clarinet, or glorious spots or stripes.

"The other plants looked at Miss Collard in disbelief, and the plant goddess asked, 'Are you *sure* that's what you want? Are you absolutely sure? Consider this well . . . I have offered you anything.'

"And Miss Collard said so fast she could barely get it out, 'Yes. Yes. Yes. Big thick and sturdy leaves are useful. They are sensible, and I just want something that will never break or give out. Just give me those and I'll be quite content.'

"Well, the collard green has a long hearty season, but it has no scent, and no flower, and no beauty to its leaves. The only thing it has is its good taste, and that makes people pick it and eat it up. When asked its one wish, it opted for more and more of what was sensible, and overlooked entirely the joyful thing."

Ruby had stopped digging to see what Ouida would come up with, and she didn't want Vesta to be hurt by the story. "Now, now," she said to her children, "it was the collard's choice, in the end."

She gestured with her trowel at Ouida and LaRue. "And lest you two think you have all the answers, remember that 'the joyful thing,' as you put it, has got its opposite side. It has to weigh out, all along, against what's useful, and practical. Both things are important and, in fact, neither one can make it all alone.

"It's fine to be a dreamer, and I'm talking to you, too, Church, 'cause the world needs dreams, but you can't be a trifling dreamer, after all." She looked at LaRue and Ouida. "The two of you might show up late to the satisfaction of your very own dreams." They all laughed as Ruby got back on her knees and started digging again. "What I'd like is for each one of you to have sturdy leaves *and* lovely, aromatic flowers, truth be told."

Later that night LaRue, still shaken by the broken milk bottle, went to Ruby to talk about the thing that had come to him a few months before, having kept it to himself as long as he could. He told her of the way his vision had built up, how he had at first tried to refuse and then accepted it, deciding that he wanted to know. He told Ruby how the things he had seen and heard and smelled had coalesced, and he was trying to figure out what to do with what he knew. And for the first time, she spoke about the insult and the punishment she had borne alone.

She gave LaRue her story, without knowing completely why she had never told it before. It was time, and it rushed from her like water, undammed. He was so much her child, she thought, and the capacity for understanding that she had perceived in him from the beginning made her want to share it with him, trusting that he would pass it on in a way that might do some good.

It rushed from her as her barriers gave way, and Ruby was aware that it was a shared past, that she told a story much bigger, even, than the two of them.

"What to do with the father's sins," she said, to him and to herself, and they talked about the incident and what became of it, that had driven her from the small town where she had grown up. She knew how LaRue would struggle for a framework in which to understand his father's wounding acts, just as she had. "What they've left us . . . who they were . . . and what they made of us. I guess these are the questions, hunh, LaRue? Yours and mine."

After telling their stories to each other, they sat together on the steps without talking, the night chill of the stone coming through their clothes, and then Ruby spoke. "Well, I'm not sure about a lot of things, Bone, but these things I know. I know something about the feeling of shame, something about where it comes from and where it leads. And I know something about making an end to it, tying it off, or at least taking it somewhere else."

She listened to him say how knowing his father and his mother in this new way made him feel, and reminded him of what could be gained from paying attention. "You've always been a storyteller," she said to him, "and remember that however painful it is, a storyteller's got to know the different sides of things."

Although she didn't ask him not to share what she had told, trusting him to figure that out, he would choose to keep it to himself for years to come. Ruby lifted her heavy pregnant body off the stone steps and went in to shut down the house for the night. As he helped her up, LaRue took both of her hands and thanked her for being in his life, and for telling him the part of her own tale that she had kept to herself. He told her he wanted to stay outside for a while, and she turned off the lights and made her way up the stairs in the dark, desperate to get to her bed and lie down, but she paused as she noticed the moonlight coming through the red and blue of the stained glass window above the door.

Telling her secret to LaRue felt right, but there was another thing she was keeping to herself. She hadn't told anyone that she had a bad feeling about the birth of her child. "I'm tired," she said, half out loud, "and too old to be having babies. I don't know that I'll make it through this. I just don't know."

11

As it turned out, Ruby's feeling was right. She would not make it through, and her baby would grow up in a house without many stories. A place that held few half-truths and few lies. She would enter the world as her mother left it, inheriting the bare, bleached facts of loss.

The family she left behind was able to function through the planned farewell events of the wake and the funeral, ordering the emptiness with preparations and established roles, dividing up the things to be done so that they were occupied. But when they walked through the front door afterward, they felt a void where she had been.

None of them could find a way across the emptiness her death had left. LaRue sat on the stoop night after night, alone or with Church, trying to figure out what to do, while Vesta blocked out her grief with the baby and Eula withdrew to her basement flat. Polaris's job kept him distracted from his grief, but Ouida lay in bed hour after hour, rising only to go to the bathroom, struck numb and inert by her loss. She just couldn't believe her mother was gone and, unable to see her way even into the next phase of the day, she retreated to sleep.

Over and over she dreamed what she had seen standing at her father's side, from the threshold of her mother's room, and she tried to lie down and hide from the things she had witnessed that night.

They had come, she and Polaris, to the doorway, brought by the change in Ruby's cries, which grew more desperate and receded at the same time, Polaris taking the stairs three at a time and Ouida rushing from her room, and they had stood in the doorway together and watched Ruby die as her child was born.

"Where is he? . . . Where is the doctor?" Eula had said over and over, her question a plea, a prayer. She had helped a few children into the world and had two of her own, but something had gone wrong because this baby wouldn't come, and with each attempt to push it out, Ruby moved further and further away from them. Eula closed the windows so the neighbors wouldn't hear the screams, and tried to moor Ruby to her by holding her hand as LaRue ran through the streets of Black Oak looking for help.

There was Vesta at the foot of the bed and Eula clutching her hand, panicked as she saw Ruby weakening, and, unsure of what to do, what to say, she whispered over and over, "Hold on for the doctor! Hold on!"

It had seemed to Ouida that her moment at the doorway was an eternal instant. She stood witnessing it all in horror, the feet coming finally and then the head, tangled in the twisted cord, and Eula's hands freeing the baby and cutting the cable of flesh. And the massaging, three sets of women's hands, until a mass of tissue came, and they were bloodstained, all, their arms around Ruby as they tried to hold her to life. Blood on Vesta's starched white dress, blood on their hands, blood on the moon as it entered the room, three women round her and Ruby's grip growing fainter and fainter. Ouida held on to her mother tighter and tighter and they had to pull her away in the end.

When they came home after the funeral they stopped to look around as they entered the front room. The house felt different, smaller and closed in, its windows and doors shutting in the grief, and they were uneasy in its stagnant dryness. "This house feels like it's stopped breathing," LaRue said, and the others looked at him. "It's the opposite of having a ghost, and just as unsettling." They went to separate rooms and stayed there for the rest of the day.

In the weeks that followed Eula kept to the basement and Vesta threw herself into caring for the baby. When it had come time to name her, the others had looked blankly at each other and LaRue had come up with December, for the month of her winter birth.

Vesta knew how to feed and change an infant, how to rock her to sleep, but she couldn't bear it when she cried, and she had no solution for her blind rooting for the breast, the smell, the touch of the woman with whom she had been one. Her hold on December was so tight that if LaRue tried to touch the child, she got upset and clutched her more firmly. He tried again and again to tell her the baby would be afraid of everything if she kept on the way she was going, but she moved intently from one task to the next, closed against his input, doing what she knew how to do.

When LaRue realized that Christmas was only a week and a half away he went out and bought a tree, and although they had always decorated it and sung carols as a family, this year he was the only one interested, and he put it up and trimmed it by himself. He placed pine boughs around the house and hung a sprig of mistletoe over the vestibule door, but no one even seemed to notice.

Ouida had climbed into bed after the funeral and couldn't get up. She barely roused herself for meals and only picked at the food Vesta brought up on trays, and she hadn't been back to her classes since Ruby's death. LaRue tried to pull her from her stupor by giving her things to do and pressing her to come downstairs to eat, but she was stuck in her own blank escape, stretching out her arms for some kind of anchor, and when LaRue sat at her bedside and tried to engage her in a storytelling bout, she yawned and turned to face the wall.

Eula stayed downstairs in her unlit rooms with the heavy drapes pulled across the windows, and Polaris went through his daily routine of shaving, dressing, eating, and undressing, so exhausted at the end of each day that he could barely make it to bed.

It felt as if everything were at a standstill. It felt as if the house were holding its breath.

LaRue knew that he had to do something, but he didn't know what, and then it came to him, as if Miss Snake had whispered in his ear, how to move forward. How to remember in order to let go.

When he had the family assembled at Ouida's bedside, he explained what he had in mind. "Not like a conventional memorial service," he said. "Not like that. Mama Ruby always said that she wanted 'festivities' when she died . . . it would be like a celebration, really, of the good parts of her life."

Vesta and Eula resisted the idea of a party, which they thought was inappropriate, arguing that people might misunderstand, that it had been weeks since Ruby "passed on," and Ouida was too numb to say or do anything at all, and although Polaris had no objection, he pointed out that he wasn't up to much in terms of planning. LaRue was determined, and neither Vesta nor Eula could amass enough energy for a fight, so they let him make his plans, worrying as he did so that there was something disrespectful about it all.

He picked a date when Polaris wouldn't be on the road, gave Ouida notice that she would be getting up, and told their friends and neighbors the date and time. And then, after shopping carefully for the ingredients, LaRue cooked a feast, lovingly, as his Mama Ruby had taught him. Standing at the stove using her cast-iron dutch oven and skillet as he took in the smells and the tastes, he felt as if she were with him, and he talked to her as he had always done. She guided him as he made her honey wheat bread and he found himself overcome by the excitement he had always felt when the dough rose, filling her big green chipped bread bowl like magic. He made her greens, with the hot sweet flavor she had shown him how to capture, and her macaroni and cheese. The stewed chicken with its unforgettable gravy and rice and the roast pork and green beans she had made on special days. He finished with the cobblers and pies whose crust he had learned from her to get just flaky enough. It was a gift, a banquet in Ruby's name, and to go with the things he had learned to cook from her, he made up a few dishes of his own. And in spite of Eula's objections, he bought liquor, from bourbon to champagne.

He asked Eula to make candles as her mother had taught her, and went with her to buy the things she needed. She spent the weekend working on them downstairs, the smells of vanilla and bayberry and beeswax visiting them on the floor above.

On the day of the ceremony LaRue stood next to Ouida's bed and talked to her until she got up and dressed. When people started arriving he waited until he saw their neighbor, Miss Etta, come through the door, and without saying anything at all, he took December from Vesta and settled the baby on Etta's lap. Then he put his arm through his sister's and asked her to help folks to food and drink. Their neighbors came—Frosty, Mr. Ike, and even Delta Simms—and people showed up who had moved away but remembered Ruby's kindness over the years.

As soon as everyone had eaten and had a drink in hand, LaRue gathered them in a circle, and invited his characters to appear. On the table that had been placed in the middle of the room were Eula's candles, all different colors, shapes, and scents, and a box of wooden matches. Church reached for a dark green candle with leaves pressed into its sides, lit it, and handed it to LaRue. "I want to start this whole thing off," LaRue began quietly, as a smile crept across his face, "with one of the first stories Mama Ruby ever told me. It went like this."

He closed his eyes, recalling his little rocking chair by the stove, and when he could feel Mama Ruby's presence, he looked around the room. "There was a strange and wonderful character called the Dustman . . . he was an important acquaintance of my youth. He seemed to arrive on the aromatic wind of just-baked bread . . . at least it seemed so . . . was it so?" he asked, caught in the rich sensations of the past. He went on to tell about the Dustman's nightly visits and the transformations he brought. "Most of all," LaRue said, "he taught me that the stars could be taken down from the sky and polished, no matter what anyone thought. Here's to you, Mama Ruby, for the Dustman, and for so much else." Each person's glass was lifted, Vesta's and Eula's too, and in spite of themselves, they smiled while they drank.

Their next-door-neighbor raised her glass and said she had a story to share. LaRue lit a candle for her and placed it on the table and the room fell silent. She told about the time she had first seen Ruby, who had been kneeling in the front yard planting geraniums as she was coming up the walk. Ruby had gotten up to introduce herself with, "Hello, I'm Mrs. Geranium," and then, surprised at what she had said, both women had dissolved in laughter. "Hard to stand on ceremony after that," she said. "After that, we were old friends . . . and I called her Mrs. Geranium for the rest of her life."

Mr. Ike from the corner store spoke up next, and told about what a hard bargain Ruby drove. She haggled, he said, just for the exercise of it, because his prices weren't negotiable, and she knew it. He always got a kick out of her coming into his store, he said, because she never allowed him to get complacent.

Delta Simms raised her glass and shifted her clay to one side of her mouth. "Miss Ruby was decent folk," she said, "and she gave me this once, filled with sage." From her pocket she pulled a piece of cloth that LaRue recognized was from a curtain that had once hung across the kitchen window. "I'll sew this into my skirts," she said, and then drank from her glass and resumed chewing her clay.

There were testimonies from people whose lives Ruby had touched only briefly, but to whom she had given a sense of her zealous, loving spirit. A woman said she hadn't realized what all Miss Ruby had done for her until she heard about her dying. She told about the time she had come through Black Oak on her way up to Chicago, and had walked in on a social club meeting at Ruby's church. All conversation had died as she entered, and she had suddenly seen herself through their eyes, realizing the things that were her best were all raggedy and faded, after all. Her shoes were worn and holey, and all she had with her was a measly little bundle of stuff, but out of the silence Ruby spoke up, asking her how she could help, and then took her in, until she could make the next leg of her journey North.

LaRue talked about Ruby's laugh, which he was fond of saying "came from her feet." "The thing was," he said, "she reached down and pulled up that laugh of hers in the bleakest of times. There was always some humor to be found in things, and you see," he said, chuckling himself, "Mama Ruby taught me about our folks' most important survival skills. She taught me about making something out of nothing, and she taught me you've got to laugh to stay alive.

"You know," he said, "that brings me round to introducing someone who very much wanted to come tonight," and Miss Snake made an appearance because, LaRue said, "she too wanted to say good-bye and hello.

"One day, Miss Snake really learned a lesson in creativity, in working with what you've got. She had awakened, this particular day, to find herself of very drab and somber decoration, and she wasn't sure how to go about raising her spirits. Her skin was a kind of gray and brown, but she was in a purple mood, and she was sidewinding her way on down the road when a big old hand reached out and grabbed for her. The hand just missed her, but it was getting ready to come after her again, and she said to herself, 'Lord have mercy. It seems I'm gonna be messed with this day.' She knew she had to think quick, and so she remembered having seen a snake that looked ordinary, like she did that day, but had the most perfect defense.

"The next thing Miss Snake did was spin herself in a coil, and rear back her head. She had seen the fiercest snake do it once, and it had been hellified. So she flattened her head, and reared up, and made as if to strike. She had no fangs or poison. She had only her wits to get herself out of scrapes. Looking over at that hand, she thought she had better do the best cobra imitation she could muster up, if she didn't want to end up someone's curiosity, living life behind a piece of glass. Well that would never do, so she went for it, and an amazing cobra she was. She out-cobraed the cobra, she thought, and she had that big hand and the man attached so scared he was gone in a flash of plaid, and she was left laughing the rest of the way down the road, thinkin' about throwin' a masquerade ball."

"Well that reminds *me*," a neighbor broke in, "of a sticky situation Brer Fox found himself in. It all had to do with a dress-up party." She went on to tell a story about all kinds of camouflaging and outwitting.

After a good bit of lying, during which many characters familiar to the neighborhood came to say farewell to Ruby, Vesta lit a candle and told about how Ruby had read them poetry when they came to live there, and she recited "L'il Brown Baby wif Sparklin' Eyes" in her honor. "I remember Ruby saying it to LaRue," Vesta said, "before he could talk, that is, because you know that ever since he said his first sentence, nobody has been able to get a word in edgewise!"

"Sister, you like to give me a hard time more than you like to breathe." They all laughed at that, even Ouida, who sat in the circle, but couldn't bring herself to join in with a story. She did light a candle and listen, as her grief, dry and unexpressed, cleaved her breast.

Next it was time for Eula to testify. "Well," she said shyly, "I've never been a storyteller, I let my son take care of that. But I would like to thank Ruby Staples. I'd like to thank her for making us family, for the way she took us in. You know, she never made me feel indebted, and I will have you know that even though it wouldn't have made a bit of difference to Ruby, I paid her back every penny I borrowed. Not for her, that is, but for me." She tapped the arm of her chair for emphasis as she spoke.

"Truth is, I could never repay her. Never. She gave me my life. I'll miss Ruby Staples . . . she saved me more than once. To Ruby," she said as she lifted her glass and took a tiny sip of champagne, and even though only some of them knew the full meaning of her tribute, they all joined in the toast, and drank to Ruby's open door.

The whole night Polaris had sat in his armchair and listened, weeping silently at times and laughing at many of the stories that were told. Vesta stood behind him, patting him now and then, and looked over at Miss Etta holding December, to make sure she was safe. Finally, when Polaris was ready, he leaned forward and said, "She was always beautiful, my Ruby, like a beacon in the night, she guided me through things." He looked at the floor and Vesta lit a candle and handed it to him while he remembered. "On the very first day I saw her, all dressed in lavender, I pointed her way and told my brother, 'See that girl . . . I'm gonna marry her, just you wait and see.' She got more and more beautiful every year we were together, as her life came to show across her face, and I was always surprised by my luck in being with her, every time I walked through my own front door.

"Now we have a child who's got her eyes and a shock of her hair, and she doesn't even know what she'll miss in not growing up with her. She's gone now," he said, looking down, and suddenly he got a rush of her skin smell that he used to breathe in, his lips at her temples. "I don't know how I'll get on." He was silent for a while and then raised his head and said, "My memory will be my light. I know it will."

He blew out his candle and took a gulp of bourbon, and then he leaned back in his chair and wiped his eyes with the back of his hand.

The room was quiet. Nobody remembered Polaris ever having talked that much. As they sat in silence LaRue thought about Ruby's secret, but decided it was not yet time to let it go. They sipped their drinks, and then he closed the ceremony by offering a gift to everyone who had come.

"Well, you know, it's something," he said, "what comes from what." And they all turned to look at him as he began. "I saw my friend Miss Snake last week, and I swear on high I learned something remarkable from her this time. You see, I bumped into her on the street and I couldn't have missed her 'cause she was a grand kind of blue, with flecks of orange along the sides. She had just eluded some entrapment or other, and we wanted to get out of the bleak winter chill to have a word. I was working on my private Good List and we stepped inside to get warm. I explained what I was doing," LaRue said, and then he told those gathered in memory of Ruby what a Good List was. "I asked Miss Snake whether she had any gifts in need of praising that I could add to my list.

"'Well, LaRue Smalls,' she said, addressing me as usual, by my full name, 'I have something to tell you that you may not think up front is *good* news, but I have a feeling it will do.'

"'Tell me. Please tell me,' I said, ''cause I am truly in need of a blessing for my list.' Miss Snake smiled as she came closer, and I leaned forward to receive her gift.

"She looked me in the eye, like the sister of mine she is, and said, 'This is what I have to offer you, LaRue Smalls. Next week . . . on the twenty-third, is what they call the winter solstice. It's the shortest day of the year.' She paused for a moment, and then went on. 'I know that may not sound like such a very big deal, but this solstice thing is the very start of winter. It's the time when living things go underground and hibernate, as they must, or heal themselves, you know, in order to come back in the spring. At this time, you see, the world begins to move out of shadow,' she said, 'to make its circle once again.' I looked up and, in a flash of blue and orange, she was on her way."

He paused for a moment. "Now that's all Miss Snake told me, but it made all the difference in the world. It's like . . . at this time, the year advances and retreats," LaRue said, looking around the room with his shining eye and coming to rest his gaze on Ouida, "and at the time of greatest darkness comes the light."

He looked at Church, who was smiling at him. "So there it is," said LaRue, "Miss Snake's gift. It's just around the corner . . . and many groups of people, as you may know, think of this time of year as the birth of the sun. And even though it seems, in the midst of winter, like things have given up and died, it's like a point on a turning wheel . . ." He made a circle with his hands and then opened them as he looked at each one who had come with the love he had in his heart, and he picked up his glass and raised it. "To the solstice. The beginning that lies within the end."

II

He walked for fifteen minutes before
he came to it. "Cross it," she'd said, and
he thought there would be a bridge
of some sort. There was none.

———

From Song of Solomon, *Toni Morrison*

12

Spring came, but the garden out front filled with hollow stalks and brittle, curling leaves. Untended and unwatered, its colors were gone. The crocus and iris bulbs came up on their own, but grew more and more pale, until their petals were an almost transparent white, and Ruby's little plot was filled with the ghosts of plants.

Gone were the colorful flowers, and gone was the woman who had helped birth the stories that had made their house live, the center around which their family had formed.

The ceremony of remembering had helped them get up and move on, but it seemed to LaRue that everyone expected to get over Ruby's death, while he knew it was something that would always be a part of them. Not somewhere they had been, and then returned home; part of the landscape of their lives.

No one else wanted to talk about her, or even think about her, but LaRue felt Ruby's continual presence. Eula went back to seeing clients, Vesta was absorbed with December's needs, and although Ouida managed to rise from her bed and return to her classes, she stumbled around as though only half-awake.

LaRue tried to fill the space Ruby's death had left with stories and songs for the baby, but he would start tales and they would die. He couldn't get Ouida to take part in any lying at all, or even get a Good List going. It was as if there weren't food enough for stories in that house. One night he turned off the radio and told them that he knew the time was coming when, like Tennessee Jones, he would have to go and start to find out where he fit into things.

"I guess Jones is such a plain name," he said, casually, "that it needed dressing up."

They stared at him blankly, and then Vesta sucked her teeth while Ouida yawned.

"Hmmm," he mumbled to himself, "said once that he was glad to have his name. Said it was the thing that made him choose to venture out . . . Seems like having a name grounded squarely in a specific piece of earth, a *named* piece of earth, just made him want to see the world."

Vesta said, "LaRue, not now. We don't have the time or the inclination for your foolishness." He began again, but Vesta kept getting up and going into the other room to check on the baby. Finally, she started to get up and he leaned out of his chair and took her wrist. "Sister, sit. I don't hear December crying, and you know, it's amazing, but babies will let you know if they need something, so just be still." Holding her wrist, he looked around the table and said firmly, "I have a story for you all to hear.

"Well, the first time Tennessee Jones went to New Orleans, he told me, he saw a sight he would never forget . . . it just seemed to sum up the South for him, that one single thing he saw." They gave in to him, and before they knew it they were rapt. They had all put aside what they had been doing and were looking at him.

"He had just left Memphis, hitching a ride on a freight train filled with metal . . . iron . . . I think it was. He didn't even check to see where that train was headed, because, you see, it didn't really matter. Just so it was headed somewhere else. Tennessee figured that, by and by, he would see it all, for he didn't plan to ever stop. He didn't believe in settling down.

"Tennessee had been saving for it, planning it in earnest for a year, 'cause of course, he had really planned to do it since he was a boy. He hadn't told anyone, not even his mama. He knew his leaving would hurt her, but he had to go, and he figured she would come around to understanding.

"It was all cold and dirty on that freight car, but his excitement warmed him, and he sat there, in motion at long last, and just savored the feeling of being on wheels. He rode all night, sleeping through the first few stops with his head on his suitcase and his coat pulled around him, and then woke up and got his things together and jumped down off the car.

"He didn't know it at first, but he was in New Orleans, and he had heard a lot about this place, where lines between all kinds of things were blurred, and where even death, it seemed, was celebrated, and there was music in and for everything."

LaRue's hands were really going, as he was deep into his story. "For a whole day Tennessee walked around and stopped to sit and watch things. He stood on the bank of the Mississippi, and walked around the Quarter, and he saw something that would change him, too, 'cause he had an experience that wasn't new, but through which the world he was leaving kind of gelled. It would always live for him, that world, but once it was turned solid, he was able turn his back on it.

"He had walked all night and it was almost light out again, and he turned onto a street so narrow and crooked it looked like a mistake. The sun was just coming up and he passed by people who had never made it home the night before, and were traveling at daybreak, toward sleep. Tennessee shook his head at how things seemed all topsy-turvy in New Orleans; you couldn't even tell who was what. And as he got about halfway down Mistake Street, he stopped dead in his tracks. There, in front of the grocery, was a colored child, no more than five, tap dancing in blackface. Next to him, a fat middle-aged white man sat on a barrel, holding out a cooking pot, collecting coins.

"Tennessee stood there for a long while. He had seen such things before, and had even tapped for coins a few times in his own life. But something about it made it seem like he was seeing it fresh. He stood there frozen in place, watching all the generations of colored men he had known performing, dancing the dance that was theirs and was not theirs, dancing for someone who could never see the way that they had claimed it, made it their own.

"That young boy was dancing for a man who was just feeding from him, like an animal that lives off another beast, and this man who fed off of him, this parasite, for that's how Tennessee put it, a parasite who couldn't really know that he had . . . and hadn't . . . made both the boy and the dance his. Tennessee's eyes met the boy's eyes and, for an instant, he was watching himself.

"Tennessee Jones turned and walked through New Orleans as if possessed, as if he was seeing things in a different quality of color. Blue, it seemed, had never been so deep and vivid; the red he saw almost seared his eyes. He combed the streets, looking at the grace and the ugliness of the South straight on. He took in everything: the twisted wrought iron, the peeling walls, the elegance and decay. He looked at each face he passed, burning them into his memory, and when he felt that he had really seen New Orleans, he headed for the train station and bought a ticket north."

The family sat spellbound, as Tennessee's anguish had become theirs, and LaRue finished up, his hands coming to rest on his lap.

"Tennessee said that after seeing that, even though he had lived with it . . . in it . . . hell, *lived it*, he had to go. And that's when his real traveling began.

"It was a sort of beginning, you might say, and you know, whenever anyone has the nerve to ask him where he's from, he says, 'I'm from Tennessee, as you might have guessed. But I was born in New Orleans.'"

All eyes were still on LaRue. "I guess it just might have been that name, made him want to see the world. But you know, it wouldn't necessarily affect everyone the very same way. Tennessee's a remarkable man . . . he surely is. I guess it could work the other way around . . . I guess it could."

Everyone was quiet for a while, and then he told them he would be leaving in June to go South. When the news had sunk in, they all rushed to state the reasons he couldn't go. Eula's voice turned shrill as she said how dangerous it was, how she knew white hatred of colored folks hadn't changed at all, and may have gotten worse. Vesta asked him if he even had an itinerary. They all said they needed him there with them to cope with Ruby's death. And finally, they told him he was just too young to go. Only Ouida, through the fog in which she still moved, had an intuition that it would be okay.

"I'll be seventeen," he said, looking at Polaris, "and you were working by then. I'm talking about a summer, not the rest of my life. Like

Tennessee Jones, I need to go for a while," he said, with tears in his eyes. "Everyone does, you know . . . have to go. I'll be leaving this summer and I'll be back in time for school this fall."

His chest was burning with the thought of having to leave them even though it was a month away, and with a fear of the unknown things he was seeking out. But he felt excitement, too, and a sense of opening. "It's like this," he said, "I have to go . . . in order to return."

They couldn't talk LaRue out of leaving, and they worried about him all summer as they waited for the cards and letters he sent from along the way.

That train trip he had taken with Polaris when he was seven had remained a part of his present. The faces of the people on the train had appeared in his stories for a long time, and he had dreamed of going everywhere he heard about, to Pill-addle-pie-a and beyond.

Ever since the night of his vision, the idea of traveling had been an obsession with him. It was as if his eyelids had been opened, and he had started, then, to comb every part of the city where colored folks lived, hanging out on street corners and at barbershops and bars, trading stories with the people he met. Watching and listening. He had traveled around with Church, talking with people about where they came from and what had brought them to the city, and they had sometimes asked them in to their evening meal, whether or not they had much to share, and LaRue found out about the work they did, their dreams. Their passions and distresses.

He had gone to churches all over Black Oak, and wherever he could find music, in search especially of the blues, listening for what fed the voices and rhythms, for the colors and the stories he could hear in the music. He had read and examined everything he could find about the South, and had been in trouble countless times for staying out late, forgetting about time when he was talking to people or listening to music. He wanted to understand what he could about his people's pasts, and he had decided that he didn't care if his journeying would happen little by little, he was going to see what he could see.

After Ruby's death, LaRue had known that the time had come for him to make his first trip alone, away from home. His pain at losing her hit him, unannounced, as he was caught by a smell, a color, a sound. He paused and saw her hands and heard her voice, and he couldn't believe that she was gone. "It just can't be true, it can't," he thought, "that I will never see her again," and he didn't know how he was supposed to move her to the periphery of his life. But while the rest of the family was fumbling for a route that led directly somewhere else, LaRue sought a path that could bend back.

The next spring when things thawed from their winter stillness, freeing tadpoles that had been caught in white-clear ice, pushing sleeping things above ground, LaRue decided he would leave. He wanted to go to the places from which his family came, and he put away the money he earned doing yard work until he had enough for his train fare. He was going to see the plants and animals Ruby had told him stories about and try to piece together the fragments Eula had given him so that he could understand something about what her life had been like, to imagine the tree where she had found refuge high up and the candlemaking in her mother's little kitchen. And he wanted to try to see the place where the white man's laugh had changed everything for her family, pushing them north where she would meet up with Ontario Smalls.

As he stepped up to board the train he remembered what he had felt like as a child with Polaris just behind him, his large hand on his shoulder. LaRue had looked up at him in his dark blue porter's uniform and cap, proud of the shiny metal buttons of his uniform, his polished shoes, and his steady dignified smile.

He climbed the grated metal steps to the train, and saw a car full of brown and black and tan people. His people, with their belongings stuffed on the racks above, on their laps, under their feet. He made his way down the aisle to an open seat, lifted his bag to the rack, and sat down with the box of food his mother had made for him, its aroma mingled with the chicken and salt pork the other folks on the train had brought. For them, there would be no dining or depot service, and no sleeping cars to stretch their tired legs. They would have to struggle for pride as they squatted and stood in the roadside grasses that served as a bathroom. For them, there were only the worn seats where they sat bundled against each other, from which they would rise, stiff, after sleepless nights imagining those who had found privacy and rest in their whites-only berths.

LaRue ran his fingers across the wine-red threadbare velvet seat and the marred wood of the armrests, the pale grain showing through where it had once been stained dark. As he leaned forward to look for his family through the open window he remembered flowers in a field from years ago, and then the whistle blew and the train jerked forward. He sat back in his seat as he waved, and then shut the window against the soot that blew back into the colored car, placed as it always was, right behind the engine.

As he made his return to the places he had never been, he thought about the trains that had begun to move his people en masse in the opposite direction, carrying them, with all their mythologies of the cities for which they were bound, into the unknown.

He thought about other generations traveling that same path on foot, following the brightest star and praying for open doors along the way. Their urgent drive to be free had made up for bloodied feet and hungry days and nights that held probable death and possible salvation. Heroes, the ones he came from who had pushed on in darkness across alien terrain, despite trackers and their blood-hungry dogs. Despite raised and welted flesh, healing angry, angry as they staked everything. It was stealth, and risk, that had moved them. And these things that moved them still.

LaRue thought, too, of the journeys North his parents had made and imagined Eula's family boarding a train in her town, taking what they could with them and leaving the rest behind, that laugh echoing, echoing, the whole way there. And his father, about whom he knew next to nothing. Who was he, this man who had shaped them so, who seemed to rise, still, from the darkness of his mother's basement flat, cowing them with his raised fists? "Who was he?" LaRue would ask as he traveled to the place Ontario Smalls had hated and loved.

He went through towns and places you couldn't even call towns, and when he was as near as he could get to Eula's birthplace, he got off and went the rest of the way on foot. When he watched the train pull away, his pulse started to race and he had to fight the urge to run after it and reboard. He stood and watched it fade away. Venturing from the little lean-to that served as a depot, he suddenly felt the heat, and a panic, an urgency to get on his way and find out where he was. He noticed a patch of bayberry and, as he got down on his knees to smell it, his mother and her candles flashed through his mind. And then he thought of Ruby.

He wanted to weep at the thought of her, at the understanding, that came in waves, that she was gone. Gone, the one who had really told him who she was. He sat down next to the bayberry and thought about how Ruby had shared with him the thing she had been keeping, since girlhood, to herself, trusting him with her secret, with the punishment she had suffered and the way she had made it her guide. Sharing the burden that was also his.

He wanted to weep, but he tried to focus on what she had given him, and he stood up, turning slowly in a circle as if time had stopped, and remembered Ruby's words. "Pay attention. Not just to the words, but to the feeling tones. Pay attention, LaRue."

He gave himself up to where he was, starting on the road then in a different way, and began to really see the landscape around him. He saw leaves breaking through the cracks in an old stone wall and a cluster of fragile star-shaped flowers with broad glossy leaves too heavy for their slim stalks, which had taken root in the slope of a dying tree. He saw the vegetation along the road and the places people had rooted themselves to the land. Though he had few facts to start with, he let his imagination go and pictured his mother learning to read at the kitchen table of a house he passed, or choosing scents for candles she had learned to make.

As he traveled he also thought of the things Ruby had told him about the country town just outside of Black Oak that she had left without her family's blessing when she turned nineteen. She had given him so many details of the place, what things grew there and what leaves could harm and heal. The smell and texture of the soil and the funny characters who had lived in the place. Everything seemed so familiar when he got there that he half-expected to see the very people whose exploits Ruby had repeated walk by and say hello.

She had told him how she learned to distinguish dangerous from not, and what the boundaries were, as they learned to get along in the woods. There had been snakes that rolled over and stiffened like staffs, insects that devoured their own kind, and plants that could help flesh knit together or take a fever away. It was as if a whole world had opened up for him and he was astounded by the beauty and mystery of the countryside.

He found a room for the night in Eula's hometown, and when he settled down in bed he was tired, and thrilled, and yet he felt a kind of hollow of longing for his family. He hoped he had done right in leaving, and imagined what each one of them was doing. His mother was down in her room, he was sure, and Polaris was asleep with his arm stretched across the bed where Ruby used to lie, as LaRue had seen him the night before he left, pushing the door open gently to check on him. Vesta dozed lightly, her shoes by the bed, ready for December's cry, and Ouida was reading or lying under the breeze of her open window, thinking of the future, he hoped. Church, he knew, was drawing somewhere by whatever light he could find.

The next morning he abandoned his stiff collar and his tie and put on the work clothes he had brought with him, and then he slowed down his pace and spent several days there, getting to know the place and its inhabitants. He took his meals with the family that had rented him the room and in the evening he sat on the porch with them, stunned by the completeness of the dark, talking or listening to the animal sounds that restricted sight seemed to amplify. He rose from his bed one night, awakened by the full green heavy smell of rain, and leaned out of his window to collect and taste it from the cup his fingers made. He spent a whole day waiting for a heron that lived on a nearby lake to take off and, struck by its rise, he felt mothered, and understood that things existed for many reasons, and only one of them was use.

All along the way people wanted news of up North. "Do you know my cousin, Retter? She's up there, too, workin' in some kind of shoe factory, cleanin' up. What's it like there . . . in your eyes? I hear tell there's jobs for everyone, and decent places to live . . . schools and stores and whatnot." He met people who had been saving for years to go North, and who had to sneak out of town to avoid being killed or jailed for causing unrest. "Ain't you goin' the wrong way, son?" one man asked as he passed him the *Chicago Defender*. He met people who were building, still, for their risks, and some who would never leave.

He took some chances at first, but he learned how to carry himself and where not to be. A case of poison ivy and a nasty spider bite taught him to take stock before acting, and he got a lesson in fear from a pair of pale eyes when, off in a dream world, he took too long to step out of the way.

In each town LaRue came to he walked around and talked to people, looking for odd jobs or for a lead on something he could do for a while. It didn't take long for folks to offer him a bed for the night, directions, or a meal, and he found out how those towns survived by mutual support.

LaRue was willing to do just about any kind of labor he was up to, but he liked work that took him outdoors best. As he worked his way toward seeing what picking cotton was like, he found seasonal work picking tobacco, onions, green beans. He was slow at first, and had a hard time keeping up with the other workers, in part because he kept looking over, measuring himself against their pace. He soon caught the rhythm of the work and built up his strength.

He stayed on a job as long as he felt like it and until he earned enough money to move on. He left one plantation in a hurry when he realized he'd been flirting with a woman who had a jealous husband picking a few rows down. And in one town he sat up half the night telling lies and drinking whiskey, and awakened the next morning to find his money gone.

He showed up for day work picking cotton and met up with a sharecropping family that was trying to make it into the next season. They made room for him in their daily cycle of thankless work, giving him a pallet on the floor of their shack and a share of the food that barely went around, in exchange for a part of his wages. "Did you notice the moon?" he asked them one night after dinner, and the man who lived there stared blankly as he drank from the mouth of his whiskey bottle. "The moon? What moon?" The moon was just a break from labor, to be followed by another day of work.

LaRue lay on the floor with them and looked at the stars through holes in the curled and yellowed papers that covered the walls against the weather, pieces of their headlines sprawled above his head.

He picked cotton with them and his fingers, raw and cut at first, began to callous before he moved on. And as he bent over the rows and worked with the family, their rage became his rage, mute and consumptive, rage at the cotton that had been lifted up into god. His hatred and his anger grew as he picked, built as the sweat dripped from his darkening skin, and he looked at the ravaged women, aged in their youth, who picked cotton as their mothers and grandmothers and on and on had done, and the anger of generations rose up until he could hold it no longer, and he hacked helplessly at the roots of the plants as he had seen others in their unspoken misery do, hacking to destroy their fluffy whiteness; he cut at one plant and then the next until he fell to his knees among the split brittle stalks and the masses of white fiber that were spotted with his blood.

He thought of Ruby telling him the story that was hers, and understood more fully the way in which it was his, as well. How that story of reduction and punishment spoke not only of his clan, but was bigger than he knew.

At night LaRue saw a broken bottle taken to a neighbor's face, and a quick knife flash, as rising tempers were fed by alcohol. He saw his fellow workers turn their rage on each other and themselves, saw their violence entwined with their love, and it made him reel with recognition. And he saw a woman sit, night after night when the work was done, with her feet planted firmly apart as she pulled faces with her knife from discarded bits of wood. She looked from the jagged bottles, to the cotton, to the moon, knowing, knowing all the things people are capable of, taking it in and saying nothing as wood shavings fell about her feet.

He moved on from the cotton fields, passing places with sawmills, and clay mines tunneled out for miles underground. He spent a week learning to make barrels from a cooper and another chopping trees. He passed the whole summer in those green places, working with his hands and harvesting, gathering what had been planted the fall before in faith, in concert with the rain.

And just before his traveling came to a close, there was passion, among the summer's rites. A woman who had let him a room came and introduced him to the feel of skin and the taste of mouth, came to him and they made a sweet agonizing climb. She opened an entrance in him and they took their time in the forgiving night, making a pact for slow and patient love in a world of obligation and strife.

When he left her he went, finally, to the place from which Ontario Smalls had set off to find work in the city, and without knowing what it had really meant to him, LaRue saw the green to which his father had dreamed a return.

As he walked the path along the edge of the woods, stopping to look at a plant he had never seen, or the life woven together to make the web of the forest, he felt respect. He was awed by the fretwork of light that came down through the trees, and the heavy rich decay of the earthen floor, where his imagination told him unexpected things moved blindly in the moist dark. He barely breathed as he took in the mystery, captivated by the chaos and the order that were there.

Searching, he found some pieces of the past for holding on to. He found beauty in the place from which his father, and perhaps his, had come. And he learned something more about the sources of his pain.

He paid attention that summer, and things that had been hidden were revealed. A serpent he had thought to be part of a tree moved and overtook its prey. A leaf fell to the curving river where he stood, and looking down into the water from the edge, he saw the layers of living things in its depths.

The tall pines bent in the wind and he listened to the voices of trees, firmly rooted yet dancing, and to the no sound. To the balance.

He was perched on the crest of the earth's ripeness, its summer bearing fruit, and he was amazed. He felt as though he were at the middle of the world.

* * *

As things grew quiet and settled in the long August days, LaRue thought about going home. He felt the lengthening and the shortening of the light, the shifting of green into gold.

Just before autumn, he headed back to Black Oak. Unannounced, he walked through the back door one evening right before supper, dropped his bag, and lifted the lid to each of Vesta's pots. Everyone was speechless for a moment as LaRue looked around the room, sensing himself returned and among them, yet apart. He didn't know how he would be able to tell them about his summer, about the things he had given and received.

"Wishbone!" Ouida cried out as she leaped from her chair and put her arms around him. He went around the table kissing each member of his family, and came to a man he didn't recognize, and paused, as the man said, "Now wait just a minute, I'm not that type of guy. Shaking hands will be quite sufficient!" and discharged an explosion of a laugh.

LaRue focused on the stranger with his penetrating look, and then Ouida said "Oh . . . Junior, this is my brother, Bone . . . Wishbone . . . this is Junior Biggs." LaRue shook his hand and noted, to himself, that something about Junior struck him as wrong. His face looked too loosely connected, like one of those group drawings they had made growing up, folding a piece of paper so that the nose, the mouth, the eyes were drawn by different people. It seemed to LaRue that there was nothing unifying his face, and he had to concentrate on it, hard, to make it come together.

When LaRue left the room to look in on December, Junior asked Ouida what kind of name Wishbone was, and what was wrong with his eye. She hushed him, afraid LaRue would hear, and put Junior's questions out of her mind.

LaRue stood in the doorway of the baby's room, where Vesta had hung many of the samplers she had made in that fury of embroidery before December's birth. He was struck by her growth in the last three months but, not wanting to wake her, he stood and looked at her for signs of Ruby. Since she was asleep, he couldn't see that she had been given Ruby's eyes. Suddenly, Vesta was beside him, pulling his arm so that he would leave before he woke her up.

When he got back to the kitchen, he lifted the lids to Vesta's pots again. "Stop that," she said. "You know it's tacky and bad manners to stick your nose in other people's pots. I hate it when you do that."

"LaRue," Ouida said, "go on and leave her alone. You know how easy it is to get her going. Seems like all I have to do sometimes is breathe."

"Okay, okay, Sister. I promise I will not do it again," he said, as he lifted the last lid, "because you know the last thing in the world I would ever want to be is tacky."

"Mmn mmn mmn," he continued. "I see you're making brussels sprouts. And without consulting me. Well, I'm going to share with you the *only* recipe for brussels sprouts, which I learned on my trip, so next time you can make 'em right."

Vesta sucked her teeth. "You've never liked brussels sprouts, LaRue, and in fact I remember you absolutely refusing to eat them." She turned away, but LaRue had the attention of everyone else, even Junior Biggs, who sat at the table watching him like he was a creature from another galaxy.

"Well I didn't know about *this* way of making them. Now listen closely, because once you hear this recipe, you will never want to make brussels sprouts any other way." Despite her fussing, Vesta went and got a piece of paper to write the directions down.

"First thing you do is wash them, individually and tenderly, pulling off the yellowing leaves, because they tend to be bitter . . ." he instructed, demonstrating with his fingers. ". . . gently, very gently, making sure you get out every little grain of sand that might be hiding among the overlapping leaves.

"Then, you soak the sprouts in a mixture of one part chicken broth, three parts water, and one part vodka . . . Yes, vodka, or as our people say: *vot*ka. Yes, did I forget to mention that this is a Russian way of making sprouts? I think Tennessee Jones learned about it on a trip to the Steppes.

"Anyway, while your sprouts are soaking, you prepare a mixture of onions and bell pepper, which you sauté ever so lightly in a big flat pan, so that things are all spread out and cook evenly. Then, once your sprouts have soaked in this mixture for seventy-two-and-three-quarters hours, you take them out and rinse them. Put them in a large bowl and sprinkle salt, pepper, a touch of coriander, and a dash of hot sauce on them.

"Next, you add them to the pan with the onions, and it is crucial to add them a few at a time . . . one by one would be even better," he said, glancing at Vesta, who was bent over the table, while she took notes, "and then you add the very teeninchiest bit of water, and a few more drops of *votka*, to your mixture.

"Cook your sprouts slowly, gently, with the top on, until they are just soft enough. You can tell they are the right degree of soft by inserting a fork right at the base. If it sinks right in, they are perfect. Remember, there is nothing worse than a mushy, mealy sprout.

"Next, you spoon them gently into a bowl, and pour the juice from the pan right over them. You then sprinkle, ever so gingerly, the slightest bit of grated cheese over the top, and wait until it is a little bit melted." He paused and licked his lips for emphasis, noting that everyone, even Vesta, was now hanging on his every word. "Then, there is the final touch. And you must get this part right.

"You pick the bowl up, careful not to spill a drop, go over to the back door, open it, and toss the whole gotdamn thing out the door.

"And that's the *only* way in the world to make brussels sprouts."

After they had laughed and given thanks they began to eat and Vesta said, "Well, LaRue, did you run into Tennessee Jones on your trip?" He knew she had missed his stories and, laughing, he said, "As a matter of fact, Sister, I did run into Tennessee Jones once or twice. And you know, he told me a story I'll share with you."

LaRue wanted to tell them something about his journey. What he really wanted was to tell them what Ruby had shared with him just the year before, so that Ouida and Vesta would be able to know the part of her to which he had access. He wanted them to be able to make some kind of backward trip to claim a difficult piece of the past, but he didn't know this man, Junior, and it was too soon. He would wait, he decided, and he would know when the time was right. Tonight he would tell a different story.

"There was something Tennessee saw," he began, "when he was working to make a road. He had been looking for work for a while, just like I had, when he heard that some people were clearing a forest to make a road. Neither one of us knew a thing about felling trees, but work was work, we figured, and we both decided to give it a try. This place was just buzzing with activity when we got there, and they sure were hiring, 'cause it seemed like they just couldn't get enough workers.

"They were cutting down everything in sight. These tall majestic grandfather trees were all around, and they practically commanded respect. Those tree-cutting folks seemed to Tennessee like they were termites or something, Tennessee said. Hungry for wood.

"Well, one day Tennessee was hauling away a bunch of roots and stumps, and that road was sure getting built, 'cause you see it was progress coming to that place, this flat red stretch of road running through the woods like a scar. Those men who were building it said it was gonna put the little nearby town on the map, and they were tired of being a no-count little town. They had a whole set of schemes for getting rich, if they could just get people coming to their little town.

"All of a sudden, as he was carting away those roots, Tennessee heard a huge crash in the distance, louder than any trees he had ever heard fall before. There was a break in the work and Tennessee decided he would go and see about it. When he got there, he was struck stone dumb by what he saw."

LaRue stopped in mid-sentence as he saw Junior Biggs brush Ouida's arm. There was something so intimate about it, with a proprietary edge, he thought, and then he noticed a glint of gold on her ring finger. He looked at Junior, trying to get a hold on his face, and then forced himself to go on with his tale, despite his alarm at what he had seen.

He went on. "When Tennessee Jones got there the tree was cracked open, and he could see deep inside its jagged-edged wound. He dropped the torn roots he had in his hands and bent down to look into the tree. He could see some of what had happened to that tree, because, you know, a tree tells its story, too, tells it through its rings, the thick spring bands and the thinner summer ones. He started counting them then, as everyone else stood by.

"The men who had felled it looked at him like he was crazy, and then one of them laughed at the look of loss on Tennessee's face and said, 'It's just a tree, and there's plenty of 'em that's got to go in order for this road to come through.' But Tennessee imagined the landscape without those big old beautiful trees that had rings and rings within their trunks as testimonies to their time here on earth, and these men with the saws were just passing through. They had a job to do, bringing progress to their town, Tennessee Jones told me he thought, as he got back to his feet, just before he quit and moved on.

"He had lost count at three hundred rings, when his boss had told him to get back to work, and he couldn't get over the sight of that tree, all opened up, while the men around him laughed, with no appreciation of the life in that trunk.

"That tree might have been there since before colored . . .since before white folks were there, Tennessee said, when Indians worked the land. It had been here through three, four hundred winters and springs.

"And Tennessee thought about all the things, the history that tree had lived through. Who knew whether it had been made a punishing tree with the hanging of dark men and boys from its limbs? Whether battles and accords had been worked out there? How many conversations of love and remorse had happened under its canopy . . . whose initials had been carved in its trunk, declarations of endless love? Or how a young girl had climbed into that tree, claiming its shelter, its quiet, for herself, and perhaps dreamed.

"Maybe a great quiet poem had been written in those branches, or sweet fruit eaten in the pocket of a private afternoon. Simple things, you know, that might have gone on there. Simple things that fed that poem.

"Tennessee didn't know what all had happened there, but he thought it might have been like that with the other trees he had helped to fell and pull from the ground. That big one did it . . . convinced Tennessee he had no business making that road. The way he put it was," LaRue said, "It was like a witness tree.'"

When LaRue was finished with his story, which appeared to leave Junior perplexed, Vesta rose from the table and said, "Dessie, she'll be waking up soon."

"Dessie?" LaRue asked, and Ouida smiled and filled him in. "That's what Vesta calls her, Bone. You know she could never go for a name as strange as the one you thought up."

"Well I guess not," he said, "I guess not, but she's still December to me." And then LaRue reached for his bag and pulled out the things he had brought back for his family. "They're nothing fancy," he said as he unwrapped them. "Found things, not bought . . . just so you'd know I was thinking of you while I was gone." He also had something for Church, whom he would track down later so they could talk about what had happened while he was gone.

Vesta came back in the room and he gave her the first one. It was a bright red cardinal feather, tinged with black. She took it from him and stroked it, pushing the silky threads up so they clung together, and then down, fringing them out. "It's lovely, LaRue, thank you so much." She could never say how much she had missed her brother, even though she knew she didn't understand him, and she cherished the thing he had found and called hers, though she would have never thought of bending to pick it up herself.

Next he pulled out some bayberry he had picked from the roadside for Eula, and for Polaris a piece of quartz.

He brought stories of the plants and flowers he saw to Ouida, along with a graceful branch, which he said was from Tennessee's witness tree, that was the shape of a sidewinding snake. And to the baby, December, who, in his absence, had become Dessie, he brought a rattle a woman had showed him how to make by filling a dried gourd with seeds.

For himself he had saved three stones collected along the way, one striated with reds and grays, one chunky with glittering ore, and one worn smooth by the river that had been its home. He wrapped them up and put them in a dresser drawer, along with a cotton plant stained with a dark brown spot of his blood.

13

LaRue's alarm at Junior Biggs was well founded. They were barely into the new year when Ouida agreed to marry him and the wedding plans took on a life of their own. Although the ceremony was set for June, nearly six months away, it seemed to be the only thing the future held.

That time seemed like a blur to LaRue, and he would always remember the marriage through the omen of the wedding cake.

A debate about every aspect of the cake extended for weeks on end: the recipe, the design, the flowers on the sides. Great thought was given to dimension, to color, to the number of tiers, and LaRue watched Eula, Vesta, and Ouida sketch it, plan it, change their minds and begin again. The judgment of what should go on top was left for last. They conferred endlessly, and for weeks Vesta interrupted conversations with "What about life-sized flowers . . . or no, a bell . . . for the top?" There was the baking, the assembly, the decoration, late into the night before Ouida's special day. They had considered and arranged for everything, and the only variable that couldn't be controlled was the wave of summer heat that swept Black Oak.

"So much . . . so much to do," he heard Vesta say to December again and again as the big day approached, and she strove to do things the way they were supposed to be done.

Their lives were consumed with decisions: which kind of invitation and who to invite; which kind of paper and which kind of print; whether engraved script was worth what it cost. They debated which kinds of flowers should make up the bouquet and which should be displayed around the house; where to place the aisle and which music to play; what food to serve and how it should be arranged.

Vesta had organized all of the preparations, delegating responsibilities that she wrote down on paper for each one of them.

She had LaRue busy with his list up to the time the guests arrived. He was cooking, running errands for flowers, and doing other last minute things. Tying ribbon to the stairway banister. Unwrapping gifts, arranging chairs.

For months the wedding plans had driven the life of their house.

The cake. Three tiers balanced delicately on hard sugar columns, with vines of pale pink roses climbing the sides. After presenting it to LaRue proudly, Vesta put it in the kitchen so that it would be hidden until the moment when it would be unveiled.

The dress. Ouida had gone for a series of conferences and fittings with the seamstress, a friend of Eula's who sewed for white people. The dress had folds and folds of luminescent ivory fabric and Ouida was fastened in by a string of tiny satin-covered buttons that ran all the way down the back. LaRue was sure they had spent way beyond their means for the entire affair, but it seemed that all judgment had been suspended for this event. He heard the reason again and again.

The declaration. Over months of frenetic preparation it had seemed to drift through the air, repeated until it sounded like a child's song or a warning to LaRue. Every girl . . . The day every girl . . . the day. He heard it said so many times it seemed to take on a spirit of its own, to emanate from the house itself. Whole life . . . whole life . . . whole life. "The day every girl dreams of her whole life."

Ouida was immersed in all of it, her time of glory, her moment, when she was for a brief time the center of the world. LaRue saw that the idea of the wedding and the planning that would put it in motion had gotten bigger and bigger, gaining in momentum, while Ouida, overwhelmed, grew dwarfed at the node. And throughout the preparations he had sensed that mixed in with her wonder and excitement, there was dread.

His lasting memory was the image of the cake, testament to a thing gone wrong.

Now she was back, one year and one month later. It had taken her that long to leave Junior, and she must have had to try to stick it out. And then, like the wedding cake, she had surrendered to what was, and had come back home.

Polaris had answered the door the night she returned, thinking at first that she was there for dinner, a habit that had become more and more regular. And then he saw the suitcases. He was puzzled, never having understood what she had seen in Junior, but unsure, nonetheless, about the meaning of this coming home. Unable to talk to his daughter about any of this, to be involved in the way Ruby would have been, he just tried to be available with what he could give.

He didn't push for an explanation, and he didn't see hurt or sadness in her eyes as he stood there holding the door. She looked fine, Polaris thought, and there was a firmness about her, as if she had settled something inside. Polaris held open the door, not understanding, and said, "Come on in, baby . . . let me help you with those bags." He figured she would tell him what she was going to tell if and when she was ready.

When LaRue found out she was back he thought, instantly, of the cake.

In the months after his return from the South, he had asked Ouida again and again why she wanted to marry Junior Biggs. He had watched and listened to Junior for a long time before confirming what his gut had told him from the start, and in paying close attention he detected the small diminishments Junior wrought. He laughed at Ouida's opinions as if they were charmingly inane, and talked, always, always, about himself, pretending helplessness around her, announcing that he couldn't find something and awaiting her rescue.

Junior gathered his views from the newspaper and when he heard someone in authority express an idea, he made it his. LaRue noticed his habit of glancing around at people's faces to gauge the effects of his words, and it was the fact that he didn't seem to be anybody on his own that concerned LaRue the most. It wasn't that he disliked Junior, he told the family. There wasn't anything there to dislike.

But because Junior was what every one of Ouida's and Vesta's friends had been told she wanted, Ouida had felt powerful pulling him. He was defined as handsome, with an aquiline nose and "water hair," not straight exactly, but obedient if properly wet, and from a prominent family, owners of the first colored drugstore in town. "Big niggers," as LaRue said mockingly. What nobody came out and said was that the thing Junior was best at was having a good time. LaRue asked her if she couldn't just take him for that, for the fun, and not tie her life up with his. But she needed, in the end, to make him more.

LaRue had wanted to understand why Ouida had chosen Junior, but whenever he asked her about it he had felt as if his words weren't connecting up with her, as if she were redirecting all doubts and uncomfortable considerations to a place outside herself. "What about your teaching?" he asked as he took her hand, and when she didn't answer, he continued. "Have you just given up on what's yours, Ouida? Have you?" She didn't respond because she didn't have an answer and didn't feel up to looking for one.

Long after Vesta had stopped going to parties, Ouida had still been intoxicated with the social whirl, and LaRue found out that it had been at a dance, years before, that she had met Junior. She had resisted his interest until she emerged from her daze of sleep to attend a party with a friend, the summer LaRue was gone.

When Junior had first tried to court her, years ago, the other young women in her set had made a fuss, and told her he was one of the Biggs family that owned the first colored drugstore in town. They told her how he had been away to college, and was a good catch, and Ouida had thought he was sophisticated because of the fancy cigarette case he carried and the fine shoes he wore. He had been persistent, but she'd had many attentive men to choose from.

And then she discovered Junior like a sleepwalker reaching for balance finds the wall. From the barely remembered blur of a party he had emerged, stepping out, dancing, from the music and the people and the spinning, an apparition she had barely perceived through the gauzy curtain of grief between herself and the rest of the world. She had blinked as he came forward from the crowd, an incarnation to fill her need. Ouida could think about Junior and dream up a kind of dream with him, and remove them, both of them, from the spin. She could lose herself in him, stepping, half awake, into a waiting role that looked, from her stupor, as if it had been created just for her.

Wanting, needing, to believe in his power to change things for her, Ouida had decided to love Junior Biggs, and then proved it by sleeping with him. She'd had to believe him when he said his self-control would protect them, and then he had begun to press her into choosing a wedding date. When she had put on the ring LaRue had noticed before she had accepted Junior's proposal, she had liked the way it made her feel, its statement to the world that she had been chosen and desired. Ouida delayed setting a date for as long as she could, resisting the momentum that was already building, and finally agreed that they should marry in June.

The preparations were started and the cake was underway.

When the day of the wedding arrived, they were all busy completing the tasks on their lists. After tying ribbons and flowers along the banister of the stairs from which Ouida and Polaris would descend, it was almost time for the guests to begin arriving and LaRue decided to go see if she was ready. He saw her tension, and a sadness behind it, when she answered his soft knock. He entered her room and sat on the edge of the bed, and she turned away from him and worked at arranging her hair. She had seemed to move through that morning in a fog, bathing and perfuming herself and getting buttoned into her ivory gown. "Help me with this, will you, Bone?" she asked, and he got up and secured the crown of stiff wire and prickly white roses in her upswept hair, careful not to stick himself on the few remaining thorns.

It was then that he noticed the twitching on the left side of her mouth.

"Ouida," he said, taking her hands and pulling her to sit beside him on the bed. "You know it's not too late to change your mind. I'll go out there and tell everyone, if you want to stop it here, and you don't even have to face them or feel embarrassed." She continued to look away and tucked in loose pieces of hair.

"I mean," he continued, "you're not getting married for them. You're getting married for you." She turned to him, finally, and shook her head. "I know you don't understand, Bone, but not everyone's strong."

"You're strong, Ouida. I know you better than anyone. I know you by your stories. I know just how strong you are." He had been fighting anguish at her predicament ever since he had met Junior.

She looked at LaRue and then sat beside him on the bed. After a long silence she said, "We've started something, Bone, and now it's in motion, like one of those locomotives Papa rides or something, and I don't know how to stop it." She looked down, unable to tell him about her carnal guilt. "I can't change my mind. Not at this point." Standing up and going to the mirror, she said, "I need someone to love me, LaRue, and Junior Biggs can be that one." She put the finishing touches of rouge and powder on her face and stared at her image in the mirror.

When Vesta peeked in to say that all of the guests were seated, Ouida gathered her bouquet and went to the doorway, waiting for Polaris to join her and deliver her over to Junior Biggs.

LaRue remembered them stepping into the living room and the guests exclaiming "How lovely," awed at her beauty, at her confection of a dress. And there was Junior, up ahead and proud, awaiting her arrival at his side. "Every girl . . . the day every girl . . ." LaRue heard it, resounding, with a life of its own. As she and Polaris marched through the guests LaRue had given her a furtive, sidelong look, and he would never forget how her smile, read by everyone as happiness, looked frozen into place, and he could see that twitching, like a desperate pulse at the side of her mouth.

She looked so uncomfortable, he thought, and he didn't have any idea how her sweaty feet chafed against the hard new toes of the ivory satin shoes that pitched her body forward. He didn't even know that laced into her corset, damp and restrained, she struggled to breathe as the whalebone stays dug into her flesh. Numb and overwhelmed, she wondered herself if she was in there somewhere, or had just disappeared into the yards and yards of suffocating satin and lace.

She had felt like hard baked sugar, in danger of being mistaken for decoration and lifted onto the achievement of a cake herself, solving once and for all the dilemma of how to top the creation that had plagued them for weeks, only to have someone try to break off an arm and nibble it away, unobserved.

"How beautiful," the guests exclaimed as they mopped their sweaty brows, "how beautiful she is."

It had been a day of record, leaden heat, and colored women all over town had cursed the elements as they wrestled with their hair, whose will the humidity had brought out. There was hair rebellion in Black Oak, and many surrendered and pinned on hats. Hair rose. It curled up tight. It frizzed. It fought their brushes and pomades and straightening combs. It refused.

Sweat dripped down people's spines and folks were stuck to the slim wooden chairs that had been rented and arranged in rows. The guests tried to fan themselves with whatever they could find and when one pulled a framed sampler off the mantel and tried to stir some air with it, Vesta had come up, snatched it from her hand, and returned it to its rightful place.

And then Rhea Winters began to hand out the fans she always carried with her, advertisements for the Winters Brothers' Funeral Home. People pushed and reached over each other to get them, desperate for relief, and they beat the air with those fans, which bore a picture of Leverett, unctuous and beckoning, ornate gothic script announcing the motto that was an eternal part of Black Oak.

LaRue answered to himself, "Why not . . . why the hell not . . . with class?" There they were, trying to get through Ouida's wedding and commemorating the effort at a graceful, dignified burial in the process.

It was so hot people started to lean, and then Mamie Banks fainted, hitting the floor with a thud, just as Junior said, "I do." Ouida dropped her bouquet and LaRue laughed into his handkerchief until Vesta silenced him with a vicious look.

Before Ouida knew it, the ceremony was over, her hands were once again full of flowers, and she was standing in a receiving line. She imagined she had answered "I do" in the appropriate place, but she didn't remember. It had been a blur, and now Junior stood holding her elbow, asserting dominion over what had just become his.

The cake rested on the sideboard, an achievement, a display of painstaking planning and work. A three-tiered monument of sweet white and pink. But that day had been so hot the icing had begun to run before the cake was even cut. It looked more and more exhausted and the hard baked sugar bell on top, too heavy for the melting cake, had begun to slip a little and then listed and sank partway into the cake until it collapsed the tiers below and became a shapeless mass.

And the most amazing thing, thought LaRue, was how the guests pretended it wasn't happening, and exclaimed at its utter loveliness. He caught Ouida's eye just as the cake gave in, and thought she looked as if she didn't know whether to laugh or cry.

Vesta was so upset she lunged across the room in her pale pink dress, a concession to the bride's white, grabbed Dessie from Polaris, and stomped upstairs. Nobody wanted to move the fallen cake into the kitchen, so it sat there, a mound of white, the bell on its side, with everyone acting as though it didn't exist. LaRue helped himself to a plateful anyway, and said it still tasted good. When Vesta had recovered her composure she came back downstairs to tend to serving the other food. It had meant so much to her that everything go just right, and LaRue tried to comfort her, but she turned her back and ordered him to leave her alone and go entertain the guests.

Ouida freed herself from her dress with Eula's help and put on street clothes. She tossed her wilting bouquet and left for their new flat on Junior's arm. The day every girl dreamed of was over and, eventually, the guests left and the family, exhausted from all the buildup, deferred cleaning up until the next day.

Even Vesta should have known better, but she had ceremoniously packed up the bell from the wedding cake and stored it away, so that Ouida would be able to pull it out in years to come and reminisce.

Here they were, a little more than a year later, with Ouida back home and them trying to sort it all out. She had stayed married for about as long as LaRue had predicted, and there she was, returned to the room she had shared with Vesta growing up. LaRue knocked and they told him to come in, and he sat on the floor between the beds, leaning against one of the mattresses. He didn't really have to ask why Ouida had left Junior, because he had known from the first that the marriage was doomed to sink, just like the frosted bell. Vesta needed to know why.

"What was it, Ouida?" she asked. "Did he cheat? He lied, right? . . . Did he hurt you?" She had asked the unthinkable before she could censor herself.

"No . . . no, Vesta, he didn't do any of those things." There was a long stretch of quiet, while Vesta stared at her.

"Well, what?"

"What, what?"

"Well, he must have done *something*, for you to move back home?"

Ouida didn't answer.

"He must have done something that . . . that . . . crossed the line."

"It's nothing he did, Vesta."

"Well, what then? What is it, if it's not something he did?"

"It's nothing he did, Vesta. It's who he is."

"Who he is." Vesta repeated Ouida's words.

"Well, yes. Who he is and who I am."

"But," Vesta asked her, looking blank, "did you try?" When she got no answer, she went on. "Did you try to be a wife? I mean . . . to make him happy . . . to cook a nice dinner and keep a nice home . . . all those things?" Vesta had noticed, the times she had been to Junior and Ouida's flat, it had been in a state of troubling disarray.

"Well maybe I'm not cut out for it, Vesta . . . for being a wife."

Ouida felt it was too much to try to explain how she had realized, right away, that it was wrong. She thought of all the things she had realized, without being able to explain. How after the big production of the wedding she had felt foolish, and had had to try, at least, to make it work. Not only was the role wrong, "like having on too-tight clothes," she had often thought, but she had soon found out just how irresponsible Junior was, how, although his family's business had helped him develop a taste for nice things, he had no sense of balance about them. He spent the rent money on fancy shoes, or lost it playing cards.

Once legitimizing the union had absolved her of her carnal guilt, her interest in sex had seemed to die, as well. Without having any other experience to compare it to, Ouida had realized Junior was a selfish man, who went through a few predictable preliminary maneuvers in bed and then satisfied himself. She didn't know if most men were like that, and she didn't know how or whom to ask, but she didn't think it would do.

Marriage was supposed to give a center to her life, but as soon as they were settled in their new flat, Ouida felt exiled. She lay there in the night, after Junior had rolled off her and gone to sleep, opening and closing her hands, which seemed to ache, consumed with a sense of sadness, wondering what she could dare to try and have for herself.

The truth was, the thing that had made her leave had been a small enough thing. She had taken a good look at Junior that morning as he sat in his pajamas eating the breakfast she had made. When his milk glass was empty he had looked at her helplessly and said, "Ouida, I'm out of milk," and he was suddenly a huge infant, and Ouida stared at him, almost fascinated, and asked herself if she was going to spend her life taking care of a man she didn't love. She looked at him, his eyes plaintive, his hand holding out his empty glass, and imagined an expanse of colorless years raising Junior Biggs.

It was a small enough thing that, after a year of trying, showed her she couldn't make it right all on her own, that what they had was insufficient to make her stay. She packed the suitcases she had brought with her and left. She wanted nothing else he had.

Vesta had started scratching while she waited for Ouida's answer and got only silence. "Well, if it's a secret," she said, "then you need not tell . . . If it's got something to do with your private . . . with . . . bedroom matters, that's not something I need to know anything about."

Ouida was silent still. She could never communicate how big it was and how little it was to Vesta so that she would understand. She looked at LaRue for help and, as always, she saw gentle understanding in his eyes.

"We all have things we live with," Ouida thought to herself, "and some we bear alone."

14

Once she was back home Polaris helped Ouida pay for training as a manicurist and she got a job at the Marquis Barbershop in downtown White Oak, where the staff was colored and the clientele white. LaRue thought it strange how they had her seated behind a table in the window of the shop, all dressed in white like a virgin or a nurse, her shiny implements spread out before her. She seemed to be an advertisement, a high-yellow girl with long hair, displayed in the window to draw white businessmen in as they passed the shop.

The first month after she had left him Junior came by several times and begged her to come back to him. "You're my wife," he said, as if that was argument enough. She told him firmly that when she left her family's house it would be for a place of her own, and tried to make him see that she wished him no harm, but was finally waking up. Eventually, he seemed to grasp that he was wasting his breath and stopped coming, and a few weeks later Ouida heard that he had a new lady friend.

LaRue never stopped asking Ouida what she wanted to do instead of normal school, and she told him she was first trying to get on her feet. But he noticed that she never seemed to be reading anything, and he couldn't get her interested in doing much lying. When he tried to ask Vesta how she thought Ouida was doing, she looked at him blankly. "She's got a job, Bone. She's grown-up now. There's no time for that stuff anymore, just like I don't have time to sit and talk that foolishness we used to talk because there's so much to do." She got up to check on Dessie and then returned to the list she was making of her tasks for the week.

When she had put aside enough money, Ouida moved from the

family house into a small flat of her own. It was only two rooms, with a makeshift kitchen made up of a small cookstove and an icebox. Because she was intent on decorating the flat herself, the only pieces of furniture she had were a bed, a gate-leg table, and two straight-backed wooden chairs, which she had found in the family attic and painted cerulean blue. She found other odds and ends up there: a brass lamp that she polished and topped with a shade, a pair of candleholders, and a couple of chipped cups and bowls discarded as flawed over the years.

She brought along her rich fabric collages that had once hung on the bedroom walls but had been folded and put away when she left to be Junior's wife. She made curtains out of fabric found in Ruby's chest of remnants, and brought family pictures and pressed flowers and dresser scarves. She took the tree branch LaRue had brought from his trip down South, and another crooked piece of wood that he had painted purple and green, like a spotted snake. And she brought the quilt with a pattern of fans, each at a different stage of opening, that Ruby had been working on when she died.

Even after she moved Ouida still came by the house for meals and often stayed overnight, as if she was learning gradually how to be on her own. LaRue was glad to see her get her own place, and he helped her paint the walls lavender and light blue and move in her few things. While they were painting, she talked to him a little about how she still missed Ruby and about her marriage to Junior, but again and again they hit unyielding places in their conversations when she shut him out.

He thought about the way Ruby had helped people lay down their stories and their troubles and he remembered that she hadn't pushed, but had given them the room to say what they had to say. He figured Ouida would tell him by and by, maybe on one of those early evenings on the stoop, the place of so many confidences and tales, when she came for dinner.

One day LaRue came home and found her sitting there and in a talkative mood, but he still had the feeling she was carrying a weight she just couldn't release. He knew she needed to talk, but wasn't able. When LaRue asked her what it was, she answered angrily,

"Nothing. Nothing at all," and called through the front door to Vesta in order to avoid his probing.

Vesta came outside with Dessie and pulled her on her lap. Before she was even settled, she had started in on how much the baby had grown and on every little sound she had made and thing she had done that day. LaRue interrupted a soliloquy on how many inches her hair had grown and what grade it was going to be.

"Come, December," he said, "and let's talk a little bit."

Vesta pulled the child closer and said, "I was just going to put her down, LaRue. It's not a good time."

"Nonsense, Sister . . . it won't hurt to let someone else hold her and talk to her . . . isn't that right, December?"

"Dessie. I call her Dessie. And you have to be careful . . . she's into everything these days . . . walking and getting her little hands into things . . . watch it, don't let her slip down the stairs . . . watch it . . ."

LaRue's anger at Vesta rose, as she made it next to impossible for anyone else to spend any time with the child. December relaxed as LaRue rocked her and asked her if she wanted to meet his friend, Tennessee Jones. She was content to sit on his lap while he lulled her with his tale, and once she started to fall asleep, he returned to Ouida and what she wasn't telling him.

"You were telling me . . . or not telling me something, Ouida, about what's going on with you."

Vesta looked at them and asked, "What? What are you talking about?"

"Nothing," Ouida answered sharply, "nothing at all."

Vesta hoped Ouida wasn't in yet another fix, but it wouldn't have surprised her in the least, as she told LaRue often that Ouida had a talent for trouble that challenged her comprehension. "More secrets." she said, shaking her head. "As I said before, it's entirely possible that I don't want to know."

"Not a problem," Ouida answered, hotly, "because you shan't."

LaRue glared at Vesta while he rocked December, and said, "You know, trouble has a way of just refusing to stay out of your way. Sometimes you think you've avoided it, but there it is, a part of things, like the planets . . . or thunderstorms."

They stared at him, knowing he was leading into something bigger. Neither one of them knew if they were ready for something difficult right then, so they said nothing. But LaRue felt in his gut that the time had come to tell some of the things he had kept to himself, and he thought that maybe if he could tell his stories it would help Ouida tell hers.

"There's this thing I've been wanting to explain to the both of you, about my trip down South," he began. He rocked December on his lap. "This trouble kept raising its head, nudging me more and more, and I tried to look the other way, but it did no good. I know you noticed I was acting kind of strange . . . some time ago." Images of the past flashed before him and he spoke again. "The lady running down the street . . . the broken glass." He paused and saw recognition in their faces, and saw, too, their fear at discovering what it was.

"And then . . . I never could stand the scent of that perfume Mama wears. I was smelling and hearing and seeing things that had happened long ago." He paused and they could all feel the sky moving into evening, and the darkness it delivered, settling down.

"What things," Ouida asked tentatively, "did you start to hear and see?"

Vesta felt something bad coming and started to fidget, but LaRue went on. "These little things kept knocking around inside, demanding my attention, and however hard I tried to ignore them, they would not go away. I kept them to myself as best I could, those little pieces of memory, because I didn't know what they meant all together and it didn't seem like it was something good that I was trying to face . . . in spite of myself. I tried to hide from it, but one day things shifted and it all came together."

"What," Ouida asked tentatively, "did you start to hear and see?"

Afraid of what was coming, of the things she had tried to consign to the past, Vesta started not only to fidget, but to itch. She was shifting back and forth on the steps to try to soothe her fevered skin, waiting for an opportunity to take Dessie back from LaRue.

LaRue spoke then of the vision that had come to him on his way home from work, of how he had seen Ontario Smalls in the figure of that window-washer, and how, in a dizzying instant he had been returned there, to their running and his falling, to everything in between.

Vesta heard him begin to speak it and said, "No," silently, said that she could not admit Ontario Smalls into her present. She had spent so much time trying to block out the noise of what had happened, so that while LaRue was talking she distanced herself by dimming his voice, as if she were turning down the volume knob on the radio, until she could barely hear what he said, could only see his mouth moving and hear muffled sound coming out. After all, she had been trying to banish Ontario Smalls for a long time now, and whatever it was LaRue thought he needed to tell them she didn't want to know.

When her itching overwhelmed her and she could stay put no longer, she stood up and held out her hands to take Dessie from LaRue and after he half-stood up to settle her into Vesta's arms, she went in to put her down. LaRue had tried to argue with her and then had given up, deciding that if Ouida could listen, he would tell her both stories, his and Ruby's. He would tell her how he had sat on the stone steps and received the past that had happened before memory and was happening still. He would tell Ouida about the unifying pictures and sounds, and the entrance that had been opened in him that had set him on his own path.

Vesta stood inside the door and listened for when it would be safe to return to the stoop. The memories she couldn't banish were enough, enough, were all she could accept, and they still came, now and then, along with the fleshy wings and doorways of her early years. That they came in pieces didn't help, for she knew the whole within which they fit. She knew the entire story, of which the shattered bottles and purple bruises, the perfume and the inlaid birds were only parts.

Vesta came back outside after LaRue had finished telling what he had learned about his father. Ouida had his hands in hers. "I've told you my story," he said, "but that's not all, because you see, when this happened I didn't know what to do with what I had come to know, and Mama Ruby listened. And then, it turned out that she, too, had a secret to tell."

Vesta panicked, not knowing what to do. She had thought when she sat back down that he was done confessing, and here he was opening another old scar. Ouida stared at LaRue, wanting, and not wanting, to know.

"What I'm trying to say," LaRue continued, "is that with family it doesn't have to be that way. Sometimes we can tell our secrets, and in the telling, heal the wounds they've made. And sometimes, the revelation of other people's hidden stories is about our own pasts, too.

"Mama Ruby told me something before she died, and it meant everything to me, because it turned out that it had a lot to do with my life . . . it helped me to think about my own dilemma, see, and I have wanted to tell you both countless times. And to let you know what going South was partly about. They are family truths, and all parts of the same story, I think."

Vesta wanted to get up and go at the same time that she wanted to stay. She told herself she didn't want it, she didn't want to know about any more pain, but was compelled by the power of the mystery as LaRue went on. "It turned out that when Mama Ruby was sixteen, she made a kind of passage into the hardness of the world, as something that had been growing between her and her father culminated, finally, in a single event.

"Her father, who everyone called Papa Drake, though you'd never know that or much of anything else, since she never talked about her family at all . . . well he was a sharecropper. He worked the cotton fields owned by a white man named Dewey, or *Mister* Dewey to the colored folks. Mr. Dewey owned most of the land in town and, in fact, his family had owned most of the ancestors and some of the living residents of the colored part of town. Well, as a measure of Mr. Dewey's character, he used to lash out harshly at his mules, tearing into them with his whip even when they were going as fast as they could. Animals . . . people, especially those who were female . . . everything existed for his use.

"Well, Papa Drake was always jumping to do whatever Mr. Dewey wanted and whatever he said. He was deferential in a way that hurt Mama Ruby deep down, showing what he called, 'the proper respect.' Well, on this one day Ruby and four of her sisters and brothers were on their way to the field to chop cotton, and they were running late. When they got there, Papa Drake was already chopping, and Mr. Dewey was sitting in his wagon with a couple of white men. When they saw those men everyone except Mama Ruby jumped off the wagon and ran to the field to start on that cotton, in fear of Mr. Dewey's wrath.

"But you see, that day Mama Ruby had decided to take her time. Infuriated by his presence, and the suggestive and insulting way he spoke to her and the other girls and women who worked his fields, she got down off the wagon slowly and began to file her hoe. She decided that she would show him he didn't own her, and she would take her sweet time.

"Mr. Dewey sat there with the other white men for a long time and watched her sharpen that hoe, and when he saw his cronies looking at him . . . watching to see what he would do . . . he leaned forward in his seat and said, just loud enough for her and Papa Drake to hear, 'You're already late, you black bitch, and you better get your ass in that field.'

"Ruby didn't respond, but stood there, filing the hoe a little bit more, and she saw that field of blank white cotton turn to red. She felt herself slide past reason . . . past common sense. When Mr. Dewey leaned toward her and said with quiet malice, 'Now,' Mama Ruby felt her red rage go white again, and raised her newly sharpened hoe as she said, just above a whisper, 'This black bitch is ready for you. Come right on.'

"Everything was absolutely quiet. The other children had stopped working and were standing by, in a stretch of silence that seemed to age everyone, Mama Ruby said. And in that soundless eternity, Papa Drake, who had come closer, sensing trouble, and heard the whole exchange, looked from his daughter to Mr. Dewey, and then back again.

"Mama Ruby watched him look from her to the white man as if in slow motion. 'Get in that field, girl,' he said, finally, looking past her, 'fore I whip your hide.' And he watched until she was bent over chopping, and then looked at Mr. Dewey, who was sitting there, waiting for an apology, and gave him what they both knew was his. 'I'm sorry for her, Mr. Dewey . . . I just can't seem to do nothin' with that girl.'

"Bent over in that row Mama Ruby heard her father's words, and she wished she could have taken it all back. She would have given anything she had to have been able to reach out and pull back the whole of it: insult, response, and apology. All. She wished she could just unravel it, and everything else that had ever happened to her, and begin again. She had sassed that white man in front of his friends, and she knew that that was something he could not allow. Her father had had to put her in her place.

"Mama Ruby knew, she really did know, that her father hadn't had a choice, that if he hadn't rebuked her openly someone could have paid with their life. Ruby knew exactly what time it was," LaRue said, looking at Ouida and Vesta, "and she knew it wasn't a question of right. Although it tore her up, it wasn't that she blamed her father for what he did in front of the white man. It was what he did afterward that wounded her so.

"You see, Papa Drake held it against her, and never let her forget. And he never once told her that he was sorry for what he had to do, that the world just wasn't supposed to work that way. She was only a girl, she told me, only a girl, and he had needed to punish her for his own inability to make it work a different way.

"The whole family was afraid of him, because he was an unyielding, angry man, and it seemed like his hardness showed in his face, which was thick and cracked like old leather. Her mother couldn't see past her fear of him, whose word was law, and Mama Ruby couldn't even talk to her about how helpless she felt.

"There had never been any tenderness for them, Mama Ruby said, as if he did all the bending he was capable of in the rest of his life . . . spent it up in his dealings with white folks. In fact, she could not recall her father ever offering a kiss, and could remember only one, single thing that had been given to her and her alone: a blue woolen cap with dark red trim, a gift when she was five or six, was the one free gesture of affection she could recall.

"It was as if that kind of love was just too expensive, especially with respect to her, for Mama Ruby had always felt that her father had separated her out from the rest of the family as a focus for his rage. 'You're headstrong and you'll never amount to anything,' he had told her, from the time she was a little girl, as if he hated her for her refusal to learn her place, for the resistance he could not afford in himself.

"And on that day in the field, when she was sixteen, the thing he had been building up against her all her life just blossomed, and consumed everything else. She said, as we sat on the stoop in the moonlight three years ago, as if it had happened yesterday, 'Seemed like he meant to break me, no matter what it took.'

"Papa Drake gradually allowed the other children to leave the farm and seek other lives for themselves, but Mama Ruby he kept at home. 'You'll never hold a job . . . you don't know how to get along with white folks,' he said again and again, and Mama Ruby had wanted schooling, but he had forced her to leave just before finishing high school. So she stayed there cooking and cleaning and sewing, helping her mother with the other kids. Afraid. Afraid of the form his punishment might take.

"But Mama Ruby knew that as long as she stayed in that little town, accepting what her father allowed, she would never be free of his punishment. In fact, it had grown so big and wide that she couldn't even see around it. She would be forever trying to win his approval, and hers was a debt that would never be paid.

"It took her three years after the incident in the field to get the strength to go, but at the same time that it wounded her, it clarified things, and when she left, she left without a word.

"Mama Ruby said she wondered sometimes if Papa Drake felt guilty about the way he had treated her, and if that feeling bad just fed the whole thing and made it worse. She wondered what had made him give in to the meager part of himself, but she guessed, in the end, that it was the only way he knew to survive into the next week . . . the next day . . . the next moment.

"Well, she carried it with her always, the weights of his punishment and of that initiation she had had. And you know, when I think back I'm sure I could see her reliving it sometimes, maybe on those quiet Sunday mornings that were her own. She said she felt it come alive inside of her, like grief, at unexpected times. It was unresolved and unforgiven, what had gone on between them, and she never saw Papa Drake again, but what she did with it was this: she tried to claim what he had done as part of her story, and use it as a kind of guide.

"Once accepting the truth of how her father had treated her, she tried not to repeat what he had done. She said there was part of it that was for letting go of, like the ashamed, separate way it made her feel, and that also, there was a part for holding. And in a way, it was something she worked at keeping her eye on, so that she would never forget to reach for the bigger part of herself."

Vesta held her knees tighter and Ouida brushed the tears from her eyes. Neither one spoke.

"So we talked," LaRue said, looking at one sister and then the other, "about wrongs done. The wrongs of our parents. The wrongs of the world out there. Our own wrongs. We talked about some framework for them . . . some way to understand. We talked about, in these various lines we're part of, what we have inherited . . . and what we'll claim."

In the days and weeks that followed LaRue's revelations, he wondered what difference it had made for his sisters to know another part of who he was and who Ruby had been. Ouida had at first seemed distracted and hurt, and he knew she was thinking about the things he had said, but she had only spoken of it briefly. She had joined him one night on the stoop and said how much she missed Ruby and how many things she would tell her if she could. She told LaRue of the afternoon when they had washed and peeled apples together, when Eula and her family had sought refuge in their home, and they traded stories about her, as if they were making a picture that was more and more whole.

Vesta never raised the subject of the secrets again, and tried to push them back inside with all the other painful and private things she wished she didn't know. Her life went on as before and she resumed going to church with Eula as soon as Dessie was old enough to take along. She continued to work in Foundations, and during the day she never even had to go outside, as the store had built its own cafeteria so that downtown White Oak wouldn't have to see colored women eating lunch in its restaurants. She watched the clock, marking time by lunch and coffee breaks, and thought of Dessie, who was cared for by their neighbor, Frosty, on days when Eula had hair appointments. At four twenty-five Vesta began to pack up her things and at four-thirty she was walking, with her co-workers, through the door. Toward home. Toward Dessie, the very thing for which she had always longed.

It seemed she had prayed for a doorway all her life. Conjured it in the unremembered night and tried, later, to grab hold of those wings and passageways that slipped away. And then this baby had come, feet first, bearing the blood of loss, and once Eula had freed her from the choking cord, Vesta had stepped forward to take her child.

She had been appalled by the blood and the heaving, by the sight of Ruby exposed. By her pain and the tearing of flesh. "My God," she had thought, "there must be a better way to get born." But she had been there, holding out her arms to take the child of the woman who had saved their lives.

And this child seemed to be for her. For Vesta, who had been so long exiled. And the love she had felt for her in that moment of stepping forward had grown and grown, so that she knew a bond so strong she lost track of any separating lines.

Vesta had been asking if it was a good day or not for as long as she could remember. She had been cleaning up after people and buttering bread to try to make things right, and here was a creature who looked to her for everything. Filling her need was something Vesta was sure that she could do.

Caretaker.

It was Dessie's infancy that Vesta had loved best, once she had gotten her past the search for a full breast, and she moved toward her at four-thirty each day. There were solutions for her tears and there was the look of satisfaction on her face when she was fed and sleeping. She marveled at how little it took to amuse babies, and at how loyal they were.

Dessie was her way out of herself, that crossing she had wanted in those girlhood nights, and she didn't have to wonder what, what to say, because whatever she said was new and right. Dessie's accomplishments felt like her own, and she took joy and pride in each thing the child learned to do, her first teeth and her first steps and her first words the most important things that happened to Vesta in those years. Dessie was the center of her life.

Witness.

Above all, she tried to make sure that nothing bad ever happened to her. She watched over everything she did and when it looked like there might be trouble, she stepped right in, removing things that might trip her, things that might slow her. Clearing the way.

In a world where so much could happen, where so very much could go wrong, she vowed to protect this child.

As long as she was there to ensure it, the sky was safe.

One Sunday, Vesta was putting the finishing touches on a cobbler and getting Dessie ready for church. LaRue sat in the kitchen with her, reading the journal he had kept during his summer in the South. It was his turn to make dinner, but Vesta had already finished the dessert, and was instructing him for the tenth time about when to take the cobbler out of the oven.

"I heard you the first nine times, Sister, and I believe I taught *you* how to make peach cobbler. Which church are you going to this week anyway?" he asked. He was intrigued by her visits to different churches, and sometimes he went along, but she had her limits on where she would go. She never went to any of the storefront churches that were cropping up all over town, and LaRue figured she would end up where she and Eula had started, at the Episcopal church. Formal and restrained. Known.

"This week I'm going to the Black Oak Baptist Church, the one that Frosty goes to. She says they have the best choir in town."

"Well tell me how it is, and don't forget to look for the Winters Brothers. I know they'll be there." They had an ongoing joke about the astounding presence of those funeral home fans at just about every church in town.

"Hey, listen to this, Sister," he said as she straightened up from checking that the cobbler was centered on the oven rack. He had come across something he had written during his trip. "There was a Shiloh Baptist Church in that last little town I stayed in. And it was there that I met a man named Phoebus who was planning an escape to Chicago, which he spoke of like it was the Holy Land.

"And it was an escape for real, 'cause if his sharecropping boss found out he was leaving, he might have killed him, or had him arrested for inciting a riot . . . that happened, you know, to the cousin of a woman I met . . . and here I've written about that six-year-old-boy who waited every day for news from his uncle up in Cleveland, who had gone in search of a factory job and hadn't been heard from yet. He asked me what language they spoke in Cleveland, and you know, that boy thought of it like a fairy tale land, peopled with kings and dragons.

"And listen to this, Sister," LaRue continued, looking at his journal. "That little boy told me he . . ."

Vesta interrupted him with, "Look . . . look, LaRue, she's trying to say my name . . . it's coming out Besta, but that's what it is . . . Yes, and you're my Dessie, aren't you, sweets?" Even though LaRue had only begun his story, Vesta gathered Dessie up and left for church, leaving LaRue to think about the migration north on his own.

When she got there she relaxed and sat back against the pew, waiting for the service to begin. She watched people come in and greet each other, sharing news of the past week and chatting about their families and parish business, and although she didn't recognize a soul there she felt swept up in the mass of believers. Maybe it was the fact that she wasn't acquainted with anyone there that liberated her. She didn't have to worry about being known but unrecognized, recognized but excluded. She didn't have to concern herself with what anyone there knew or thought about her. She was a voluntary stranger who, for the afternoon, did not feel strange.

As the congregation settled down in their seats and a hush fell over the crowd, Vesta pushed a piece of candy into Dessie's mouth to keep her quiet and closed her eyes.

The choir began its cry and neck muscles distended as the congregation strained forward. Though many of them held hymnals, they looked beyond their texts. They sang in a chorus threaded with blood, from a music of past lifetimes, and the next. Though many sang with eyes closed in apparent solitude, they painted a group mural of interlocking voices, in variegated tones of blue.

Vesta leaned forward, palms upturned in her lap. And then she gripped the smooth wooden edge of the pew in front of her with her right hand, while gently moving the heavy air with the Winters Brothers' fan in her left. She felt herself dropping from within, limbs sucked, unresisting, into a deep internal shaft. Was it a doorway, after all? A doorway in?

Sliding back until her shoulder blades met the ungiving pine she began to disconnect, opening her eyes to focus on the fused panes of colored glass and dropping her hands to her sides. There was music in the rhythms around her, in the swaying of each back bearing its own trouble. Gazing up, her face and her white-clothed body flushed with crimson and deep blue light. Her hands closed around Dessie's small sticky fingers, and then she awakened to sudden movement all around her.

She returned to the dry blankness of knowing the way things are. To the whiteness of her life. It was what she seemed, always, to come back to, as if the transitory moments of relief she worked for faded, inevitably, to a barren plateau.

When she got home she found LaRue still wrapped up in his journal. Absorbed in reading and daydreaming, he had lost track of the time and forgotten the cobbler. Vesta was furious, despite his profuse apologies, and talked about the scorched dessert non-stop, until LaRue decided to skip dinner and went upstairs to his room.

He was disgusted with himself and he felt Vesta was right when she called him trifling. Among the many things she said in anger was the prediction that untogether as he was, he would never find a girl. He vowed to be more attentive to things like time, to get a handle on his imagination and stress the practical. After all, he was almost grown and would be leaving for college in less than a year. Maybe he never would get it together, he worried, and maybe now that Ruby was gone there would never be anyone else besides Ouida and Church who would understand and accept him. Maybe he never would find love.

15

"Families can go *down*, you know," Olive's mother, Rhea Winters, said as she leaned in her direction, speaking with a gravity reserved for threats of pestilence or war. Olive pulled her torso away from her mother, even though she was all the way across the room, and Rhea Winters settled back into her chair, her warning delivered.

She had said it again and again in the same way, as if a gear were engaged and a pattern set in motion, and each time, Olive wondered at first what her mother was talking about, and then started when she saw her meaning. No matter how many times she had said it, Olive was shocked.

When she thought about LaRue, she never saw the person her mother criticized. She loved the skin and the full lips that Rhea scorned, and the unencumbered way he walked. She loved the mischief in his eyes. And she loved the lies he told.

The first time she saw him, the summer before he left for college, he had been walking across the street whistling when he saw her and stopped. He was fond of saying that the thing that caught him was how imprisoned she had looked as she waited in that outfit that was so "unher." He said that he could never have walked past the incongruity of her starched outfit and the wildness of her long sprawling limbs, without finding out who she was.

As he smiled at her and crossed the street, she lowered her eyes in the ladylike way her mother had taught her, and straightened her hat and gloves.

"LaRue Staples," he said as he removed his hat and bowed, "but they call me Wishbone. Bone for short." She kept her eyes lowered, as she had been taught, until he craned his neck to look under her hat. "I do believe you have the longest legs I've ever seen. Have you got them folded double under that Sunday dress?" She smiled in spite of herself, and tried to cover her mouth with her white gloved hand as he continued, "Why even your knees are lovely . . . the loveliest I've ever seen. Whatever *is* your name?"

She tried not to, but she couldn't keep from looking up, and when she saw the light in his iris, she couldn't help but smile. Gateways, his eyes seemed to her, to somewhere familiar, yet unknown.

"Olive," she stated matter-of-factly, and he waited for more, eyebrows raised. "Olive Winters."

"Mmmn," he said, looking directly into her eyes. "I didn't know that Olives grew in winter. A gift of summer, I always thought they were, but you've proved me wrong."

She didn't know what to say, but she smiled. She really smiled. "Well, and do you know the meaning of your name, Olive?" he added, leaning closer.

"Excuse me?" she said, and he responded without taking his eyes from hers. "Do you know the meaning? Do you know where olives fit into things?"

"Why no, I don't guess I don't know," she answered slowly. "They're those little green things to me, sometimes with little red wicks sticking out, what do you call 'em, pimento, I think. They grow on trees, I think . . . or is it vines. No, I don't guess I do know much about them," she said, looking away and clasping her white-gloved hands.

He had laughed as he leaned against the wrought-iron railing. "Well, you see . . ." he began, "it was all about deliverance . . . deliverance, and a rainbow. You know the story, it's one of the oldest told." He began his tale, and when he got to the building of the ark, and the gathering of two of every sort to be kept safe by a covenant, Olive realized what story he was telling, and began to add bits and pieces of her own.

"Were there roaches on the ark, too?" she asked. "There must have been more than two . . . more than two of them must have snuck on that ark, abundant as they are today," she exclaimed, and they both laughed.

"There were definitely roaches, too, and maybe a few extra snuck on. Anyway," he continued, "once they were all safe on the boat, the rains began."

"Well, Mrs. Noah sure must not have been no colored woman, 'cause she'd have been worried about her hair," Olive interjected.

"Let's just say she had more important things on her mind . . . if that's conceivable, that is . . . so anyway, they spent forty days and forty nights holed up in that ark, and with no radio and no going outside, I figure they told each other some whopping lies . . . now that I think of it, that's probably where lying started . . ."

She stared at him, wondering what kind of creature it was who had just entered her life.

LaRue continued. "They sat there on that ark, trading tales of Brer Rabbit . . . and of course, Brer Roach. And I figure there was some sweet talking going on, seeing as they had forty days and forty nights to renew their love . . . Oh yes, I'm so sure there was some lovin' goin' on."

Olive interrupted him again. "Well, if all that was goin' on, there must have been some fussin' too." She started out shyly, looking at the step in front of her, but finished the sentence with her eyes meeting his. "Lovin' and fussin' seem to go together, far as I can tell."

And he thought, as he listened to her, that he might have met his match.

"Must have been some fussin' too. *Anyway*," he continued, "when the waters abated, the ark had come to rest on the top of a mountain, and Noah sent out a dove, to look around and see what was doing. The dove came back without landing, as, you see, the earth was still covered with water, but when he sent her out again, she returned bearing an olive branch in her beak. And that's how Noah knew that the waters were down, and it was safe to leave the ark . . . It was a rainbow that greeted him, and the promise of seed and harvest . . . cold and heat . . . night and day."

They looked into each other's eyes for a while, and then he leaned toward her and whispered, "Are you my sign, Olive, that there is dry land up ahead?"

She looked at him for a long time and, without even realizing it, she nodded.

"Winter olives . . ." he whispered, " . . . imagine such a thing."

All summer they sat on the stoop, ignoring Rhea Winters's frequent trips to the window to observe them, and tried to top each other's fantastic tales. "I've got one," he would begin. "Did I ever tell you the story of Ida's Fish Hut?" he said as he leaned back against the stairs and began.

He and Olive had invented a pair of reappearing characters: the Powell twins, LeFoy and Footney. LeFoy was six feet seven and almost white-skinned, while Footney was four feet eleven and dark. And the most remarkable thing about the Powells, which LaRue pronounced "Pow," as he had always heard black people do, was that, despite their differences in build and skin color, their facial features were just alike.

LeFoy liked nothing better than to sit around and do some 'fendin' and provin', but he was short on common sense, while Footney, who had his mind on scheming and oversporting, was always getting them in a jam. "Well it just so happened," said LaRue, "that Footney was tryin' to convince Ida, who owned a little eatery, to bring him and LeFoy in as business partners. It was a little hole-in-the-wall, about the size of your mother's hall closet, and not nearly as neat."

"It was fried fish," she added, "that Ida sold at this spot."

"Yes. Hell yes. Long as there is grease and fish, our people are gonna be fryin'it up . . . So one night, when folks were wrapped three, four times around the block, waiting in line for Ida's fish, a shot rang out. And LeFoy and Footney Powell just happened to be in line, waiting on their Friday night mess of whiting, and to put a plug into Ida about making them part-owners in her hut. Footney had his bottle of hot sauce in his inside coat pocket . . . he never carried it in his outside pocket, lest he be relieved of it before he got his fish."

"The aroma of that fish," Olive said, "sweet and hot as it came out of Ida's vat of bubbling grease and cornmeal, traveled for blocks, and folks would get off their stoops in a trance and head that way, against their very own wills, it seemed sometimes. Now Ida did positively no meetin' and greetin', and there was no need to ask what you wanted, 'cause there was only one thing on the menu: *fish*. When it was your turn, you walked up to the counter and she looked you straight in the eye with her no-nonsense look that had an edge of hostility in it, pinching shut her I-don't-play mouth, that top lip darkened with the shadow of a mustache, and said, like a challenge, 'How many?'"

"Well," said LaRue, picking up the tale, "on the night of the shooting, Footney and LeFoy had waited for two hours and seventeen minutes to get their fish. They were three people from the door when a scuffle ensued and two shots rang out. I heard tell it had something to do with misappropriated fish . . ."

Olive slapped her thigh and laughed. "You know you need to stop, Wishbone. You need to just stop."

"Well about a week later, Footney was called to testify, having been the one to see the incident most clearly. Footney walked to the witness stand proudly, filled with a sense of his importance, both in having witnessed an unusual and disturbing event, and in being asked to tell the tale in court. Dressed in a borrowed suit, he raised his right hand solemnly, exposing a whole expanse of bare wrist, as he had forgotten to put on his cuffs, and swore to tell the truth.

"After he sat down, he responded to the first question by stating his name slowly, enunciating each syllable and pausing to make sure everyone got it. He glanced at LeFoy across the courtroom with a self-satisfied look, and waited for the questioning to begin.

"After all the preliminaries, placing him at the scene and establishing his competence, the prosecutor asked Footney, 'Sir, where were you when the first shot was fired?' Footney looked at the judge and replied, solemnly, 'Your Honor, I was at Ida's Fish Hut.'"

Olive began to smile, feeling the story coming to a close, and LaRue slowly wrapped it up: "Well, then the prosecutor knitted his brows and asked Footney, 'Okay, that's fine. Now, sir, let me ask you this. Where, exactly, were you when the second shot was fired?' And Footney said, quick as a flash, 'I was home.'"

Olive fell out laughing, as he delivered his signature. "I swear on high that tale is true . . ." and she finished it for him. "If not for me, for sure for you." And then they were quiet for a while, stirring around inside for other tales.

"I've got one," Olive said.

"Let's hear it then," he said, still chuckling at their joint ingenuity.

"There was something that happened to LeFoy and Footney Powell that had to do with pork," she said. "You might have already heard about it. What? You don't believe me? . . . Well just listen and I'll tell you what I know . . ."

Rhea Winters refused to speak to LaRue. When she saw him, she just said, "Mmmn," or sucked her teeth. LaRue tried to lighten things up and make Olive laugh about it, saying things such as, "Trying to get a conversation going with your mother is surely a challenge. You can rub two words together and not be able to kindle a blessed thing." And when Rhea had failed to respond to his polite greetings for several weeks, he began to speak for both of them, asking and answering the questions customarily asked.

"Well how are you, LaRue?" he would begin, facing to the right, and then, turning left, "Why, Mrs. Winters, I'm doing just fine. How nice of you to ask."

Rhea Winters glared at him without speaking, and after he left, she never failed to mention that she had seen families go down.

One night, when he arrived to see Olive, her mother opened the door just enough to tell him that she was out, and then shut it in his face. That sliver of light, extinguished suddenly by such a small act, the pressing of a palm, had stunned him. LaRue had stood on the porch for a moment before he could descend the stairs.

Ashamed of her mother's rudeness, Olive invented explanations to give LaRue. She told him that her mother had been ill, and that her medication gave her certain lapses. LaRue told Olive that it didn't bother him, but he knew the meaning of Rhea's looks.

After three months, Rhea told Olive to invite LaRue to Sunday dinner. She was sure that he would demonstrate, in such a setting, just how inappropriate he was for Olive, and she figured that without her resistance, the relationship might fade.

LaRue arrived with a bouquet of flowers, for which Rhea barely thanked him, and they sat down to eat. After Rhea said grace, they ate without speaking, as they always did. LaRue kept looking around, waiting for something to happen, trying to figure out their foreign, silent way of sharing food. The silence was punctuated only by the little sharp sounds of silverware against china, and the monotonous clicking of Rhea's false teeth. As soon as the meal was over, Leverett Winters excused himself to return to work. During coffee and dessert, LaRue couldn't take the clinking and clicking, the way Rhea dabbed at the corners of her mouth as she looked through him. Without altogether meaning to, he blurted out, "Eagles."

Rhea's clicking teeth fell silent as she stared at him. Olive smiled to herself. "I think often of eagles . . . at times like these." Rhea stared at him hostilely and said, "MMMn." He continued.

"I believe it was Tennessee Jones who told me . . . yes, it must have been him," he said, glancing at Olive. His look told her that he knew it was a pretense, that her mother would never accept him, and he continued, "He would have had occasion to learn such a thing on one of his trips out West. So it was, he came to find, one piece of time he spent in the wilderness, that eagles have the most curious ways."

Rhea still looked at him scornfully as he talked. "You see, strange as it may seem . . . and I swear on high it's true . . . they mate for life. And each year they lay just one egg, in a nest that sits in a most dangerous place, on a crag, or balanced just so, in the crack of a cliff. Amazing, that they place their most valuable thing there, that which is worth their lives, for you see they care for this one baby eagle even at the expense of their own lives, even if they must starve.

"Somehow, they believe. They believe that it will be okay, and live with some kind of faith in the way of things. Exposed to rain and wind, the bird survives, with their care, until it is ready to fly. Mama and papa eagle don't fret, because it is the way, and never has a baby eagle risen and not flown. It all happens, just so, when it is time. And mama and papa eagle can see baby eagle go on to do the very same thing, passing down their gifts . . . twin gifts, really . . . of trust and flight."

Rhea Winters never heard the end of his story, for when he was almost finished, she got up and started carrying the dishes to the kitchen and scraping the plates. After he left, Rhea started washing and polishing the silver they had used for dinner, in accordance with her oft-stated principle that you must keep nice things up. She had seen the way they looked at each other, like conspirators or something, and decided to act.

She began with his name. "What kind of a name is 'Wishbone' for a grown man . . . or for a child, for that matter," she said to Olive as she shook her head. "Why it's . . . it's undignified, just like those no-count country niggers coming up here and ruining the things we've worked for, wearing their work clothes on the streetcars and speaking who knows what, it's not English, and living all packed into these flats like sardines . . . anyway, who . . . who, I ask you, would take a man seriously who had such a name?"

Olive laughed. "I like his name, Mama, and its origins are special, whatever else you think."

Rhea knitted her brow. Her husband's funeral home gave them an intimate knowledge of other people's lives that Rhea Winters never hesitated to use. She had been holding the circumstances of Ontario's death as a trump card, to show Olive when necessary, to make her understand fully just how inappropriate LaRue really was. She could see it was time to play it. "You know, dear child, that I have never told you the true nature of that union between Eula and Ontario Smalls. I have wished to shelter you, but after all, as they say, the splinter is most often like the stick.

"The facts, hard and cruel as they may be, are these. Ontario Smalls was a man who raised his hand to his wife. He hurt her so bad one certain night, not long before he died . . . and I might add that *that* was a fitting end . . . that Eula Smalls was reduced to running, bleeding, through the street, bleeding and running, and half-nekked . . . it was shameful, don't you know. And something else that I have no doubts about, there is more to that than meets the eye . . . A man hits his own wife like that, he must have had some kind of reason . . ."

"Stop, Mama. Just stop. You don't know a thing about it, and anyway, it's not really your business is it, so let it go. If you're interested, why don't you just ask LaRue Smalls?"

Rhea Winters stopped for a moment while she finished up the flatware, and then continued. "All I know is, Olive, and I don't mean them harm, is that they are different. They are. Living in that crazy way, two families together so you can't tell who's who or what's what. Do you want to live that kind of way, Olive? No, I know you don't . . . Now we've done everything a family could do for you, Olive, and you must hold things up. You can do better, find someone who will provide for you rightly, and give you babies that won't be dark . . ."

At that, Olive threw her towel on the table and started to leave the room. Rhea's voice rose in volume and pitch. "You just remember," she cried, a piece of half-polished silver in her hand, "families can go down. They can!" And alone, she said softly, to herself, as she polished away the silver tarnish furiously, "Why I've seen it happen right before my eyes . . . they can . . . they can."

16

Just as LaRue was getting to know Olive, Ouida was having her own summer of discovery. She was finding out about choosing, and about a woman she had never expected to know.

Her kisses were like nighttime secrets, and Ouida swore that her laugh, like the rain, made things grow. Zella Bridgeforth touched her somewhere timeless, held her, compelled her with her rhythms, and Ouida answered her call. She chose her, after all, but the path that led to Zella took her, first, through other choices.

The summer of 1926, the summer they had met, Ouida would later think of as her "swan song." She had swung her corset-cinched body along the streets of the city with long steady strides, smiling but never meeting the eyes of those who paused from whatever they were doing to partake of her radiance. Just divorced from Junior, she was finished, finally, with trying to will their union into rightness.

As soon as she had landed her manicurist job and rented her flat, she had surveyed the range of the possible from the vantage point of her manicurist's table, feeling, for the first time in her life, that she owned the choice. From the spin of options, she made assessments. And she did some choosing.

She chose Johnston Franklin, the middle-aged white man who stopped in the shop on his business trips from Louisville. He came in and stared at her while waiting for a chair, and she met his glance, her chin in the air, and kept working. While he sat for his haircut and shave, he asked Alton, one of the barbers, who she was. When Alton didn't answer, Johnston Franklin turned in the chair, his face half-covered with lather, and addressed Alton with a demanding look. Alton turned away and stirred his soap, assessing the cost of defiance. Finally, he said, "I think she's married, sir. Least that's what I've heard."

Johnston Franklin laughed and said, "Well I'm not interested in her husband. What is her name?"

Alton stirred his soap some more and then answered, "Ouida Staples. Miss Ouida Staples."

Ouida had noticed the exchange and could see Johnston Franklin coming her way out of the corner of her eye, but she refused to look up. She sat at her table humming while she polished and arranged her instruments, the edge of his gold fob, a crisply creased pant leg, and the tip of an expensive shoe just within view. Finally, when he realized that she wasn't going to look up at him, he sat down and ordered a manicure. She took his hands and began her task.

"I understand your name is Ouida," he said, "and that's an unusual name." She lifted her eyes slowly, as if it was an effort, assessed his face in an instant, and returned to his hands. The barbers watched to see what she would do.

"And how *are* you today, Ouida?" Johnston Franklin tried again.

"Oh, I'm just fine," she answered with a hint of insolence as she lifted her eyes, "sir."

"Well . . . I don't recall seeing your lovely face in this establishment before . . ." Ouida kept filing, silently.

"I come in here every month or so . . . here on business, quite regularly, and I will certainly make it a habit to visit this establishment more often." She filed his nails silently, thinking how soft and pale his hands were.

"Well . . ." he ventured, "this town sure is different from my home . . . it's the city, all right, and I do like, now and again, seeing something besides trees . . . of course, this town doesn't compare to New York . . . now that's a different story, that's the real city. Have you ever been to New York, Ouida . . . Miss Ouida?"

She shook her head, and kept working on his nails. And receiving neither information nor interest, he jerked his hand away as she was finishing up, paid his bill, and left. He returned the next week, and the next, watching her from the barber chair, and when he was finished being shaved, he came up to her and leaned over her table until she met his eyes. Matter-of-factly, he said, "It would be my pleasure if we could spend some time together . . . tonight, perhaps."

She looked at him, her head tilted, and measured the choice. She saw a square pink face, not so different from many she had seen, well fed and well tended, and even though it wasn't a face that moved her much, she thought she could look into his restless moss green eyes for a little while. It was a face that held the promise of things she couldn't afford, and their delivery with a kind of homage.

She glanced over at the barbers, Alton and Regis, who watched the whole thing unfold and waited for her to resist sweetly, and their expectations bred defiance. The other barber, Flood, never looked her way.

"Not tonight," she answered as she stood up and went to tend to some other job, making him wait until she returned to tell him when.

It was a timeless play, the choreographed conquest of strange exotic prey, and Ouida was willing to play it for a time. It was a variation on a role she knew, and even though she was familiar with the script, she liked to think that it was she, in fact, who controlled the hunt, fooling the hunter into thinking things moved along by his design. She figured she could learn something about the rest of the world from Johnston Franklin, about the places he visited that she had never been. She liked the challenge. She liked the gifts he brought. And she liked his liking, too.

Their first night of sex, Johnston Franklin had undressed completely and was waiting for her in the bed when she came in from the bathroom, and she had stood, fully dressed, and looked at him. "Well, you certainly are direct, Johnston Franklin. You get right to the point."

She found herself calling him by his full name, even in bed. And after they had sex he talked to her of his business trips, of meetings and sales and the shops and restaurants he had visited. It was as if just being around Ouida made something in him loosen and spill out, the things he held separate from the rest of his life. Eventually, he started discharging the details of his day, his aspirations and his self-doubts, as soon as he saw her, and he talked all the way through undressing, right up to their first embrace.

He was captivated by her beauty, and her knowledge of its power, and he had seen it in the way she made him wait that first day he saw her, and had wanted it for his own, sensing there was something, some kind of magic, that she knew. He wanted to know it, too.

He wanted to know about the way she lived life up close. While he heard things and looked at colors and shapes from somewhere outside of himself, he could tell that when Ouida did something, she was right in the middle of it. He asked her to reveal to him her eye for things, and he asked her to give him the rich details she saw. "Tell me a texture," he would say, as they lay in the rich linen of his hotel, and she would begin to describe some fabric she had seen.

"Silky, like a river in sunlight, and purple, with flaws that aren't flaws, but just the way of the cloth. And it feels purple, Johnston Franklin. You know how purple feels? Rich, with a grain that's both kind to and hard on the fingertips. Now it is your turn," she said, lying back on the pillows. "Tell me about the trees you have at home."

"Okay . . . well . . . let's see," he said and then stopped. "I can't," he protested, but she continued to prod him. "Okay, okay. The trees in my front yard are oak trees. They are live oak trees."

"Live oaks." she said.

"Yes. Live oak."

"Well, that doesn't mean a whole lot to me, Johnston Franklin. Are they shaped like fat stodgy men, or lithe like young girls? Are they dark, and do other colors show through in spots? Are they sheltering, or does the rain get past the leaves? And what does the bark feel like to the touch . . . does it stand away or cling to the wood?"

He leaned back against the pillow and tried to imagine them. "They're shaped . . . like oak trees are shaped, I guess. I never noticed. And they're green . . . and brown, like I suppose most trees are."

"Well, how does the trunk feel?" Ouida asked.

"They are like . . . they're live oak, that's all. I don't know what else to say," he stammered, as she shook her head and argued. "I know what you call them, Johnston Franklin, but what are they like to you?"

"We had them put in a long time ago . . . they're what everyone has . . . and they're old . . . and big . . . and they have leaves, like all trees. I don't know what else to say. I don't know, that's all I see."

Ouida looked at him, propped on her elbow, and then slid down under the covers and went to sleep.

Johnston Franklin visited weekly for several months, but Ouida began to withdraw from him as she felt him trying to hold her closer and closer, like a butterfly in a Ball canning jar. Waxed paper stretched across the top. Breathing holes punched through.

The last time they met, on one of his regular forays from his wife and family, he held onto her as she got up to leave, and demanded to know where she was going. Ouida pulled her arm free and gave him a decimating look as she got her things to leave. When she glanced back to look at him for the last time, she saw a child whose fingers held traces of the black and orange dust of captured butterflies.

When it was just about finished with Johnston Franklin, Ouida chose the barber, Flood, who drew her with the economy of his attention, and looked at her from underneath his eyes. The other barbers flirted with her all the time, and played at asking her out. "You shore is one fine-lookin' woman," Alton would say, leaning on the arm of his chair as he waited for his first customer, shaking his head. "When, just when, are you gon' marry me?"

"After she marry me and I leave her," Regis answered, "'cause you know a woman fine as she is don't mean nothin' but trouble. I prefer the ugly ones, truth be told, 'cause that way you're glad when they leave you."

She laughed at them playfully, and said, "You two are just no good. What about that devoted little lady of yours at home, Alton?"

"She would understand. She know I just married her 'cause I was waitin' on you."

Flood never joined in the joking, and he barely even smiled. Ouida didn't even know if he was married, and as she wasn't looking for a husband, she didn't care. He never looked her way when Johnston Franklin came to the shop, and he never shaved him or cut his hair. He prepared all of his own lotions and tools, neither accepting nor offering help. He traveled solo, with a hardness about him that she wanted to work soft.

When Ouida had passed between barber chairs one afternoon in search of towels, and brushed against his arm, he hadn't started, or looked at her, but she had seen the muscles in his forearm tense as he gripped his comb. After that she found reasons to go by his chair. Knowing that she would have to go after him, and thrilled by the pursuit, she brought him a cup of tea one morning and left it on the counter behind his chair. He let it sit all day, never thanking her and never drinking it. She did the same thing the next day, and the next, until, holding the cup with both hands, warming his palms, he lifted it to his mouth and drank. And as he lowered the cup, he looked at her with desire, and a trace of contempt.

The next evening, she waited until Alton and McGraw were gone, and she and Flood were left to lock up. Fiddling with his scissors and combs, he slowly cleaned up his chair and the floor around it, while she arranged and rearranged her manicurist tools, unable to speak. He went for his coat and hat and headed for the door. As he reached for the doorknob, she spoke.

"Flood?"

He stood with his hand on the knob and his back to her and then he turned, and she said nothing as he stood at the door waiting for her. They walked to her flat, and as soon as they got inside the door, they tore at each other's clothes, and took each other on the bare floor, as if it couldn't be helped, as if it had to be that way, the hard urgency a hurting they both wanted to feel. As soon as it was over, he dressed and left without saying good-bye, and Ouida didn't think of the risk she had taken until it was too late.

At the barbershop, things didn't change on the surface, and Ouida knew little more about Flood than before. What she did know was that the heat, the tension between them would make him return, and she waited for him to come to her again. At times she wondered if she had dreamed it, until a week later, she had stood watching him after Alton and McGraw had left, and he looked at her and grasped the back of his chair tight, until the leather squeaked. She knew he wanted her again; and again, he waited at the door.

In their fevered loving, Ouida saw Flood surrender, silently, to something in her. She wanted to be the one who reached him, against his will, the one whom he couldn't help but come back to, the one who excavated his pain, his need, and for a time, she was willing to exchange peace for the intensity of the fight. Again and again, she tugged on the one string that joined them and she reeled him in.

When this was no longer enough, Ouida had tried to push it further, to find out who he was, but the two of them were stuck in a moment in time, repeating again and again the same act, moving nowhere. By the time she heard Zella's call, she was letting go of what she had, and didn't have, with Flood, and she chose Zella, rain-voiced, in whom she met herself.

The first time she saw her, Zella was standing on the corner waiting for a streetcar as it began to shower, and Ouida watched her digging in her bag from the barbershop window for something to shield herself, cursing as her hair got wet. As soon as she had pulled out a newspaper to cover her head, she had tossed it down and stood there laughing as her head got soaked. Ouida glanced up and saw her as she was putting her instruments away, and moved to the window to watch as Zella lifted her arms and face to the rain and shook her head, opening her generous mouth to taste the falling water.

The next time she saw her, Zella had come into the shop for a haircut on the weekday allotted for colored customers, and Ouida had watched her enter and approach Alton's chair, struck by the way she moved with authority over space. She was tall and slender, and a few years older than Ouida, almost thirty. Her skin was copper-colored and her hair was a mass of dark ringlets, but it was her large flashing black eyes that were remarkable, one smaller than the other. When she walked over to Alton's chair and sat down, he came around to face her and declared, "Now you don't need a shave, and I know you not even thinkin' 'bout cuttin' off all that pretty hair, so just what are you doin' in my chair?"

Zella frowned and gave him a look that was a challenge. "You cut hair, don't you," she stated, rather than asked, and Alton nodded. "Well," she said, "I suspect you cut it like your customers ask you to, is that right?" and Alton nodded again. "Then I suggest you get busy with your scissors and crop mine just above my cheek. Right about here," she said, gesturing with her hand.

Alton argued with her for a while, but he gave in when Zella said, "Why is it that colored folks feel every bit of our hair ought to be on our heads! If we were as concerned with what's in our heads as we are with what's on them, we'd be a lot further along."

At that, Alton had to laugh, and he took up his scissors. He shook his head as her hair fell to the floor, and exclaimed what a shame it was the entire time, and after Zella looked at the finished product in the mirror, she got up, paid him, and left, nodding to Ouida on the way out.

"Well," Alton said, as she was leaving, "Girl, bet' not mess with that one. I know her peoples, and she ain't quite right. What I mean to say is . . . she ain't normal."

When Ouida stared at him, wanting to know more but afraid to ask, he continued, "I know she'd like a sweet young thing like you all for her own. Her kind, they like that."

"Now that's a lovely woman," Zella said to herself once she was outside. She turned back and caught Ouida's eye through the window, and there was between them a moment of recognition, whose power made them turn away.

Ouida went to the family house that evening and stayed the night, and Vesta sat on the edge of her bed working lotion into her face while Ouida was brushing and plaiting her hair. "Vesta, I met someone who's different," she ventured, unsure of herself.

"Different . . ." Vesta replied. "What does that mean?" And Ouida paused. "I don't know. Different, somehow. I don't know how to explain it."

"You gotta do better than that, Ouida," Vesta said. "It's late and I'm not up to reading minds tonight."

"Well . . . she gets her hair cut short, and at the shop," she began, to which Vesta raised her eyebrows. "I don't know, she's kind of not feminine, but she is feminine after all." Vesta just looked at her.

Ouida told Vesta what Alton had said and then she stopped brushing and asked, "What do you think, Vesta? You know anything about these things?"

Vesta didn't and so she shook her head. "I've heard of people like that, but no, I don't know at all about that sort of thing. I can say, for sure, though, that it sounds like trouble to me," and then she finished up with her face, turned her bed down, and curled up facing the wall. But she lay there in the darkness considering what Ouida had said, and it was a long time before she fell asleep.

The next time Ouida saw Zella, two weeks later, she had thought about what Alton and Vesta had said and she was ready for Zella's greeting, but not for the way she made her feel, like a dry part of her was being watered. "Rain," she whispered to herself, "Rain."

After her haircut, Zella sat down at Ouida's table and said, "I think I'm due for a manicure." In fact, she had never had a manicure, but something in Ouida's response to her glance had pulled her there, and she had to see what her voice sounded like.

"My name is Zella," she opened, and Ouida responded, "Ouida . . . Ouida is my name."

They smiled and Zella asked her what kind of name it was and where she got it. She said, quietly, "It was passed down. Or so my mother said." As Ouida worked on Zella's hands, she noticed how strong and worn with experience they looked and felt, and she wanted to know where those hands had been.

Zella began to feel the need for a weekly haircut or a manicure, and she and Ouida found themselves sitting for hours talking while she surrendered her fingers to Ouida's, and felt something in her tear loose. Each time she left she told herself on the way home that she was risking her heart foolishly, that in the end, she would be destroyed. She knew, somehow, that Ouida had known only men, and she told herself that she could never have her and that she had to stop going. But she always found a reason to return.

She stayed one time until the barbershop closed, and the two of them kept on walking down the street toward Ouida's flat. They stopped to buy fruit and when they got to the flat, Ouida made tea and offered Zella one of her chipped cups, and then they sat in the nook she had made next to the kitchen with her cerulean blue chairs, telling about themselves until their hands, both reaching for the teapot, touched.

"Say yes," Zella whispered.

"Yes," Ouida answered. "Yes."

They sat in the last light of the day as it thickened and became gold, entering through the window, coming down to them, meeting them. Lowering itself into their laps, the golden light thick with all that the day had held. Light not merely for seeing, but for touch. For love.

It was almost dawn again. Almost light, but not yet, not yet. Zella rose from the bed and went to the icebox to get a pear. She sliced it into wedges and removed the seeds, and little beads of juice stood out on the cool inner surface of the fruit. She knelt beside the bed and said, quietly, "Close your eyes."

And she turned a wedge of the iced fruit, turned it, to Ouida, and the open cool innerness of the wedge met her lips. Ouida sank her mouth into it, giving in to it, and Zella fed her, after she was spent, but not really, not quite, not yet, as the fire rose in her again, mingling with the ice-hot wetness of the fruit, into an ache that had to be quenched even though it was getting light, pale light, pale and thin and tinged with blue, thin, but not yet, not yet, and it had to be now, even though there would be time for it all again and again and again across the years, it must be now and now and now.

17

During Ouida's summer of discovery, Vesta tried to counteract the bareness of the house by planting flowers out front. She was overwhelmed by the myriad of things she could plant, by the distinct needs each growing thing had and the tending each required. LaRue helped her choose some flowers, but when she said she wanted to plant them herself he stepped back and let her be in charge.

She watered ritually, whether the plants needed it or not. Instead of listening for what the garden told her, whether the ground was already moist from rain or the sun so hot the plants were thirsty, Vesta watered every day. She liked weeding, which made her feel as if she was correcting ills, but she sometimes got carried away and yanked up offshoots and seedlings from her plants. It was frustrating that some things she planted wouldn't bloom until the next year. The problem was, none of it looked like anything to start with and she just didn't believe.

Somewhere around the middle of the summer she began to lose interest and there were fewer and fewer flowers, but as they faded and withered Vesta came up with a solution. She selected the thing that was easiest to grow and filled the little garden with it from front to back. Once she had it under control, she turned her attention to Dessie and to LaRue, who was preparing to leave for college that coming fall.

He was the first one in the family, the first one known to many of the residents of Black Oak, to go to college. They were all proud of him, his family and his neighbors, who had known him since he was a mischievous child. They knew he was a rule-breaker, but they loved him because he was theirs, and wanted him to do well for all of them in that distant, alien world for which he was setting off, even though some of them were a little bit afraid, like Vesta, of what could happen when you reached too high.

Olive had finished school the year before and was working at the family funeral home until she could find a better job. Although she did mostly clerical work and didn't have to deal with corpses or coffins, she yearned for something better. She had been a good student, but had never seen herself as college-bound, and her mother had never encouraged the idea of continuing in school. Instead, Rhea reminded her that men didn't want women who were "too educated," and she should be trying to get a husband who would take care of her so that she didn't have to work.

Olive didn't know what she would do if her future was a vast expanse of mournings and ritual departures. A death-watch. She didn't want her place to be with the gone and the grieving, and she sat in the office ordering and receiving supplies, writing out bills, balancing the accounts of the bereaved as her father dressed their dead in his subterranean workroom. Olive hadn't yet figured out how to do it, but she had decided she would get out.

By mid-summer, Olive was able to tell LaRue about her mother's raging against him. Since she was a child, she had heard the rules spelled out: dark skin could be balanced by social status or money, but blackness, alone, placed a man beyond consideration. Now she disclosed, for the first time, how her mother had made her wear a clothespin on her nose at night and told her "hold your mouth in" whenever she laughed too freely and showed the fullness of her lips. How she had been encouraged to choose a man who would "lighten her children up" and warned never to drink black coffee when she was pregnant, unless she wanted her babies to come out dark. And how she had always been told to "act like a lady," never to emerge from the house without makeup and perfume, to hide her long and bony legs and "do the best with what she had."

He listened quietly, and then took her hand and told her that he loved her. He said he adored her legs, that they had been what drew him to her. "You enticed me, Miss Anansi," he said, invoking the spider about whom he had heard tales all his life, "with those miles of toast-colored legs . . . when I saw them I knew I was done for . . . and your nose is the best nose I've ever seen, it's just absolutely yours . . . and really, 'Live, I like everything about you . . . and I love the way you smell," he said, brushing her neck with his lips. He never had been able to bear the smell of perfume, and had asked her from the beginning not to wear the flowery, store-bought smells. Burying his face in her neck, he told her once again, "I like you plain, as you are. I like the smell of you."

LaRue had sensed what was going on with Rhea Winters, without being told, and after talking to Olive he went home and sat on the stoop, thinking of Ruby. He imagined her response, and was sure she would come and sit down next to him and say one simple thing. She would look him dead in the face and say, "Wishbone, that woman is the little end of nothing. You and Olive better go on about your business, now, and live your lives." And then they would laugh and look at the stars in silence.

It was then, as he thought of Ruby, that he decided to ask Olive to come with him when he left for school.

While LaRue was preparing to leave for school and take Olive with him, Ouida and Zella were coming to know each other.

"Bulldagger is such a . . . a brutal kind of word, Z," Ouida said, turning to Zella in the night. She had first heard it from the mouth of one of the barbers at the shop and it had been used to describe Zella.

"Brutal words for brutal people," Zella responded, with a caustic edge that made Ouida draw in her breath.

Ouida had noticed people's eyes on them. As she stood buying fruit and vegetables one weekend, she had felt two women watching her and had tried to ignore the building sense of fear and anger within. Finally, she had finished with her selections and lifted her head proudly, as Ruby had taught her, to meet their curious eyes. "Good morning, ladies," she had said with a smile as she left.

It had shaken her a little, what she had seen in those eyes that watched her like she was a creature, deformed. There was a flash of violence she had detected, and suddenly, she saw that she was a member of another hated group. Sometimes she passed a mirror and stopped to look at herself for traces of some kind of differentness, traces of the things other people seemed to see, and half expected her features to look warped, explaining the reason for the rage whose depth stunned her.

She looked at familiar parts of herself, her hands, her mouth, as if they deserved blame for their acts. One side of her wanted to say to strangers, "No. It isn't like that!" and explain the beauty of what she and Zella had, and the other side wanted to deny it altogether, to run from the part of herself she was opening up.

Turning inward, they sought solace in the quiet country of their private love.

Because Ouida never discussed her personal life with her father, it was easy not to talk about what was happening with him. She knew that he preferred to think of her as virginal, even though she had been married, that this was something he would much rather not know. When she confided in Vesta that she and Zella were together, Vesta stared at her, fidgeting and scratching, and shook her head.

It made Vesta dizzy, just the idea of such a blind and unknown path. For weeks she tried to reason with Ouida, pointing out all the risks, and when her warnings went unheeded, she refused to discuss it at all, gradually ceasing to resist Ouida's choice, but refusing to discuss it again. As if to make up for the recklessness she saw around her, Vesta adopted an extra vigilance in her own life. She started cooking double, and making go-plates for Ouida to take to her flat. She planned and replanned what she did. She made lists. She ironed extra hard.

Ouida would never tell Eula about Zella unless she had to, even though she realized that she had probably knew it from hearing others talk. But she would catch the woman who had been another mother to her for almost as long as she could remember evading her glance sometimes as she did dishes or sat at the table with her sharing a meal, as if they were separated by an interplanetary breach. In those moments Ouida talked to Eula until she met her eyes.

Ouida thought LaRue would understand, and she figured she would tell him at some point. She longed for the chance to speak to him sometimes, because she didn't think she would even have to explain it. At least she wouldn't have to justify her love. He would know Zella was good, just as he had known the inverse about Junior Biggs.

While she tried to come to terms with the secret of her love for Zella, she also struggled with telling Zella about her other night visitors. She wanted to tell her about Johnston Franklin and Flood, but she didn't know how, and Zella was fighting fears of her own that she would have to find a way to face.

One evening in the post-dinner quiet, the heat pressed down on them like a ceiling. It was too hot to eat, too hot to touch, too hot to talk. Zella stood up and said, "That's it." She went to the bathroom and started running a bathtub of cool water. "Come on, Ouida, I've got a plan."

They lowered themselves into the water, sighing with relief, one at each end of the tub. Zella had brought fruit and books and they propped their heads up at the ends with pillows. There they lay until dusk brought relief from the heat or their skin began to wrinkle up. They looked at each other periodically and burst out laughing.

One night that same summer, as LaRue and Olive sat outside the Winters house, LaRue said, "Olive . . . if you could be any kind of animal in the world, what kind of animal do you think you'd choose to be?"

"What kind of *animal?* I don't know, LaRue, I never gave it any thought."

"Well, think about it now. What animal would you be?"

"My favorite animal . . ." she started, but LaRue interrupted her. "Not your favorite, not the one you would like to look at or be around, that one we'll discuss next. The one you see yourself as, if you could be any one at all?"

She thought for a while and then said, "I think I'd be a bird, so I could sing and fly. There must be nothing that compares to flying, don't you think?"

"Yeah," he said. "Flying must be something, but you know, I'd be a serpent if I had my choice."

"A serpent . . . you mean a *snake?* All slimy and creepy, and eating mice whole. I hate snakes, LaRue, so I'm glad that decision's not yours to make."

"Well, just listen, girl, and I'll tell you why. The snake has been around since the beginning of time. It is what you call grounded, living as it does in absolute intimacy with the earth, while you and I must rely on our feet . . . which in my case, however, is no minor thing, big as my understandings are . . ." Olive kissed him playfully, and he continued. "The snake has learned, over the generations, to change color, and has developed warnings like the rattle . . . and the venom it has to protect itself. The snake is a survivor.

"But most important of all," he went on, "when it gets finished with the skin it's wearing, it sheds it, crawling on out of the past and into the future. It is life and it is death, Olive, and that's the serpent's gift. The gift of renewal."

Olive looked at him, her eyes wide, receiving what he had to say.

"Well, you may fear her, 'Live, but you damn well respect her. The snake is my girl."

"Your girl. LaRue, what are you talking about?"

"Well, let me tell you the story about the strength of Miss Snake, and I believe that will illustrate my point. Because of all the powers I've mentioned, plus her amazing and inventive colors and patterns," he said, explaining how Miss Snake can move from midnight blue diamonds into magenta batik and telling about some of the skins she had worn, "the other animals of the forest envied her to no end. They didn't quite understand her, and they tried to turn their envy and their terror at her beauty into scorn.

"Periodically, they tried to get together and keep her down, and they developed all kinds of theories about why she was less apt at this or that. Some despised her because she lived on the ground, and hadn't elevated herself, like other species had, and Lion said she was 'primitive,' having remained as she had been since before time. And you see, Miss Snake was beautiful and different, in a disconcerting way. So one day, there was a get-together of the other animals, a kind of inter-animal conference, if you will. And the topic for discussion was how to dominate Miss Snake.

"After a long, very civilized formal-type discussion, Lion spoke up. He roared, as he felt was fitting for the king of the jungle, which he considered himself to be. He showed his teeth before beginning a long pompous speech. 'It is just below the cranial area, where we know the snake is weak . . . for of course, anything associated with the cranial is inferior in . . .'

"'Oh Lord,' said Spider, from his web in the corner, 'get on with it, will you, or we'll be here all day!' Lion sneered at Spider, but then the others echoed Spider's cry. Lion looked around in anger and smirked. 'It just so happens that I am acquainted with the weakness of the snake: if it is grabbed just behind the head, it can't bite, and this is the way to dominate and conquer this beast.'

"Well, after some further discussion, they agreed on an elaborate plan to grab Miss Snake behind the head. Fox would get her attention, so that Goat would have time to create a whole mess of commotion and signal Lion to jump down from a tree and clamp his big old lion teeth right behind her head. They all clarified their roles, and at the agreed time went to the appointed place to wait for Miss Snake to amble by.

"The next day, Miss Snake set out for her morning constitutional, and they were all waiting. She wore her finest rattle, and skin of checkered orange and red. She had no idea that they were waiting for her, but Miss Snake was always prepared. They underestimated her, because she was as aware as they were of where her vulnerability lay. When she got to the appointed place, the other animals started to act their roles, and she heard all manner of carrying on.

"As things got louder and more confusing, Miss Snake realized that she was being ambushed. She looked up and saw Lion perched above her in the branches of a tree, and she thought that if she coiled around herself and moved in a circle, they wouldn't be able to find her head. Miss Snake flew into a circle, so quickly she surprised herself . . . she was looking, that day, like a ring of fire . . . it was something to see!

"Her attackers leaped back, in shock, afraid and confused, and some, like Deer and Rabbit, took off in a flash, thinking there was a forest fire taking shape. Miss Snake was an unbroken circle, and Lion didn't have the vaguest idea how to find her head. And if he couldn't find her beginning or her end, he couldn't catch her, could he, Olive?" He waited for her response. "Could he?" he said as he laughed. "I swear on high, this tale is true . . . if not for me, for sure for you."

He leaped off the stairs, seeming to fly. "Next time we'll discuss favorite animals, but for now, see you soon, big baboon . . ."

And Olive, rising to her feet, said, "After while, crocodile . . ."

And LaRue, in front of the next house, backing slowly away, responded, "That's the word, little bird . . ."

Olive, at the door, said "Later, like an alligator . . ."

LaRue, halfway down the block, his repertoire exhausted, making one up, shouted, "Uh . . . take it easy, light and greasy . . ."

Olive shook her head and laughed as she watched him reach the end of the block. "An unbroken circle," she whispered to herself as she turned to go inside. "Now how about that?"

On the night that they left for the Alabama college town a few weeks before the start of school, LaRue scrawled out a note for Rhea Winters and left it above the immaculately polished buffet that held her silver tea service. It said, "We'll be back between night and day."

LaRue wrote it and stuck it in her beveled crystal mirror with the gilt frame, knowing that the day is always becoming night, the night becoming day, that he had left her waiting for a fixed point in time that would never arrive.

When they got to Alabama LaRue found a couple who took them in for a little bit of rent. "Friends of Tennessee Jones," he said. And it was in that borrowed room that they began their life together. If he stopped and thought about it, LaRue was afraid sometimes that he loved Olive too much. He fought against pulling away from her when he felt that way, but he was afraid, afraid sometimes that he would lose his way.

They made love those Alabama afternoons in a bed with one leg shorter than the others, under sun-washed deep blue medicine bottles that were lined up on the windowsill. Tentatively, awkwardly, they found the way into each other and learned their bodies over the course of that first August. But even in their fumbling, even before there was grace, there was recognition.

He opened to her and she to him, and they found themselves meeting in the sweet, throbbing center of a prayer.

The bed rocked and they laughed.

The light struck cobalt and it made them want to cry.

LaRue longed to do anything, everything for her, and he was amazed by all that he felt. He touched Olive. Her hands, her mouth were on his skin, and he couldn't believe, couldn't believe the beauty of the unencumbered, spontaneous her, couldn't believe the things he could read in her eyes. He was astounded by what was received, what was received as he gave.

They built their love up slowly, so slowly, that it seemed to have been happening forever, and in the instant it took her to get her breath. Olive reached for anything to ground herself and her fingers found the wooden spools at the head of the bed. Slipping her hand through the rungs she gripped the turned wood, gently, firmly, mooring herself, and then she went into it, to where he was taking her, further in. To where he was taking her to meet herself.

To the threshold they went and stayed, just short of the crossing, for what seemed like time beyond time, and there they balanced, arriving forever, and became their trembling.

He wanted to give in to her and to his own joy and suffering, to it all, for in the middle of his pleasure there was his fear, too, at how they burned, how they burned. At the way she looked into him, beyond his face, her eyes showing love that was tender and fierce, and there were instants when he had to fight a pulling back, when he almost thought he couldn't, couldn't bear to be known that way.

But Olive looked in his eyes, into the wedge of light, in that moment, that sweet and terrible moment of recognition, and LaRue felt her scorched into him, and it was then that he let her take him, in the cobalt blue. It was then that he let her take him. It was then.

As he gave himself over to her, LaRue pulled away everything that she could hide behind, and Olive surrendered to all that it was and all that it could be.

"Say my name," she whispered, and he did. He said it, over and over, chanted it in the wash of deep blue light.

They were barely moving, and in total flux. She was her own, completely, and she was his. It was too much to bear, and it would never be enough.

18

Four months after they left, LaRue and Olive were on their way back to Black Oak for Christmas break. Vesta and Eula had been cleaning and making special foods the whole week before they were scheduled to arrive and were waiting for Polaris to bring them from the station. Vesta stood at the window, wiping smudges from the glass, as she watched for a sign of the car.

For the first time since Ruby's death, Polaris had bought a Christmas tree, which stood in the corner of the living room, waiting to be trimmed. Dessie touched the long Scotch pine needles and inhaled the dark, fresh smell of the tree, while Vesta kept an eye on her from the window post and mumbled about Polaris being late.

During the train trip home, LaRue and Olive had talked about the changes in their lives that made it seem as if they had been gone a lot longer than four months. When they had first arrived in Alabama Olive had looked for a job, but all she could find was evening work cleaning offices at the college. She soon started sitting in on classes with LaRue and a few weeks later wandered into a biology lecture and found herself fascinated with the slides of plants and cells projected on a screen at the front of the room. She went to all the classes she could manage before her afternoons at work started, but she was reluctant to enroll. She said she just wanted to find out all about the plants and animals and draw them in her notebook, without the pressure of writing papers and taking exams.

She finally found permanent work as a switchboard operator and LaRue juggled various enterprises. He started a service picking up people's clothes for laundering and ironing, waited tables at a local men's club, and shelved books at the college library.

Olive tested him on his course material before his exams and he rubbed her back when she got home. She read the books he was assigned for his courses and they talked them over. They cooked together, making up recipes that called for whatever it was they had on hand, and on Sundays they took walks in the country and made love with the sun beating down on them, deep in the grass. He put scarves over the lampshades and they danced around their room.

Although they were busy and barely making ends meet, they both felt as if the world had suddenly been widened, within and without. LaRue was fleshing out his understanding of the South and learning more about his cultural history, but although they had found a new realm of experience in their college town, they still felt like misfits sometimes. Married and working, they weren't quite a part of the social scene at the bastion of the colored elite. Since not fitting in wasn't new to either of them, they turned to each other, and to books.

LaRue decided that he wanted to be a writer. As he read more and more he was convinced that it was his job to collect, tell, and invent his people's stories. When he wrote and told her this, Vesta could hardly believe he had chosen nothing practical to study, and was acquiring no concrete skills. Throughout his college years she would ask him, "Don't they have an agricultural program, where you could learn about . . . I don't know . . . about planting and farming, or couldn't you learn how to run a small business? Or how to build things, even, how to build roads or houses. Something, LaRue, that you could *use*." She either wanted him to be skilled, or to choose a profession, but as far as she was concerned, he had no real goal in mind.

Olive and LaRue talked the whole trip home about what the last four months had been for them and once they got to the house, Vesta fed them and plied them for the details about school and life in Alabama. LaRue had waited until they got there to tell everyone they had been married by the Justice of the Peace after getting to Alabama. "Oh no!" Vesta cried at the missed opportunity for a wedding, and LaRue stared at her, incredulous that Ouida's experience hadn't demystified wedding ceremonies for her. She apologized, insisting that she was happy for them, but "just surprised," and then turned her attention to assessing Olive as a wife.

She could tell right away that Olive was warm and that she loved LaRue. Moving toward him unconsciously, her fingers brushed his arm or smoothed his eyebrows with such gentle caring that it made Vesta ache to be touched. But they cut up so much, Vesta observed, and got swept up in such silliness, arguing about what LeFoy and Footney would say or making up names for each other until they were falling off the couch in laughter. That night, as Vesta put Dessie to bed, she thought that Olive might not be what she had hoped for in a wife for LaRue. What he needed, she thought, was a no-nonsense woman who would balance out his weaknesses, and as nice and loving as Olive appeared to be, she seemed just as flighty as LaRue.

The next morning Ouida came over to help put up the tree and have their traditional Christmas Eve celebration. Radiant and edgy at the same time, it seemed to everyone that she was holding something back. Although she had been afraid to bring Zella, she couldn't stop thinking about what she was doing and feeling. As she wrapped presents and stirred eggnog she imagined how Zella's hands were occupied and she felt her in flashes, wondering whether she was filled with thoughts of her, as well.

She tried to picture what would have happened if, like LaRue, she had brought her new love home to meet her family. Only Vesta had an inkling of what was going on, as she had told her that night about meeting her "different" girl and confided, later, about their love. Ouida was sure Vesta had heard the gossip and tried not to think about it, but as she reached to take Dessie from Vesta she saw her pull away, slightly, as if she wasn't sure who she was, and it pierced her in a white-hot shaft, the judgment contained in a split-second look.

Later she sat on the floor with LaRue and Olive and made ornaments out of pine cones and shells with Dessie, aware of Vesta's watchful eye. They folded and cut paper snowflakes and strung cranberries and popcorn with her, despite Vesta's fear that she would stick herself, or put pine needles or something more harmful in her mouth. Vesta kept coming to the doorway of the front room, her stirring spoon in hand, to make sure that all was well. LaRue had them all laughing at his imitation of a nutcracker, and then everyone stopped and listened to him and Ouida trade stories about LeFoy and Footney's holiday celebration, and the truth about why mistletoe inspires folks to kiss.

While they were hanging their ornaments on the tree Ouida caught LaRue looking at her. She hadn't realized she was humming and swaying back and forth as she found just the right place for the little stuffed moon she had made years and years before. The light was shining through his eye as he watched her. "You're glowing," he said, smiling now, and she laughed, looking directly into his gaze, answering, "Yes. Yes, I am." She turned to get another ornament, a yellow maple leaf she had once helped him sew from scraps of felt and velvet they had found in Ruby's remnant box.

They told the history of each thing they hung on the tree as it was lifted from the ornament box, and then LaRue held Dessie up in his arms while she added the things they had made that day. They asked Olive how her family had celebrated Christmas, and noticed that she had blinked tears away and answered, "Nothing . . . there was nothing special really," as she imagined the elaborate decorations, the display of china and silver, and the party her mother must now be holding for the prominent citizens of Black Oak.

Neither Eula, nor Polaris, nor Vesta was sure what to make of this gangly girl who was clearly LaRue's family now. They thought they had her figured, and then she did something to throw them off. On the one hand, she looked proper and ladylike, but underneath that there was something else. She helped cook and set the table and wash dishes, and her speech and demeanor were polite and sweet. They were sure she was quiet, and suddenly she got going on something she had read and talked a blue streak in her gravelly voice.

Olive tried to keep the deep way she felt everything reigned in, as Rhea had taught her, but since she had gotten together with LaRue she had more and more trouble maintaining that tack. If something struck her as funny, she laughed her deep husky laugh right out loud, and if she was troubled it was all over her face. She loved to dance and her body responded to the music that played on the radio, uncensored, in a way that disturbed Vesta. Olive tried to hold in her feelings for LaRue, and then found herself raising a sprig of mistletoe and kissing him right on the mouth, as Vesta and Eula looked at each other in a moment of shock before they looked down. Although there was a kinship with Ouida, the others didn't know what to expect from Olive. The one thing that was clear about her was her love for LaRue.

They all went to bed that Christmas Eve exhausted from catching up on the last four months. Everyone was tipsy from the eggnog, which LaRue had spiked with bourbon. Eula and Vesta had pretended they didn't realize, and went back for cup after cup, and then Ouida and Olive and LaRue stayed up talking and telling lies, laughing into the night. Everyone slept soundly and Vesta was happy that her loved ones were all accounted for, again under one roof.

The next morning Dessie heard LaRue downstairs and went running. "Rue," she called out to him from the top of the stairs, and he answered, "December? Is that my favorite girl?" and before Vesta could stop and call her she stepped forward, missing the top stair, and fell four or five steps. She hit her head before he caught her, halfway down the stairs, and held her in his arms. Vesta had seen it from the hallway, had seen Dessie's tiny feet and the bottom of her skirt, had seen her falling and falling and falling down what seemed to her like an endless flight of stairs and had reached out to steady herself against the door frame and then sat down on the floor.

She knew that the worst had happened and she sat in the doorway trembling and afraid to look up. She heard nothing but silence and looked up to see, not the ceiling, but an expanse of blue sky. And then LaRue was holding her, trying to quiet her shaking. She looked at him without really focusing on him, and then he put his arms around her and she wept. "She's all right," he whispered as he rocked her. "Sister, she's all right." Olive brought Dessie up the stairs so that Vesta could see that she was okay and she drew her close, unable to let go. Olive and LaRue were crouched on the floor with them at the top of the stairs and finally, when Dessie began to cry, they had to pull Vesta away.

Vesta seemed disoriented for the rest of the day. Through the opening of gifts she looked shaken and then she threw herself into cooking the Christmas dinner and enacting the ritual turkey carving and passing of the foods they had each year. The lighting of candles and the grace. She spoke little during the meal and barely cracked a smile at LaRue's recollection of Miss Snake's latest adventures.

When Ouida returned to her flat after Christmas, she called Zella immediately. She couldn't believe how she had missed her over only a few days, and they had their own holiday celebration that night, exchanging tokens offered in keeping with their agreement that they had to have been found or made. Zella gave Ouida a sachet she had made from dried flowers and a poem, and Ouida gave Zella a bookmark she had woven from ribbons and thread.

Zella was overcome, every now and then, with a fear of her own. It came in the midst of some routine thing, as she combed her hair or poured hot water over tea. And it rose, pounding in her, the terror that it would all go away from her, suddenly, because of an ugly comment, or because she was just something Ouida was trying out that she would finish with someday. And at those times she withdrew until she felt strong enough to come out of her solitary world.

Having known since puberty that she wasn't really interested in men, Zella had spent tortuous girlhood years playing the expected role anyway. She had gone on dates and even been engaged. Throughout, she had had her secret liaisons with women, and had finally come not just to accept herself, but to celebrate who she was, years before she met Ouida. But she had mastered the practice of keeping a distance from people, especially fellow students and workers.

Zella had moments of panic at the reckless way she had let Ouida, who had known no woman before her, right into her heart. She went fishing to try to sort out her feelings and she went to see the Saras, two women who had shared a house since girlhood in the nearby town where Zella had grown up. Both with the same name, both unmarried, they had lived together for so long, in the same house, that they had become an institution. People speculated about their relationship early on, but they were so much a part of things, and betrayed no shame or embarrassment, that their living arrangement ceased to be an issue. Doubtless some chose to think they were spinsters, spurned long ago by some nameless men, but deep down inside everyone knew this wasn't true. Newcomers to the neighborhood would ask across the fence, "Well, what about those two women? Are they sisters, or what?" And the people who knew them would answer, "Oh, that's just the Saras. They're family, that's all."

Although her mother had refused to discuss whether the Saras were lovers or friends, thinking the mere suggestion of the issue obscene, most folks in the neighborhood said that if the two women had lived together for twenty-five years, they didn't know what the hell the difference was.

Zella had done cleaning chores and run errands for them since she was a child, and they had been like godparents ever since she realized it was women she loved. She went back home to see them, seeking advice, and told them about the new woman who was changing her life. They mostly listened, and asked her to bring Ouida to meet them.

Ouida, meanwhile, was dealing with her own fear. She still hadn't been able to tell Zella about Johnston Franklin and Flood, whom she had seen recently. She felt so at ease with Zella that she tried to bring up the thing she was hiding, but she heard a kind of alarm in Zella's voice and decided to forgo it. She didn't figure it really mattered now and anyway, it was her private past, even if there had been some overlap. It was nothing she was proud of, nothing that was really for sharing, and she decided to keep it to herself.

These hidden things would soon be told, though, and it would be harder than she thought. Once revealed, they would be cloaked again, becoming parts of a layered secret that would change everything, scarring memory and flesh.

They would be told, if only to Zella, these pieces of Ouida's past that were embedded in her turning point of losing and getting, to whose memory she would forever wake.

19

Her flesh spoke. Testifying with knotted scars along the hips and knees, angry healing flesh that had faded over time and was joined by the wrinkles and folds of age.

Without, the scars had grown familiar and indistinct. Within, there was the perfect imprint of her desperate choice.

It stayed hidden, mostly, in waking, but survived in that storage space within that holds impressions of our singular griefs: the stamp of a parent's death, the shape of first love, the contours of unspeakable loss.

Sanding the edges of the past in order to move on, Ouida had secreted the sharp memories, mostly, in her private archives, but unannounced, they surfaced, coming to her again and again in her dreams.

There was the gritty scrape of metal against flesh. The smell of blood, and the cold hard distance in his eyes.

There was the cracked plaster of the ceiling where she had focused her pain.

And there was the single grimy lightbulb, swinging from a twisted cord.

Recorded, all, with the memory of the circle that Zella's arms made around her in the backseat of their borrowed car. The depth and width and curve of it visited and woke her in the late afternoon, always in the same way, taking shape in her stomach and then spreading, as if pouring itself into a waiting mold.

After a morning at her sewing machine, joining and ripping out seams and resewing them until they were perfect, she got up to fix her lunch, grasping the edge of the table, and lifted herself with fingers numb and stiff from work, balancing with one hand while she reached for her crutches and tucked them under her arms. She flexed her fingers as she leaned against the kitchen sink, and looked out of the window through African violet leaves. Once she had made her lunch and eaten, she lay down for her afternoon rest, pulling Ruby's unfinished quilt over her legs.

She drifted into sleep and woke, gasping, drawing in her breath and with it the memory, taking in the sharpness, that it be borne. She woke to it, to her panic and her shame, to the memory that lived. To the losing and the getting. To the memory that was the shape of everything she would never be, and everything she was.

When her period had been late for a week, Ouida told herself it would come, that she had never really been regular. When a month had passed, she shifted between panic and denial, trapped and without the inkling of a route toward help. When she saw her naked profile in the mirror one morning, she could no longer hide.

Stepping into her panties, she caught a glimpse of herself, and let them drop as she straightened up. She looked from mirror to flesh, and touched slowly, with fingertips first, and then with her whole hand. She returned to her image in the mirror and then backed up and sat down on the edge of the bed.

She sat there for an hour, stunned by the reality that was, somehow, hers. She was hit by a wave of disbelief, even three years after her death, that Ruby was not there, and as she thought of what to do about it, she knew that she needed Zella's help. She waited until they lay in bed that night, their legs entwined, to ask. It was then that she spoke of her other night visitor.

"Zella, you know that luggage with my monogram, that I said my uncle sent me? And the organdy hankies in my top drawer?"

"Un hunh," Zella responded, half asleep with her face in Ouida's neck.

"Zella, listen. I have something to say," she declared with quiet urgency as she nudged her arm.

Zella raised up on her elbow and looked Ouida in the eye, a pinpoint of dread dilating in her stomach.

"Well, they didn't . . . they didn't." She looked away, and it seemed that she actually aged in the time it took for her to turn back to Zella's face. "I didn't get them from my uncle at all."

Zella stared at her, unwilling to help her finish what she had to say. She tightened her jaw and braced herself against the coming blow, as Ouida finished. "The white man brought them. The one from Louisville."

Zella was too stunned to absorb anything besides Ouida's last syllable, resounding over and over again in her head, "ville . . . Ville. . . . *ville*." And then she felt the tip of rage as Ouida finished.

"Zella, it's been two months since my last period. I need your help."

Zella looked at her, mutely, as the confession came out in a rush, and rose from the bed. And as the numbness faded, the full range of her feelings passed through her. She turned away from Ouida, who sank into her pillows silently. Zella paced the kitchen floor and then sat, facing the window. Hours later, she came to bed.

She stayed, as she knew she would, and reached to turn off the light. They faced opposite directions, their backs not touching. During the night, Zella turned to look at Ouida's sleeping face, emptied of stress but pale and tired, and wondered how she had let herself love so, against the one rule she knew about never getting close to women who love men. She studied the face that she had trusted with an anger that had chilled into something distant and analytical, searching for hints of dishonesty in what now appeared to her to be a mask.

How could the person beside her be so foreign, and yet so known? How did it happen that way? It all seemed a message to Zella of what she could not have. She turned to look at her over and over and asked how Ouida could do this to her. And then, somehow, in an instant, as she studied the face that seemed altogether emptied, she felt that what was happening was happening to them, and accepted the love she felt.

When Ouida woke the next morning, Zella was sitting at the table fully dressed, drinking tea. She had stayed. When Ouida saw her there she felt a surge of panic, but as she came into the kitchen, she saw a cup of tea waiting for her. She sat down, and they looked at each other silently. Zella spoke, "Ouida. What do you want to do?"

Ouida shook her head and said, "Before we talk about it, I have one more thing to tell you. So that it will be clean." She looked straight into Zella's eyes and said, "There was another. There was the barber, Flood."

Zella looked at her, from what seemed like far away, knowing somehow, through her jealousy, that whatever else Ouida had been doing was about something other than love. And so she nodded, and pointed to the cup of tea. As Ouida sat down to drink, Zella set out the choices: the one, crazy, that she felt her way toward in darkness, and the other, reckless, the terror of which was known.

Zella told her later how she had counted up three windows and stood staring for ten minutes. She left, got a block away, and then came back. She stood at the curb looking up, pulling her coat close and wondering how she could climb the stairs, and how she could not.

She had gone first to her aunt Mandy, who ran a boardinghouse for young women. She knew not to say the word abortion, and formed her question carefully.

"Where can a girl who's in trouble get help?"

Her aunt smiled slightly, relieved that the rumors she had heard about Zella were either untrue, or had only represented a phase. There was an awkward pause, and then Zella spoke.

"Not *me*, Aunt Mandy. I'm asking for a friend."

Mandy's smile faded, and she lowered her eyes, ashamed, and told her how to find out what to do without really asking.

Zella had memorized the address, and had gone there after work. She looked up at the window and finally opened the door, moving toward the third floor with decisive steps. She stood facing the grimy yellow door while she got her instructions in order, and knocked. The door opened as far as its chain would allow to reveal the face of a small black woman with piercing eyes.

"I'm here about the goods. About getting them unloaded. WB sent me."

The woman's eyes moved down from Zella's collar to her feet, and then back up again, taking in her tailored clothes and polished shoes. She stopped at her face and spent a good bit of time there, and when the anguish in the eyes told her that it was love that had brought her there, love and desperation, she decided that it was not a trap.

"The goods are your'n?" she asked, roughly.

"No. My friend's."

The door closed for a moment, while she removed the chain, and then she grabbed Zella's arm and pulled her across the threshold. "Sit down while I tell you what to do."

Zella dwarfed the slim wooden chair and looked around the room. Bits of old rugs were pieced together to cover the floor. The place smelled close and the windows and shades were drawn. The strange, rough woman stood in front of her and shook her finger in her face.

"You go, after dark, tomorrow, at seven at night, to where the Old Stone Road and the street without no name meet, and you make you a right turn. Go to the big elm tree at the next fork in the road, and there will be a black car waitin' for you. Now you tell the man in the car that you come 'bout the cargo, and give him the money in your envelope. He'll take you to the place."

She finished with the most important part. "If you ain't got the money, don't come."

Zella rose and left the room, her eyes meeting the stranger's long enough for her to see something else beneath the harshness of her way. The small gnarled woman touched her arm before she closed the door, and then, alone again, she muttered to herself, "Lord watch over you, child."

Zella descended the stairwell, the grim green walls marked with fingerprints along the banister, and wallpaper that stood away from the walls at the corners and baseboards. She stopped at the foot of the stairs and touched the wall as she tried to make out the pattern. Faded almost to smudges were traces of spring bouquets.

She went next to withdraw the money from the bank and took the streetcar to the Marquis, where she waited until Ouida finished doing a manicure and pulled her aside. As she explained the plan, Zella couldn't help looking at Ouida's stomach, bound tight with a laced corset. She gently tucked a lock of Ouida's hair back in its chignon and left. The next step was to borrow a car.

They met that evening at Zella's flat, and said nothing of the next day. Zella ironed and folded a stack of clothes and tried not to think of the coming day. She tried to bury her anger in order to give Ouida strength. She had never really thought, when she allowed herself to consider it, that she, alone, could have Ouida; she had always been afraid to ask her to define her feelings, afraid of things against which she had no power, things so different from her. She had felt, somewhere inside, that she couldn't have her because Ouida was connected to something else, and at the same time she knew that she did, she did have her, and that whatever else there was that Ouida belonged to, the thing that bound the two of them was different, and was strong.

At work the next day Ouida's hands trembled so much that she could barely finish her first manicure. She kept having to excuse herself and go to the tiny makeshift space with a toilet and sink that they made for her in the men's barbershop. She sat on the edge of the utility sink and tried to get calm, but she felt as if she had to keep a careful distance from the center of herself. She felt as if her life had gotten mixed up with someone else's.

She mumbled to herself and returned to her table. Alton kept coming over to ask her if she was all right.

The horror stories she had heard came back to her in snatches as she waited for a customer or held a strange, white, uncalloused hand. She thought of the stories she had heard of butcherings in dirty rooms and bleeding from careless hands, and she imagined the profound shame her mother would feel. And she returned to the thing becoming inside of her, not knowing how to think of it, but knowing that it couldn't be.

She remembered the day Vesta's family had moved downstairs, Eula sewing by candlelight when the light bill couldn't be paid, eggs for dinner and run-down shoes. Ouida had just begun to shape her life, and she couldn't give that up. For a man who wasn't willing and whom she didn't want? For all kinds of isn'ts and might-be's. Zella had offered to raise it as her own, had said that they could do it together, but she couldn't even see her way clear to think about that.

She knew that she would have to risk her life to save it. Her hand strayed to rest on the almost concealed roundness of her stomach, and she tried to put aside her fear.

Zella picked her up at five o'clock, and they drove through an empty landscape caught between winter and spring, bleached of color. Pools of dark watery ice swallowed weather-worn bits of grass, while other patches were still dry from freezing.

Ouida sat clutching her pocketbook, looking straight ahead, until they came to the fork in the road, and she lowered her head. It was dark now, and they got out and went to the window of the other car, and Zella stepped forward and repeated the code words she had been told to say. The man took the envelope that Zella held out, looked inside, and opened the back door from the inside. They climbed in, and Zella took Ouida's hand.

They rode in the dark for forty-five minutes, going in circles, Zella thought, and pulled up next to a shack surrounded by pools of mud and gravel. Ouida would never lose the sound of the tires coming to rest on the rocky side of the road.

As they were led inside, a man asked, "Which one?" Zella and Ouida looked at each other and Ouida stepped forward. He pointed to a door and Zella started to follow, but the driver stepped in front of her and said, harshly, "Un unh, lady. You can't go in." As Ouida walked down a filthy hallway, she heard a scream, and stopped for a moment to look back at the door behind which Zella stood, clutching her handbag, before she moved on.

As she came to the end of the hallway, Ouida looked around for something that reminded her of a doctor's office, and then she realized that this was where she had been headed all along. The man who had met her at the door told her to undress, and handed her a sheet. "Put that over your bottom half," he said, making no move to leave. She stood and stared at him until he left the room, and when he came back, she was standing in front of the table wrapped in the sheet, holding her clothes in front of her. He took the clothes from her and motioned for her to get on the table. He took her feet and put them into loops of rope that hung from the ceiling. And he never washed his hands.

As he parted her and felt inside with his finger, she sucked in her breath and tried to go somewhere else. Then there was cold metal pushing in, and a pain that she would never be able to describe, as he began scraping with the curette. The entire time that he was with her, he chewed on a cigar.

And she focused on the grimy lightbulb that swayed above her, wrapping herself in her cries.

She could hear him messing with a can or bucket, and the sound of metal against metal as he put his instruments in an enameled basin. He took her feet out of the loops of rope and stood over her for a moment and said, matter-of-factly, "Some bleeding is normal." He shook his head then, and said as he went through the door. "It's over. You can get up now."

She struggled to get up, as Zella came through the door to help her dress. They had left a cloth and some pins on the table, which Zella helped her pin to her underclothes and pull on.

The whole way back to their car, Ouida rested her head on Zella's shoulder and concentrated on getting home. No words were spoken as they got out of the man's car and into their own.

She had soaked through the pieces of cloth they gave her before they had gone fifteen miles, but Ouida told Zella not to worry. "He said there would be blood." But Ouida remembered a night of blood-soaked hands, of blood on the moon, and reeled with fear. Zella stopped the car twice to change the cloths and tried to stay calm.

Ten miles later, Ouida began to whisper, "It's not right, Zella, it's not right," and Zella looked back over the seat and felt a rising panic. She pulled the car over and grabbed at the newspapers on the floor of the backseat, arranging them under and around Ouida to soak up the fevered blood, chanting one of Tennyson's verses they had both been made to memorize in high school.

"'It little profits that an idle king . . .' Say it with me, Ouida, come on now . . . 'By this still hearth, among these barren crags . . .'" Zella recited.

Ouida kept up for the first few lines, as Zella tried to start the car over and over, missing her timing with the clutch.

"'I cannot rest from travel, I will drink . . .'"

Ouida whispered, anchoring herself with the long-remembered words. But she heard rushing water in the distance somewhere and, looking for the source, she raised herself up and then slipped further and further down as her head fell back to the seat.

"'. . . alone, on shore, and when . . .'" The water rushing, she knew she heard it, and she turned around, searching in sunken darkness around her, and heard the faint whisper of Zella's voice.

"'. . . have suffered greatly, both with those who loved me and . . .'"

She heard the water, and she could hear Zella. And then she let go.

Zella managed to get the car started, and raced back to the city, going over and over their options. She knew that they could not go back to the shiny black car where the road divided, and that even if they could make it back there, they would never be able to find the shack again. She picked up the verse again, reciting now for herself. "'. . . To rust unburnished, not to shine in use . . .'"

Ouida found herself turning round and round in search of the water that she heard, and then saw the mouth of a tunnel, which she entered, alone, no longer linked to Zella's voice.

She followed the water sounds through the dark tunnel, feeling her way along the sides of the passage with her hands, and came to a little cave, carved from the side, a hole almost, half underground but with an opening above, which seemed to blossom into itself, jeweled green and soft with the moistness of moss and unruly grass, water spilling down over the edges of rocks, once jagged, and now eroded smooth. The earth, wet and heavy, held the blooming place like a secret, and at its opening, Ouida stood.

Zella had almost reached the edge of town, speeding as she continued reciting. "'. . . as though to breathe were life . . .'"

Ouida yearned to sink her fingers into the clay, to touch the tangled roots it hid, to feel it against her and the water raining, beating on her skin.

She stood at the mouth, stunned by its dark and wild beauty. By its secret. And she reached out her hand, to find, between her and the water, a set of iron bars.

She wanted the place, needed it, and thrusting her hands between the bars, she tried to reach it, tried but couldn't reach, but tried, reaching and reaching.

Zella had to think of a doctor who would accept her explanation of a miscarriage and take the risk of helping them. The only name she could come up with was Dr. Miles, a family friend. As she drove, she focused on reaching the safety of his house.

When they got there, he told her that he couldn't. Just that he couldn't help, and she had pushed her hand into his closing door and refused to leave until he gave her the name of someone who could. She ran back to the car and drove to the address, her foot shaking so violently above the pedal that she almost couldn't drive, unaware until she got there that he was not a doctor, but a veterinarian.

And he had tried to help. When Zella had knocked at his door, he had answered with a dinner napkin still tucked into his collar. "Yes, may I help you? What's wrong, child? Don't just stand there, tell me what's wrong."

She took him to the car, where Ouida was stretched out on the backseat, surrounded with bloody newspapers and he stood on the sidewalk looking up and down the street. "Help me get her inside."

Once they were inside, he told her what kind of doctor he was, and Zella just stood there and looked at him with her mouth open.

He gave her some medication and told her to go home, afraid to send her for a doctor. "What I do in this office is one thing, but I cannot allow you to go to a hospital. They will know exactly what you've done." Before they left he asked if they were sisters, and Zella's silence was the only answer she gave.

Ouida woke in a hospital days later, to the sound of a door, shutting? Opening? She wasn't sure. In the quiet of the night, it seemed as if it was the only sound there was.

Reborn in the still blankness, and unsure, Ouida found herself, again and again, waking to the sound of that door.

She returned from the memory shaken, stunned with the past's consumption of the present. The memory would revisit her, a month later . . . a year later . . . in that plateau of the day that has been left unclaimed by tasks. And every time she woke from it, she recognized the smell of rich wet earth.

20

When Ouida woke, in the stillness, in the blankness, Zella was beside her. She had slept at the hospital in a chair by the bed until Ouida wakened, and then she came daily, reminding her that there was life.

After the bleeding slowed, the one who had, after all, opened his door to them helped get Ouida home and then disappeared. Zella had tried to nurse Ouida at home, but she grew weaker and more delirious as the infection spread, unchecked, through her fevered blood, and when she finally resorted to the hospital, Zella knew she had to say that she had found Ouida in that state, bleeding from self-inflicted wounds. She knew she had to withhold information despite the fact that Ouida was near death and her joints were stiffening, and so she didn't tell what had been done. Didn't tell about the scraping and the cutting, clandestine and unclean.

When Ouida woke days later to Zella and the sound of that door, she tried to fight her shame, but there it was. In the ceiling crack of that seedy room and the man with the dangling cigar who had had those hands and that metal inside of her. And in the strangers, the money changing hands in the night, the doors that closed. In the blood and newspapers in that borrowed car, the kneeling in the midst of it, holding to the poem she had learned as if it were prayer.

Because it was hidden and sordid she was ashamed, and the lies felt folded and stuffed deep inside to replace what had grown there, cushioned and secret and hers. Ashamed, Ouida wasn't sure she had a right to grieve for the child that might have been, wasn't sure what she had a right to, after all.

Because she and Zella made a silent pact not to tell what had put her in the hospital, a careful, heavy silence descended around the whole thing. When Vesta and Eula and Polaris came to visit and glanced at Ouida with questions in their eyes and a fear at the answers they might get, the looks they received told them not to ask out loud. After a month in Black Oak's hospital it became clear that the doctors had done what they could and an operation beyond their capabilities was required. To give her a chance of walking again, they moved her to an East Coast hospital where a new type of surgery was being tried.

Zella took a leave from her job and transferred to a teacher's college in the town where Ouida was sent. She found a room with friends of friends, and came each day to the hospital when it looked as if Ouida had given up, bringing what she thought would make connections to the outside world.

She came with textured things for Ouida to touch. A curved shell of bark that Zella said felt like mountains on a map. A smooth piece of carnelian, orange shot with amber fire, that was cool to the touch, and a rough, irregular piece of lapis that looked just dug from the ground. Pine needles encrusted with pungent sap and veiny maple leaves whose edges curled and crumbled as they dried.

And she came with pears and chocolate and crystallized ginger with its sweet burn. Things for tasting. Things for the mouth.

Her clothes were performance, and Ouida waited each day to see how Zella had put herself together with touches of opulence. She combined fabrics with rich textures, making them hers, and touched off her soft muted wools with vermillion scarves, or strings and strings of beads that she carried off like no one else could, inspiring folks to stop and tell her, "Girl, you *wearin'* that suit." Whatever she wore, she wore with drama, and anyone who was paying attention could see that she enjoyed this expression of herself.

"The whiteness here I just can't stand," she said one day as she came through the door, pulling a four-foot scarf of raw ocean-colored silk from her bag. She put it in Ouida's hands and together they felt the welts that were part of the weave and then sat, each holding an end of the rippling sea scarf, and Zella told her of the day's events.

And then she slid the white curtains all the way to the sides of the rods and draped the teal cloth across the top.

She brought strands of glass and silver beads that knocked together like music and read to Ouida from her favorite books. She told tales from the outside world, bringing little dramas she had witnessed into the hospital room: descriptions of people she had seen that day, the unique shape of a cloud, the way the wind had lifted a hat and carried it across the street.

She came with beeswax candles and burned them against the rules.

She came with life, this woman who tasted rain, and when people asked if they were sisters, she answered, "Yes."

In her dreams Ouida returned to the cave she had discovered in the back of that borrowed car to find a blooming wetness replete with fragile orchid petals opening, audacious, with their wild markings, against all that could happen in the world and all that could be wrong.

Zella learned about the grotto when Ouida mumbled from sleep about falling water and darkness and awakened with her there, reading or holding her hand. She told her about the place, but refused, still, to discuss the infection and its toll, or the unsuccessful operations that had not prevented her legs from stiffening. She talked about all the things she would do after she walked out of the hospital, and even when they told her she would walk with crutches, she pretended it wasn't so.

While she dreamed of the verdant growth beyond the iron bars, she returned in waking to the wilderness that threatened her life.

Zella thought she saw small signs of progress until she came one afternoon and found Ouida turned to the wall, withdrawn. For days she lay like that, her face against the white wall, refusing to look at Zella or to speak or eat, her already wasted body growing thinner. It took Zella days to find out what had happened, and then she could only tell her bit by bit about the new layers of shame and anger within.

She told Zella, finally, how the team of doctors had appeared, suddenly, announcing what a challenging case she was, and discussing her as if she weren't there, in terms of what could be salvaged. And they had had her disrobe and struggle slowly, painfully across the room, supported on either side as she pivoted and swung her stiff legs around while they studied their work. She had walked back and forth, a naked specimen, before forty, fifty pale predatory eyes, hearing comments about her beauty, ravaged and laid bare for them to see. When she could finally tell the story, her face still turned to the wall, Zella climbed on the bed and held her, unconcerned by the curious and hostile looks she knew they would get.

Ouida had turned from the wall and told Zella how she had been displayed. But she wasn't free, yet, of the stagnant torpor that was claiming her. Zella worked each day to pull her out of it, but Ouida never talked about the pain. She didn't speak of how she would master walking or make future plans. She didn't even talk about getting up from her bed or leaving the hospital, but retreated, once again, to the refuge of sleep, and Zella tried to think of something that could pull her back into life.

Below the surface, Ouida felt unlinked. Afloat in a world cleared of smells and colors and sounds, she sometimes couldn't fully hear what was said about and to her, and when she did, she often felt as if she was experiencing things from far off, through a filter. She went to her grotto and she pleaded from half-opened lips for the strength to meet her body's pain and for answers to the questions in herself.

She wished for her mother, who she knew would somehow help her if she were there. Ruby, who had borne a sense of disgrace and punishment Ouida had not even known about until two years before. And she thought about LaRue, to whom she had always felt connected, wondering where he was, where he was after all. "How do I go on from here?" she thought. "How?" One day she turned to Zella with wild eyes and said with a dry, burning voice, "What do I know about this, Z? I don't know anything at all."

When she had left for the East Coast hospital, Ouida had told Vesta and Eula and Polaris that she wanted them to stay in Black Oak, that Zella would send them updates on her progress. LaRue didn't hear from Vesta until months after Ouida was first hospitalized, and even then, her letter spoke only of an undefined "sudden illness" requiring a transfer to a hospital "out East." He hadn't been back to Black Oak that year, and had stayed so absorbed in his own life away at school that he had failed to realize how much time had passed without hearing from Ouida and, reluctant to upset his studies, Vesta had resisted telling him anything at all. Although she finally did write to him, he couldn't get her to be more specific about what had happened or what Ouida's condition was, and having never met Zella, he couldn't turn to her. When he could get no further information, he made plans to come. On his spring break from school he made the trip out East to see what was what.

When he came through the door of her hospital room and said, "How's my bestest girlfriend?" Ouida reached out her thin arms to him and whispered, "Wishbone. Wishbone, I can't believe you're here." When he asked her what had happened she wrinkled her forehead and closed her eyes, and he panicked as he thought about the sleepwalking after Ruby's death, from which she had only recently emerged. "My God," he said to himself, "don't go to sleep again." She looked at him from the stupor of medication and withdrawal, and then closed her eyes, waking later to find him still there. She rambled on about orchids growing out of every wild place in her dream. Out of the grotto walls and sides of other growing things. Out of her own mouth and eyes. Out of the dark, wet smell of decay.

When Zella arrived after class, he was sitting by Ouida's bed asking her about the orchid-filled place. When she had entered the hospital Ouida's nurse had told her he was there, and when she saw his back a jolt of panic passed through her. Panic at coming disapproval, coldness, a failure to recognize her place in Ouida's life. And then he turned and smiled at her so warmly, the light shining through his eye, that she had a feeling that whatever his understanding, it would be okay.

"You must be LaRue," she said, holding out her hand, and he smiled at her black fedora with its red and purple feathers and said, "You're wearin' the hell out of that hat!" They laughed and Zella told him her name and added, "Of course, I feel like I already know you

. . . and Tennessee Jones . . . and Miss Snake . . . and all the rest of your family."

The way Ouida lifted her hand from sleep for this woman, and the way she took that hand, told LaRue there was love between the two of them, and it wasn't that he understood its shape, but that he would try to know about it, about Ouida's love for this remarkable-seeming, vital woman. He would try to know about it, but he would wait for her to tell.

He sat with them quietly while Ouida drifted in and out of sleep, and while she was dozing he asked Zella what had happened, what had gone wrong. She told him there had been an infection that had stiffened her legs and a series of operations to try to make them bend. She told him how they had been urging her, unsuccessfully, to begin to walk. Ouida woke up, smiling when she saw him, and said, "Tell us a lie, Wishbone . . . we need one. A lie or a Good List . . . we're dying for something like that around here."

"Let's see," LaRue said as he thought of the start of a tale, "I think Miss Snake had something to say once about this whole pain and illness thang." Zella smiled at his pronunciation of the last word. "Thang," she said, and he answered, chuckling, "You know thang is much more serious than thing. Thang is the ultimate thing." All three of them laughed. "Anyway, what happened was this. Miss Snake had a brush with blindness, and it happened in the middle of a desert sandstorm. This particular time she was colored a pebbly tan, so that she could blend in with her surroundings and avoid attack. She looked like she was all this pale, pale brown, but if you studied her *real* close, you could discern a subtle pattern of spirals on her back.

"Well, a sandstorm arrived on the scene, unannounced, and swept through the desert, wrathfully, turning everything upside down. Miss Snake was hit by something and came to find she had been blinded in one of her eyes. All she could see with the other was swirling beige. The whole desert was the same color: the sand, the rocks, the plants, and to Miss Snake's horror, she couldn't find her way. It was so much the same it looked like white looks . . . like the absence of things.

"She couldn't burrow under the sand, because the storm was so violent it was picking up whole dunes and depositing them somewhere else. And it's a fact, you know," he said as an aside, "that the whole Sahara Desert moved to a different location and all the maps of Africa had to be redrawn as a result of that storm."

Ouida sucked her teeth and whispered, "Bone, I had forgotten what a true liar you are."

"I swear on high," he responded, "better lyin' than dyin' . . . Well Miss Snake remembered that she had seen the shelter of an overhanging rock a day or so before, and if she could just find it she wouldn't be dashed up against a boulder or hurt by the storm. But try as she might, she couldn't distinguish a single feature in the barren landscape that was churning around her like a dry sea. Eventually, as she trembled there in the vast beigeness, she realized she'd better use her wits. And that's when she began to listen very carefully to what was around her. She calmed herself inside and took stock of the situation by feeling and listening and smelling and tasting the world around her."

LaRue paused and then continued. "Once she had made that shift, she began to detect small differences in the things that had looked all one color not so very long ago. She inched her way along, her senses other than sight fully alive, and made her way to a rock. Maybe not the one she had seen before, but one that provided shelter, nonetheless.

"And that's how Miss Snake got out of that fix, finding her way slowly along what had been an undiscovered path . . . a path of her own making . . . to shelter. I'm not sure she ever regained the sight in her eye, but she told me that even though it was hard to have her vision cut in half, there was something . . . something else that came out of that desert sandstorm." His hands were open, the palms turned up.

He took Ouida's hand, kissed it, and whispered in her ear, "Remember, Ouida . . . on the other side of what there isn't is what there is." And then he gathered his things to go.

Zella decided to go with him, and as they were leaving the hospital LaRue asked her to tell him about the operations and she gave him more details about what had happened in those hospitals, and how his sister was lucky to be alive. When he asked where the infection had come from, she paused and said that she thought that was something Ouida had better tell herself. "It's not that I don't trust you . . . it's just that it's hers."

The reminders of life that Zella brought, along with LaRue and his lies, helped Ouida make a claim. For a few days after he left she barely roused from sleep, and then Zella came one day and found her alert and awake with the pain she had known and would be fighting for a long time. Zella sat down by the bed and they looked at each other without speaking.

Ouida's eyes were so clear that Zella could see into them. Her face, gaunt and pale, bore traces of what she had been through, and Zella thought she was more beautiful than ever before, her face the face of a woman, not a girl. A woman who was learning about life. For a long time, neither of them said a word, and when Ouida spoke it was to ask Zella to help her into the caned wheelchair and take her out to the porch. It would be cool outside, Zella reminded her as she tucked blankets around Ouida in the chair. Her slender, stalklike neck looked like it could scarcely support her head and the tips of her fingers traveled into the soft hair at the nape. Ouida said she knew it was barely March, and winter had not yet relaxed its hold. "I asked the nurse what month it is," she told Zella, "and somehow, without realizing it, I have missed a whole cycle of seasons. She told me it's March, and I want to be out there today, if just for five minutes, to feel things waking up." They went outside, then, and Ouida looked around slowly, taking everything in.

She found herself in the thawing. In the entrance to spring.

She had been there almost a year before, on that dark road where she had gone to try to save her own life and ended up in the circle Zella's arms made around her, covered with fevered blood. Ouida leaned her head against the back of the wheelchair as the past with its many layers, hers and her mother's and countless others', known and unknown, rushed to the surface to become part of her present. She closed her eyes for a moment and tried to get her breath, and then she opened them and smiled as she pointed up.

"Look, Z," she said, "at that awning up there. It reminds me of jack-in-the-pulpits. Have you ever seen one? I used to . . . I used to know a story about them . . . how did it go . . . ? Something . . . something about that striped partial cover, and the wonder of what lies beneath . . ."

She paused to think and then went on. "I know . . . I can remember it now, it was a story I made up for LaRue . . . he couldn't have been more than ten, and was already challenging me to beat his lies. So I told him about the jack-in-the pulpit's hidden reward."

"Tell it to me," Zella said, as she sat on a stone bench and stroked Ouida's hand. "Tell it to me now."

"Well . . . it needed a shelter, you see, for its fragile, inside parts, but it also wanted those who were so inclined to notice, to be able to appreciate its beauty . . . and so let's see, what did it do?" She paused and reached back for the story.

"Ah yes . . . it came up with this solution. Not a complete protection, that would close off its beauty completely from the world, but an awning." She described the flower, gesturing with both hands. "You might not even notice it, thrown off as you might be by its cluster of big, solid green leaves. But if you're really paying good attention, there's this small secret, beautifully striped in a purple the color of eggplant or of deep brown lips that have been kissed throughout the night . . . a dark kind of ancient green . . . and white.

"You might not take the time to look beneath the awning," she said softly, "if you're hurrying on your way." She brushed a tear from her eye and missed one that fell to the cold stone beneath her. "But if you are moved to peek underneath the striped hood, you'll find this erect stalk, thrusting up out of a well of delicately veined leaf skin, looking like life itself, and the awning making a liplike curve above and around . . ." Ouida laughed at her story of patience and discovery, and Zella didn't know how long it had been since she had heard her laugh like that.

"Tell your friends," she said, turning to face Zella with her clear, shining eyes, "I done told mine."

Ouida started, after that, to really try to walk. She began to accept what had happened to her, and what her role in it had been and not been. She forced herself to look at the scars on her body, about which she had been vain, and to touch the raised flesh that was now a part of her story. She accepted that in her life she was going to have to fight going to sleep, and now that she had begun to be rooted out of herself, she made a decision to make of things what she could.

When Zella went to Black Oak to take care of business, Ouida asked her to bring back several things when she returned: a box she had covered with a collage of paper and fabric that held the tree branch LaRue had brought from down South, and Ruby's fan quilt, its fan pattern arrested halfway along its length. And she wanted Zella to find whatever photographs she could locate at her flat.

A week later Zella returned to find Ouida staring at the imprint of an ear on the inside of her upper arm when she knocked softly and entered the hospital room. "Look, it's my ear," she said as she touched it with her fingertips, and laughed. "Isn't it funny?" She had turned on her side while sleeping, resting her head on her arm, and she said it looked like she'd been listening, hard, while she slept.

Zella touched the imprint on Ouida's arm and put the African violet she had brought on the windowsill and they sat together and went through the things she had found at Ouida's flat. Ouida looked at a photograph of Ruby and noticed the determination in her stance, the fight in her eyes, and remembered the story LaRue had shared when she had left Junior Biggs and moved back home. When she thought of her mother she recalled a laughing, gentle woman with great imagination, but there was evidence of another part of who she was in the way her head and shoulders were lifted and in the manner in which she rested her hand on the railing at her side. Ouida caught a glimpse of what it was that Papa Drake had had to punish. "Proud," she said aloud, "proud fighter," and it occurred to her that that was what a colored woman had to be.

Zella had found one picture of Polaris in his uniform, standing next to a train. His bearing was stiff and dignified, but his eyes had the unreadable look he wore, always at work and often at home. "Papa," she said as she looked at the picture, realizing how little she knew this man who had protected and provided for her, realizing how much between them would probably never get said.

There was a photograph of Ouida, Vesta, and LaRue taken at about the time she and Vesta had graduated from high school. LaRue stood between them, his "bestest girlfriends," his arms linked through theirs, one foot on the ground and one in the air as if he were about to rise in flight and step from the flat sepia paper of the photograph.

And there were two prints of Ouida and Zella, taken that summer that had just passed. In one they were posing in vests, knickers, and spats, holding a string of just-caught fish between them. They smiled, self-mocking at the butch role they had assumed for the photo. In the other, they sat side by side in loose bathing jerseys, their thighs just touching, the shapes of their breasts revealed by the clinging wet cloth of their suits, and the intimacy of the picture made her almost need to look away.

Ouida put the pictures in her collage-covered box with the branch from LaRue, and then told Zella that she needed her help getting a start with the crutches that had been propped in the corner behind the door for the past month.

For the next few weeks she fought to walk with the crutches, finding a place inside to put away the hurt, the strain of moving muscles that had been inactive for almost a year, the ache underneath her arms and in her back. As she worked at walking she dreamed of the dark and secret place, but she always woke with the loamy wet smell of the earth on the other side of the iron bars.

A tangle of flowers and plants grew on the walls, rose out of open roots, and the floor of the cave was sodden with things slipping into decline, browning leaves and stems degrading into soil and from that, pale beginnings pushing up. There were orchids and climbing clematis vines. Queen Anne's lace, and poppies, and all the flowers she had ever lied about. There was foxglove, with its markings that alarmed, and wild, showy trumpet vines, those "in-spite-of" flowers Ouida loved.

The air was heavy and moist with lingering rain, and there were dark pools of water where she could see scarlet and yellow and sienna leaves floating just below the surface. There were wildflowers she could not name, and little bits of blue amid the expanding green. And if she looked hard, she found jack-in-the-pulpits, their dark stripes curving in protection of their fleshy, hidden gifts.

Night after night Ouida went there, and then she pushed her fingers through the bars. She pushed, the barriers giving way, and woke in a clean wash of moonlight with the grainy feel, the fecund smell, of earth on her hands.

While Ouida recovered, Vesta worried about her and waited for news from Zella, but she was consumed with raising Dessie. In those days, she often said she didn't dream, and she guessed she was just too busy. Although in other times she had awakened conscious of fading doorways and wings; she woke then, to the flat, uncluttered present. She had no stories or lies to give the child who had become hers, and she wasn't much for sitting on the floor and making things, or acting out parts and reciting poems. What she had to give was her constant presence. That and a network of ground rules and guidelines that amounted to a body of law.

Vesta was always saying things like "If you touch that, it will fall," or "If you play with that, you will be hurt," so that from early on, Dessie had no doubt how things connected up. She knew that "balls were for bouncing," and "forks and spoons, not knives, for eating." She was clear on which things were open to her and which weren't, and among those that weren't, the proper uses. There was absolutely no question what a chair or a sofa was for. It was not for standing and reciting poetry; it was "for sitting."

LaRue returned to Black Oak angry at Vesta after visiting Ouida in the hospital. He didn't understand her decision not to tell him what had happened to Ouida, nor her failure to do anything about it. She hadn't even pushed to find out what had gone wrong. He knew, also, that he was angry with himself for becoming so separated from his family that what was going on with his "bestest girlfriends" could have escaped him. He tried to figure out how to talk to Vesta about Ouida, but she evaded him every chance she got and when he saw the way she was with Dessie, his irritation grew.

He remembered how not so long ago, she had pressed him for details about what went on away from home, trying to impose her rules on him, or to at least set forth clear boundaries, and he realized how much her questions had felt like warnings. She had asked about race relations in the Alabama town where he and Olive lived, and if he was careful about how he carried himself and where he came and went. She asked whether he was working hard and what grades he expected to get. What classes he was taking and what kind of job he planned to seek. She asked where Olive worked and how much money she earned. Whether she cooked dinner regularly and whether it was good. She asked what he intended to do after graduating and when he would be coming home.

She worried about him, she often said as she twisted her fingers, she worried like a mother might, and he had felt, so often, that she was drawing everything from him, and he had had to fight for air. He recognized her suffocating presence as he watched Dessie sitting on the floor between Vesta's knees to get her hair brushed and combed and plaited. And he watched Vesta removing a chair, a book, a toy from the child's path as she made her way across the floor. When the child, unwatched for a moment, got herself entangled in a pile of yarn and embroidery floss from the sewing basket, Vesta was on her feet, freeing her from trouble as soon as she spotted it.

"She would have worked her way out of it on her own," LaRue said to Vesta, "if you had given her the chance." Holding Dessie with one firm hand while she restored order to the sewing basket with the other, Vesta looked at him resentfully and asked why, if she was there to do it for her, she should stay in a fix. "Besides," she argued, "she's got to learn not to touch everything she sees."

Unable to stand the sound of Dessie crying herself to sleep, Vesta had moved her into the room with her, and often anchored herself around her small, sleeping body. Unwilling to watch her struggle and err, she did whatever she could to make things smoother and safer for her. And she tried to make up for Ruby's absence and the fact that Eula had never said she loved them by reminding Dessie of her devotion every chance she got.

"Don't forget it," she said, holding her so close it made her squirm. "Don't forget . . . don't forget that I love you." LaRue watched them as, sewing basket returned to neatness and locked, she held the child close, and he couldn't help but notice that Dessie's eyes darted, as if she were trapped. It made him think of Foxglove, and a story from long ago.

The next day LaRue overheard Vesta's stern questioning: "Which is it . . . is it the truth, the whole truth, or did you fib?" Her voice seemed on the verge of splintering. "You can't have it both ways," she said. "You can't." She was pushing Dessie for an answer about whether she had disobeyed her rule against before-dinner snacks. "Now which, which is it going to be?" She threatened her with making her kneel on the cold, rough floorboards in the pantry. "A child's got to learn," she said, "A child's *got* to learn."

That night at dinner LaRue decided to tell a story about LeFoy and Footney. Eula and Polaris seemed glad for the reappearance of the twins, and settled back over dessert to hear a lie or two.

"The brothers were sitting on the stoop one evening," LaRue began, "as Footney explained a plan to buy a large quantity of soap and resell it at a huge profit. He stopped short in his explanation when he realized that LeFoy was somewhere else entirely, and waited silently for him to return. He tapped his foot while he waited, and it grew faster and more insistent as his patience wore thin, but his brother, leaning back on his elbows, stared up above the buildings into the sky. Finally, LeFoy turned his head slowly to face his brother and said, 'Footney . . . do you think there are degrees of truth?'

"Footney looked at him, shook his head, and realized they would get no further with the development of their soap-selling plan until they had a discussion of the topic with which LeFoy was now obsessed. He sat down next to him on the step and said, 'Degrees of truth. And what, may I ask, does that mean, LeFoy?'

"'What I mean to ask,' he answered, 'is whether a thing's got to be either true or untrue . . . yes or no. Whether, for example, there's such a thing as a half-truth . . . or a part-way truth, you might say.'

"Footney looked at him. 'A half-truth,' he said.

"'Yeah. And if there *are* degrees of truth . . . if there, indeed, are . . . can you measure it in geometric terms, so that three hundred and sixty degrees of truth equals total truth?'

"Footney wasn't sure what LeFoy was getting at, but he answered, 'Well, maybe so, when you put it that way. I know I used to tell Mama some itty bitty teeninchy lies. Things that didn't really matter in the scheme of things.'

"'A forty-five-degree lie,' LeFoy said, gesturing the spread of the angle with his hand.

"'Yeah, well I never met anyone who really wanted or could stand the complete, unfiltered truth, and I guess sometimes a little teeninchy lie is the better thing to do, all things considered."

"'Well, what do you know that's three hundred and sixty degrees true? Things shift around and get all complicated, you know. Things are sometimes true and not true at the same time. And then again, in some sense maybe all things are true, just not in the same way. It's still a thing that lives in the middle, but not an end thing,' he said, stretching his arms apart.

"Footney took this opportunity to break in and guide the discussion back to his topic. 'It's a slippery thing, this whole lie and truth thing. Very slippery . . . kind of like soap . . .'

"LeFoy wasn't ready to move on. 'Or,' he said, pushing Footney's patience to the limit so that he stood up and kicked at the wrought-iron fence, 'not a one-end thing. Both ends maybe, but not one.'

"LeFoy went on. 'And if truth's not an absolute, a lie can have a truth in it, too, don't you spec? Most everything's got truth in it . . . or maybe things kind of *hold* truth. Only thing I can think of that's three hundred and sixty degrees true is that there's no such thing.' LeFoy sat there for a while, looking at the stars, and Footney was relieved that he was finally going to be able to get on with explaining his scheme."

"Still tellin' your lies . . . *still* tellin them," Vesta said as she got up and started to clear the table as soon as LaRue was finished, and then she went upstairs to check on Dessie.

The way she dealt with the baby made Polaris uneasy, too, but he had always let Ruby deal with raising the children, and he didn't have the strength to face it and figure out something better. He had to tread carefully with Vesta, as the child had become her province, and she seemed to need to be in charge of her. He was so grateful to have Vesta and Eula there to help with the baby, and he was so tired, working on the road for longer and longer stretches, trying to supplement his regular wages with extra work as money got shorter and shorter. He had an uneasy feeling about some of the interactions in his house, but the way things were arranged and divided up between men and women was what he knew, and it seemed easier to go along with it than to fight it.

While Vesta's behavior concerned Polaris, it made LaRue crazy. He waited days for a chance to talk to her about it, and about Ouida, and she evaded him until one night when he came into her room while she was putting Dessie to bed. He sat on her bed until she turned to face him and then he pulled her into the hallway and pushed the door closed. "We have to talk about Ouida, Sister . . . you didn't even tell me what was going on."

She yanked her arm free but he continued. "There are a lot of things we need to talk about, and you know it as well as I."

Vesta hushed him and warned him that he would wake the baby, and when he refused to move she agreed to go into his room and talk. The feeling that someone was mad at her always gave her a sense of disarray and her heart raced wildly now in anticipation of either an explosion or cold withdrawal. She tried to prepare against it by straightening up, standing to rearrange the things on her dresser, her fingers shaking slightly as she awaited his anger.

When he pressed her about why she hadn't told him about Ouida's illness and she said she hadn't even known, he asked her how that could have been so. Having no real answer and not even able to think clearly, she looked at him without speaking and began to scratch her arms. He could tell that she knew about Zella and had decided to keep a safe distance from it. And he could tell that she knew that the secret Ouida kept was a disturbing one. One she preferred not to know.

He wanted to ask her where her own life was headed, and he turned the conversation to Dessie. "You can't live for her, Sister," he said gently. "You've got to have your own thing."

"She *is* my own," she answered. "Who else's is she? I'm what she's got and she's what I've got. We're each other's own."

"Sister, you know what Miss Snake would say, about what's yours and what belongs to somebody else?"

"I can imagine what she'd say, or what you wish she'd say, in any case . . . Wishbone . . . the one who wishes for everything . . ." She shook her head at him and went on. "And I haven't got time or room for it. You'll always be tellin' your lies, see, but I haven't got room for your wishes or your made-up stories and tales. I live in the world, LaRue Smalls . . . now go on home to your poetry and your wife, and leave me to the things I've got to do."

She left him sitting alone in his room, listening to her hard, precise footfalls on the stairs, thinking that he would have to stop wishing something for Vesta that she could never do. He would have to stop wishing his own wish for her. "I guess Miss Snake could teach me a lesson, too," he said to himself, and realized that Vesta was right about something else, too. He lived somewhere else now, and he needed to go home.

21

When Ouida's discharge from the hospital was imminent, she and Zella decided not to return to Black Oak, but to go to a place where they wouldn't be weighted down by so many silences. They chose a city near Black Oak, and Zella went ahead to find a job teaching high school English and a place for them to live. Vesta let her store their few pieces of furniture in the attic, and after they moved into a ground floor flat, Zella put a plan in motion to build a house without stairs, using the money her father had left her from the family catering business.

When they moved into the house they were the first colored on the block, and neither of them would forget the way the next-door neighbor stood just inside her door, her arms wrapped around her body, and watched. It took her three years to speak, and then she did so as she was moving out. "Good-bye," she said coldly, as she passed Zella on the walk and got in the car behind her moving truck. "Good-bye."

As they had driven up that first time, Ouida had been overwhelmed by the expanse of lawn out front and the real backyard. She had collaborated with Zella on the design and had been to look at it while it was under construction a couple of times, but it was something else to drive up, watching from the car window that frosted over with her breathing, and see it as theirs. Zella had helped her out of the car and steadied her on the icy walk as she swung her stiff legs around, and when she opened the front door for her, they had stopped right inside on the mosaic-tiled vestibule floor and looked around. They hadn't had much furniture at first, but the oak floors had been beautiful, and the diamond-paned leaded windows sparkled, and there were all kinds of things, bookcases, tables, and cabinets, built in.

It was a house with no stairs for Ouida to climb, with bedroom, kitchen, sewing room, and living room on the main floor, and two more rooms upstairs for visitors. Although it took them a long time to furnish it, they delighted in each little thing they got for their house. Zella went back to Black Oak to get her books and the few pieces of furniture that had been passed down to her, and the little treasures Ouida had brought to her first flat. Zella found secondhand furniture, which Ouida recovered, and they rehabilitated and repainted other things they came across, laughing at their devotion to "the great Negro art form of making somethin' outa nothin'."

As soon as they could, they ordered a new sewing machine for Ouida and set up a workroom with furniture she could easily negotiate. Zella saved up money for the one thing she decided to buy new, the carved oak desk and its chair with spooled arms and an umber leather seat. And one day she showed up with a stray kitten she had found on the way home.

Although Ouida mastered her crutches and moved deftly around the house, she sometimes looked so exhausted that Zella had to restrain herself from alarm. Ouida lost her balance and fell, but refused Zella's help getting up. It took her a while, but she inched her way to her feet, holding on to the furniture that was nearby. "You won't always be here," she said to Zella, half in anger and half in love, "and I've got to do for myself." Zella could hardly bear to stand by and watch her struggle, but she let her do it herself and the strength she saw in Ouida's eyes made something in her turn over, made her realize she would risk anything for her. "I love this woman," she said to herself, and turned away to hide her tears.

While Ouida worked on applying the great Negro art form inside of their home, Zella turned her efforts to the garden as soon as it thawed. She planted cuttings that people gave her and experimented with packets of seeds. She planted crocuses, at Ouida's urging, and invested in flowering bushes and trees. "More wild," Ouida would say from the screened-in back porch. "More wild, like a country garden," and she would chuckle at how she used to tell Ruby to make sure there were no shears, that there was nothing sharp at all around for Vesta to get her hands on, or before they knew it the shrubs would be trimmed into neat little cones and squares. She looked at the forsythia Zella had planted at the back, its fountain of brilliant yellow stars shooting up and out, and said, "If my sister Vesta were here we could kiss that plant good-bye." Flowers sprung up in the grass and she liked it that way. The fire-lit orange of the devil's paintbrush and fringy magenta blooms whose heavy heads tilted on their slender stems.

At the colored high school, Zella kept aloof from her colleagues. While Zella taught, Ouida started the dressmaking business that would help support her for the rest of her life. They began with a few contacts in their new town, and had business cards printed. As people told each other about the creations Ouida made, which began with patterns but were enhanced with little touches of her own, her clientele grew.

During her last month in the hospital she had thought about how as children, she and LaRue had fantasized about all of the places they would go if they were able, while Vesta had held back, skeptical of the idea of travel. They had talked about sea voyages to places where different languages were spoken, and trips over land to see deserts and mountains, but as Ouida had prepared to leave the hospital, she knew that she would probably never go the places she and LaRue had dreamed about, except in books.

Once Ouida had decided to live, Zella had brought her things to read and she had been hungry for them. "Girl, you eat books," Zella told her when she saw how quickly Ouida finished what she brought. Ouida remembered the excitement she had felt entering the school library as a girl, and how she had told her mother she was going to read everything in there before she died. She had loved to stand at the shelves and run her hands across the varicolored spines of the books, their call numbers like mythic codes, and imagine those whose hands had bent back the covers and frayed the edges of the pages before her. When, exactly, she wondered, had she stopped reading? She couldn't place it, but she knew she would never let it happen again.

Since going out was hard to manage with her crutches and her trouble with stairs, Zella brought her things from the library at the beginning of each week. Ouida listened for the sound of the car pulling up on those afternoons, excited to see what she had for her, and Zella came in with the books Ouida had requested and others she thought Ouida might like, and she sat and touched them as she had in those girlhood days, excited by the edge of discovery.

There was the smell of the books and the buttery feel of their old leather bindings worked soft from use, the gold imprinted lettering worn away in places. The heavy pages, thickening along the edges and creased in some spots. Places, best loved, that had been returned to again and again. Ouida imagined, just as she had as a girl, their histories of being read.

In the afternoon when she was done with work she lowered herself into her rolled-arm chair, in the space she had created for reading, and pulled the footstool close with one crutch. On the table next to her was a shoe box she had covered with fabrics, glued on and overlapping in waves, the retted teal silk Zella had brought to the hospital overtaking pale yellow brocade, and seamless pomegranate satin along the border. In that box, next to her reading chair, she kept a collection of ordinary things: her carnelian, her lapis lazuli, and other rocks she had found; pieces of bark, dried petals, and fallen leaves.

A crescent of yellow light was thrown by the lampshade against the wall. She got herself settled comfortably and draped Ruby's quilt of opening fans, still unfinished, across her legs, reclining in anticipation. And then she opened her book and let the story take her, reading aloud sometimes to get the rhythm of the words, losing all track of time. She flagged special passages with pieces of paper so that Zella told her her favorite books looked plumed.

"Saved," she thought to herself. She felt awake and saved.

She got dinner started in the late afternoon and when Zella got home they finished making their meal together as they talked about the day's events. They developed passions for certain foods and experimented with concocting sauces and marinades. Zella became adept at smoking and marinating meats and with LaRue's written instructions, Ouida learned to make Ruby's peach preserves. And then there was barbecue, of which Ouida was fond of saying it was not possible to get enough. "Have you ever heard of enough barbecue?" she asked. "*Enough* barbecue?"

On Sundays they slept late, cuddling and talking in whispers with the cat sleeping up against them as the sun came through the cracks in the venetian blinds and made them tiger-striped. And then they read the paper together over breakfast on the back porch or before the fire, claiming the time for themselves apart from the rest of the world. As they began their life together, Ouida felt a sense of the possible. It seemed to be wide open: who she was, and who she might choose to be.

Once Ouida and Zella had been settled for a while into their new home, Eula and Vesta brought Dessie for a visit. It had been over a year since they had seen Ouida and they knew traveling would be hard for her. Polaris couldn't get away, but Ouida promised she would be home for Christmas. LaRue told Eula and Vesta what to expect regarding Ouida's legs, and Vesta didn't sleep, worrying about whether she would say the right thing and be able to act comfortable around Zella. She wasn't sure what to bring up and what to leave unspoken. "How does one act in such a situation?" she wanted to ask her mother, but she wasn't sure it was a good idea to raise the topic at all.

When Zella answered the door there was an awkward silence, followed by a burst of exuberance. "Oh my," Vesta cried out. "Such a lovely house!" It seemed to take her a minute to realize she should enter, but finally she crossed the threshold, holding Dessie's hand. Despite what LaRue had said to prepare her, she was shocked by the image of Ouida on crutches and after hugging her she turned quickly away and asked for a tour of the house.

Once they were settled into the guest rooms on the second floor, Ouida and Zella showed them around. When they came to the sewing room, Eula said how wonderful it was that she was continuing with the skill Ruby had taught her, and remembered her stitching in the evenings. And then, as they left the room, she pointed out how Ruby had altered the dresses Mrs. Franklin had given her, pausing to look directly at Ouida to let her know her refusal to thank her benefactress personally remained unforgiven.

In the weeks leading up to their visit, Ouida had been nervous about something else. She didn't know how Eula and Vesta would respond to what was obvious about her and Zella. Sharing a bedroom and sharing their lives, they were a couple. Unable to deal with such revelations to her father, she had discouraged Polaris from coming and promised to visit Black Oak soon. She couldn't forget the time she had reached for Dessie that Christmas and Vesta had pulled away. When they first moved into the house, Ouida had insisted on their having separate twin beds, so that if someone needed to, they could think of them as roommates. Zella had told her that it was a hopeless ruse, but she had gone along with it. Even if people knew they were lovers, Ouida argued, it would reduce their discomfort.

Vesta tried not to look at Ouida's crutches as she praised the house, and Ouida talked to Dessie, who looked painfully shy. Ouida was surprised by the change she could see in Eula, who seemed as fragile as a porcelain bird, and had so much foundation on her face that it looked like a mask. And the most disarming thing about her was that she looked so much smaller. Ouida was certain that she had shrunk.

Eula's skirt was loose and the cuffs of her blouse seemed to swallow up her hands. Ouida offered, gently, to take in her clothes and Eula accepted, and when Ouida held the garments up she couldn't believe what she saw. She had shrunk several inches in height and was several sizes smaller around. All in all, Eula seemed brittle and diminished. Her scar seemed more prominent, and it looked to Ouida as though she was caking on her makeup to recapture with lipstick, mascara, and rouge the woman she had been. She asked Vesta how long it had been going on, and could tell from her response that it was something she hadn't allowed herself to see.

Ouida and Zella noticed a tentative quality in Dessie, as if she were striving to do things just so. She was indecisive, as if she were performing for points. And Vesta, watching them out of the corner of her eye, was polite and pleasant to Zella. She asked questions about her family and her interests and her job, but she seemed to be more comfortable with either one of them alone, and stayed completely clear of anything to do with their relationship or Ouida's disability. Ouida knew she was doing her best and that her attempt was a testament to her love for her, but throughout the visit Vesta remained guarded, and once or twice Ouida caught her eye unexpectedly and recognized in it fear.

That night Zella read Dessie the stories that had been her favorites as a child and despite her five-year-old caution with strangers, Dessie warmed to Zella in no time. She was at first afraid the cat would scratch her, but once Zella introduced them and guided her hand onto the smooth fur of his back, Dessie couldn't seem to stop petting him. Ouida watched the two of them with wonderment, realizing, suddenly, that she had never seen Zella with a child. While most adults talked down to children or tried hard to translate to them, Zella sat on the floor and related to Dessie like a peer.

It all looked so normal, Vesta thought as she lay in bed that first night, Dessie asleep in the twin bed next to hers. Somehow, she had thought their life would seem alien or grotesque, and yet it looked like any family's life. There were plants on the windowsills and an afghan thrown over the end of the couch, she thought, and Ouida and Zella sharing the same inside language for things and smiling and frowning at each other and saying, "Hand me that bowl."

She didn't know whether to be comforted by that, or to feel more afraid, for if it wasn't something far, far off, how close was it to home? Vesta looked over to make sure she saw Dessie's chest rising and falling. "Honestly," she whispered, "I don't know what to think." It was familiar, this life of theirs, and still she wanted to weep for Ouida, who had had the chance at everything, and had turned it into this.

She didn't know why or how it had happened, but she did know that this was her sister, who had woken each day calling her "Morning Glory" or some other silly name, who had taken her hand that very first day when she saw her from the couch, orange in hand. Who had braided dandelions with her and made sure she'd been invited to that first and only dance. All these things came rushing at her in the dark quiet, including shame, because she knew that LaRue was right to be angry with her for staying away while Ouida was sick. This was the same girl who had lost sense of time chasing after blue flowers in a junkyard and then spilled them at their feet. She couldn't understand it and she couldn't talk about it, the illness or "the other thing." She didn't even know if she could really accept, deep down, the idea of Ouida being with this inscrutable woman. But she and Ouida were as much sisters as any she had ever known, and on her she would never turn her back.

As they sat on the porch the next morning, Vesta said, "I still think it's the impatiens that are the loveliest," and Ouida explained that they were annuals, and she had only planted things that would return the next year. "Well, whatever . . ." Vesta went on, continuing the debate about flowers that they had started as girls. She and Eula spent a good deal of the visit discussing and planning meals, and as they sat and considered what to have for dinner, they imagined, also, what kind of weather they would have. They compared the temperature to those of other years, and debated, over the course of each day, whether there would be showers or not. When it got hot Dessie and Zella ran barefoot through the backyard in the rain and Ouida watched them from the porch, her palms pressed up against the screen so that her fingers dripped with the heavy-scented wetness.

Dessie talked to the cat and made up new names to call it. She picked flowers for the house and helped Zella with her digging and weeding, under Vesta's watchful eye. "Don't get your dress dirty," she called out to her as she snapped green beans into a cast-iron pot. Eula directed Ouida in making a batch of hair oil and Ouida tried to get her to lead a candle-making session, but she said she had forgotten how. And each night they all turned in early, as if the effort of being together had worn them out.

One day Zella got Ouida into the car and they all went for a drive. Zella pointed out the sights, with Vesta comparing their new home unfavorably to Black Oak. Then Zella took them to the outskirts of town, where there were still unpaved roads and wildflowers grew free. Ouida braided a crown for Dessie from the flowers, while she and

Vesta remembered, silently, when they had done the same. They stopped at roadside stalls to buy fresh fruit for preserves and pies, but Ouida and Dessie sneaked so much of it on the way back that there was little left. Ouida was so tired when they got home that she could barely make it into the house.

The next day Ouida and Zella were sitting on the back porch having breakfast, taking in the smell of coming rain, when Vesta came out and said she was afraid Dessie was getting a cold. "Must have been that going barefoot, that drenching she got." She announced ominously that the child was "prone to infection," and decided to return to Black Oak a day early.

In their wake their visitors left a distance between Ouida and Zella. The two of them stood in the doorway waving, and then couldn't seem to find each other. It took them a day or so to make their way back from the removed politeness they had assumed for the benefit of others.

When Ouida answered Zella shortly the tension sang in the air and, overwhelmed with her fears, Zella exploded, accusing Ouida of being ashamed. The resentments she had felt since finding out about Ouida's other lovers surfaced then, and before she could control herself she said things she didn't mean. She charged Ouida with feeling sorry for herself and the life she had been dealt with her, and Ouida rose to her feet, leaning on one crutch and tossing the other across the room. "And I'm a burden," she shouted, "I'm just a burden to you." Tears sprang to her eyes as she said she knew it was Zella who felt sorry, sorry for her.

They both sat down then, in the silence that followed, and Ouida spoke. "I made a muddle of things, Z. Of going on to school . . . and choosing Junior and being vain through it all, just moving, without thinking, along a set-out path. And the others, too, Flood and Johnston Franklin, and getting in trouble like I did. I realized as I lay in that hospital between living and dying, just how much of a muddle it was.

"I spent nights cataloging the mistakes I made and sometimes they lined up so close together there was no light shining past. And once something had pulled me through . . . beeswax and retted silk and a blinding desert storm . . . I tried to understand that they've all been part of the way here . . . And those wrong turns I made after leaving Junior were at least signs of life. Lord knows life with him was a kind of settled death."

She told her about Junior, then. About the collapsing wedding cake that was so funny and not funny, too. About how his request for milk had been the very last straw. "You know, Zella," she said, "I saw him on the street about six months after I left, and it seemed so amazing that I'd been connected to this man. He had this delicately pretty woman on his arm. She looked like that china doll Vesta and I had, with the big painted glassy eyes that roll up into the head, and she had this frozen look of happiness on her face, like she was gratified to have been selected, and when I looked at her I saw something of myself, because you know that's what I presented to the rest of the world, despite what was underneath. And the truth was, it was like . . . like, I don't know . . . like too-tight clothes, I've always said. Tight right under the sleeves here, so I couldn't even raise my arms."

She tried to tell Zella what Johnston Franklin and Flood had meant to her, the lessons she had been able to find in them, and her need for that heat she had felt. She tried to let her know that they had not been threats, but other parts of who she was. And she tried to reassure her that although she didn't fit smoothly, just where Zella fit, it was her she had chosen and her she loved.

The next year, the whole family went to Alabama for LaRue's graduation from college. Ouida and Zella drove and met the rest of them there. She introduced Zella as her "friend," and her father nodded and took Zella's hand. He asked nothing, as Ouida expected. All he said was "Pleasure to meet you, Miss Bridgeforth."

They were excited at LaRue's passage, and both timid and proud in the awesome world of college where he had ventured without them. Vesta made lots of little comments about how LaRue could go on and become a doctor or a lawyer if he wanted, but nothing could ruin his sense of triumph. He knew what a central role Olive had played in his accomplishment, and they seemed more in tune with each other than ever. They entertained the family with stories about his classmates and adventures they had had while away from home.

LaRue and Olive came back to Black Oak to look for jobs, but they planned to stay at the house only temporarily, until they found a place of their own. LaRue knew that Vesta would have trouble seeing him as a grown, married man, and was aware that they had to make a home of their own and that their place couldn't be Vesta's place, which was what the house had become.

"Good planning," Vesta said about their move. "Just in time for all those jobs in poetry that are opening up."

LaRue tried to make light of her comment, but it added to his anxiety about the Depression. He knew that Vesta, like everyone, was worried about what she saw happening. People were losing their jobs and getting less pay for what they had been doing for a long, long time. Vesta had gone on a canning binge and was stocking up on all kinds of provisions that wouldn't spoil. Although she fought it, Ontario exploded into her memory, raging over eggs and cheese, and she turned her energy to hoarding anything she could imagine reusing if things got worse.

Although LaRue and Olive hadn't expected great opportunity in Black Oak, it took them both a long time to find jobs. She could find no work as a telephone operator and the only other experience she had was at the funeral home. She finally found a temporary job processing applications at a relief office, while LaRue got work as an elevator operator. When that ended, he found a position through one of Eula's clients as a valet.

Vesta returned to the Episcopal church she had attended with Eula while growing up and stayed put there, going every single Sunday with Dessie in tow. When her hours at work were cut back, threatening something she had thought of over the years as a certainty, Vesta woke up throughout the night. She rose at the first hint of dawn as if she had too much to do to stay in bed a moment longer and had perpetual bags under her eyes from sleeping fitfully. She talked about everything coming apart at the seams. She expected the worst.

One day LaRue opened a closet she was filling up for emergency situations and stood with his mouth agape. It was stocked with paper bags, tins, and glass jars of every shape with lids to match. Paraffin and stacks of newspaper. Twine and spools of thread and remnants of cloth, rolled and pinned into neat little bundles. She had mended hand-me-down clothes for Dessie to grow into and tucked them away in her closet, where they would be ready and safe, and had laid in jars and jars of hair oils, lotions, and soaps she and Eula had spent a weekend making. There were jars of strawberry jam she had canned and hidden behind the fabrics for just-in-case.

LaRue could see her in the front room sitting with her needle and thread, embroidering furiously, making one sampler after another, as if she were warding off coming hardship with the simple bright phrases and the numbers and alphabets that marched across her canvases, unchanged over time by privation or catastrophe. She was counting out her little squares and making tiny, perfect X's in the evening light, Dessie at her side. Togetherness Is Bliss. Home Sweet Home.

22

LaRue was fond of saying that there was no feeling like the one you got from quitting a job, that beautiful double-edged freedom of not knowing what would happen next. This time he had sensed he would be fired before he got a chance to resign, but had felt powerless to do what was needed in order to be kept on. With little talent for deference, he was unsuccessful at the only jobs he could find.

He had been far too conversant and self-possessed a waiter at the men's club downtown, where business went on so much as usual that you would never know there was a Depression going on. His boss had told him after a week that he was uppity, that he made the clientele uncomfortable, and the manager had stood staring at him in angry disbelief one day as he filled a crystal wineglass and asked a patron what he thought of recent political events. He couldn't seem to carry himself the way that makes a person want a valet. Daring to talk to his employer like a peer, he brought up topics and expressed opinions about things that had been in the news. And at the string of chauffeur jobs that never lasted long, he betrayed something considered incompatible with serving others.

Now it was happening again. After he pulled into the driveway and adjusted his cap in the rearview mirror, he tried to arrange his face with just the right expression of formal docility and got out to open the passenger door, but shining through his mask was the smallest spark of amusement in his eyes. His gentleman employer got out of the car and paused at the door to tell LaRue that he was fired. It was done quietly, politely, by the gentleman with the flat blue eyes. It was done on the doorstep before LaRue reentered the house, and the next thing he knew, he was out of work.

He came home that afternoon to a refrigerator and cabinets that were just about empty, and stared at the only two things he found: a little bit of rice and a can of corn. He laughed at how Ruby had called such makeshift meals "Surprise," and he changed clothes and started scaring up a dinner from what was there.

As Olive came through the door, she called out to him, "Hey, Bone, you're cooking. I didn't know we had anything left in there to eat." He had set the kitchen table with a lace cloth, candles, and the china Vesta had insisted on giving them as a belated wedding gift. He draped the dish towel over his arm before turning from the stove to face her. "Tonight, my dear," he said as he pulled out the chair for her and bowed from the waist, "we are serving the specialty of the maison: Wind Puddin' and Walk-Away-Bread."

Olive laughed and dropped her purse to the floor as he continued in a precise and formal voice. "It is prepared with just a hint of patience, and garnished with a bit of good humor."

As he sat down, he felt better. He had made her laugh. And when they were finished eating, she told him she had been laid off.

He looked down at the table and fidgeted. "Well, I guess there's no need to keep my news to myself. I wasn't going to tell you just now, but I lost mine too."

Olive shook her head at him and the tears rose to her eyes. She couldn't believe he had lost another job, and even though she loved the part of him that didn't buckle under, she wondered, angrily, who he thought he was. "Do you think, Bone, that your father *likes* turning down beds for white folks? Do you think he likes carrying their bags, and answering 'Yes Sir' and 'No Sir'? We all have to put food on the table, whatever it takes."

He didn't have a response, and they looked at each other and shared a bittersweet laugh. "Looks like it's time to make a Good List," Olive said. "What do you think?"

"Oh, it's never a *bad* time for a Good List, but the time when you need one most is when nothin' at all is right.

"Well then," he continued, "let me see if I can start it off, and you can go next. Let's see," he began, "it's not raining. We'll start with that."

"Okay, that'll work. And what's more, the trees are a beautiful gold."

"Yeah, winter's coming," Wishbone added, "and that's not something for the Good List. White folks might just include it, but everyone with good sense knows that our people don't belong in this part of the world."

Olive cut her eyes at him and said, "Bone, you got to do better than that. You haven't added a goddamn thing. By the time you're finished, I'll feel worse than I did!"

"Okay, okay, 'Live, I wasn't through. I was gonna say winter's coming, but spring's not far behind. Your turn," he challenged.

"All right . . . we're healthy and have a roof over our heads . . . 'Cept for that leak in the back bedroom, that is."

"But there's only one leak, and it's a small one, too. Put that on the list, 'Live. There, it's your turn again."

She looked at him and started laughing. "The one thing you better put on the Good List, LaRue Smalls, is the fact that I haven't left your silly ass yet."

"I thank the gods daily, my dear," he said softly, taking her hand across the table, "and it still just astounds me," he added as he looked into her eyes. "Olives in the wintertime."

As he came around the table and held her, he knew she was angry and he knew she was partly right. He wondered, silently, what Miss Snake would do to get out of this fix. He was worried, and he knew that laughter would soften things for a while, but that he would have to start working on a scheme.

After several weeks of looking for work, LaRue found another chauffeuring job at the house where his friend, Rencie, was the cook. He tried hard to stay silent and clear of his employers, but he sat in the kitchen and cut up with the other "help," and he and Rencie worked out a couple of hustles that kept both of their families from hunger, at least.

Rencie was allowed to take home to her kids only the leftovers that didn't amount to an individual portion, and the mistress of the house watched her closely. So the first thing she did was present herself as ignorant of proportions. "I cook by feel," she declared, closing the subject. The mistress frowned at uneaten food, and tried to hold on to amounts that she said were enough for another meal, but Rencie saw them sit in the icebox and spoil, as her own children complained of hunger.

So she and LaRue began to help each other out, smuggling extra food out of the house by collaboration. Rencie would wrap the leftovers up and put them out back, as if they were garbage, and LaRue would intercept the packages and deliver them home. And one day, LaRue had come home especially proud of their ingenuity. He had smuggled half a sweet potato pie out under his hat.

For a few weeks, Olive got up at seven and went out looking for work. She knocked on doors, phoned everyone she had ever worked for and practically everyone she knew for leads, and circled possibilities in the newspaper. She told prospective employers that she would do anything she knew how to do, and would learn anything she didn't.

When LaRue got home she recounted every aspect of her fruitless search for work, replaying interactions in excruciating detail, and he found himself dreading the moment when he would open the door and she would start pouring out what happened and would see the hopeless desperation in her face. He encouraged her and tried not to let on how nervous he was in order to build her confidence, but all he heard in the street was that times were worse than hard.

One day Olive sat in her window and watched the eviction of her neighbor, Maisie. As her things got put on the street, Maisie stood outside shaking her head in humiliation, as little by little the private bits and pieces of her life accumulated in a ragged heap. Her table with one splintered leg. Her armchair with the upholstery on the arms worn through. Her clothes and her chipped cups and her beads, all trash to anyone but her.

Olive trembled as she watched it happen, and then she went outside and told her that she and LaRue couldn't take her in because they were barely able to feed themselves, but she could leave her belongings with them, until she found a place to stay. She piled up Maisie's things at the end of the hallway, with a corner of the heap just visible from her bed, and at times, waking in the night, she was startled by the shape they made.

Olive began to get up at seven, dress, and spend the day at home reading, listening to the radio, and doing household tasks. She took a daily walk through the neighborhood asking about work, and called the same people again and again. And when the quiet closed in on her, she would suddenly jump up and wash the kitchen floor or wax the cabinets, talking softly to herself as she worked.

But she got up later and later each day, eyeing Maisie's things from her bed, dressing just before LaRue got home from work. Finally, Olive didn't see the point of getting dressed at all, and she began to spend the day in her nightgown. She started having a drink of gin "to unwind" when LaRue came home, and eventually, beforehand, in order to be in a better frame of mind when he arrived.

Her slip into numbness started earlier and earlier in the day, until LaRue came home one night to find her passed out across the bed, whispering in her restless sleep, "Can go down . . . families . . . can."

They had the same conversation about her drinking over and over, and she renewed her promises, amid tears, in the morning light. LaRue fought the guilt he felt at driving her to it by failing at so many jobs, fought the feeling of lessened manhood. And he tried to help her. He tried.

He phoned her from work, even when it was against the rules, or he had to sneak away to place the call. He dashed into the kitchen while waiting to make a delivery or drive someone somewhere and stealthily picked up the phone. Or he took a few extra minutes to stop during an errand and dial the house, afraid of the sound of her voice. And she answered with great resolution that she was all right, but then met the closing afternoon light with a couple of drinks, and by the time LaRue reached home, it was the new, different Olive who answered the door.

Somewhere between her first and second drink, Olive surrendered. When he was there, he saw it begin with a tightening around her mouth, and as the morning lost its promise and slid into the flatness of the afternoon, her mouth hardened, until she went to the kitchen and poured herself a drink.

When he was there, she stood up casually and then turned her indignation on his pleading eyes. It was all she had, her anger at his questions and at his wanting, wanting something that she didn't have to give, and so she flashed her pain and anger on him with a harshness she had never shown before, disarming him and freeing a path for herself toward oblivion.

Her eyes seemed to age as she concentrated on her glass, tilting it so the ice slid from one side to the other, tipping the balance. Nothing broken or upset. Liquid smooth. Night after night she fought it and gave in, until anesthetized, she constricted her world to a tunnel from here to there that was wide enough for one.

LaRue tried, at first, to ease her pain with stories, with updates on LeFoy and Footney, and the travels of Tennessee Jones. But one day when he came in and told her he had seen the damnedest thing at work, she lashed out quietly, without even looking at him, "Spare me your goddamn lies."

She came to spend each night in the dark living room, alone, softening the edges of her private hell, and rather than fight, he retreated upstairs to the bedroom as he saw the tightness and its antidote that followed close behind coming to claim her. Just as surely, in the morning she offered apologies and renewed vows. She asked him if he couldn't call her at set intervals to get her through that flat part of the day, the part that was neither rising nor falling. And he said that he would try.

She asked him not to bring liquor in the house, and then sneaked out to get it herself.

And most of all, she asked him to overlook it all.

LaRue spent entire nights without sleep, terrified and unmoored. He couldn't find the person he knew in the woman Olive was becoming and he felt unsure of who he was without her. He couldn't stretch the money he brought home to pay for rent and food, and that was partly because she chipped away at it to buy her gin. His family, who had pulled through so many things, was scattered and had troubles of their own. And his stories seemed to have dried up inside.

He heard Rhea Winters's clicking teeth as he lay awake at night, and thought that maybe she was right about him. Looking into the hall from the weighted dark, he thought he saw Maisie's things expanding at the end of the hall and he thought morning would never come.

He thought the leak in the back room was getting bigger and bigger, spreading a stain in the ceiling that puffed out like a yellowish bruise, and began to talk about that leak as though it was the main thing wrong, as if with its repair everything else would line up neatly in place. Night after night he lay awake wondering if Miss Snake and Tennessee Jones had abandoned them. Wondering how to help Olive, how to give her something to stay sober for, how to make her laugh. When it rained he put pans under the back room leak and got up to check them throughout the night.

Consumed by the whole of what was wrong, LaRue stumbled for a way. The Depression was the only story, how things would get a lot harder before they improved. He tried to make a Good List, but couldn't even begin, for although a pound of flour cost a nickel, that was a nickel they didn't have. He thought, obsessively, about that leak, and some days he was so preoccupied with doom that he was either late for work or too distracted to perform. His education had been useless, it seemed, just as Vesta had said, and although he wanted, wanted to repair it all, he was overwhelmed by the enormity of the ills, and couldn't even make a start.

LaRue wanted fix it for Olive, to bring her possible joy. He wanted to wrestle with her troubles for her. He wanted to, but in the end he realized it wasn't his. It wasn't his to do.

When he accepted that he couldn't do Olive's living for her, and she wasn't yet able to pull herself out of her alcoholic stupor, LaRue moved out, at her request. He paid the rent before he left, and promised to do so until she got on her feet, and then he moved back into the family home.

He hadn't been gone seventy-two hours before Rhea Winters appeared. Sitting at the kitchen table, barefoot and braless, scratching her uncombed head, Olive looked up at the sound of the screen door squeaking and saw her mother walk into the kitchen talking, as if she were continuing a conversation that had been interrupted the day before.

" . . . And well, I didn't think you'd be up this time of morning on a Sunday. You're up all right, but I see you're not dressed, and look at you, flopping all around up front like that . . ." Olive sat open-mouthed, as her mother put her bag down on the counter and reached for the coffeepot. "I thought a cup of coffee would be just the thing."

As Olive watched her chattering and measuring coffee grounds into the percolator, even she couldn't believe her mother had shown up like that after five years. Never having received a response from the cards and notes she sent, Olive hadn't even been certain her mother knew where they lived.

She watched Rhea move around the kitchen rearranging things and straightening up, talking all the while about news of people Olive hadn't even thought about in half a decade. "Now I've damn sure got a reason to drink," she muttered to herself as she gulped the coffee she had laced with whiskey when her mother wasn't looking. She stared at the thickness of her mother's middle, and the way the gray was taking over her head. It was unbelievable, Olive thought, the whole damned thing.

Rhea Winters was at Olive's all the time now, and for a while, that made her drink harder. She laughed bitterly at her mother's scorn, and made up elaborate reasons for LaRue's absence. And Rhea never let up lecturing about a more appropriate man. "I knew he would turn out no good, and you see, he drove you to this . . ."

When LaRue called or stopped by to check on Olive, Rhea intercepted him at the door and said that everything was under control, and that Olive was "resting." Incapable of facing him, Olive didn't object.

Olive wondered if her drinking made her mother seem larger and more insistent, and every now and then, when she was sober, she tried to concentrate on her mother's face to make sure she hadn't imagined it. She watched her take over from a distance, cleaning and recleaning the house, planning how to dispose of Maisie's things, and although she was rankled by her mother's presence, the care she provided eased the disconnection from her troubled world.

In the middle of one night, Olive woke from a dream of cobalt blue, and rose from her bed in search of a drink. Walking to the doorway of the kitchen, lit by one yellow bulb, she saw Rhea in her nightgown, scrubbing the counter. The hands that had never touched her with love worked back and forth against the counter, attacking a discolored portion of the wood. Olive leaned against the door frame and watched her mother for a long time. She followed her hands as they applied ammonia and bleach to the stains that had been there so long they had become part of the wood, and she saw the tight concentration in her mother's mouth, a mouth that she couldn't remember ever kissing her.

She saw all at once, in the figure of Rhea Winters, the cost of meager living, and realized with a jolt, that in her own way this was what she faced. She thought about her family, people who had spent their energy and survived on the rearrangement and presentation of death, about the business her father, Leverett, had inherited, how he had always bragged of his talents at covering scars and rejoining flesh, at the peace he could arrange. After he was finished, he had said, no one could tell what had brought on the end. He was good at packaging the dead.

As Olive watched her mother scrubbing in the shadows, she realized that unless she could find a way to answer "Yes" to life again, her future, like Rhea's, was with the dead. She didn't know how she would manage to stop drinking, but she resolved, as she looked at her mother, to try.

She walked into the kitchen and Rhea jumped. "My goodness, you scared me! What on earth are you doing up?"

"I got up to pack your things," Olive said, deciding in that moment the first step she would have to take to get back her life, "because it's come time for you to go." Olive turned to leave and her mother grabbed her arm. "Go? Go? Look at you, child! You're a mess. You need me, and I'm not leaving until I'm finished here."

Aware, suddenly, of her hair, her disarray, her own funk, Olive touched her temples and the stains on her nightgown with her free hand, and then tried to disengage her arm, but her mother grabbed her tighter and turned her around to face her, and then, instead of pulling away, Olive looked into her mother's eyes from her own red-rimmed exhaustion and pushed herself against the body that in her memory had never held her, once they were of separate flesh. She pushed herself into her mother, clasping her body to hers, knowing how Rhea would recoil at the smell, the heat of her. "Feel me, Mother, feel me," she whispered urgently to the face that turned from hers. "I am part of you." Rhea fought her, but she continued. "We have breathed the same air . . . you fed me with your blood."

Her mother looked at her in horror and tried to push her away. "Feel me now, for once . . . feel my need, Mother, my need to be loved, my need to be turned loose. Feel me, please, for God's sake, take me to you now, finally, so that you can let me go!"

Rhea Winters pulled further and further into herself, repelled by her daughter's breath and the pores and blemishes on her unwashed skin and by the rough, nappy edges of her hair, wanting to clasp her to her breast, but unable, because it wasn't what she knew. The part of her that said, "Too much, too much," was triumphant, and she succeeded, finally, in freeing herself from Olive's grip, and went upstairs to pack her things.

Olive managed to stop drinking and to take each dusk patiently, and when she had been sober for a month, she went to LaRue. He called her regularly and brought her food, but he didn't expect to see her at his door. When he opened it, she said, "Hey. Saw Tennessee Jones today."

They stood together in the doorway and she said to him, "Remember cobalt, Bone? And that bed with one short leg?" They laughed and he told her "Yes," he did. He did remember. "Remember how hot that summer was?" she asked. "How at a certain time of day the afternoon light came down across us through the deep blue glass?" And LaRue nodded. "Blues can be cool, but not that blue . . . that was a liquid hot kind of blue. Hot and clear and rich," she said, leaning against the frame of the door. He looked at her long coltlike legs and thought how much he had missed her and she said, across the silence, "I love you cobalt, Wishbone, I love you cobalt blue."

In that night, Olive came to him. And he seemed to be a doorway. She wanted to give up her pain, and she knew that he could take it. To open herself so that something in her would crack and it would pour out, all of her that was hidden, flowing molten and into him and then she could say what she couldn't say in the light. She wanted him to heal and unheal her, she wanted to be alive, to say take me take me oh take me and make me, for this moment, whole. Do me and undo me, all.

He seemed to be a doorway, and she entered. She wanted to say how sweet it was, but how sweet and not sweet it was was past saying, and so she rocked him to her with whispered chantings, and her moaning did leak out of the openings they were making and did turn to tears, and she wept for herself. She wept for herself and she wept for him. She wept for them both, separate and together, in that dry coal dark night that was now wet, her once-hidden weeping below her and above her and around. For the wanting and the joy, the drive to be known and safe from knowing. For the pain of waking.

She entered. And locked together with LaRue it seemed to Olive as if all her efforts, all her efforts at living her life, were at once small pathetic fumblings and heroic leaps. They came to each other in that night, and after, she held him to her and said, "I'm looking, Bone . . . I'm looking for light."

Once they were back together, Olive told LaRue how Rhea had arrived without saying a single thing to bridge her five-year absence. When he asked her what had done it, what had been the thing that let her know she had to break free of her mother and her drinking, she described what she had seen from the doorway and told him about the images of death that Rhea's cold, fanatical hands, scrubbing futilely in the yellow-shadowed night, had brought home to her.

After she had finished, LaRue told her what he had been through while he was gone. Having returned to the family house in a daze of grief, he hadn't been able to tell Vesta or anyone else what was going on with Olive. Vesta picked at him to find out and then, preoccupied with her own responsibilities, she left it alone. He hadn't known whether he was coming or going, he told Olive, and he wasn't sure how he had made it from day to day. And then he was fired when he was caught with a pocketful of stale dinner rolls, and he couldn't get over the pleasure his transgression gave the man he worked for, who must have been waiting a long time for the chance to throw him out, who called LaRue a "useless nigger." LaRue found that that was exactly how he felt, and after he lost that job he spent his days in the street hustling little moving, carrying, lifting jobs for whatever bit of change he could get.

The days he had spent looking for work on the corner among the men with whom he had grown up telling lies, who helped each other out with news of odd jobs and tried to get through the bleak times with laughter. There were surges of lying, followed by dry spells, when they felt too depressed or hungry for invention. LaRue had spent time on the corner listening to the ingenuity of the others, but he had had no stories of his own to tell.

The nights he had spent trying to figure out what he would do if he didn't find work, awakening in anguish over that tunnel of alcoholic disengagement and rage that he knew something about from before memory, where Olive seemed to be living. He had awakened hungry and he had awakened thinking about that leak in Olive's back room. And then, after a string of days with no money coming in, he had awakened and left Black Oak, this time without a goal, in order to get away from where he was. "I was running . . ." he told Olive, " . . . running from my life."

"But where did you go, Bone? Where did you run?"

"I didn't go anywhere far in distance, 'Live. And I didn't have any end in mind. I hitched a ride with Wilson Blue, from down at the corner, who was going west to look for work, and I got out in a little town about fifty miles from here. I followed a river north for a few days on foot, just trying to clear my head and get a handle on what was going on.

"Somewhere along the way I seemed to have lost a sense of where I fit into things, and didn't know what to reach for anymore."

Olive hung her head, ashamed of her own role in LaRue's pain. "I'm sorry, Bone," she said as she took his hand. He slid his fingers through the spaces between hers and went on.

"When I got out of Black Oak I felt like I could breathe again, and I stopped when I found a quiet place, to try to reach back and go over what had been important to me in the past. I thought about Mama Ruby a lot . . ." He paused and his eyes were wet. " . . . about what she was . . . what she is to me. The little things, you know, that survive, like how she looked at me with such love and confidence, like nothing I did would surprise her, and I think of her hands often, how they were long and graceful, and worn from gardening and working. I always thought they were so beautiful . . . hands that did things.

"I thought about how people stopped by our stoop to give up their secrets, and Mama Ruby helped them do it, with their dignity intact. And you know, 'Live, Mama Ruby always made me feel that the stories I created were the most important things, not nonsense, you know. And like I could be whoever I chose. But I haven't felt like that lately. I haven't felt like I could be anything, and then there's this hunger . . . the hunger of these times, it grinds at you, and you're not sure where to look for what you need.

"Seems like our people have always been able to tell tales, even in the worst of times, as if the stories just rose up, willful, refusing to be killed off, and that maybe, some of the very best stories come out of hard times. Well, I don't know why, but my head had just gone blank, and I couldn't even think of how to start a tale. It was like I had bought those definitions of myself in other people's eyes, in the man, for example who caught me with those dinner rolls. And that definition read 'zero.'

"So I left, and when I returned to Black Oak I got a tip from someone at the corner about a possible job. Man, I must have really looked desperate for work . . . anyhow, I went to this lamp factory and they hired me, though it's only temporary. It is work, though."

When he brought up her drinking Olive winced and looked away, but he kept talking and eventually, she took another step toward facing it by calling it out loud. Once they had brought it into the open he thought it was time for something else.

"Well, 'Live," he began, "you asked when you first got here if I had seen Tennessee Jones. Well, as a matter of fact, we traveled together for a good part of that trip I took." He paused to see what Olive's face revealed, as the last time he had tried to tell her a story, before leaving, she had pushed him angrily away, rejecting his "lies." Olive smiled and settled her body against his chest. "And how was old Tennessee?" she asked. "I've missed him somethin' fierce." This time he looked at her and saw love in her eyes.

"He's makin' it, but these times are taking their toll on him just like they are on everybody else. I ran into him when I was just about ready to come home and it turns out he was headed in the same direction I was, looking for music and for work. There was a place, you see, where he wanted to hear for himself a woman who sang the blues. 'You know what the blues are, my brother, LaRue?' he asked me, and then without waiting for my reply he said, 'The blues is the basement. And that's about where we're all livin' these days.'

"Well it turned out that Tennessee had been that way before, and we traveled together for a time, mostly on foot, and for a few miles now and then we jumped on a railroad car. Tennessee wanted to get out and walk before long, though, where he didn't feel cooped up. 'I'm in no real hurry,' he told me, 'and I like this part of the country, its middleness and all.'

"We decided to travel together as far as a little town he knew, where he said I could get the train back to Black Oak. We had a lot of catching up to do, for he had been zigzagging all over the country and had quite a few stories to tell. Having none of my own to share, I was prepared to do a lot of listening. We decided that, at a certain place right before we came to the town where the train ran, we would go our own ways.

"We spent quite a few days with each other, taking our time getting up that road. Tennessee told me his latest tales, and he showed me, too, how the tips of the pine trees that rose around us like dark, majestic witnesses bore soft needles of a fresh pale green. He pointed out how the dry ocher that started at the points of long narrow leaves crept up and up and up the wide part of the growth. He hunted mushrooms, pointing out the ones that were safe to eat, and he taught me the names and powers of the wildflowers that grew in the most unlikely places along the path. When we caught fish in the river and cooked them over a fire we built he showed me how to clean the scales and remove the bones, and while we were fishing and cooking we remembered Mama Ruby and thought about how she would have loved to be there, cooking up that fish.

"It rained in torrents one night and we took shelter in an abandoned lean-to. And when we picked up the road again the next morning, everything smelled dark and wet, and we walked into a trail of yellow-green pollen, washed into the road by the showers the night before.

"We finally came to the place where the road split and Tennessee pointed out my way to me. And suddenly I felt tired and scared, and it looked like an endless lonely path, muddy and rough.

"From the top of a hill I looked down to try to see where it stretched up ahead, and there was not even a town in sight and the road was winding as it climbed and fell again and again. I asked Tennessee if there was a shortcut, 'cause I just didn't feel like I could make the trip. My eyes filled with tears and I thought, 'I don't even have my sweet Olive with me, and I don't think I can make it by myself.' And Tennessee looked at me and took my hand in his big rough deep brown ones and listened to me questioning whether I could make the trip and begging for a shorter, easier way. He reassured me that I could make it to that town and that, indeed, I would. And then he said, 'I'm afraid, my brother, that there are no shortcuts. You gotta go the long way 'round.'

"Tennessee hugged me and took the other fork then, and I stood still for a while and then got on that path, long as it was, and I did make it to the town where the train ran.

"What he told me sounded inside, 'Live, the whole long, hard way home, and I swear on high what he said was true. It's really the only way . . . the long way round."

23

LaRue and Olive each struggled with their rough and winding roads. They found ways to bring bits of money in, but things got harder and bleaker before they eased up. Vesta lost her job in Foundations altogether, Polaris had to moonlight doing mechanical railroad work when his pay was decreased, and work at the lamp factory ran out for LaRue.

They were all worried, but they found ways to pull something out of nothing. Like everyone else they knew, they made it on credit, until Mr. and Mrs. Ike went under themselves. They saved things that in other times would have been discarded and put them to use in different ways. They bought inferior produce instead of high-priced canned goods and grew a few things in their little city gardens. They put up fruits and vegetables in canning jars and traded them with neighbors. They tried to come up with new ways to fix the starchy foods they could afford and, often, they settled for one meal a day.

Neighbors exchanged what they had in goods and services, with Eula doing hair and Vesta mending clothes in exchange for coal or for help patching the roof. Black Oak pulled together for a strike against escalating rents and people worked for meals and bonded in their common strife. Some of them gave in to violence and some folded and everyone's patience wore thin, but they tried to lean on each other. They talked about how hard things were, finding something in their situation to laugh about. "Times are so hard I caught Miss Snake eating her own tail," LaRue began, opening up a contest with whoever would play.

They all tried to change the ways they thought about using things, remaking old clothes and inserting egg cartons into shoes with holes in the bottoms. LaRue searched for firewood and other useful things in abandoned buildings and junkyards, and he organized rent parties. He believed in celebrating their ingenuity as Ruby would have done, and was always trying to get a Good List going, but Vesta couldn't see much that was funny or positive about the way things were, and she spent her energy strategizing and thanking God for her closet cache, where she had been saving things for just such a time.

All she knew was that she wanted everything for Dessie, and saw the possibility of disaster everywhere she looked. She wanted her to have plenty to eat and restful sleep, a warm home, and nice, quality clothes. She rationed out everything they had, striving to create a life free of worry and sickness for Dessie. Anxious with how she saw their provisions shrinking while their needs grew, she realized with horror one afternoon that she was screaming at the top of her lungs at Dessie for leaving a light on in an empty room. In Vesta's restless nights solids crumbled and fixed things slid out of place. Water dried up or ran out of reach. She dreamed again in those nights, she dreamed of a doorway leading out.

Olive and LaRue both looked hard for work, and she promised herself and him that she would stay sober. They took Church in for a while when he couldn't get by on his own and he and LaRue hired themselves out as a cleaning team and picked up day work at the corner gathering place. Olive finally had no choice but to go to the welfare agency for help, although dodging the caseworker's unannounced checkups almost drove her back to gin until she and LaRue decided they would have to live apart for her to keep her aid. They found her a room with a family in Black Oak and made up a story about how LaRue had deserted her.

Because she couldn't make it on aid alone, she looked for additional, undeclared work and eventually found a job cleaning the house of a woman for whom Eula had done hair. LaRue fought against the sense of failure that the arrangement evoked, while Olive resisted the desire to drink. More than once she bought a pint and brought the bottle all the way to her lips before pouring it down the drain. Evenings were the hardest times, restlessness overtaking her as the day's light dimmed and she closed her eyes and imagined the taste of gin, hot between her tongue and the roof of her mouth, and then the loosening, things sliding into place to make an integrated whole that she could penetrate, momentarily, before the blur of her life resumed. She tried to hide what she was going through, but LaRue entered her room once and found her staring at a drink she had poured. Their eyes met and he looked at her long and hard before he left without saying a thing. "Hers," he said to himself, practically chanting. "I know it's hers to do."

After six months on aid she found part-time work at the paper box factory and moved back to the family house. Since nobody could make ends meet on their own, they decided to continue to pool their resources. Now and then they opened their door to someone else, as they had to Church, who contributed what he could in exchange for shelter and food. It was a time when everyone got by through reliance on friend and kin.

But those times drove Vesta right to the edge, and she lived the rest of her life as if privation had either descended, or was on the way. Spending a dollar would always be excruciating and she would talk about money incessantly, evaluating everything in terms of monetary value. Even once the Depression was over and she had her old job in Foundations back, she hoarded every penny, "because one never knows."

LaRue finally came through with a scheme that got them past the worst of times. After over a year of scrimping and living with the family off and on, he and Olive enjoyed a brief period of plenty, until he realized, with her help, that he had lost his way. He said that although he had been introduced to his idea by Footney, he had learned from Miss Snake that a crucial part of scheming was knowing when to quit.

"Quick, tell me a number, Olive, there's someone on the line." LaRue stood covering the mouthpiece of the receiver until Olive had given him some digits off the top of her head. "Here you are, my good man. I am certain, this is the one for you today . . . Okay, thank you kindly, and enjoy your winnings. I'll collect from you tomorrow."

More and more desperate for cash because he and Olive had a child on the way, LaRue had come up with a strategy. He had noticed that no matter how hard times were, folks still scraped together money to play the numbers. Betting on a number was a crucial indulgence. An investment in hope, in chance, and LaRue figured that he could hold himself out as prescient, he could be a part of that hope. He placed an advertisement in the colored paper. Within a space three inches square, underneath a drawing of a turbaned head, it read:

Swami Jones
Your Chance for Prosperity
Phone Now and Cash In

LaRue rented a place and got an extra phone number and circulated the word that Swami Jones could divine the number and, needing to believe in the idea of that, people began to phone in. When they called LaRue told them what he felt the number would be. It hit often enough to make folks keep on calling, and when it hit big, they sent him a little extra to express their gratitude.

Vesta didn't know about his swami scheme at first, but when she went to dial the number herself, she realized whose it was. Horrified at his dishonesty, she threatened not to speak to him until he stopped. But LaRue wasn't about to stop what he had started. For four months he was able to feed his whole family with meat and to help Church get back on his feet. He was putting away money for the baby they were expecting, and with one scheme leading to another, he had also come across some hot oriental rugs and jewelry, and was enjoying buying Olive some fine things.

Having been to the edge of herself, Olive recognized that LaRue was in trouble. At first she doubted what she saw, thinking he was fuller and wiser than she was, and then she didn't know what to do about it anyway, for she was undergoing her own nightly battle against gin. But Olive was right, he was fighting his own demon, intoxicated with the success of the swami scheme, feeling powerful. He liked the game, playing the role of the character he had invented and asserting prescience. And he liked having money in his pockets, more money than everyone else. For just about four months, he felt larger than life.

Worried that he had lost track of something important, Olive finally spoke to him in bed one night, by raising the question of lying. She told him she'd been thinking about his story on degrees of truth. He laughed and recalled the reactions of LeFoy. And then she said, "Well, Bone . . . you know there may be degrees of other things, as well." He looked at her silently until she went on. "Some things may be more right than others," she said as she bit her fingernails nervously, "and the line may be hard to find. Some lying may shade into wrong, both for the liar and the lied to."

He knew what she was saying, and he didn't want her to read him that way. He didn't want anything to ruin the spell he felt. "You sound like Vesta," he shot back at her irritably, "looking at the world like it's made up of black and white." He turned his back to her and faced the wall.

"Maybe, she said, "but I don't think you've got to worry that there's a whole lot of Vesta in me. Bone, you've got to think about what this particular swami lie is doing to people who've got no money to spend on manufactured hope. And then," she said, her hand resting gently on his back, "you've got to think about what it's doing to you."

She left her palm on his back and felt the rise and fall of his breathing through her hand. "Even if the world doesn't break down black and white, LaRue, you can't just take up residence in gray."

Not wanting to listen, he avoided Olive for days, even staying out all night once. When he came through the door the next morning she was in the kitchen making coffee and she looked at him and said, "Think. Think what Mama Ruby would say." He tried to lie down in bed, but couldn't stay put and got up, dressed, and walked the city streets. He covered all of Black Oak and many parts of White Oak, too, trying to figure out something, though he wasn't sure what. He felt disoriented, as though he didn't recognize the streets he had traveled all his life. He knew what he was doing had gotten out of hand, but he hadn't wanted to come home.

Times without money, they were mighty grim, he thought, and often it seemed to him as if the only news there was was bad news, as if the promise had sifted out of things. It took some work to keep your eye on the good news, the news of the winter solstice and its promise of light.

He didn't want to think about it, any of it. It was so much harder to try to understand where lines got drawn. There had been liberties with the truth that felt right to him, and even when he had gotten started in the swami business, that had seemed like harmless invention. He had chosen to see what he was giving, rather than taking, with his scheme, to see it in terms of hope. But he knew he had declined to see part of the picture, and that the whole was more complicated than he had wanted to know. He had to face his own temptations, and at least ask himself, in a deeper way than he had done, what was right.

He heard Tennessee Jones talking to him about shortcuts and the long way round, and went home and took Olive to him and she knew he was back.

His life as a swami had lasted four months, and he had helped carry his family past hardship, but conditions seemed to be easing up. LaRue had been able to put food on the table and despite her objection to the setup, Vesta had never refused the benefits it reaped. But he had lost sight of who he was, until Olive, who had known the underside, jolted him back into reality. It wasn't a clear line, he thought, between lying and truth; it was even less clear than he had thought. About that much, LeFoy had been right. "I swear," LaRue had said out loud as he made his way back home, "I swear on high."

Although Zella's job as a teacher was secure, her salary was reduced, making it hard for her and Ouida to get by. To make matters worse, even well-to-do white people weren't having new clothes made, and Ouida struggled for work. At the recommendation of one of her clients, she had started working through one of the WPA sewing rooms, with Zella picking up jobs for her to do and bringing them home.

Ouida tried to focus on simple, unwavering things. She took her time in the morning, immersed in each aspect of the unfolding day. She liked opening the back door to get the bottles of milk, feeling the cool of the thick glass bottles against her fingertips. She put the coffee on and while it brewed she checked her windowsill of African violets, gently removing soft fuzzy leaves that were yellowing and filling the little trays beneath the pots with water. The cat approached her to be fed and she looked forward to the feeling of fur against her feet.

The hardness of times seemed to inspire in them unparalleled passion. She and Zella made love unexpectedly. They made love in the afternoon. They made love like their lives depended on it.

Over their ten years together the fire between them had waxed and waned, assuming its own rhythm, but overall it had evened out. In those days of hardship, Zella rediscovered her joy in the way Ouida's throat flushed crimson in passion and the perfect lightness of her touch, while Ouida noticed, again, the taste of Zella's mouth, basic like rain, and the flashing of her jet-black eyes, one larger than the other.

They were days of renewal. Days of wonder and release. When they were together, in each other's arms, it felt as though there were nothing else in the entire world. The two of them at the center, all else spiraling outward, as if it were distilled, all that they had for each other concentrated into one pulse.

Loving with no end in mind, that said what we have is now, what we have is this. And they had made their rituals to get them through.

Zella liked to bathe at dusk, and sometimes Ouida would come in and find her in the tub after work, scrubbing at the day that had passed as the daylight deepened and disappeared. Then Ouida would light a candle and get settled on a seat next to the tub, her legs stretched out straight ahead, and soap her, while everything outside of what they were doing fell away and they slipped into whispering.

They would end with Ouida soaping Zella's hair and massaging her scalp, building to the moment Zella loved best, when Ouida filled a bowl and she tilted her head back and there was a cascade of water down, down over her head and her shoulders.

They pretended Zella was a lost fish who had happened into their landlocked urban bathtub and had stories to tell of the things she had seen. The living coral that grew a world in its spines and fans and openings, brilliant colors and electric fish. And finally, when the bath was done, she would ask for help getting back to sea. Zella often told Ouida that the entertainment value of her companionship was "through the roof," and that was why she loved her so.

They had their imaginations and they had each other, and together they made ceremonies and made a daily life. There was sometimes trouble, as their tensions and their passions led to arguments and they clashed over ideas and politics, over faucets left running and wasted food. Both sensitive, both easy to bruise, they worked hard at loving each other well.

They had each other and they had their friends, and tried to help people in need by inviting them for meals and shoring up each other's spirits. They had card parties and poetry readings and charades with their expanding group of friends, other sharers of clandestine love. Gathering regularly, the group had celebrated the move from muted tones to full voice, as waves of unencumbered expression had swept the house.

They reminded each other to praise the gifts, and Ouida introduced Zella to the Good List. "These times are hard," Zella used to say, "but oh how textured they are."

At each day's close Ouida liked to be the one to struggle, slowly, through the house and shut off the lights before they went to sleep. And once in bed, she inhaled the quiet that settled down. Leaning over, she smelled Zella's hair, smoothing it back from her temples, and settled back into her pillows, listening to the sound of her own breathing.

* * *

Olive went through three miscarriages after LaRue gave up his swami scheme, and it kept her from thinking in terms of the future. Because she needed a chance to recover alone, she began to encourage him to find a way to travel again, arguing that time apart was the only way to save what they had. She reminded him of how, when they had first been reunited, he had told her about rediscovering his thirst to see the places that were drawing colored folks from the South, in order to put together the smaller pieces of that story into a kind of mosaic, like the intricate wooden tableaux his father had made.

Olive had been hired to do telephone surveys for the WPA and Ouida helped Vesta apply and pass the test to get work on the WPA sewing project. She preferred this public work to a private job, which would require more hours away from home and, therefore, from Dessie. At first she had only been able to find work on a crew that helped with city sanitation work and she had painted, chopped grass, cleaned, and tended trees. Finally, she had been one of the few Negro women hired to do inside work.

While he brought in money doing odd jobs for some of Eula's clients, LaRue tried to think of a way to do what Olive suggested. He began to make scrapbooks, like the leaf album Ouida and Vesta had helped him put together years ago, to keep a history. He made a big thick carved wooden cover for it, attaching photographs with little silver and black slotted corners to the heavy dark pages of the book. Some things, like greeting cards and posters and newspaper articles, he pasted in, and some things he sewed in with colored pieces of yarn and Vesta's embroidery threads. And then he heard about the Federal Writers Project, as the thirties came to a close, and applied for a job, aware that his chances for getting anything except menial work were slim. One of his college teachers helped him get a spot, on the basis of his experience as a teaching aide and editor on the school newspaper.

While Vesta worked in the sewing room and helped organize other relief efforts, LaRue set off for his alma mater, where the Alabama project was begun. He and other writers, aspiring and established, fanned out throughout the state to collect folklore and testimonies of ex-slaves. They took numbered highways and unpaved back country roads in order to find out about the customs and legends in each part of the state. They stopped in cities and one-horse towns to learn about local songs and ballads, sacred places and celebrations. And more then once LaRue ended up telling the people he met about the adventures of Tennessee Jones and Miss Snake.

When he was sent to find those who had been slaves, he found himself amid his own people's living history, asking preordained questions on birthplaces and birthdates, ancestors' origins and names. As instructed, he probed for recollections of the foods that had been cooked and the clothing sewn and worn. He asked about self-education and crafts, and about the work that had been done. When he got to auctions and punishments he found that his hands shook as they tried to use his pen and his eyes flooded with generations of tears, and then, somehow, when they spoke of ceremony, he felt renewed. When they shared with LaRue the ways they had strived for living art, he felt joined.

It was strange to him sometimes, taking notes on the things they shared, on the things, written down now and classified, that had made up their lives, and although they met, LaRue and the elders to whom he spoke, across age and privilege, and things seen and unseen, he wondered what they thought of him, as he visited the way they lived and then went home.

There were times he spent on the road that would return to him for the rest of his life. The afternoon he passed with Bertha Crosby, under tall dark pines, when she shared her meal of corn bread and gravy and together they spread newspapers on the tree stumps they had pulled between their knees and ate, and she talked about the children she had had, and about the house versus the field, and about how she had lost her husband, who had tried, three times, to run from being owned. About the first time she had seen that man she had loved, bending over water, his back arched just so, and the last. She told LaRue about conjuring and nighttime integration and sent him away with a small hand-sewn pouch of herbs and a prayer that he would be safe.

One day he spent with a man who no longer spoke in words at all, but offered tobacco, and LaRue sat smoking while the silent one pointed to birds as they lifted into blue. One night he got lost and made his way along a foreign road, praying against fire, praying for deliverance, praying to find his way. He spent a week at a harvest festival, where he heard chanting and pieces of language that seemed foreign and merely forgotten at the same time. He danced and drank dandelion wine, and he minced barbecue, telling big lies all the while, and he helped sew a rooster on a quilt.

He sent postcards to everyone from along the road so that they could follow his journey, and he came back talking about the Depression adventures of Tennessee Jones. He had collected all kinds of information about Alabama and facts about people's lives, but he had found out, mostly, about himself, and he had learned to listen better than before.

24

Although the Depression lifted, LaRue and Olive were still having a hard time. Despite the months Olive had spent alone while LaRue was on the road, the babies they had lost seemed to have taken with them all sense of possibility for her, and while he pretended, sometimes, that her despair would go away, her sadness was always with her. Sometimes he wanted to turn away from her, for he, too, was grieved, but he knew that as bad as he felt, it was harder for her still to let go of the baby who had been a part of her inside self, to whom she had channeled blood and air. Although he knew that he couldn't say he really understood, he was aware that breathing as she breathed, it had been building from her, with her, for an entrance into life.

Olive began to talk to LaRue about finding something to do that was hers, alone, and he tried to support her, while hoping that she wouldn't have to leave him altogether, to gain herself.

The talk on the corner, excited and hopeful, was of the high-paying work available farther north, in Detroit. People said they were going "up there where it's better," where there were jobs in the auto factories that were now munitions plants, as the "arsenal of democracy" drew another wave of Negroes north. While LaRue went there to see what the situation was Olive moved in with Vesta. She decided to join him when he wrote and told her there were adventures there for both of them, and they paid a few dollars a week to share a two-bedroom apartment with another couple.

LaRue had boarded the train with a sense of adventure, and had written to Olive excitedly about their prospects, but he suspected that what it amounted to was something else. He heard folks talk, cynical already, of how they had thought there wouldn't be sheriffs who beat up on them, and hadn't figured on storekeepers acting rude or insulting. They hadn't realized they wouldn't even know their neighbors, or that things, like heat, would cost as much as they did. Amid the ice and snow LaRue met someone who said, "You've heard people say 'when hell freezes over'? Well, it seems like that's just what's happened up here." But they focused, instead, on the hope for which their destination stood. LaRue heard men he met looking for work say, "At least the county hospital takes you, whether you got money or not." He heard them say that no matter what they had found, back home there were low wages and sorry excuses for schools. They couldn't return; there was nothing back there for them.

LaRue was hired soon after his arrival at a bomber plant, but work for Olive was harder to find, as many of the jobs that were available weren't open to Negro women. At one place she went to apply, the white foreman told her that her presence would lead to discord, as there weren't enough Negro women to make up a separate shift and no one could expect the white women to use the same bathroom as her. Another told her that, what with his wife working out of the home, Olive's help was really needed to clean houses like his. Finally, she was hired at the tank factory, but there was only one other Negro woman in her division who worked the same shift and, as usual, she felt utterly alone.

She worked at night, dressed in rough heavy men's clothes, making ammunition, and she didn't tell LaRue how dangerous the work was because she had tried so hard to get it and decided she wasn't giving it up. As dirty and strenuous and dangerous as it was, she felt as if she was getting to see how men lived. The wages were the best she had ever earned, and together, she and LaRue were making enough to save and return to Black Oak much better off.

Since he had no sense about how to handle money, had "no concept of it," she used to say, she deposited both of their checks and left out what they would need to get by. Arguments were inevitable, as he tried to get them to live "a little more, just a little more in the moment," and she had a plan to buy a house in mind. He felt like whatever happened, they would make it work, somehow, but she never meant to face eviction and a leaking roof again. If she had anything to say about it, Wind Puddin' and Walk-Away Bread would be inventions of the past.

One day LaRue met Olive as she emerged from the blackened windows of the plant. They argued over whether to spend a little extra money for a movie. Olive stood up and put her hands on her hips and said, "LaRue Smalls, I tell you what. Miss Snake paid me a visit yesterday just as I got off work."

He had to laugh. "Oh, is that so? Miss Snake's visiting you now, is she? I'm not so sure I believe you, 'Live, so prove it by telling me what she had on."

"She was a grayish-black this morning, the color of a newly laid road."

"That doesn't sound like Miss Snake's style to me," he said. "You must be lyin', 'Live, 'cause that's much too drab for her."

"Mmn hmmn, well it just so happens that she had a point to make. As I came out of the plant and was blinking my eyes in the bright morning light, she sidled on up to me and said she had been waiting for me to emerge. She said she knew about my struggle with you and money, and she had a little story to share that would warn me about you, LaRue Smalls."

"Miss Snake? My girl? I can't believe she would betray me like that." He was chuckling at Olive's nerve in making up a lie about his character and he couldn't wait to hear what she came up with.

"Well," she countered, "Miss Snake is also a part of my family, even if it is by marriage. And after all, we have a whole girl thing between us. It so happened that she had recently been on an important, but thankless, mundane errand that had taken her down a dark road, and she was dreaming a dream of all the adventures she was going to have when she finished. She had been fantasizing, she told me, about dancing and singing, and in celebration of the fun to come, she was all decked out in bright oranges and greens. Well, there she was, uncamouflaged on a dark, colorless road, with her head in the clouds, and she wandered straight into danger and ended up in the biggest fix you could ever imagine."

"What kind of fix did she get in, 'Live?" He was getting a kick out of her story, and wanted to draw it out.

"Well just never you mind. The point is . . . nice as it is to be carefree and jump headlong into something . . . nice as it is even to court danger sometimes . . . we've got to balance being practical and being adventurous dreamers."

He took her hand and kissed her, and she whispered, "I know something we can go home and do that's absolutely free." He looked at her, a glint of afternoon light in his eye, and smiling, they hurried home.

When the war ended and munitions plants closed or were returned to their previous uses, while new automobile factories were being built outside the city, LaRue and Olive went back to Black Oak. Polaris had retired and every now and then Eula went to someone's house to do their hair, but beauty parlors had taken over. The two of them had settled into a kind of union of their own, held together by shared trivia and items from the newspapers that they sat and read together in the evening quiet. LaRue could see that nothing much had changed for Vesta, and she was so wrapped up in planning Dessie's wedding that he couldn't help thinking of the momentum that Ouida's marriage preparations had taken on. LaRue tried to talk to Dessie, but she seemed even more distant from him and Olive than she had been before.

It felt good to get back to Black Oak. As soon as they rested from their trip LaRue went in search of Church, who had enlisted in the Army after a long stretch of not being able to find work. He hadn't really known what he was doing, he told LaRue, hadn't realized what it would mean for him, but he had found out quickly, he said, and he had a story to tell about that, and drawings he had made while he was gone. They went to the neighborhood bar and talked about what they had learned while they were away. A crowd gathered around them, others sharing their lies as well, and among them was the owner of the town's Negro newspaper.

Church told his story about his real initiation into the war, speaking quietly of something that happened to him when he was shipping out for France. He was a member of the Air Corps Service Unit, which, of course, like every other part of the armed services, was segregated, and he was stationed somewhere in Texas, where the men in his unit had become a sort of family, brothers really, called to serve in the righteous fight for things just. Assembled from different places, Church had found that they were unified by their exile and by shared and spent blood.

They were on a train, preparing to ship out, and in their slow journey through America's own battleground, they wound through block-long drowsy towns, past brown women shelling peas on their porches and white men who watched them, turned inside-out with hate. Past genteel plantation homes, and fields of cotton where you could still smell blood. Finally, the train moved into a night of solid darkness, and no one slept.

Each one of them was looking inside for some inspiration that would propel them toward death with patriotic zeal. Each one thought of something that was his own. Church said he could feel it in the darkness, even though no one spoke. Letters written and received and girls they had given their pictures and kissed good-bye. Meals prepared with loving hands. Church said he kept thinking of furniture adorned with those tatted doilies Eula made . . . and the comforting, familiar Sunday rituals at LaRue's house.

The train crept up to the station, lurching forward before stopping, and the men stumbled as they rose to grab their things. They filed off the train and entered the station as a white cadet clapped his hands until the men quieted down. He said that, since the station restaurant was "Whites Only," they could not be served. The men were directed over to a group of wooden benches along the side of the restaurant and the cadet disappeared and then returned with three Negro waiters from the dining room, whom he told to hand out the brown paper bags that held their meals. They opened them up to find lunchmeat sandwiches inside and, disgusted, they began to talk of what people at home might be eating, greens and ham and smothered chicken, macaroni and cheese and potato salad. And then, as

Church happened to look up, something snagged his vision and he froze.

Time stopped and he stared, speechless, stilled in complete understanding and at the same time, disbelief. Church paused in his telling and practically whispered the last part, as the folks in the bar leaned closer. Through the glass of the dining room that had refused to serve them, he could see German prisoners of war being served on china and starched white cloth.

It was quiet when Church got finished talking, and after they drank silently the others shared their own war stories and LaRue told about the huge munitions factories in Detroit where entire sections of a building turned out wheels for tanks or ammunition or propeller blades. He recounted how he had spent a year making airplane wings and explained his task, motioning with his hands. How he had lifted and riveted the pieces of metal of the same size over and over and over again until he had lost track and was doing it by reflex. And how then the person next to him had repeated the next task in line for an entire shift. He never got an idea of how a whole airplane was assembled, as his job had been to piece together only sections of wings.

He told tales about people he had met in Detroit and places he had seen, embellishing their names and their mannerisms to make the stories live. He told about the building of the first freeway and the giant iron stove, and he let them know all about the characters of Paradise Valley.

They asked him about race relations up North, and LaRue described how he had seen people cross over a line in themselves until rioting broke out. He had felt like he was reliving that summer of his youth in Black Oak, that summer when color exploded and patience and tolerance pulled tight and then broke. And he told about the day Olive and her friend had gone to the restaurant at the department store downtown after shopping, dressed in their best dresses and heels, in white gloves and hats. It had been a special, planned celebration and they were excited as the host showed them to their table, so excited that they didn't notice the reticence, the frigidity in his tone. They were brought silverware and the water, and that was that. They waited . . . and waited . . . and waited. For an hour they sat there, realizing, finally, that they would never be served, and suddenly nauseous, Olive rose from her chair and ran to the bathroom to throw up.

His companions shook their heads and LaRue said, "Isn't that something? Heavy duty . . . things up North." And as the fragile morning light took over for the yellow glow of streetlights the tale-telling broke up and LaRue went home to climb in bed and fit his body around Olive's.

The next afternoon the newspaperman came to the house and asked him if he would like to write a column where he could tell his stories. At first LaRue resisted the idea of it, but he said he would give it some thought. He wondered if he was up to the task, but, after discussing it with Olive he decided he should try it for a week or two and told the newspaperman he would work on a story for the next edition.

As LaRue tried his hand at writing his first newspaper pieces, Vesta and Dessie worked at making the wedding she had dreamed of all her life a reality. Although Eula didn't feel well and was too tired to be very involved, Vesta made up for her absence by taking on more and more of the planning herself.

Dessie had lived her life by plotting out each move she made along a predetermined path, and there was little give in her idea of what her wedding should be. She had been selecting fabrics and china patterns and flowers since she was a girl, carefully planning out each detail of the event that she was determined would happen, like everything else, at a certain age. She had wanted to have her first date at sixteen, her first kiss the following year, and to be married, her virginity intact, by the age of twenty-one. A month short of her twenty-first birthday, she had married and left Black Oak.

Dessie was determined to have a "regular" name, and the security the proper husband brought. She didn't want to be a foreigner, and she didn't want the chaos of the past.

You could see from her skin tone and slanted light brown eyes that she was Ruby's daughter, but something in the tight set of her mouth told you she was Vesta's child, too. Dessie assessed her own good and bad points endlessly, concluding that her trim figure and small waistline were balanced by small breasts. She weighed her shapely legs and narrow feet against the eyes that she considered strange in color and shape, preventing her from being really pretty, but she knew she got a lot of points for her mass of long brown hair, which she wore pulled back, the hairline smoothed with Eula's oil, into a neat twist.

She wore ladylike skirts and pastel twin sweater sets, just like the other young women in her social group. She painted her mouth with muted lipstick and her nails a seashell pink. Whatever they were wearing and doing, Dessie wore and did. If they spent their evenings at the Biggs's drugstore, that was where she could be found, perched at the marble counter with a soda. She was well liked and, to Vesta's relief, she was included in outings and parties, where she sat with her girlfriends and traded secrets and fantasies about the kinds of husbands they wanted and the number of children they would have.

Like most of her friends, she had had a sweetheart serving overseas who had written to her. Despite the fact that she barely knew him, she had liked getting his letters and answered with upbeat, newsy notes of her own. She had liked having a soldier boyfriend who wrote to her, but she didn't plan on a future with him when he returned. She had had other things in mind.

Her early pleasure in Zella's company had gradually given way to caution, even though no one ever spoke to her directly of hers and Ouida's love. It had taken her until well into adolescence to figure out that they were lovers, but she knew, from as far back as memory took her, that there was something considered not quite right about the two of them. The silence around their relationship was heavy with discomfort.

Zella had sent her beautiful books, and at Christmas she had always bought the fabrics from which Ouida had made her special sweaters and clothes. For each gift they gave, Vesta directed Dessie to write a thank-you note: "Dear Ouida and Zella, thank you so much for the lovely dress" . . . "thank you for the lovely sweater" . . . "thank you for the lovely skirt." She would say where she had worn it and mention some detail about the gift that she especially liked. But she realized, gradually, that they were foreign, and she didn't want to be a foreigner.

LaRue looked at her one day and was struck with how polished she had become. From the things she said he realized that he didn't know her at all. By the time she had started to grow up he had been around only sporadically, but he remembered sitting with her while she traced pictures, laying sheets of transparent paper down and painstakingly copying the images underneath. He had tried to get her to draw freehand, once Church had noticed that she had a feel for color and shape, but she preferred to get the details exactly right. He had asked her about the animals and trees and houses she drew and they had made up stories together when she was young.

As a little girl she had loved to hear his lively voice and watch his hands moving as they helped to tell a story, Olive urging him on with questions to flesh it out. The unrestrained laughter that happened in their presence delighted Dessie as a child, but as she grew older she began to be afraid that the crazy things he wrote for the newspaper marked him as a foolish misfit. Still, he sometimes got to her, in spite of herself, and suddenly her mouth loosened, transforming her face. As he watched her addressing wedding invitations in her careful cursive hand, he began to sing a medley of the latest love songs, and she released a full smile.

Although she had shown some curiosity about the family, there was so much she hadn't been allowed to learn. And now, approaching what she was sure was the start of her life with plans and certainties, she rejected the discomfort of what she didn't know. She was convinced that everything had gone and would move smoothly, according to designs and laws.

When LaRue mentioned that Ouida had once been married, Dessie asked Vesta about that wedding, and Vesta told about the dress, the ribboned staircase, the flowers, and the yards of ivory lace. But she didn't even mention the thing LaRue remembered most. She never spoke of things gone wrong, and if Vesta had had her preference, Dessie would have thought the entire family had come into existence suddenly, without a past.

Dessie nodded, as usual, taking in Vesta's version of things, but now and then fragments surfaced from the murky recesses of memory. There was the feel of her bare feet sinking into sodden grass and a yellow-green smell as dandelions were braided into her hair. Vesta holding her too, too close. A night of moonlit blood.

The memories came without context, just came, and she clenched her jaws, turning away from the chaos they brought, and reminded herself of what it was she meant to have in life.

She had been dreaming about her wedding as far back as she could remember and it was all set in her mind: the color scheme, whom she would have as bridesmaids, and the sit-down dinner afterward. She wanted it to be like something you would read about, a fantasy wedding that would be the envy of all. When she asked Polaris to give her away he hesitated and asked her if she was sure and then said, "Well, if you are, then I'll do my duty that way."

She had wanted to marry a solid, good-looking man who would be a provider, and if he wasn't from a prominent family, that was okay, as long as he was ambitious and had promise. If he wasn't fair-skinned, that was all right, too, as long as he wasn't dark. She intended to have a family made up of father, mother, and children, and the best of everything. She wanted to marry up and out of the unconventional household that didn't look like anyone else's definition of a family, into which she had been born.

She wanted a nice house and nice things. A fenced-in backyard, and a matching suite of living room furniture, and a china closet full of lovely, hand-painted porcelain plates. Dessie wanted a dream life; she wanted it all.

When she met Emeritus Moore, she was sure he was the one with whom she could have her dream. He was dependable, showing up when he said he would, bearing candy or flowers and chatting amicably with Vesta and Polaris. She liked the fact that he had just returned from the war, and the first time he came to the house he was in uniform and he talked about the burden and privilege of service to his country. Although LaRue asked him about the Army's segregated policies, he said he didn't think it was useful to dwell on such things, and talked about the honor of the fight, only admitting, years later, that he had never "made it overseas." The thing that pleased Dessie most about Emeritus Moore was that he had a future plan. He intended to take the skills he had learned in school and the Army and go North, in search of security and a good office job.

Emeritus impressed her with his bewilderment at the characters who comprised her family, and he hadn't the slightest idea what to think of LaRue, whose first words to him were about Tennessee Coal & Iron Company Jones. Although he appreciated Vesta's precision, he didn't understand her efforts to keep things as they were. He had big goals for himself and Dessie; he aimed to be a success. In his eyes, Dessie was attractive and feminine and she presented herself well. She would be a conscientious homemaker and mother, and would help him get ahead.

The Depression had been especially hard on his family, and he never again wanted to do without. Ashamed of what he had suffered and witnessed, he kept it to himself. He kept to himself that he had watched his father make one pair of socks last a winter season by turning and folding them to rotate the worn-through parts. He kept to himself that they had had grits for breakfast, lunch, and dinner for weeks on end because that was what his mother had been able to trade for her laundering work. Those things and much much more went unspoken as he promised himself that he would never return to those things.

Although Vesta wanted the world for Dessie, she resented Emeritus. She brought it under control, because she knew she wanted the things for Dessie on which she had missed out. Because she wanted her to have a husband and Emeritus seemed a good, reliable choice, she tried to think of him as an addition to the family and experience happiness through and for him and Dessie. But when they moved to Detroit, she never forgave him for taking her child away.

In order to pursue the opportunities he had heard about, Emeritus had planned their move. He told Dessie they were going just before the wedding. That way, he would get a fresh start and leave Black Oak, where he had been poor. He was only too happy to leave Dessie's strange family behind.

Once she had had her fantasy wedding, with all its trappings and gifts, they moved. They went where they felt greater opportunity waited, to a future of comfort and maybe even wealth. Emeritus was certain there were jobs from which he could climb his way to the top and he intended to spend time in the right places and get to know the right people, to figure out the game and play it right.

After the wedding and the leave-taking Vesta threw herself into rearranging the house. Since machines had replaced the handwork she had always done in Foundations, she had retired. Although she still had Polaris and Eula to take care of and keep her company, she felt that with Dessie's leaving, the life had gone out of things. The nights, when she could go back over the things she had accomplished during the day and do needlework until she was sleepy, were bearable. But in the morning, when she woke to find that things were undeniably what they were, she had a hard time getting up. The day awaited her, blank and open, and she lay in her narrow bed, her shoes within reach, until she got the strength to rise, feeling separate. Separate once more.

25

When LaRue and Olive were in their early forties and had just about given up on having children, they had a daughter, whom they named Selena, child of the moon. They were both excited and intimidated by finally getting what they had wanted for so long.

At times LaRue thought he wasn't up to it, that he should have perfected himself before attempting to pass on who he was and what he knew. "I haven't got it right yet," he told Olive while she was pregnant, "who knows what mistakes I'll make." As it got closer and closer to her due date, he felt terrified. And he realized, once their child was born, that there was no easy way to do it, no bridge to bear him safely across.

As he stood next to Selena's crib or held her smallness in his arms, he couldn't believe the fragility of the skull that practically fit within his palm and the tiny limbs that shuddered when she cried. He felt the smooth, unlined feet that wouldn't touch ground for a long time yet. There were no limits on what she required of him, nor, he realized, on his love. It felt boundless and he tried to understand that with her, he would be able to hold nothing back.

When she cried in the night and it was his turn to change or comfort her he sometimes wanted to cover his head with his pillow and not to have to answer to anyone. And though he was frightened, both by the completeness of her need and by the depth of his own feeling, he kept in mind what it had been like to be mothered by Ruby, and vowed to pass on what she had given him. Careful not to forget the thing she had held as a guide, helping her to reach for the bigger part of herself. He accepted that he would give Selena whatever he could. That he would comfort her when she was sick and help her know the beauty, and its opposite, that comprised the world.

He also thought of what Selena brought him, of what he received. She looked to him and he heard the sea sing, realizing the times of hunger and difficulty out of which she had finally, finally, come. When she gripped his fingers he saw the magic of reflections.

Rhea Winters showed up again when she heard she was a grandmother, and Olive decided to give her another chance. She wanted Selena to know both of her grandmothers and had had a dream that the three generations of women could get together, and Selena would make it all right between the two of them. She wanted their story to have a happy ending, but it didn't take long for Rhea to start bad-mouthing LaRue and before she knew it, her fantasy had dried up. Rhea came over periodically to spend time with Selena, but Olive gave up on them understanding each other or being close.

Eula was ecstatic about finally having a grandchild and she offered to sit with Selena. Shrunken and weak, she couldn't handle the baby, even though she said she could. It was clear to everyone that she wasn't well. Everyone noticed that she had lost weight and seemed pale and tired, and that she often had to cancel appointments with her few remaining clients, but if anyone asked her how she felt she was evasive and even hostile, and neither Vesta nor Polaris felt like it was the kind of thing one pressed. It took LaRue following her down to her flat and asking her again and again what was going on for her to admit that anything was wrong.

She had been sick, without telling anyone, for a long time. It had begun with backaches, and bouts of constipation, which had worsened over the course of a year. She avoided going to the doctor, because she couldn't bear to be examined "down there," and even after she told him how she had been feeling, she refused to get help. Inside, she vacillated between assuring herself that it was nothing serious, and a fear that broke her sleep.

By the time LaRue convinced her to be examined and took her himself, it was far too late to do anything at all. Choking growths had spread around her organs, feeding from her until she had nothing left with which to fight. Throughout her illness she never complained and she continued to go to church until she could no longer get out of bed.

Although most of Detroit's factory work had dried up after the war, Emeritus had known someone who referred him for a white-collar job where he was one of only a few blacks. With the prerequisite promotion and savings built up in the bank, they felt it was time to move to the next stage of their marriage. According to their five-year plan, Dessie and Emeritus bought a small two-bedroom house.

It was this move that Dessie had been dreaming about, forever, it seemed. There was so much that she wanted, and so much that she got.

She got her Mixmaster and her pastel kitchen with custom-colored pink stove and icebox. Pink floral curtains with ruffles and a tablecloth to match. Little touches, like the box she hung on the wall for mail and the napkin holder and salt and pepper shakers, which were pretty little pastel-colored houses, with holes in the roof.

She loved entering her kitchen the first thing in the morning, and seeing everything matching, sparkling new and clean. It was all hers, she thought, every last bit of it, just like what you'd see in a magazine. She liked pulling out her set of shiny copper-bottomed pots and pans when it was time to cook, and serving meals she found in cookbooks on her china plates. Her early evenings after work were consumed with casseroles and she pored over cookbooks for the perfect meal, but whenever she got adventurous and produced something like poached salmon, Emeritus looked at it suspiciously and declared that he didn't eat pink fish, that he was a meat-and-potatoes kind of guy.

Dessie was ecstatic when she was asked to join a bridge club. She had learned to play with the hope that they would occupy the stratum of Negro society where women belonged to such clubs, and once she had joined and found that she didn't really like playing bridge, she couldn't imagine herself quitting. On Friday evenings, Emeritus's night with the boys, she fixed her own dinner and waited for him to come home. Saturday nights they spent quietly in their living room.

They hardly ever had company, besides the bridge club that she hostessed once a year, but Dessie always kept the dining room table set with her china and silverware, as if at any moment festivities were about to take place. And although he took little interest in the details of the things Dessie amassed, Emeritus liked opening the front door and seeing his home, with his wife in it, and everything nice, nice. It was what he worked hard for, what he was building, and he was proud.

She got her kitchen and her living room furniture. She got all the things she wanted, in accordance with their plan.

Once they were settled in their new home, it was time to start their family, and with that decision there were plans to make for the coming child. When she wasn't teaching, she immersed herself in decorating the second bedroom next to theirs as a nursery. Emeritus fantasized about how he would play catch with his boy, and take him to work with him and show him off. How he would teach him how to be successful and how to get a woman. How he would teach him to be a man. When Dessie got pregnant, Emeritus started talking about not wanting her to work.

She secretly enjoyed her job. She liked the kids she taught, their wonder and responsiveness, and she enjoyed getting dressed and going to her work, with a sense that something different could happen to her during her day, out there in the world. She enjoyed the lunchtime talks with her fellow teachers, and she liked making out her detailed lesson plans and correcting quizzes. At first she said nothing in response to Emeritus's comments about leaving work, keeping to herself that she was undecided about whether she would return after the baby was born.

Emeritus's promotion settled the question of Dessie's continuing to work. When she was put on bed rest and on leave from teaching he went to her supervisor without her knowledge and informed them that her health was frail, and that after his child was born she would need time and energy to recover and be a mother. He said that she would not be coming back.

He waited until the child was born to tell Dessie, and then tempered her resentment with the understanding of how important the welfare of her and her child was to him. Once he had settled it for her, Dessie decided it was a privilege not to have to work, so she got her feelings in line with this. "Emeritus doesn't want me to work," she told people, as if it were a quaint burden, having a man who cherished her feelings that much. And although Dessie knew better than to brag to Ouida or LaRue, Vesta was impressed, despite the fact that she would always resent Emeritus for taking her girl so far away.

When their daughter, Pearl, was born, Emeritus didn't try too hard to hide his disappointment. He had, after all, wanted a boy. For nine months he had imagined a little image of himself who could carry on his line. "Your name just gets lost with girls," he said.

Once she had become a full-time mother, Dessie was exhausted with feedings and changings and with rocking Pearl to sleep, but when Emeritus got home she tried to have her hair done neatly and be washed and dressed. She drew out her tasks across the long days. Washing clothes on Mondays in the wringer machine downstairs and hanging them to dry out back. Vacuuming and dusting on Tuesdays, and on Wednesdays on, on, and on.

Although Emeritus was wrapped up in his job and unconcerned with what went on with her and Pearl, Dessie worried about whether she was doing the right things as a mother. She consulted the books she had bought to see if Pearl was developing according to schedule, and as Pearl slept she worried her way into the afternoon, wondering if she was giving the baby the right amount of the things she was supposed to have. She worried about when she would have time to get her house clean the way she liked it. And she worried over how white her whites were, if their clothes were ironed well, and whether the lack of starch in Emeritus's collars was holding him back at work.

But when he came home after work he entered a house where

everything was neat and sparkling clean. The smell of dinner drifted out from the kitchen to the vestibule, where one of Vesta's samplers hung on the wall:

When We Put It
To The Test
We Always Find
That Home Is Best

When Eula died, Vesta was with her, holding her hand. The priest had been there the night before to give last rites, and then it had been a matter of waiting, as peace had been achieved. Vesta had drifted off to sleep, waking to find her gone, and after the first panicked moment of wanting to cry out "What? What has happened?", to object that she had missed the important moment after all, she didn't know what to do. She sat there for a while in the realization that everything that had been the focus was suddenly rendered moot. There was nothing, in that time just past the dying, for which to prepare. She looked at her mother, astonished at the way her mouth hung open, slack. She couldn't seem to move from the side of the bed and she couldn't seem to touch her either. There was silence, as everyone else was still asleep.

Vesta slowly unclasped her hands and did what she had wanted to do for as far back as she could remember. She reached out and touched her mother's scar.

Because she knew Eula would want a formal ceremony, Vesta arranged a funeral at the Episcopal church, where all the members of the congregation who had known Eula as a devoted attendant over the years came to pay their respects. Vesta chose a handsome outfit for her, and her best hat and shoes and gloves to bury her in, and she arranged to have a chalice engraved with Eula's name, so that she would never be forgotten.

Women from the church brought food and gathered at the house, and Vesta felt strange to be talking to people about whose lives Eula had shared the minutest details.

This time the wake was at a funeral parlor, but Vesta stood at her mother's casket and thought about the first time she had done this, at her father's family hour. She almost reached out to steady herself against the casket, and suddenly, as if the years had rushed backward and she was engulfed in layers of time that were then, and then and now, she felt her mother's gloved fingers tight, tight, around hers and her voice: "Look, don't touch." She was eight again and surrounded with strangers, even though now she knew their names.

Gasping, Vesta jerked herself back to the present and looked at her mother's hands crossed neatly across her chest, thinking that it was wrong, that those fingers that had known no peace should, instead, have been resting on the serpentine welt: her mark of loss.

Dessie's difficult pregnancy was too far along for her to travel to Black Oak for the funeral, but LaRue went and got Ouida and they all gathered at the house after the wake and told stories about times past. Those who remembered were dwindling, LaRue thought, and the only one left of that generation was Polaris, who seemed frail and lost in reverie more and more.

Since his retirement ten years before, he had led a quiet, settled life, rising at dawn to stir around downstairs making his coffee and reading several newspapers, and then he sat on the back porch or listened to the radio with Eula, neither of them talking much. In the afternoon he took a walk that ended up at a bar where he met old friends and former railroad men for a drink, but he returned by six for the dinners Vesta cooked.

In the evenings they sat in the living room, those who made up the family now, and listened to the radio. Vesta wasn't sure what it would be like to look over and see her mother's chair empty. What would she do without her company, LaRue wondered, even though they didn't talk about anything much. What would she do without the sound of her voice, chattering on and on about the small facts that anchored her in the world.

LaRue could tell that Vesta was disoriented and afraid of all that she might feel in missing first Dessie, and now Eula. The fact that she hadn't cried or expressed her feelings at all let him know that she was in trouble, and he decided to stay on at the house for a while. He saw her at the closet where she still stored the things on which she had stocked up, adding things and arranging them in neat rows. He brought Selena over as often as he could, but Vesta still seemed detached.

In the midst of cleaning the basement rooms after the funeral, Vesta lifted the top of her mother's treasured ginger jar, and saw something peeking through the dark brown petal dust inside. She reached in and pulled out the letter Eula had folded and buried decades before, and stared at the envelope, and its barely readable date. She pushed the letter back down into the jar until its corners were covered, deciding that whatever it was, she didn't want to know. She thought it better not to disturb the dead.

Later, a second letter fell from Eula's Bible, letting Vesta know that her mother had had a part of her life she had kept to herself. It was a letter, dated a mere six months before, when Eula had become housebound, and it was from a gentleman she had known at church for years. He had walked her home each Sunday, but Vesta had never suspected it was anything more than courtesy. But this . . . this was a love letter, she thought as she read.

"My dearest Eula," it began, and there was a tenderness and respect expressed that Vesta couldn't believe. She stopped reading and thought back over the years. She knew that Eula had been there, at home with her and Dessie and Polaris each and every evening and night. She had had no torrid love affair, no callers, no evenings out, but she had had a companion who had loved her. She had had this.

He said that he missed their Sundays, that without her company his day scarcely seemed complete. She had been a bright spot, adding, with her beauty and her loveliness, to his weekly day of praise, and he had the highest regard for her and wished her the best. He had signed it "Mr. Williams" and sent it through the post.

She couldn't believe it, that she had never read past the surface. All those Sundays when she and Dessie had left church right after the service was ended and Eula had stayed on, and Vesta had just assumed it was the Ladies' Auxiliary or Bible Study that held her. But she had been loved, in this quiet, simple way, and had kept it to herself, this thing that was her own.

Vesta's stopped her cleaning, closed the door, and went back upstairs, determined to tackle her mother's belongings at a later date. She joined Polaris in the living room, still thinking of what she had found.

After the family convened to remember Eula, the two of them were left alone. Although Dessie hadn't been able to come, she had sent a lovely spray of roses that Vesta had lifted from the casket and brought home. Once they had turned brittle and brown, Vesta pulled off the dry, aromatic petals and wrapped them in a piece of tissue with the letter from Mr. Williams, and stored them safely at the back of her closet.

26

Not only did Dessie not make it home for Eula's funeral, she didn't return to Black Oak for six years. She felt more and more isolated in Detroit, and less and less able to do anything about it.

She had developed the habit of moving through an idea, taking equal and measured word steps toward and away from actions and ideas. She would get caught in debates with herself about anything, in the bank, behind the wheel, in a supermarket aisle. She could alternate between which brand-name product to buy, hearing the advertisements in her head, and be utterly paralyzed until she asked a bystander for help.

"What do you think?" she said, holding her hand with the Jif peanut butter in it across the aisle, forcing a shopper to halt.

"Excuse me?" came the puzzled answer. "What? What do I think about what?"

"Jif. Jif versus this brand. Is it really true, do you think, what they say about choosy mothers and whatnot, or is it just an advertising ploy, and should we really feel stupid for paying more when it's really the very same thing?" She stood with her arms in the air.

The woman with the child crammed into the too-small seat, legs dangling through the metal cart, had taken a step back from Dessie and stared.

"Well, I don't rightly know. I reckon they're just about the same after all."

"I suppose you're right. But then again, I want to feed my family the best. I couldn't live with the thought of not being a choosy mother . . ."

"Well . . . then I reckon you'd do better buying the Jif. Yup, I'm sure of it. Jif's the way to go."

"But I'd hate to be made a fool of . . . what a dilemma . . . do you really think . . . I guess it's safer to go with the Jif." As she turned back toward the aisle, she saw the woman rounding the corner of the aisle, going so fast she grazed a large display of pork and beans as she fled.

Once she got home from the supermarket she had dinner to plan, and a house to clean. She had a garden to weed and a child who would soon be home from school to get ready for. She tried to be a good mother to Pearl, taking her to after-school dance classes and getting her all the toys and games for which she expressed a desire. By the time Emeritus got home Pearl was often already in bed, which left Dessie struggling to make things perfect.

As soon as she heard him on the porch she mixed him a cocktail and went to meet him and take his coat. He reached for the drink and went to sit in his living room chair, while she put the finishing touches on dinner. She asked him about his day and as he went on and on about what had happened to him at work she tried to be interested and attentive. She had realized when they were first married that it didn't really matter how she responded; she had a series of interjections that she offered, always in the same way, and that seemed to be just what he was looking for.

He asked for a nightly report on Pearl: whether she had done her homework and what she had accomplished in school, and he went to her door and looked in on her. After dinner he read the paper while Dessie cleaned up and then they watched a little television together before turning in. On the weekends they had a family activity, and Dessie didn't have to worry about deciding what they would do, because Emeritus took care of that. They went on a drive through a pretty neighborhood, imagining themselves in one of the houses along the lake, or drove on the winding roads of Belle Isle. They stopped for Vernor's ginger ale or ice cream at Sanders and Dessie and Pearl sat at the counter on either side of Emeritus, trying not to make a mess on the fronts of their matching mother-daughter dresses.

It was during those weekend activities that Dessie found her mind wandering to disruptive images of the past. To colors and shapes and sounds that she couldn't get ahold of, that she couldn't place. And at those times she forced herself to return to her earliest clear memory, of sitting on the floor between Vesta's knees while she smoothed and plaited her thick, unruly hair.

Whenever LaRue visited, he and Ouida stayed up late into the night talking. One humid summer night they sat on the back porch telling each other their stories of love. She confided in him that she thought Zella had been taken, for a time, with someone else. She told him how it had been healed between them, how there had been a mass of birds of paradise, but that she seemed not to want to let her bitterness go. He told her about the times he had been tempted, sorely tempted, but had made himself step back from loving someone else.

"Why did you, though?" she asked him quietly, afraid to say it too loud. "Why did you step back?"

"It's not that people aren't flawed, and there are always other people who catch your eye. That's just being alive," he said, laughing. "We both appreciate fine women." She smiled and then he went on. "You know, Ouida, I think people screw up, but that it can sometimes be forgiven," he said, taking her hand, "depending on what it meant.

"But the reason I stepped back was because if you're building a house with someone, and you love that house, you don't make it with inferior materials, even though they may cost less. You don't smoke in bed, even though that may be your biggest pleasure. And you don't neglect it or let it fall into disrepair. You tend it, maybe not perfectly, but with effort and with love.

"Olive and I have got this big old house going, and it's just full of good stuff. There's the things that go wrong with an old house, too . . . furnace breaks down and paint starts to chip . . ." They both laughed and then he exposed what was harder to talk about. "I don't know what the future holds for me and Olive, Ouida . . . she's never really had the chance to invent herself. And our needs have been bumping up against each other lately quite a lot. She'll always fight the bottle and the death she comes from, and Lord knows, I've got my shit. But right now I want to keep living in that house, broken furnace and all. It has a great wraparound porch. And I'm willing to give up some of the other stuff for the chance to sit and rock on that porch."

Ouida nodded and squeezed his hands. "You give up some of the me for the us."

"But you know what, Ouida . . . those me-you, those me-us lines are the hardest lines there are."

"Who you tellin'?" Ouida said. "Those are lifelong lines, those there, and we're all trying to get them right. Look at Vesta and Dessie for starters. When I think about it, I can't believe all the love there has always been there, but look what it turned to."

"Well, when I think about it," he told Ouida, "I feel angry at myself. I look back on it and I like to think I tried to stop it, but did I? It was as if I could see what she was doing . . . smothering December, from the time she was a little girl. It was like watching her fencing in a tree." He shook his head. "And I should have prevented it, you know . . . now look where December is, stuck with the little end of nothing, 'cause she doesn't even know how to do otherwise."

"Maybe, LaRue," Ouida said gently, for she had wondered, too, what she had done to help, "you did try, but you couldn't have stopped Vesta, 'cause she was hell bent on placing that fence. Maybe we can both try to be there for her, though. Maybe we can try to. And you know, I've heard that sometimes a tree grows right past and around an iron fence or gate that's been set down to bound it, surrounding it so that the gate seems embedded in its trunk."

LaRue grew quiet, and then he told Ouida how he had realized that he had blurred that line, as well.

They had waited so long for Selena, had tried and tried for a child, and when she came they were afraid something would go wrong, afraid that something would come along to take her from them. They had talked a lot about not being overprotective, and had pulled each other's sleeves when they noticed it getting out of hand. Somehow, though, LaRue said, the hardest thing he had done was to love his child, while letting her be herself.

One day, while Olive was away at school, Selena had been home with a cold, and they had been playing quietly. He was telling her about how his parrot friend had hopped a freight train and barely escaped being sold as part of a carload of fruit. He had explained about Pill-addle-pie-a and had gone on to one of the early adventures of Miss Snake.

"I was completely wrapped up in telling her this story," he said, "and I kept asking her what animal she liked best and would want to be. She told me she didn't have a special animal and I just kept on pressing, saying 'Of course you do, just think which one it is.' She argued with me and then fell silent, but I kept right on, determined to make her join in my thing.

"And then, it was as if I stepped outside of myself and could see my desperation to press her into doing what I had done. There I was, Ouida, pushing my little girl to be an extension of me. I froze as a piece of the past flashed before me.

"Selena sat still in her little yellow rocking chair, and when I was finally able to speak I told her I had just remembered something I had to do. I handed her some crayons and paper and told her to sit tight while I was gone, and I staggered to the back porch and asked myself, 'What am I doing? What am I doing here?'

"Suddenly, in the middle of my insisting the shape of my own imagination on Selena, I had remembered an image and in it, I had seen myself. I had had a flash of Vesta, hands outstretched across the sky, trying to protect Dessie, and blocking out the sun."

The next day LaRue sat in the quiet of the afternoon, smelling the aftermath of a morning shower, and watched Ouida brushing Zella's hair.

"I miss that," he said, and they asked him what it was he meant.

"That," he said. "What happens between women."

Ouida kept brushing and waited for him to go on.

"Doing hair," he said. "Remember how Mama Ruby used to let you and Vesta brush and braid her hair, and how sometimes you four women would have a chain going, each one getting hers done and doing someone else's. And there would be this certain kind of talking going on, hushed and familiar. Well, I would be sitting there watching in wonder, at the edge of the circle, but not quite in it, and it fascinated me, the intimacy of it."

"And men don't have that together?" Ouida asked.

"They have their moments of togetherness, but they're different. I've had them with Church, sitting together saying nothing . . . or illustrating a story, and maybe listening to music we've had it, too. But it's less about talking than for women, and the other thing is that men don't touch like that."

He looked over at the two of them, and even though they weren't touching, it seemed as if they were. They were in the same rhythm. "I've had times with Olive, when things were right between us and the world seems to stand still for a bit. And there you are together, in this secret pause that's the center, that's just yours. People have that with lovers, and even then, it's rare. Outside of that it's even hard to find, indeed.

"You two have it . . . and Olive and I do. I guess it's family, that's what it is. It's having family with someone."

All three of them were quiet and then LaRue said, "You all spoiled me, you know," he told Ouida, "you and Vesta. You let me be a part of it, and we would lie on the floor and make leaf books or talk, or give back rubs or braid hair. And for the rest of my life I'll have this standard of intimacy. That girlfriend thing, that I would never find with men."

Soon after that they started getting hungry and they went in the kitchen and began fixing dinner. That night, after Zella had gone to bed, he and Ouida sat at the kitchen table having tea. He could see that she was having a hard time getting up from the table and he told her to stay put, he would get what she needed. Refusing his help, she struggled to her feet and refilled her cup. He asked her whether her legs hurt and she told him that although they did, she couldn't focus on such things and still go on.

"Pain's an old friend," she told him, laughing. It was something she never talked about, but he wanted to know what she had to say and he asked her. She told him about the coping game she had secretly played in the hospital years ago, after he had come to see her and she had chosen life, and many times since: in an hour it will still throb; in a day it will wane; in a month it will scar; and in a year it will fade.

"There have been times, Bone, that I haven't wanted to live. You know. Better than anyone, you know how I have had to fight sleep . . . and had to struggle to make the decision to feel pain in order to get the rest of life."

He said, "Well, you did decide to wake up, didn't you? You decided to live?" She said, "Yes, I did. And I've never, in all these years, told you how it all began."

Ouida told him, almost forty years later, what he hadn't known. She told about the dividing road and the stirrup ropes above that kitchen table, and the crack in the ceiling that had haunted her for the rest of her life. She told him about her terror and about her spreading blood, and about Zella's arms. And how she had held on with the story of Ulysses's quest and stayed alive in the wet cave filled with blooming plants and moist soil, in which she had managed, finally, to sink her hands.

It felt good to tell LaRue the thing that had been Zella's and hers, and he was right there with her as she told it, as if they were in the past and present, too, as if he was feeling it with her, somehow making it his own. While she was telling him, she took the lapis stone from her cherished fabric-covered box, worn by the fingers' touch and by the years, and placed it in his palm.

"Mine's been a quiet settled life, at least in outward terms, but you've done some traveling, Bone, the kind we used to talk about, starting with that first train trip. You've been all over the country seeing what our people have been doing. I've rarely left this house, and I'm not sure where I've gotten, after all these years."

"There's different ways of going places," he said, and "we're always arriving. After all, you got your hands in that soil, didn't you? You got them in there and those barriers, they did give way."

III

. . . Yet in languid
frenzy strove, as
one freezing fights off
sleep desiring sleep;
strove against the
cancelling arms that
suddenly surrounded
me, fled the numbing
kisses that I craved.
Reflex of life wish?
Respirator's brittle
belling? Swam from
thc ship somchow;
somehow began the
measured rise.

From "The Diver," Robert Hayden

27

He said it all the time now, over and over again, fixing on a single memory of unjaded pleasure, an afternoon spent between father and son.

It had started after Polaris retired, and it was just him and Vesta in the house. Sitting around the table during Sunday supper, a little smile would break and he would start to shake his head and rock. Soon, it was practically all that Polaris Staples said.

The first time he had said it, completely unrelated to Vesta's stream of conversation about her day at work, she had stopped and put down what she was doing, and stared flatly at him.

He repeated it, chuckling to himself: "Do ya like stewed rabbit? Ain't the gravy good?" and went on eating as she tilted her head and searched for a context. When she couldn't think of one, she shrugged her shoulders and kept on eating, looking over at him every now and again.

The next time it happened, they were sitting together in the living room, when he turned to her and waited for her to look up. When she did, he said it, with the same nostalgia as the first time, his mouth rising at the corners. She put her mending down, thinking back for something that would give it meaning, and came upon a memory he had shared about a hunting trip he had taken when he was only twelve.

More than once he had mentioned it, one of the few times that he and his father had shared, a morning stolen from farm work and his many brothers and sisters for hunting, a singular moment that was theirs alone.

She recalled that his memory had been filled with the thick moist smell of the woods and the shifting patterned light descending through a tapestry of overlapping leaves. And Polaris had finally been old enough to go along.

Vesta looked over at Polaris, the smile of remembrance still on his face, and tried to see a boy's face hidden in his thickened features, trying to remember what he had shared. He had spoken of the awful smell of gunpowder, and of his fear and his wonder, as he and his father entered the unknown realm of the woods. There was the waiting, and the stalking, and Polaris's own mixture of horror and triumph at the helpless creature he had felled. He had told Vesta something about a recitation of thanks, for the bounty and the blessing. The peace that his father showed him how to make with the hunted. And it came back to Vesta, what he had told her about his father's calloused hands, showing him how to tie the animal by its feet, and the two of them returning home, side by side.

And Polaris waiting anxiously as his mother skinned, seasoned, and cooked the rabbit, while he asked her over and over again if it was ready yet. And his father had sat there waiting as he took his first bite, and asked him, chuckling, "Do you like stewed rabbit? Ain't the gravy good?"

Vesta had placed the phrase, but in the weeks that followed, it vexed her to no end that he had to say it over and over, "strumming on her last nerve." One night he sat at the table and smiled while she cleaned the kitchen, tasting it again, the sweet tenderness and smooth, brown, peppery gravy, feeling the link between father and son.

Vesta stood bent over, the entire top half of her body in the oven. She scraped at the dripped grease that had burned into the metal of the oven, pausing to spray some more oven cleaner, and she heard the sound of Polaris's chair grinding against the linoleum and his faint chuckle and began to whisper into the oven as her hand made furious scraping strokes, "Don't say it. Don't say it. If you say it, I'll scream." She clenched her teeth. "One more time, and I think I'll scream."

She braced herself.

"Do ya . . ." he launched in.

She pulled her body out and slammed the oven door. His chair thumped to a standstill and his mouth hung open. He looked like he had lost his way.

When she saw his face, she felt suddenly small, and put her spoon down and crossed the room. "I swear, the mess life gets you into . . ." she muttered to herself. Leaning over the table across from him, she gave him back his one small good thing."I didn't hear you, Papa Staples. What was it that you said?"

He looked at her blankly for a moment and then smiled.

"Do ya like stewed rabbit? Ain't the gravy good?"

Not long after Polaris got stuck at stewed rabbit, he died of a heart attack, and Vesta was left alone in the house. Dessie came from Detroit for the funeral and the wake, and then returned to Emeritus. She had announced the night she arrived, as she came through the door, that she had to get back to him and make sure that he was eating properly, and that everything at home was taken care of. Vesta turned away and sucked her teeth at that, and busied herself with preparations for the wake. Everyone could feel an uneasiness between Olive and LaRue, and he and Zella were in and out helping with arrangements, and Ouida came and stayed with Vesta until she decided what to do and where to go.

After the wake, Olive put Selena to bed and turned in herself, but Zella stayed over and the rest of them sat up into the night drinking and reflecting on the past. "How long ago was it that we all lived here together?" Vesta asked. "Must have been a hundred years."

"Well, I think it's time to sell this house and move somewhere new," Dessie said. "There's too much of times gone by in here, that is if you ask me."

"There's lots of memories between these walls," added Ouida. "We all grew up here."

They were quiet, until LaRue poured some brandy, leaned back, and said, "Remember that time, Ouida, when we were sneaking around listening in on everyone's conversations? We were gathering information for that play we were writing together, and you were taking notes with your ink pen and notebook on the way people behaved. I used to have you crawling along the floor once Mama Eula, Mama Ruby, and Papa had gone to bed. Listening for information. Soon as we saw their lights go out under the door, we'd slip out of bed, remember?"

Ouida chuckled at the memory. "LaRue, I don't know when I've thought about that. We were sure a handful, you and me.

"The time I remember best," Ouida said, "was the time Papa caught LaRue coming in the house in Papa's one pair of good Sunday shoes. Not only did LaRue have them on, but he had stepped in a pile of dog poop on his way home, and he was bent over trying to scrape it off. When Papa walked in, LaRue just opened his mouth. It's one of the only times I've known him to be at a loss for words.

"That, of course, was temporary. Papa was so mad, he stood there speechless in the middle of the floor . . . I myself could have sworn there was steam coming through his ears . . . and I just looked from one to the other, waiting for the fireworks. Papa finally said, 'Boy, I've a mind to knock you into the middle of next week.' And LaRue straightened up and looked earnestly at Papa and said, 'Well, Papa Staples, if you must, could you make it a Thursday, 'cause I've got an appointment to go to on Friday night.'

"Papa couldn't believe it. He just stood there, and there was this long silence, until someone—was it Vesta?— laughed."

"Now you know it wasn't me," Vesta answered. "It was always you that laughed, Ouida. You and LaRue. The two of you were famous for getting into trouble, cutting up. Matter of fact, everyone always expected that of you all, and they thought Dessie was good, but the truth was, Dessie smiled sweetly, said, 'Yes, mah'am,' and went right on doing exactly as she pleased."

Dessie laughed and denied it. "Now I was never a problem. I was a good solid student in school, I helped around the house, I married a good upstanding man . . ." Everyone looked at each other. "What?" Dessie said. "What? You all need to stop. Anyway, Papa was glad that he at least didn't have to worry about me. Vesta and I never gave him cause for concern."

"Who knows what concerned Papa," said Ouida. "He was hard to know. You know I don't think I ever had a *real* conversation with him."

"But he was there," Vesta said.

"Oh, he was there," Ouida continued, "even when he couldn't be around in body, he was working hard to provide for us . . . and he did love Mama, I believe."

"You know, I wonder . . . I know they still did it when we were growing up, we've got Dessie here as proof, but I wonder if it was good, if it was hot?"

"LaRue!" Dessie exclaimed. "You *would* think of that! About your parents you wonder such a thing?"

"Well, yes, Dessie . . . You know it's a universal, this making love stuff. And I wonder what it was like for them. Just a 'spousely duty,' or was it rich? I never heard them, but I imagine it went on. Everybody does it. Even *you*."

"Well, even if it did, do we have to talk about it? Do we even have to think about it, LaRue? You really do redefine tacky sometimes."

"Well say," he added, laughing, "along the lines of tacky, how's Emeritus? Is his love still potent and true?"

Vesta listened as Dessie and LaRue dug at each other, smiling inwardly at any criticism of Emeritus, while Dessie got visibly upset. Vesta mended her torn cloth and replaced her missing buttons more and more furiously, thinking of the time when she had heard Ruby and Polaris moaning late at night. She had been so embarrassed, and shocked that people that old still carried on, that she had buried her head under a pillow so as not to hear. She looked over at Zella massaging Ouida's neck and started to blush.

Ouida spoke up again. "I guess what I'm asking is, did I really *know* him? Does anyone ever know anyone else," she continued, "except for fleeting moments when you stop, caught by some familiar sound or smell or tone? And that thing that caught you is such a small thing, like a mouth raised and opened to falling rain . . ." She glanced at Zella. ". . . a small thing that makes you say, 'Yes, I recognize this person. This is someone that I know.'

"And maybe, too, it's just how fathers are," Ouida said. "But what

I mean is this: what were the things that he noticed . . . in a room full of stuff, what did he see?"

There was a long pause and then Vesta said, "In a way, I knew him best, all the time we spent together in these last years. But we mostly didn't talk; we just sat and enjoyed each other's company, without having to say a thing. I guess I can say that I have a sense of him, not from talking, but just from being together. And one thing's for certain, the stewed rabbit thing, it wasn't just nonsense . . . I remember him telling me a story that gives it some sense." And she went on to tell them about Polaris and his father facing the woods together for the first time.

When Vesta got through telling the story, Dessie said, "Funny, but it just never struck me that Papa was ever a boy."

LaRue told about the time he had ridden with Polaris to Chicago. He was only seven, but he had talked so much about going somewhere, picking Polaris's brain about how trains felt, and what it was like to watch the world pass from a square of glass, to sit there at the window as hills turned into factories and then back into lakes and fields. He had badgered Polaris for details, for the feeling of motion underfoot, and the smell of metal and steam, and one day he arranged the dining room chairs like train seats, with an aisle in the middle, and asked them to eat dinner that way, while he served them from a tray. Polaris finally told LaRue that he could come along, if he promised to behave.

"I can't believe LaRue is still talking about that train trip," Dessie said. "I didn't even come along for another decade or so, and I've still been hearing about it all my life. He's probably been all the way across the country by now, on much fancier, much faster trains . . . he's maybe even been on an airplane . . . and he's still talking about that sorry little trip with Papa, when he had to sit way back in the colored section and be treated as the child of a porter, whose job it was to serve white people. You are a puzzlement, LaRue. I swear you are. I think you've got an extra card in your deck . . . you're playing with fifty-three."

Everyone laughed at the comment that was so like her, and LaRue said, thinking of his favorite Spanish knight, "Better a card too many than a card too few."

And then Ouida and LaRue, in the exchange of a glance, decided to tease Dessie. "You know, Dessie," Ouida started, "I remember something that happened when you were a little bitty thing. You were far too young to remember."

"Yup." LaRue picked it up. "I swear on high it happened, and it went like this: now we all know Dessie has always been in a hurry. Somethin' to do with being a menopause baby," he said, turning to her. "It was as if you always felt you had to make up for arriving late. So you walked at six months, and talked at nine."

"LaRue, it's beyond me how you lie," Vesta broke in. "Nobody walks and talks that early, and Dessie was no exception."

Ouida jumped in to help LaRue out. "Un hunh. She did too. I was there when she said her first words. I think they were, 'Do you take credit?'"

Everyone laughed, including Dessie, and then LaRue went on. "I remember that time when Dessie was about five years old, and her personality was already set, as you can tell from this story

"Ouida was in Black Oak and she was on a sewing jag, and she and Vesta were taking all kinds of things apart and remaking them into clothes for Dessie. Times were hard, and Ouida wanted to have a birthday present for Dessie, so she eyed an old lamp shade, and an idea popped into her head. She and Vesta washed it and bleached it and ironed it, and then Ouida made it into a little linen jacket for Dessie. It was the cutest thing you ever saw, but Dessie didn't want that lamp shade dress. She cried and cried, 'cause she had seen where it came from and she wanted something new, but they made her wear it anyway. She pouted and pouted, until everyone on the block carried on about how pretty it was like you wouldn't believe. Then you couldn't get her out of it . . . she even wore it to bed, I think."

"Now you know that's plain fabrication!" Dessie cried. "I always liked that jacket. You and your lies."

"Oh my God," Ouida laughed. "I knew you'd deny it, but we were all there, and we know just what happened. Tell your friends," Ouida said, slapping her thigh, and LaRue finished for her, "I done told mine."

They all sat sipping their drinks, and then Dessie put hers down and said, "My vantage point is different from all of yours, because I was so much younger, and you know what I remember most about growing up is the burden of that weird name I had, which Vesta, thankfully, relieved me of. And everything always seemed so crazy around here. Vesta was there, always, like a mother to me, but I remember feeling like I didn't really know or understand you two," she said, gesturing to LaRue and Ouida. "It was like a carnival sometimes around here. Lying . . . and performing . . . I never knew what anyone was going to do . . . it was so foreign from the way other people lived."

Zella had been quiet most of the night, but there was something about Dessie that tended to make her want to start something. "Tell me, December," she said, calling her as she always did by her given name, "how *do* other people live?"

Dessie never could seem to be at ease with Zella, once she had realized the thing that went unspoken, but was always there. It just made her squirm, the thought of Zella and Ouida together, and as Emeritus said, they were beauties, both of them, who didn't have to be like they were. "If you didn't know about them," she often thought, "you'd think they were just like me." The thing she couldn't fathom was their lack of embarrassment, of shame. She thought she hid it, but her looks, her body language, said how she felt without her uttering a word. She looked kind of sideways at Zella and said, "What?"

"How *do* other people live? I sure would like you to tell me, because in my experience, there are as many ways of living as there are people." Dessie kept looking in her direction but avoided her eyes and her feet began to tap wildly, until her white pump flew off and landed in the middle of the floor.

"Well that's the truth," LaRue said, looking at Dessie's shoe, which no one made a move to retrieve, as he took Zella's hand, "and each individual sees the very same events with a different eye." He couldn't help noticing how dirty the bottom of her naked foot was. "And you know, this all reminds me of something Tennessee Jones told me about the Indians of the Great Plains. The way they would document their history, you see, was with something called a 'Winter Count.' It was a way of marking time from one year to the next, by recording, with symbols or pictures, on a buffalo hide or speaking it out loud, a single memorable happening. The sequence of recorded events was the count, and the thing was, there might be many winter counts in progress at the same time, with each person marking time by the choice of a different event.

"It's like we all have our own winter counts going, and we've chosen different things to record. Say we all made one for this past year . . . what would you all put on yours?"

Vesta laughed and said, "Stewed rabbit. That's been the overriding thing about this year. And of course the gravy, which is good." They all chuckled, knowing it had driven her crazy, and because even though it was sad, it was funny, too.

"What about you, Ouida?" LaRue asked. "What would be your thing?"

"One thing? Only one?"

"Well maybe two. It doesn't have to be *all* that happened, you know, but the essence of things."

"Okay, okay, let's see." She looked at Zella and chose one thing that had within it two. "Birds of paradise," she said, and Zella added, "Ditto," but they wouldn't explain why.

Dessie looked up to find everyone staring at her. Far away in thought about the frozen unrest she could feel at home, she hadn't even heard them call her name. She still hadn't picked up her shoe, deciding to conquer her embarrassment by pretending it wasn't there. She looked up, realizing that she could never tell them what was going on with Emeritus, and said, "Well . . . we redid the new house this year, which is good . . . and I'm just having a ball choosing new curtains and slipcovers, making it all new and fresh, and uh . . . Pearl . . . she's doing well in school, got all Satisfactories, and . . .well it's been a real good year for us."

They could all recognize, as the words rushed forth, that she was presenting a veneer, but no one had ever known how to reach her, how to make her open up. They were quiet. They sipped their drinks.

LaRue thought for a minute while he tilted his glass and watched his brandy wash the sides amber, and then told them about the shooting star he had seen. He tried to describe the star and the reverence it had made him feel so that they could see it, making his winter count. That unforgettable fiery arc of light it had made across the blue-black sky.

After the ceremonies for Polaris were finished, Vesta seemed lost. She straightened up the house, room by room, and then returned to where she had started and straightened up some more. Just as she had each week in the years since Eula's death, she dusted around the ginger jar, the letter within sunk in the powder of roses and still unread. She bought shelf paper and rearranged the pantry food. She fixed leaky faucets and bleached the grout between the bathroom tiles. She washed the windows, from the inside, and polished every piece of wood in the house.

When she finished her dusting she broke out her iron and attacked a pile of laundry. When that was done, she set in to darning and replacing buttons. But she wasn't ready yet to go through Polaris's clothes, and the door to his room remained closed.

The attic, she thought, was a project that needed tending to, especially if she decided to sell the house and move to an apartment. She would begin working on it while Ouida did some sewing, to begin to figure out what to throw away, what to give away, and what to keep. There were lifetimes of things up there, saved against the not-knowing of the future. Balls of string and empty gift boxes. Bits of wrapping paper long ago yellowed and creased. Outgrown clothes that might come back in style or fit someone not yet born.

She carried a chair up the narrow attic stairs and planted it and her bunch of cleaning rags in the middle of the floor. Standing in one place, she turned slowly, absorbing the details of the room where she had played as a child. Since then, she had only come there to put away the things either cherished for passing down, or caught in that limbo between keeping and discarding.

The walls were yellowed, with lighter scars from patched leaks, and the cloth window shades were crumbling and veiny. "It smells close and old up here," she thought, running her toe across the hardwood floor, now sprinkled with plaster dust. She walked across the room and touched the edge of a shoe box, almost lifting the faded dusty top, and moved on to brush the edge of the cedar chest. "Who knows what's in here," she thought, grasping the lid and then pulling back. "Too much. Too much."

She prodded the boxes and bags, but couldn't seem to open any of them; she wasn't prepared. Stooping under the slanted front wall, she forced the little window open and rubbed the pane of glass with a rag to see the view from there, and somehow, it was so small, the stoop and the steps and the little piece of city lawn that had been filled with flowers when she was a child. Looking down on the place where she had lived, she felt as if she could see all the comings and goings of her life that had happened since she had arrived, that night of running, at this place.

She could see her mother's wild and bleeding hair, and the flowing nightgown that stood out against the night, exposing her nakedness. And then there were boxes and furniture, all being carried downstairs, and she saw herself, holding an inlaid picture of birds. Vesta looked up to the sky, a cloudless blue, and heard the sound of something tearing, the sound of a cry.

She gripped the slanted wall next to the window and steadied herself, and then she shut the window and turned to her task. She couldn't stand there and muse on the past, about which nothing could be done. Decisions had to be made, and she was the only one to do it. Surveying the room for a place to start, she settled on a corner piled high with boxes and discarded furniture, dragging the chair she had brought with her across the room to sit down.

The first thing Vesta came to was a metal strongbox. Forcing its rusted edges apart, she found that it was filled with Polaris's things: papers, greeting cards, mementos, a few photographs. She looked in the box, closed it, and put it aside, not yet ready to confront the bits of things to which his life had been so recently reduced.

She opened a shoe box, placing it as Ouida's from the size

stamped on the end, and found a pile of Polaroids. Picking one up, she recalled the wonder of the black box that had spit out their likenesses, groups of them crowding round to see their images take shape. This one still had the little triangular piece with the staggered edges attached to the end. She looked at it, and at a few others, decided that they were LaRue's, and put them aside to start a pile for him to look through. Next was a bag of children's books that had been his, a volume of fairy tales among them. There was a box of handmade Christmas ornaments and the leaf book they had sat on the floor and made, its pages veiny and crumbling and the leaves within turned to dust. And with those things was a half-completed piece of needlepoint, an old hat, a headless doll with leather limbs.

Everything she came across held some piece of their lives . . . a small child's glove with a hole she remembered making . . . the handle of a brush . . . things that were to anyone else merely junk. However tarnished, however obsolete these things were, she was connected to each one of them somehow. She had to stop and pause every now and then on her way through the piles and piles of things they had saved, careful to maintain her footing in the here and now.

As she moved the boxes and bags, squatting among all of LaRue's stuff, she exposed the tip of something yellow, a small piece of furniture, she thought, that jogged a hazy memory. She moved the things around it until it stood alone: a child's rocking chair that was now chipped and missing its seat. Rubbing the dust and grime off with a rag, she tried to place it, and then said aloud, "LaRue . . . yes, he would get a kick out of this." Sitting down on the floor then, she forced herself to stay in the present and reached for the next box.

She began the pile for Ouida with a book of pressed flowers, a school project she had made as a girl. Most of the petals had long since disintegrated and settled into the binding, leaving only stems attached to the torn pages. Underneath the remains of flowers were identifying labels, printed with a deliberate child's hand.

She came across stacks of clippings from the colored newspaper, and unfolded their yellowing pages. The Winters Brothers' advertisements seemed to have anchored the community across decades. Those and the social announcements, "Interchangeable," she thought, from year to year. "Niggers, trying to be something they're not." These went mostly into Dessie's pile, where there was very little else. Dessie didn't like "old things" much, and had told them during her visit of the brand-new linoleum she had had installed in her kitchen, and about her Sunbeam mixer, "the best of its kind." Dessie said used things depressed her, and she exchanged them as quickly as possible for new.

Five piles were taking shape around the room, one for LaRue . . . one for Ouida . . . one for Dessie . . . her own . . . and the discards, to which Vesta added things and then took them back.

As she was getting up to quit for the day, she noticed a small closet three feet high. She thought there must be something special behind the door, but when she opened it, she found more of the same. There were books, and letters, and linen they had embroidered as girls. She lifted the tops of boxes and then put them back to tackle another day. But there was one box that was bigger than the others, and it was wrapped in tissue and tied with string.

Vesta extracted it from the pile, carried it into the room, and put it on the chair. She untied and unwrapped it and stared at the thing, and then she put the top back on and went downstairs to show Ouida what she had found.

"It's still beautiful," she said, as she came through the door with the box in her hands. "You won't believe what I found."

Vesta opened the box and dug through the tissue, as Ouida put down the finishing work she was doing on a dress. Vesta lifted something from the box that seemed to Ouida like a vestige of someone else's life. She blinked to orient herself, and then looked at Vesta. "Oh my goodness, the bell from my wedding cake."

"Can you believe it? Isn't it something," Vesta said, looking at her hands as they held it out to Ouida, who made no move to take it.

They looked at each other, and then at the bell, until Vesta lowered it back into the box and sat down. Each was quiet, returning to the afternoon when Ouida had married Junior Biggs.

"You were lovely," Vesta whispered.

"I was scared."

Vesta looked at her and answered, "Well . . . yes. I imagine you were nervous, the wedding night ahead of you and all," Vesta said.

Ouida looked over at her. "No one could have missed the fact that I was nervous . . . I even dropped my bouquet . . . but that's not really what I'm talking about."

"Well, you were a beautiful bride, and it was the loveliest of June days."

"Vesta," Ouida said, "it was hot as hell."

"Hot?" Vesta asked. "Was it really hot?"

"I promise you, Vesta, it was religiously hot."

"Oh," Vesta said, "I guess it was rather warm."

"It was so damn hot that night, that I wouldn't let Junior come near me. It was too hot for loving. It was too hot to touch. And don't you remember Mamie Banks fainting? Boom, she hit the floor, just as we said our 'I Do's.'"

"*That* little detail I've tried to forget."

"Well it happened, and it was the richest event of the day, far as I can remember . . . that and the cake." Vesta had a sick look on her face at the mention of that. "God," Ouida continued, "all heads turned toward Mamie Banks, and then back to Junior and me, as if it hadn't happened, leaving Mama Eula to fan her until she came to. And by the way, I should have known better than anyone how hot it was, all done up in flounces and lace and layers of cloth. Curious custom, it is, to arrange for the bride's supreme discomfort at the absolute *apex* of her life. There's something in that . . . something to think about, for sure."

"Well, Ouida, everyone thought you were lovely, and the perfect couple, too, what with the Biggs's money and such. It was an elegant affair, if I do say so myself."

"Yeah, that bitch Rhea Winters, who Mama Eula insisted we invite. Her, and lots of other people who talked about us over the years."

"Well, *that* day, nobody said a negative word. There was nothing to say, because it was all done perfectly, and you were the perfect bride . . . I always thought I would do it just that way again . . . and June weddings are so nice."

Ouida looked away, and lifted her sewing to take a stitch.

"I wish Mama Ruby could have been there," Vesta said softly, after a while, "to see you married and all."

And Ouida rested her sewing in her lap and thought about how she had wished for her mother that day, as Eula had flitted around playing hostess, a pink hat pulled down over her scar. She wondered if Ruby would have been silent while she went through with it, and whether she would have kept her from feeling ashamed for letting Junior push her into love the way he had, compelling her to turn it into something. Ouida had known, as she promised her eternal love and obedience, that it wouldn't last, and as it turned out they had barely made it through a year.

Polaris had escorted her through the invitees, delivering her to Junior without asking Ouida a single question. He had probably never understood what she had seen in Junior, and had felt as if he didn't comprehend anything at all that women did, she imagined. He had probably thought of himself as leaving things to Eula, with the pondering of love just not being the province of fathers.

"I remember," Vesta said, "that you even cried, and we had to re-powder your face . . . Funny, isn't it, how there are sometimes tears of joy."

Ouida looked quickly over at Vesta in disbelief. She didn't know, she didn't know at all. It had happened so many years ago, in what seemed like another lifetime, and Vesta had never known what it had been for her. She looked away and remembered her descent from upstairs into that very living room where they now sat, Junior standing in front of the fireplace, waiting for her.

As Vesta chattered on about the perfection of that day, Ouida remembered how she had felt she couldn't get her breath, all dressed up in binding white like an ornament, suffocated by the heavy lie of it all. The most important day . . . the most important day . . . the most important day. She had wanted to scream and run, but duty had propelled her down the last few stairs and through the group that stood waiting. It was what a girl wanted, wasn't it? And it was what she had earned.

"White," she thought, as she heard herself being given over to him, "for purity." The fiction had risen within her as she thought of a lifetime of persistent, joyless fumbling and a marriage to be acted, like a play.

"White," she said to Vesta, who looked up and smiled.

"Yes, you were a perfect picture. And everything was white, even the little roses in your bouquet . . . as I watched, I thought you were the perfect bride. You were radiant."

"Scared," she said, almost desperately.

"You were scared. And I was frightened, too. As I saw you come down those stairs, your hair wound all around with flowers . . . a princess really, is what you looked like . . . a princess in white . . . and I was a little bit scared because I knew that I would never be there, in front of the fireplace, with Polaris giving me away. That's what I was scared for . . . I was scared for myself. And I never was there, I mean, standing where you stood."

Vesta continued, "And as for you . . . well, who wouldn't have been afraid? No one to explain it . . . to tell you what to expect. Believe me, all of that business is pretty scary, when you think about it."

Ouida looked at Vesta as if across a gulf, and then spoke. "It wasn't what you think, Vesta. It wasn't sex that scared me, we had already done that. Sex had bound me to him, Vesta, and that's why I married Junior, because I thought I had to . . . I don't know . . . dignify it somehow. Make it right."

Vesta watched her carefully. "Mmmm. I see. Well, fear, fear of what's unknown . . . still . . ."

They sat silently for a long while, until Ouida finished what she had to say. "It wasn't the unknown that scared me, you see. It was what I already knew. I was scared, Vesta, of life without love."

Vesta looked away, and then stood up and went over to the bell. She pushed down the tissue, and replaced the top. "Well," she asked, before leaving, "but don't you miss being married? Don't you miss it sometimes?"

Ouida just looked at her and thought, without feeling able to explain, "I am married, Vesta. I am."

28

Vesta decided to distribute the things she had found in the attic. She knocked on LaRue's front door and got no answer. She knocked again, shouting his name, and he called to her from the backyard where he was fixing an old phonograph. "Sister, come on back here. I'm in the middle of fixing this record player here. Come around back."

She brought the rocking chair to the gate and said, "LaRue, I found something, just an old piece of the past, really, when I was up in the attic. I thought you might remember it. And I brought a box of other things I identified as yours."

"Un hunh," he said without raising his head, unable to tear himself away from his project. "I've almost got this thing working, and then I'll look and see what you've got there. This thing is just stubborn . . . as if it had a mind of its own . . ." He chattered on.

"Is it something from your appliance purgatory?" he asked, without raising his smiling face to hers. "The Depression years being over," he went on, "you might let go of those broken mixers and toasters that you'll never get working again . . . Now this here phonograph is almost rehabilitated, like me . . ."

She stood at the gate for fifteen minutes, while he told her all about what he was doing, and then she got fed up. "Look here, Bone. I may not have a job to go to, but I'm busy. I haven't got all day to stand here and wait for you to finish whatever foolishness you're in the middle of." At that, she carried the chair over to the garage. "I'll just put it with the rest of these old forgotten things, and when you can tear yourself away, have a look at it, and call me if you've got time."

As she left, he chuckled and said he'd phone her later, and called out to her, "Sister . . . I'm gonna play that sad sad song you're singin' on this phonograph, once I've got it fixed."

She went from there to the post office and mailed several cartons to Ouida. Dessie's things fit into a very small box.

Ouida called her when she received the packages. "Good God, Vesta," she said, "I got the boxes you sent. All this stuff I'd forgotten even existed. I've only been through one box so far. What all is in here?"

"The past," Vesta responded, matter-of-factly. "If you've got a use for it, it's yours."

The year Polaris died Olive's and LaRue's love was truly tested. She had been realizing for a while that there was a hole in her life, and for a few weeks, she had tried, again, to fill it with gin. He fought turning away and asserting that it would disappear, but confronted her to talk of what was missing. They decided that she needed to find her own way, as he had been able to do, and she enrolled in a two-year biology program in a town a few hours from Black Oak. LaRue knew that only if he let her go, was there a chance that their love would last.

He took care of Selena while she was away, and she returned on weekends or they visited her where she was. When she was finished with school she had a job waiting in a laboratory in Black Oak. He missed her terribly and was afraid sometimes that she would not return, but he kept in mind the good parts of that house he had told Ouida he was building with her, and tried to work on the things that needed attention and care. Meanwhile, to make ends meet, he worked as a clerk in an office downtown, and continued to write his columns for the newspaper about inventing a family with a different shape.

That winter, LaRue went to spend some time with Ouida and

Zella. He and Ouida sat in the kitchen, looking out at the January landscape. Despite the falling snow, Zella was out there, barbecuing ribs on the grill out back, and LaRue was mixing up a pitcher of margaritas.

Zella came through the door with a plate of steaming ribs. She put it on the counter and poured herself a drink. "What are you all talking about?" she asked, and Ouida told her.

LaRue looked at the plate of ribs and patted his stomach. "I've gotta watch out here 'cause every time I come to visit I add some breadth to my middle. You sisters sure do eat, and you know what else? This all reminds me," LaRue said, gesturing with his hands, "of a story I need to tell you. It's the history of the world, from the beginning to the present."

"The history of the world?" Zella said.

"Yeah. Listen. Just about everyone belongs to one of two groups. There's a large group of people who can't think while they eat. As long as they're eating, they will not be thinking. Well there's also a very, very small group of people that can think while they eat, and that group is divided into two subgroups. One is after power and money, and while they're eating they're thinking about how they can get more power and money. The other subgroup are what I call the Do-gooders, and while they're eating they're thinking about how there are people in the world who are not eating.

"So the way it breaks down is this. The ones who are after power and money, it takes just a few of them, perhaps hard work, and definitely luck, and they can achieve power and money. But the Do-gooders, they want to start a movement. They want to go down among those people who cannot think while they eat, and find a group of people there who are not eating. And of course, when you're not eating, you're thinking, if about no more than 'Why am I not eating?'

"So the Do-gooders say, 'Come along with us and we'll make things better for you and everyone.' And things start getting a little bit better and a little bit better, and pretty soon, those people begin eating, and you know what happens?

"They stop thinking! And the movement is over, to begin in another time and another place. And that's the history of the world."

Zella and Ouida were laughing so hard they could barely talk, but they did manage to say, in unison, "Tell your friends."

LaRue talked with Ouida and Zella about the changes happening in the world. For his columns he was sent to cover stories on burning and looting breaking out from coast to coast. He told Ouida and Zella about the times he had marched and the things he had seen, how he had listened to street corner tellers of tales all his life and now he had heard street corner prophets who were calling for a reshaping of the world.

Zella told him how their neighbor had watched them in silent rage as they moved in and had never spoken in all the years they had lived side by side, and LaRue said, "Well, that's part of the story of these times, but there's this, too. I ran into Tennessee Jones and he had a tale to tell. He was in Detroit when things blew," LaRue said, relating what he knew of the riots that had happened there.

They talked about the explosions of rage they had seen in their lives, as if things moved in cycles. How each one had been born of anger and frustration, and had ignited in an instant of crossing over. But this one, the one Tennessee had seen in Detroit, was different. It was about race, but about having and not having, too, LaRue pointed out. "In this one, we attacked each other . . . and ourselves. Tennessee knew a black man whose store was burned, because he had more than the brother down the street. "I'm here to tell you," LaRue said, "these times are different. They're different, and yet very much the same."

LaRue went on to tell about a lesson Tennessee Jones had learned a long time back, about having and not having. He told about the time when he had earned the "Coal" part of his name.

"He revealed to me the scar he had to show for it," LaRue said, "one he had acquired when he was heading North, looking for work. A man all dressed up in starched collar and suit whom he ran into at a train station had talked him into coming to work in the coal mines.

The wages were higher than many he'd been paid, and he didn't guess the living would be worse. And it wasn't until Tennessee got to the mining town that he found out the part of the story that hadn't been told. He had been hired to break a strike.

"He had ridden to the little mountain town with a trainload of colored men, and none of them had realized what was in store. When they pulled to a stop there was a mob of desperate-looking, angry white men waiting for them with picks and shovels and rocks.

"Tennessee and his brothers had meant those white men no harm, and had in mind only to feed themselves and their families. And, as you know, we weren't welcome in their unions anyhow . . . some concept of unity, Tennessee said. Well knowing that, the mining bosses had shipped them there, had set these men against each other for the company's ends.

"As they got off the trains, the white miners warned them, and then the rioting broke out. They shouted 'Scab!' as they attacked; Tennessee said it was a roiling blur of hungry men who thought they had pinned down who the enemy was. Many of the colored men were killed, and it went on for days, as some found places to hide and went on and took the work, and the white workers didn't give up trying to either kill them or drive them from that town. Tennessee was caught in the fight that first night, and someone had hidden him and patched him up. He escaped, but he carried a deep scar on his cheek from a coal pickaxe.

"He was staggered by the way the violence had exploded, in a manner he recognized from his growing up. But he said that once he knew why he'd been brought there, he had to move on. He had a feeling about how working folk were bound together, 'cause he saw the condition of a white worker's family that took him in, saw that their cupboards were empty just like his, and their children were in rags.

"And Tennessee said he realized something he hadn't known about how things fit together. Another small, but vital piece about his place in things."

* * *

Vesta didn't know what to think of the things she saw happening. She only left the house when she had to, and she didn't have Polaris to talk to, so she called LaRue all the time, saying, "LaRue, all hell's breaking loose." The styles, the nudity, the open kissing and touching, the casual unguarded approach to drugs left her openmouthed. The people she saw on television looked to her as if they had come from another planet, and Vesta felt like a holdover from times gone by. If the past wasn't for her, neither was the present. Vesta didn't know where she belonged.

The televised shows she saw left her trembling and speechless. She saw the marching and the raised fists and militancy being born. She saw young people saying what they would and wouldn't take, and calling themselves "black," which she argued wasn't accurate. It wasn't that she felt a kinship with white people, for they, she had always known, were from alien terrain. But she held out that it was brown, it was brown that described her, and that no one was black.

"The world's at war," she said, "and all hell's breaking loose." And there was yet another war going on, one in a long line that she had lived through, but this one was long and drawn out and nobody she knew even seemed to understand the why of it. All they knew was that their dark sons were leaving to fight it and never coming back. Everything she saw in the paper and on TV was bad, and more and more Vesta declined to know it. Eventually, she stopped watching the news and read the paper selectively. "Let's face it," she said out loud, "the news is bad."

For the six months after Polaris's death, the house gave Vesta something to do, and then she decided it was too big for her to live in by herself. She had cleaned and rearranged and weeded out old things and had come, gradually, to occupy less and less of the house. The basement flat they had moved into when they first came to live with the Staples family had long ago been made separate from the upstairs and rented out. After Polaris was gone Vesta had closed off the upstairs bedrooms to save on heat. Next she had had the heavy oak pocket doors that hadn't been used for years pulled out from their resting places in the walls, and closed off the front of the house, as well. She slept on the couch, confining her movement to the kitchen, dining room, and living room, and entered by the back door.

As she tried to adjust to being alone, she found that Black Oak had changed and there was hardly anyone she recognized on her block. She hadn't even paid attention to the way time had been passing, and she found that the faces around her had changed. One day she realized there was no Mr. and Mrs. Ike's at the corner, and as she sat out front on summer evenings as Ruby had done, she saw that nobody stopped and chatted as they walked by.

She took a new look at her neighborhood and found that the young people who hung around unsettled her with the hardness and insolence in their eyes. When she said "Afternoon" to them they didn't speak back. No one seemed to address or even look at each other and, in fact, Vesta realized that everyone she saw in Black Oak emitted a kind of wariness and mistrust that had not been there before. She felt frightened walking in her own neighborhood, and had heard a story about an old lady being knocked down and robbed of her county check.

She looked for the Black Oak she knew, for some face or storefront that was familiar, and on her way to the bus one day she thought she saw LaRue at the corner spinning some lie, but as she stopped and squinted, one of the men stepped forward and she realized with a start that no, that was another time, that something had shifted while she had stopped paying attention. She heard one of the young men say something about an "old lady in white."

It hit her suddenly that she was the last one left, not just in the house, but in the whole neighborhood, and that the house held too much, too much of the past. With LaRue's help she found an efficiency apartment in a safer part of town and after moving the things she hadn't distributed or sold, she settled in, just before her seventy-first birthday.

LaRue tried to talk her out of taking so much stuff, reminding her again and again that it was only a one-room apartment, but Vesta insisted that she could always get rid of things later if she had taken too much, and jammed the place so full of furniture that she could hardly get around. She took the mahogany dining table and buffet, the Persian rug, and the plastic-covered couch and coffee table with the plate glass to protect it. She also took her spooled oak twin bed and matching dressers, which were in one corner of the single room. And she brought all the little decorative things that had been amassed over her years in that house. Tiny china figurines of French ladies and crystal bud vases. Little wooden boxes and brass plates. And, of course, all over the place hung the cross-stitch samplers she had been making all her life.

LaRue thought he could barely breathe once they got everything in the apartment, and he bumped his shin three times just trying to get across the room and into the kitchen. He suppressed all critical comments, though, and reassured himself that although it might be cluttered, it would be clean. And after all, it was Vesta's apartment, and the only place of her own she had ever had.

For several nights the strangeness of her surroundings kept her awake, but she drew on the familiar things around her, looking over at her dresser and the cross-stitch sampler on the wall, running her fingers over the bumpy surface of her quilt where the edges of different fabrics met, and her disorientation began to pass. She crept out of bed to get a brandy, moving stealthily, as if hiding from herself, and propped up against the headboard with pillows, she sat and sipped while she watched the lights from passing cars move across the wall. She could hear the running motors and the tires before the lights arrived and she imagined the places they were coming from, and the warm, familiar homes that were lighted for their returns.

The night of her birthday, after a visit from LaRue and calls from Ouida and Dessie, Vesta sat on her couch, turning an orange in her hands, feeling the tiny depressions in its smooth, polished skin. Returning to that night of her childhood, that night of broken bird wings that had ended with a gift.

Once she had been there, to that night of her past, she tried to stay tethered to what was. The uncertainty she felt in her new surroundings subsided a little more each day and she settled into her life without Polaris, or anyone else, to care for. She found that she didn't feel like cooking for herself and took to eating TV dinners and anything that came in a can. During the day she watched soap operas, her "stories," she called them, and LaRue was mystified by how involved in them she became, speaking of the characters as if they were people she knew. Finally, he thought to himself, she had found a kind of storytelling she could give herself over to, and he teased her that these sagas, also, were lies.

Her commitment to daytime drama was interrupted only by her delivery of last rites for her church, a service she had started performing at her pastor's request. He encouraged her to be involved with the church in this way, and she grew busy with visits to those facing death.

The phone rang and she was asked to go to a woman who had wasted slowly, over several years. She got into her corset and sitting on the edge of the bed, pulled on her stockings, preparing herself for what she would find when she got to the woman's house. She said the words that would be offered later in the quiet, steady voice that made her suited to her task.

After dressing she set off energetically, fueled by a sense of purpose, prayer book beneath her arm, crucifix hanging from her neck. But as she approached their front doors she dreaded crossing the thresholds of the dying, dreaded the intimacy that wounded her as she entered their lives and detected the smell of beans or fried meat recently cooked, that lingered in the air. It was unbearable, seeing the soiled underthings soaking in the bathroom bowl, stepping over the wheel of a toy or a forgotten shoe with its broken lace and twisted tongue on her way to deliver peace.

When she saw their eyes, afraid at the coming passage, she was always alarmed and clutched the polished metal that hung from her neck, mooring herself with prayer. She sat by the beds of those she had been sent to help, leaning over their wasted bodies, and restored peace.

There was comfort for Vesta and for them, too, in the pattern of her recited words, in their rhythm as they left her lips. There was faith in the repetition, in the delivery, that would move them along.

At this wasted woman's house she found three generations of family rendered numb by grief, and a score of unfinished tasks. There was a pot of boiling water on the stove and half-peeled vegetables along the drainboard. The vacuum cleaner stood in the middle of the floor, trailing its cord across the room, and children were half-dressed and running around. Vesta tried to do the thing she came to do, and then she left.

As she came down the walkway, hearing the door close behind her, she could feel the autumn leaves crunching beneath her feet on the half-raked path. She could suddenly see the little apartment where she now lived, and wondered how it would look to a visitor who might come to her with the kind of help she gave. They would be greeted by no disarray, no shoes slipped off carelessly beneath her coffee table, no nylons discarded by the bathroom bowl. She kept good order in her house and when her time came, all would be neat and clean and attended to. She imagined what state LaRue's and Ouida's houses might be caught in and she had to laugh. And Dessie's, which she had always thought meticulously cared for, but in which she sensed some unnamed trouble she dared not think about.

She considered her loved ones as she touched her silver chain and crucifix, and she prayed that they were well and safe.

29

That year autumn seemed to last forever, but the cold did come down, just before Christmas, coating everything with ice, glazing trees and brick walls and iron railings. It seemed as if the world had been encased in a clear stillness, marked by frail white cracks. Everything felt cold, and touch that lingered too long brought with it a frozen burn.

That year, when the cold finally came down, late but with a vengeance, Dessie felt her life a winter, with no spring in sight.

Season of decline, it seemed to be eternal, with no stirring up ahead. She was trapped in impotent despair, trapped in silence, and there was ice around her, all that ice.

She wanted to be able to tell someone, but how could she admit what her life with Emeritus had become? She wanted to be able to ask how it had happened. She didn't, didn't know.

She couldn't figure out if they had inched toward it slowly, over their stone years together, or whether there been one big thing she had missed that had caused them to slide into such unhappiness, like a peg fitting a hole.

Dessie knew that most of her family had never liked Emeritus, and she didn't want to provide another reason for disapproval by even hinting at her unhappiness. Those who had liked him didn't like bad news, and she realized, as she sat alone one night trying to make sense of all that ice, that she didn't have a single friend she could tell. The ladies in her bridge club didn't want that kind of revelation, bringing doubt to their own good things, and they didn't share the details about their lives anyway. Not, at least, the negative ones. There was no one, no one she could tell.

She sat and wondered how to trace back what had gone wrong and realized that she couldn't even place, exactly, when they had stopped having sex. She tried to pin it down, but couldn't, and the bigger question, anyway, the one she spent more and more time on, was "Why?"

Certain that she had been a good wife, she went over and over the list of her accomplishments in her head. She had had a child, and even though it wasn't the boy Emeritus would have preferred, he was pleased that Pearl looked like him. "She's just like a little me," he liked to say, "running around and getting into things."

She had kept a nice house, one he could bring friends to proudly, and his dinner was always waiting for him when he got home from work. She had learned to cook the things he liked, and to present them well.

She had kept up her figure and when Emeritus got home she was always dressed and had her makeup on. She had been faithful about getting her hair touched up, so that he had never even known it wasn't naturally straight, and when it had started to gray, she had had that taken care of, too.

She had even given up her job as a teacher because he didn't believe his wife should work, and that had not exactly been her choice. And despite her resentment, she had relented, and even when they had had trouble paying the bills, he had not budged from his stance. She had given in to him, telling her friends, with perverse pride, what Emeritus did and didn't "allow" her to do.

She had built him up, she thought, to feel that she was behind him, no matter what he did, and that was the part that most rankled her now, that she had flattered him, inflating what was really commonplace.

Dessie ground her teeth and clenched her jaws until they ached as she made her mental list, which was growing by the night. She chewed on her fingers, already dry and cracked from the cold, until they bled. She scrutinized her life with Emeritus for each thing sacrificed, each thing borne, as she sat in the living room after Pearl was in bed, waiting for him to come home, as evening stretched into solid night.

She tried, instead of being angry, to think of where she had failed, where she had gone wrong.

"Sex," she thought. "It must be sex." And as she examined the past she concluded that in that province, she had tried to please him too. She had done it as often as he liked . . . surely she had. She had been willing, but not eager, as he had ideas about what was fitting for ladies. She remembered that one time she had been moving further and further down his belly with kisses . . . it embarrassed her to think of it . . . and there had been his hand on her neck, stopping her, and the look on his face as she lifted her eyes to meet his. Shock, she had seen, at the end she had in mind. "Not for a wife," he had whispered urgently, "that's not for a wife."

It had been okay with her whenever he had wanted to have sex, but she hadn't ever pressed him. She had never approached him openly, but had answered his want and liked it, not too little and not too much. If he had been steady, he had not been imaginative, and she had often quieted her own need, feeling slightly ashamed, once he had rolled off her and drifted to sleep. Although they hadn't "done it" much in recent years, Dessie figured, from what she read and heard, that that was what happened.

When it had been months since he had touched her, she tried to rouse him in the night, pressing his shoulder once from behind, and he had pulled the covers up around his neck and turned away. He wouldn't even talk to her. He just turned away.

Though she fought against it, she remembered little bits of the past, like cracks of light that shone beneath a closed door, that she didn't know how to place. She saw Vesta reaching for a bloody newborn and clutching her tight, tight. A full round moon coming out of shadow in a winter sky. She let her guard down and a field of cotton went red. Walls and walls were lined with oranges and then she saw a multicolored serpent coiled in a circle, tail in teeth. Disturbed by the images that came to her, she shut her eyes and clenched her jaws, trying to banish the random, chaotic things she saw.

And some nights, as she lay and tried to sort out the different qualities of darkness in the night, she felt she had to restrain herself from getting up in the freezing cold and feeling along the walls of their house with her dry, split fingers for openings. She thought, those endless winter nights sealed in their frozen glaze, that she could hear her hunger vibrate from the walls like wires, taut and humming, humming in the empty space inside herself. The singing of her imprisoned blood.

She needed it filled, needed it quieted with flesh that didn't measure, but came for what she could give, and looking at Emeritus's back in his pajamas with their grid of little brown medallions, inhaling his cool citrus cologne smell, she thought she would choose anger, or flesh that fought against her, over those pajamas and that flat back.

She lay in her bed and dreamed of faceless lovers who could take her need and her pain, and she developed a wanting for that so bad her jaws ached, as if they were wound tighter and tighter at the joints. She wanted sex, then, in a way she had never thought about, wanted a him who would come to her without the measuring and lick her clean of the failure and despair, wanted him in her mouth. She wanted the edges of teeth against her skin, and the salt traces of sweat and the smell of the long day that hadn't been washed away. To be locked thigh into thigh, wrestled free from the hurting.

Dessie was appalled at the fantasy growing within her night by frozen night, monstrous in her eyes, appalled that it was there and at the same time stoking it, calling it up. She wanted to take and be taken and she wanted it to hurt, smaller, now, so that it could stop the wide, full wounding that was taking over her life.

And her need, it chained her; for as long as she wanted him Emeritus had the power to say "No."

When she finally asked him if he was having an affair he denied it, and then he gave in and told her the truth. He apologized and promised to stop it, but some nights he still came home late, and at his office there was no answer. He reassured her, finally, that it would run its course, that his father had done it, and his father before him. He told her it was the way men are. "I have no intention of ever leaving you, Dessie," he told her. He told her he "didn't believe in divorce."

December was reduced to waiting. Longing, while he said "Yes" to someone else, and she thought, "Maybe he loves her. Maybe she's something I'm not."

She grew to hate Emeritus, and the worst part about it was that instead of making her want to leave, it caused her to hang on, because the shell idea of him as her husband was all she had left. Hers was the sharp, foul-tasting hatred of someone trapped, not just by Emeritus, but by the way she saw her life. Her anger ate away at her like acid while she sat in her newly upholstered chintz living room chair and made a list. All the things she had done for her marriage. All of her virtues and charms.

And then, in one sleepless night of wanting, her outrage, her indignation, her fear shifted and she turned them out as well as in. They became her weapons, and with these she made her second list. From the chintz chair that matched the couch and drapes she sat grinding her teeth and biting her cuticles, and thought up ways to make him pay.

She cooked the foods he hated, and washed his bright clothes with his whites.

She threw away one of each pair of his socks and rejoined the survivors with ones that didn't match. She loosened one button on each of his stiff white shirts so it would come off that day, and watered his brass "Employee of the Year" plaque until it rusted. She emptied his ink pen and unraveled the hems of his pants.

Dessie was reduced to little triumphs, gymnastics of will. She spent hours devising ways to get back at him. Ways to ruin the things he treasured, ways to make him feel unloved. When she left the living room one evening, she unscrewed the lightbulb and took it with her to the bedroom, leaving him sitting with the paper in the dark.

At first Emeritus saw Dessie's efforts as disruptions of the order of his house. He liked to have everything just so and admonished her for the way she had let things slip, for what he chose to see mostly as her carelessness. And then, when he realized her intent and the care she had taken with her sabotage, he felt a kind of triumph. Blind to the crisis building in her, Emeritus was impressed by his own power, so that when she took the lightbulb with her, he merely laughed.

She wanted to know why he treated her the way he did. Had he ever loved her, she wondered, and if so, what had made him change? "Why does he do it?" she asked herself over and over, "Why does he treat me this way?" She turned it over and over in her mind, shivering in that winter ice. If he had been able to respond to her honestly, he would have answered, "Because I can."

Not only did Emeritus not understand what Dessie was going through, he didn't even really think about it. He was sure she would get over it eventually and that things would return to the way they had been.

When summer came, Ouida and Zella decided to drive up to Detroit and see Dessie and Pearl. As always, they considered the visit an undertaking made in spite of Emeritus.

From the first time they had met him Ouida and Zella had thought him small. And Zella had seen that thing that she had learned to read in people's eyes that spoke of wariness and distant superiority. He looked just past her, but she caught it anyway.

He had always been uncomfortable around them, especially Zella, who didn't try very hard to hide her contempt for him. He dealt with their relationship by acting as if it wasn't so, and the understanding he had come up with was that Zella had preyed on Ouida, and that she, being "lame," hadn't had a choice. "Now I feel for your sister," he said to Dessie, "but the other one I just don't understand." And he couldn't get over the fact that they were both such attractive women. Dessie buried the curiosity about Ouida and Zella that made her afraid, and she never would have discussed it with Emeritus.

"You know what goes on between them, and, well," he said once, "I don't even like to think about it, but I'll tell you what it isn't . . . it isn't right. And I definitely don't want to talk about it."

Although Zella was always threatening, privately, to wait until that one time Emeritus finally looked directly at her, and seize the opportunity to kiss Ouida deeply at the dinner table, they both worked hard at not letting their intimacy show while they were in Detroit, and everyone stayed clear of anything that had anything to do with their love.

This trip, like the one the year before, from which they had returned home exhausted, was part of Ouida's effort to hold on to an idea of family after Polaris died.

After their arrival, they rested and then assembled for dinner. Somewhere in the background, there was a humming sound.

Dessie seemed to be pulled taut and about to snap, and there was a tightness to her voice, joined with the bitterness Ouida had heard over the phone. Despite Ouida's efforts, Dessie wouldn't tell her what was wrong, but something sounded like tightening, tightening wires.

"What's that sound?" Ouida asked. "What is it, Dessie? It's a kind of vibrating sound, a humming almost."

"She hears it," Dessie thought hysterically, "she hears it too," and the idea of it brought tears to her eyes. She got up from the table and retreated to the kitchen so no one would be able to tell, but she returned and said nothing, and Emeritus just sat there stabbing his food with his fork and chewing his pot roast, well done by his mandate, thoroughly. "I didn't hear a thing, Ouida. You must be losing your grip." He looked over at Pearl and told her not to eat so fast.

His criticisms and his dinner table rules never failed to take Ouida's and Zella's appetites away. That and the silence. Whenever anyone started to speak, Emeritus interrupted and either told Dessie to get more gravy, more pot roast, more peas, or told Pearl to finish her vegetables, to chew thoroughly, not to talk with food in her mouth. Ouida, who had grown up with laughter and storytelling at the table, found the dinner table experience excruciating, and Zella would have been hard-pressed to name anything at all about Emeritus that she didn't find hard to take.

Ouida thought she heard the humming again. A sound like tightening wires, plucked now and then, and it made her focus in on the things around her. She noticed that Dessie's fingers were ragged and scabbed, and she had bitten them raw. And she noticed those hands shaking as she tried to cut a piece of roast in response to Emeritus's demand. She was having a hard time cutting it and her eyes filled with tears, and Ouida noticed that as he witnessed her discomfort, a smile, a smile of triumph, formed on Emeritus's face.

Ouida struggled to swallow, and couldn't stop looking at her sister's fingers, holding a knife and fork from the fine Reed & Barton wedding silver she had been so excited to get. She looked over at Emeritus. "What's he doing to her," she asked herself, "is he beating her, is that it?" Ouida tried to eat another mouthful of food because she knew Dessie would take it as a criticism of her cooking if she didn't. Her head was spinning, and she knew Emeritus was hurting her little sister somehow, and although she imagined there had been hurting that had always gone on in little and even big ways between them, there was something different happening here.

"My sister . . . my sister," she thought, and she remembered her entrance to the world with blood on the moon. She remembered, all at once it seemed, Vesta and oranges, and images from so long, so long ago, her mother washing apples and Vesta's shoes by the bed and her night silence and Eula's fingers on the scar, and she wondered if Vesta knew what was going on in that house, and she wondered what it was that was going on, what he was doing to destroy her, and it was too much, and she wondered how she had chosen this man, and yet asked herself how else it would have ever been, and her head was spinning and she had to tell herself to open her mouth and breathe. This was her sister, though she hardly knew her, had never lived with her, and, my God, she looked at her and she saw her mother and her father, and she felt, with shame, that she had never really done for her and that she would have to do something, do what she could, now. And she had to try to breathe as she gripped her knife so hard her knuckles paled, and she would kill him, but she wouldn't have to because Zella would do it first and she realized that he was addressing her and she didn't even know what he'd said.

She stared at Emeritus and answered, "What? I didn't hear you," struggling to get the words out and to ignore the sound of the vibrating wires that seemed to bounce from the walls of the room.

"What did you say?" It came out as a whisper and then he smiled and pointed at her with his fork and repeated it.

"Doesn't look like you're too keen on Dessie's pot roast." He smiled and sucked his right front tooth.

Ouida couldn't answer. Looking down at her plate, she forced herself to eat, and thought how she had to find out what was going on in this neat little house with its floral centerpieces and its matching slipcovers and drapes.

After dinner Zella put Pearl to bed and Emeritus withdrew to the living room and left them to clean up, but Ouida knew he would never go to bed and leave them alone that late at night. He had sometimes seemed reluctant to leave them alone with either Pearl or Dessie, as if whatever she and Zella had together was contagious. He tried to stay just within earshot. Ouida knew she would have to wait to speak with Dessie until the next morning when he left for work. She talked to Zella that night and found that she had noticed it all, too. Neither one of them slept much and as soon as Dessie fixed breakfast and both Emeritus and Pearl were gone, they appeared in the kitchen and sat down.

They didn't have to push too hard, after all, as Ouida put her crutches aside and, leaning against the counter, pulled Dessie into her arms and Dessie began to shake and then the tears flowed and she sobbed, relieved that she could let it go. When she finished crying Zella helped her sit down at the table and poured her some coffee, and she told them what had been going on.

Ouida immediately launched into the merits of putting Emeritus out, or of Dessie's leaving herself. She started making a plan until she realized, from the look of horror and surprise on Dessie's face, that she had no intention of doing either one. Ouida lowered her hands to the edge of the table and the three women sat and waited, for what, they didn't know.

Zella tried to keep quiet, but finally exploded. "Why don't you just leave the bastard . . . didn't you ever think of that, instead of letting his disrespect ruin your whole *got*damn life?" Ouida's eyebrows went up as Zella's voice went out of control for that one syllable. Zella looked at her and continued. "Right now he owns you, straight out has the title to your life. All that bitterness and evil has made you his."

Dessie just looked down at her fingers, cracked with dried blood where she had bitten and chewed them, and cried. She knew she wouldn't leave.

"But why, Dessie, why?" Ouida asked her. "Why on earth would you stay?"

Dessie looked down at the kitchen table set with its new matching place mats and napkins, and answered, "I fit here." That was all she said.

Dessie had asked herself the same question, had thought about what it was that kept her there, and had looked around at her life. She had looked at the house they had bought together, which was appointed comfortably, just as she liked. It was the kind of house she had wanted. A nice house. And it was filled with all the latest things, color-coordinated and matched. She had looked at the fence around it, and the flowers planted in neat rows out front, her house and her garden with its red and blue flowers. It felt as if it was where she belonged.

They made up a family, she and Emeritus and their child. She was a mother and a wife. She was Mrs. Moore to the neighbors, and at the corner store. She was Pearl's mother, and she was Emeritus's wife. It was her place, this house and this family. It was where she fit.

30

Ouida called Dessie weekly after leaving Detroit. She felt her sister's crisis moving toward a crescendo, and was so upset by the calls that she found herself taking long naps. Dessie sounded as if she were suffocating, she thought, or gasping for breath, and Ouida wanted to turn away from it, as she had done before.

She had never understood her, she realized, not her demure rectitude nor her inertia. She and Zella had been rendered speechless by her declaration of how she "fit" with Emeritus, and it had been days before they could even address it in words. When Dessie had said it, Ouida had felt the gap between her and her sister widen into an uncrossable gulf. She and Zella had left that week, when it was clear that Dessie was going to stay and the tension with Emeritus had reached an unbearable height. To Dessie's dismay, Zella had stopped even trying to hide her contempt for him, sucking her teeth and rolling her eyes at his comments, while Ouida fantasized about elaborate ways for Dessie to escape.

She dreamed of ladders lowered from airplanes and intricately plotted night flights. Camouflaged escapes and downtown shopping trips from which Dessie and Pearl would never return. And then, finally, she and Zella realized that they could no longer be in that house, that they needed to go home.

It angered Ouida that Dessie never called her and she used to say, "You know, the phone works both ways." Each time she hung up after talking to her she told Zella it was the last time she would call. "I'm old and tired, Z," she said again and again, "and I can't help."

But then she would lie down seeking sleep and see her sister from that doorway where she had stood as she joined the world, the mother who had just birthed her taking leave. She would see Vesta removing all obstacles from the path of a baby with Ruby's slanted gold-brown eyes and full head of hair. When she realized how uninvolved she had been in her sister's life she felt guilty, and tried to think through why she had let it be that way, whether there was something that made her inaction okay. "There were no stories for her," she told Zella. "No stories at all."

Even before she had gotten old she had been too tired, she guessed, or maybe she had been old early. Maybe that was it. She knew her exile from her family had been self-defense, in part. She had gone to Black Oak for holidays and fulfilled all the formal obligations, but she knew what Vesta really thought from the way she had responded when Ouida had first told her about meeting Zella, before she had started guarding herself. She remembered, although she had tried not to, remembered like it was yesterday, that time when she had reached for the three-year-old Dessie and Vesta had pulled back just slightly, just enough for Ouida to see that flash of mistrust and reluctance in her eyes. It had happened in an instant, but she had seen it. She had seen it and would never forget.

Ouida decided that as awful as she thought Dessie's choices were, she herself had taken no responsibility for showing her a different way. She had let Vesta take over and raise her, and it was hard to reconcile the realization with what Ruby had taught her and the example she had been. Now there was her niece Pearl, in whose life she might make a difference. And yet it was true, it was true that even the horror Dessie was living, the sound of humming wires and the small, pathetic efforts at sabotage, made her want to lie down. But despite her vows not to call, and the numbing ease of sleep that drew her as it always had, she continued to pick up the phone.

One October night months after their visit, Dessie called for help. She had become unable to eat or sleep, and although she was consumed with punishing Emeritus, she said she seemed to be the only one suffering. Ouida tried to get more information to assess how near the edge her sister was, but Dessie just rambled on about ice, and said over and over, "It feels like winter. It feels like winter everywhere."

It got harder and harder for Dessie, until she was calling daily, but couldn't seem to leave. Ouida figured her own listening meant something, but she couldn't come up with anything that helped Dessie, who grew more and more desperate to make a move. Finally Dessie was calling and couldn't seem to say anything, but wouldn't get off the phone. And then Ouida had a premonition of light, and asked LaRue to go to Detroit.

LaRue drove all night and arrived in Detroit the next morning. He had to ring the bell for half an hour before Dessie got out of bed to answer the door. She had stopped getting up and dressing altogether a few days before, telling Emeritus she had the flu. He had already left for work and Pearl was at school, and LaRue knew he had about eight hours to help Dessie decide what she wanted to do and pull together a plan.

Once he had made a pot of coffee he asked her if she knew what she was going to do. She stared at him until he told her to drink her coffee. She shook her head and started to cry as she spoke of the winter's freezing burn, and then she seemed to realize how extraordinary it was that LaRue was there to help, and pulled herself together to tell him that the only thing she knew was that she had to leave. The next question, with which she needed help, was "How?"

She told LaRue she didn't know where she could go and when he asked about whether there were any of her social club ladies or other friends who would help, she just laughed. He made a call, to one of Tennessee Jones's friends he said, and found a place for them to stay for a few nights. He began asking what she wanted to take with her, without pushing, and when she couldn't seem to answer and looked panicked at the need for further decision, he took things from the closets and drawers one by one and asked her if the items should stay or go.

When they had a few bags packed and loaded in the car for her and Pearl, LaRue convinced Dessie to take a bath and fixed some food. When she emerged from the bathroom they sat down to eat, and he told her the story of the beginning in the end, the story of her solstice birth. She hugged him and when he stood up and got their coats she stood and looked around the living room.

"My things," she said, shivering, "LaRue, he'll get all my things."

He waited in silence while she looked at her drapes and her sofa, at the pair of lamps and end tables, and her porcelain statuettes. He waited while she looked around at all the things that had been hers, and then she turned her back on it, walked through the door, and said, "Ice. All that ice."

When Pearl came out of her school, LaRue and Dessie were waiting for her. They explained that they were leaving and that she would hear from her father soon.

Dessie didn't sleep at all that night. She smoked one cigarette after another and trembled at the anger Emeritus would feel when he got home and found her gone. She couldn't believe she had done it, and she went in and out of being so disoriented that it felt as if she were walking underwater with slow, slogging steps. Every time she drifted off to sleep she woke suddenly, with a start, to the sensation that she had lost her balance and was heading for a fall.

LaRue was on the floor next to her, getting very little sleep himself. At about 3 A.M. she said, in the darkness, "What did you think of him, LaRue? Really, what did you think?" It was a question she had never before brought herself to ask.

"A hood ornament."

"A what?"

"A hood ornament." He struck a pose to show her. "That's what he always reminded me of, on one of those fine old-fashioned cars."

She wanted to defend Emeritus, to make it not true by not knowing it, and at the same time she knew what LaRue meant. They laughed, and Dessie tried again to go to sleep, but kept thinking of her husband's rage at what she had done. What she didn't know was that he never came home that night.

LaRue had lay there in the dark reminding himself that he had to be careful. He wanted to jump in and rescue her, to handle it and make it all right for her, once Ouida had told him the things that had been going on "for God knows how long," but he knew he had to keep in mind how to help guide her, while making sure the trip was hers.

The next morning he woke to find her curled up and crying, trying to purge the unplaceable memories that were coming again. He sat next to her on the couch and held her. "Now you get to find out who you are," he told her, "who you can be if you choose. I'm gonna stay on a little while in this here Motor City, and see what's what. What it was our people came here for, or better, what they got when they came. And that way, I'll make sure you're on your feet, my solstice girl, before I go home."

The next Sunday, while Pearl and Dessie were napping, LaRue left the house where they were staying and decided to go for a short walk. He saw familiar street signs and landmarks that he recognized, and then he walked on, lost in thought and realized, much later, that he was a long way from where he had begun. He had been thinking about Selena and what kind of choices she was making for herself. He wanted to call her and urge her to come home, but he knew he would have to deal with his fears for her well-being without expressing them to her, and that he didn't have her answers, anyway. "This being a parent," he thought, "is something else." And then he considered being a son . . . and a brother . . . and a friend, and he had to laugh. "It's all hard work," he said, calling her up as he chuckled to himself. "Don't you think, Miss Snake?"

LaRue heard the singing of a voice blue and weary, but still full of fight, drift out from an open window. He heard clapping and rocking from a storefront church. And he heard drums, as a stranger's long bony fingers beat the music for a ritual dance on overturned bucket bottoms from a set of crumbling steps.

And there was Miss Snake, waiting for him, coiled in a labyrinthian knot. He looked at his companion and touched the lapis stone from Ouida that he wore around his neck. He joined her and she guided him through a bewildering maze of winding streets, her skin a deep, rich red, and they could still hear the music as they traveled, could hear the music that they carried with them down, down into the heart of the city.

They went through the smoky hull of Detroit, seeing in the distance the downriver plants that made steel and parts for cars and trucks. Caught in the spools and wires that caged the sky, the orange molten heads of smokestacks burned, spewing their dark venom across the plain.

Folks were out, en route to church or merely seeking air. They had taken time off from the steel mills and the auto plants, or the holes they had made in their lives, and moved a little toward each other. On some streets, the mouths of cremated houses gaped in incredulity. On others, tightly sealed bungalows were interspersed with wooden frames that leaned tentatively against the sky.

Stores had their rippled iron pulled down across their fronts, their rusted, painted iron gates closed and locked. Concrete. There was the rubble of burned-out buildings, the gashes in the earth where there had once been life.

The land and the people were scarred.

The morning sun seemed to take the edge off things, so that jagged windows and overlapping planes didn't cut so sharp against LaRue's heart. Some streets were comatose, enfolded in a quiet pallor, sleeping on the bridge between life and what comes next. And weaving in and out of the rubble of Belleterre Avenue came the elastic stretch of a pair of long legs, moving to the joycry of a portable blues.

They walked the city, he and Miss Snake, and saw places where anger had burned across the city and left its mark: "Soul Brother" . . . "Soul Brother." Frantic announcements to try to stave off looting and fire, letters scrawled across the fronts of stores not so long ago. Remembering what had erupted in his boyhood days in Black Oak, LaRue ran his fingers across those angry letters on brick and saw walls scarred dark by fire, and it felt to him as if it had happened just yesterday, and would come again.

His land and his people were scarred.

The hopes that had fueled their journeys north, were they ashen, now that so many were dead and dying on the other side of the world? Wasting behind concrete and iron bars right there? Did people still carry places of promise inside, he wondered, or were they slipping from militancy into despair? He knew his people, knew what they had survived, and knew most clearly that they would surely need the Great Black Art Form now.

He came to a place where two streets met and felt suddenly tired. "Let's take a rest, Miss Snake," he said, "I'm older and much more tired than I thought." They sat down then on the stones of a decaying wall and LaRue tried to get his bearings. He asked Miss Snake which way to go and she didn't answer, but lay beside him, glowing a deep blood-red. Were they lost, he wondered? Were they lost?

He closed his eyes for a moment and on opening them he saw Ontario and Eula standing in a massive field dotted with yellow flowers. In the midst of recaptured green they were looking at each other with some small measure of the tenderness that must have once been felt, and then he saw Polaris in his uniform, setting off with his father on his very first hunt, the shine of his buttons creating blinding stars of light.

He saw the men from down at the corner whose stories he had sat and absorbed while growing up, and the soldiers from Church's train trip, witnesses to that china and those linen cloths, who never made it back. He saw Bertha Crosby holding out that pouch and Crenshaw Wells as he sat quietly with Ruby, trying, still, to get his tale told.

When he saw Ruby they exchanged a look that held in it all the possibilities she had taught him, all that they had shared. She sat erect, her eyes and her spirit penetrating, and she looked a little bit like everyone he had ever known. She had a braid down her back and the smooth face of a young girl, yet eyes that protruded, ancient and full with all that they had paid attention to. Her hands, resting beneath her breasts and then stretched out to him, were deeply etched with lines.

LaRue saw Church Newman coming down the street, carrying a sketch pad under his arm as he passed through the lifeless landscape. LaRue waved to his friend, who had never been recognized, but had always practiced at his art. Down another block he could see a battlefield of corpses lying amid the jungle green, and down another there were scores of dead bricked into prisons, sitting with watchful eyes as they waited out their measured, living deaths.

They were there at that crossroads, all of his dead.

Resting his elbows on his knees, he paused, his head of gray and thinning hair in his hands, his tears falling on the broken sidewalk and glass beneath his feet, and when he raised his head he had no idea where he was.

Was he lost, he wondered, and if so, which way was the way back? He could no longer see his companion beside him and he rose, finally, leaving behind another layer of innocent skin, and turned around to retrace his steps. When he was halfway home it began to rain and he didn't try to shield himself, but received it, walked through it, making his way back.

Dessie felt strong as long as LaRue was in Detroit with her, but once he went back to Black Oak, she slid into despair. He had helped her find an apartment and they had talked into the night, with LaRue telling her all kinds of things about the family and tall tales that had doubled her over in laughter. He spoke, too, of the thing Ruby had carried. He spoke of running and offered fruit. From his pallet on the floor he talked of the open road, and their collective history of risk and stealth. Of the price of cautious living and Vesta folding into white.

She asked him not to leave because she was afraid, and when he asked her what she feared, she told him she had no script. "It's the openness . . . the chaos of what I might feel and what might come," and it was then that LaRue told her what he had learned decades ago from Tennessee Jones. He told her about the long way round. Before he left he had been able to be her doorway, and the next part was hers to do.

The thing that had helped her decide to go was her realization that if she was too weak to leave for herself, she could leave for Pearl.

When she tried to examine the history of her life with Emeritus, she couldn't get a handle on anything about it. It all seemed to run together. The things that had always defined it had slipped away, and when she thought about what kind of father he had made, she realized that he had been a figurehead. A pose in chrome. When she thought of them as a family she pictured the portraits they had had taken at the studio downtown and placed around the house, but she didn't really know what it had been made of, the life she had chosen. "Pearl will never really have a father in Emeritus," she realized, "and at least I can save the one parent she has."

She thought of the kind of mother she had been, how she had made sure Pearl was healthy and safe. How she had tried to give her everything: dance lessons, music lessons, horseback riding and ice-skating and parties with presents and clowns. She had tried to give her everything, but she couldn't really think of what they had done together. They hadn't played or talked or read together, and they hadn't made things up.

She looked back, and unsure of where she had been, she had the impulse to erase her years with Emeritus, which looked more and more like lost time. Passing whole nights without sleep, she cried until her eyes were swollen and red, and when she did drift off she woke suddenly, panicked at what had happened and what she had done. She underwent a nightly battle over whether to call him or show up at the house, but the thing that kept her from going back was the fact that, despite his expression of his intentions, he had never called or come to see Pearl in the entire three months she had been gone.

When Emeritus finally did show up he tried to intimidate her, but she looked at him and all she could say was, "Fuck you." So shocked that he didn't have a response, he stared at her as if he thought she had been possessed by the devil, and recoiled. She said it a lot over the next few months, and she found that her jaws hurt less and less. She tried out all the curse words she had ever heard others use in the privacy of her new flat. And she remembered the stories LaRue had told her, and laughed as well as cried.

The next thing she had to do was look for a job. Since teaching was the only skill she figured she had, she went to the Board of Education and got an application. She worked on it for a week, unsure of her answers, and when she came to the part for listing previous jobs, she had only that first teaching job to put down, which had ended years before. She didn't know how to account for the intervening years, and so she put "Homemaker" in the empty space and submitted it, terrified she would be hired, and terrified she wouldn't.

She hired a lawyer and had him draw up the papers for divorce. Her hands shaking as she took the pen, she looked over at her daughter and signed her name. She would have to think about whether to hold on to the name Moore, which Pearl shared, because it seemed, for some reason, that she couldn't let it go. She would give some thought to that.

She read stories to Pearl and together they made up new endings. They had left most of her games and toys behind with Emeritus, so they improvised. They drew pictures and took apart old necklaces Dessie found and restrung them in unexpected patterns. They started a dress-up box with old clothes and shoes and jewelry and Pearl put costumes together from that box and they had shows and plays and a parade. They closed their eyes and pointed to places on the secondhand map Dessie had bought and then talked about the people and animals and landscapes of the spots they had picked.

When her disordered pieces of memory came she tried not to fight them so hard, and they began to fit together more and more.

Over time, Dessie realized that she didn't need to erase her life with Emeritus in order to move on, as there was much, she was sure, that had come out of it, even if she couldn't see it yet. For one thing, Pearl had been born of it, and they were becoming closer and closer. She was beginning to realize that Emeritus was part of her path, and she addmitted the rest of her history, chaotic and unplaced, into her present life. She was unsure, still, about most things and her days often started with fear and doubt as she tried to meet the unscripted future.

One thing she was certain about: she took back the name she had been given by LaRue. December. The name of her winter solstice birth.

31

Ouida stood at Zella's casket, slightly bent, leaning on solid arms. Her ceremonial wig hugged her forehead where the elastic gripped too tight, and the toe of one foot rested, poised to pivot, on the polished floor. She stared, struggling with an impulse to peel back the expression of arranged peace, searching for the woman she had known. She looked for the dark eyes that could flash caustic or tender. For the warm flush of vibrant copper skin. She looked for Zella in the face before her.

The mouth once carved and full was pinched shut. Hair once worn loose had been set into waves and dips of unsettling symmetry. All of her features looked insistent, exaggerated by the funereal makeup that, seeking desperately to recapture life, only makes more real the passing on. As Ouida stood staring, groping for the past, she opened and closed her hands over the worn rungs of her crutches, gathering close the fragments of their forty-seven years.

Ouida looked for Zella and it came back to her, the summer after she had left Junior Biggs, when they had met. In her memory that summer, that summer that had been hers, inhabited a soft violet space. As with all treasured time, the lens had gradually softened, rendering indistinct the sharp edges of growth, polishing smooth the glory of her freed beauty. She returned, for a moment, to her choices.

There had been Flood, tormenting her with his restraint, his hardness, and Johnston Franklin, with his linen and embossed leather, barter for the pulse of life she gave. And then, to everyone's astonishment, there had been Zella, in whom she had sensed something unplaceable from the first.

Had it been the disregard in the set of her jaw, or the untamed richness of her laugh? Maybe it was the way she had tasted rain. Ouida remembered sharing the knowledge she had thought was secret with Vesta, the late night revelation that she had met a girl who was "different."

It wasn't long before she had heard Zella spoken of in curtained words, in phrases of whispered violence. BulldaggerBulldagger-Bulldagger. Sealed by a switchblade fold of hands and an abruptly turned back. But her fear had been heightened only for an instant, and the warnings had washed right over her. She had reached through the ugly words, past the fear in other eyes, scattering an arc of their beaded unshed tears. Reaching anyway. Reaching because of. Reaching for the knowing.

There had been polite speculation at first about the nature of the friendship, but others had found solace in her enjoyment of the company of men. As she and Zella grew closer, some distanced themselves from the taint of the "unnatural," and more and more, she and Zella had found themselves speaking in conspiratorial tones. Heads shook slowly in condemnation, and leaned closer for details. Couldsheisshedoesshe? Those photos of stilted poses that had yellowed over the years in dusty attic boxes betrayed a subtle intimacy that would have rendered inquiry unnecessary.

How many distant arcs had spiraled off that early meeting, fused from passion and nearly disarming understanding? Arcs like arms that would flail and smooth and push, and draw them in again across the years.

It was Zella who had helped her stem the fevered blood of that stagnant day, that night of rent flesh, stopping midway through the barren landscape of dry ragged brush and fallen leaves to arrange the discarded newspapers. And that was only the beginning. Over time, she had cradled her in those places that they inhabited alone.

It was Zella whose legs had been there when her own had stiffened. She had moved to be near her that year in the East Coast hospital, and had built her a house without stairs.

Ouida remembered approaching their house for the first time, after leaving another hospital where she had spent two years. She had seen it from a block away, through a little circle rubbed from the frosted car window. They had been the first colored on the block, and she would never forget the look of choked rage on their neighbor's flaming face as she opened her door and stood watching them struggle to move in. The hostile stares persisted until the area began to change, and they could finally release the breaths they had held for decades. One more reason to keep to themselves. One more silent space.

They had spent forty-two years together in that house, washed in the prism of afternoon light that spilled in from the window of tiny stained-glass panes. They had watched so many things pass from their living room chairs. Joe Louis and "Amos 'n' Andy" in the magic word-picture times before TV. Assassinations that had left them speechless. Stonewall and the slow gains of sixties' marches. And Bob Gibson's Cardinals. And "Porgy and Bess" on the hi-fi, relegated later to the basement. And all the little changes wrought by mornings and dusks. There had been many an outburst in that room, where discussions were never tame. She would hold forth, gesticulating with impassioned hand-phrases, while Zella waited quietly for the chance to slice in with sharp concise rebuttals. How many times had she hoisted herself up, snatched her crutches, and disappeared before Zella could come up with a response?

She thought, too, of the kitchen sink, where she had stood so often, continuing with the daily tasks that move life forward, and she was sure that if she added up the time she had spent there it would amount to years, passed in that familiar pose. Crutches abandoned, she stood with arms firmly placed. As she washed and chopped, she looked out through her collection of African violets, sifting time. Assessing and reassessing the past. Imagining things to come. Zella would enter and stop short, struck by the strength of her pose, mumbling, "I don't know who's disabled and who's not."

They had taken cooking seriously, and unlike the women of today, she had never really worried about getting fat. "You can't get too much of a good thing," Zella used to say. Both had their specialties, and they were always feeling some craving coming on. Zella made homemade soup with everything left over thrown in, and seafood was an undying passion. But no matter what season or hour, it had always been time for barbecue. She remembered how they had sat devouring a slab one evening thirty years ago and pledged, hands raised to the heavens, that they would never stop eating ribs. And Zella had sometimes gotten a notion to barbecue in the middle of January, and Ouida would find her outside cooking in her beaver coat and boots.

There had been regular gatherings in the early years, with Zella or LaRue mixing and passing round the designated cocktail. They had spent three weeks on margaritas once, stuck on a double-edged Tequila rush. There had been chitterling parties on the back porch. And bridge games that extended into night, stretched by the requisite bout for biggest talker of shit. Twin titles, "Bridge" and "Shit," which Zella often won.

There had been such carrying on. She would never forget the time LaRue had visited, and had joined into the discussion of the *Kinsey Report* to say that such theories were originated by the great Roman philosopher Julius Octavius Flavius. He had had everyone going, taken in by the casual nature of the lie, until Zella went for the encyclopedia. You never knew what was fiction and what was fact . . . he wove them together deftly, scorning the effort at distinction.

Poetry readings and games, and the contest for "Homecoming Queen" that the girls had judged. And that unforgettable Sunday morning after a party that had left the floor littered with sleeping bodies, when Lanie Johnson had awakened them with a lamp shade on her head to serve bacon and eggs.

Early on, Zella had put aside the styles prescribed for women, preferring pleated trousers and button-down shirts back in the forties. Ouida remembered the first pair of trousers they had bought. Marching into the men's department at the main store downtown, Zella had scandalized the place. And then, moving directly into lingerie, she had satisfied her passion for lace and silk. She had been thought so daring. So bold. And so many other things with which she did not concern herself.

Zella had considered herself tough, walking alone at night, convinced that attitude was a foolproof repellent. And to her colleagues, she had been a teacher, nothing more. No one had asked about the missing pictures of husband and kids, or visited her at home. She had mastered the protective device of distance early on, so that it was clear that things private were forever closed topics.

But no one knew how gentle she really was. For Ouida and their animals, who loved without judgment or condition, she would have rearranged the stars. She had treated their cats like her own babies, feeding them only fresh liver from the deli down the street. "They live better than we do," she used to say, feigning outrage at their indolence, scolding them for not getting jobs.

Former students of all ages stopped her on the street . . . she had run into one last spring, a student who had become a teacher herself. The brilliant ones flourished under her tutelage . . . and none forgot her. People were still telling the story of the sleeping student who awoke to find a sign reading "Rest in Peace" hanging from her neck.

And while Zella was at school, Ouida had turned to profit her gift for shaping fabric into clothes, tucking and pleating silks for white ladies who could afford such customized things. She had felt at peace only when creating, and was mostly glad to have the time to herself. But sometimes her loneliness had been something tangible, her companion. The quiet time was punctuated only by the humming of the machine and her outbursts at mistakes. She was swept up with profanity for a time, calling out curses with increasing fervor.

Seeking always, always, to quiet restless hands, Ouida had mastered the entire array of needlecrafts. Her fingers took off like hummingbirds, as if to make up for what her legs could not do. She had quilted, clothed, sweatered, and afghaned her family, so that December and Pearl had seldom had store-bought clothes. Sewing was something Ruby had given her, and she could still see her quilting in dim evening light. She had meant to pull her weight with Zella, honing her one marketable skill, the joining of needle and thread. She had never wanted Zella to look back and wonder if she had been saddled with an invalid.

In quiet times, they had read. In recent years the books that Zella couldn't manage to bring had arrived by the book-mobile that visited "shut-ins" once a week. She liked to mix up the classics and the latest offerings, and kept a record of what she read, charting her journeys into other worlds. Many a time she and Zella sat up far into the night discussing their favorites. Sharing stanzas from Robert Hayden and Keats. Arguing whether *Finnegan's Wake* was worth the try.

And they had fought, venting anger in curses uttered with sweeping arms. Wounding with immediate regret. But then, they were devout about everything they did. Her jealous passion had erupted more than once at intruders, real or imagined, and there was a dent in the dining room wall to memorialize one explosion. The cut-glass pitcher had sailed through the air in slow motion, of its own volition, it seemed, just missing Zella's head. Ouida had reached out to snatch it back, and then stared, shocked at what her hands had done.

Afterward, there had been silence as they turned aside from their brush with loss. After walking around it for an entire day, Ouida had quietly gone for the broom and dustpan and had swept up the broken glass. They had been speechless for days, and then one afternoon Zella had returned from school with that bouquet of soaring birds of paradise . . . there must have been two dozen . . . and left it on the bed.

They had moved past the pain, but she had tucked it away with the other disillusionments, cordoned off with her indignation, in a place not too far back. Accessible. Where she could reach it to probe the soreness, or pull it out for view. She knew now how little it had mattered, and regretted that she had nurtured it so long.

Some of the best times she could remember were the Scrabble bouts at the folding card table they kept in the vestibule. Both determined and fiercely competitive. Both holding out for the seven-letter word. They had had to institute a timer to keep decisions from stretching into night. In spring and summer they had taken the board to the shaded porch with cool drinks to ease the heat. To watch for the landing of wings and the drifting down of forsythia clouds.

And there were those recent summer visits to see December and Pearl in Detroit. They set off at dawn with waxed-paper-lined tins of fried chicken and deviled eggs that were gone within an hour. They played word games and Twenty Questions as they drove. They came, like the seasons, for long spells at a time. One day in early June they would pull up to December's two-family to find Pearl on the stoop relaying cries of "They're here" to her mother out back. Bedrooms were switched, furniture rearranged, and projects begun. Summer curtains took shape in the dining room workshop where Ouida sequestered herself on cooler days. Pound cakes, preserves, and watermelon pickles appeared, as she swung around the kitchen impassioned, determined.

Neither Vesta nor December had asked questions. They had listened silently over the years to the things carefully selected for sharing. They figured that what their sister chose must be okay, and when they heard the word "lesbian," they never thought of her. In decades of long-distance holiday calls and letters, neither one of them had failed to include Zella. Maybe they had loved her like a sister, but they had kept their distance from the hazy spaces where strange love lived.

On their visits, Ouida and Zella had guarded December's ignorance carefully, displaying just enough affection. Stilling touch. She had wondered often if sudden rage lurked below the surface calm. But in the rare moments when intimacy bled through, when their fingers brushed or she caught something in their eyes for which she had no comfortable name, December turned and busied herself with straightening up.

With Pearl, the nature of Ouida's love for Zella was never broached. In their zealous protection of her niece's innocence, in their attempt to keep this child from the dangers of things sexual, they had sealed her off from understanding. The not telling grew, until it was larger than the reason why. And soon it was herself, and not her niece, that she protected. She didn't know what the exposure would mean for their love. Would it keep? Would it keep? Would she hesitate before she hugged? Would she pull away behind her eyes in confusion? In anger at her prolonged ignorance? In horror at the shame that implicitly accompanies such silence. Because she could not risk this magic, she was an accomplice in the hiding. Here she had chosen not to speak. She had chosen not to be known.

Disapprovals had never been voiced at family gatherings. No open disdain, even from those with connections more tenuous than blood. Just a veering from all dangerous ground, and the cool whispers that faded on their approach.

At times she had longed for open scorn. For the honesty of direct confrontation. And she had tried to use her mechanism for physical suffering on the psychic pain. To apply the coping game that she was already playing now with death. In an hour . . . a day . . . a month . . . a year. But she found that unarticulated condemnation made wounds that burned freezer-sharp. Wounds that would never make scars. Wounds that would never heal.

She and Zella had grown old together. Their loving had aged, too, "like wine," Zella said, turning gentle and knowing and rich, and Ouida remembered when they had first found gray pubic hair. They had laughed, saying it was time to get rid of those tired old things. And she had been shy about her scars at first, covering her nakedness even when alone. But Zella had embraced it all, seeing beauty even in her mangled joints. There had been wrinkles, sagging breasts, and sometimes a passing glance in the mirror that made you stop and look for the girl you had been. In forty years of Sunday afternoons massaging and lathering Zella's hair, she had watched it move through shades of gray into solid white.

And then the stroke came, suddenly, after all the years of encroaching decay, with so little concern for easing them into death. It had hit with violence, knocking her from her chair, so that before she realized what was happening, Zella was lying at her side. Zella had lingered a few weeks, recognizing no one, in a place where antiseptic dispositions and artificial cheer were the only weapons against certain death. Ouida had managed to struggle there to see her only once. With all of her illnesses, she had outlived Zella. They had never imagined it like this.

She stood there at the casket, back suddenly in the present. Although only a few moments had elapsed, their years together had passed before her in their richness. She glanced across the room of heavy drapery and slim armless chairs, completing her formal goodbye. And then she moved on, past the section where Zella's family sat, to stand, with LaRue, next to the close friends.

The parlor filled with eyes that evaded hers, unsure of the response to match the occasion. As she looked around and arranged her crutches to leave, she felt trapped within the walls erected by their fears.

From the beginning, they had been consigned to narrowed space. To cubicles with proportions that seemed just right to those safely distanced by the refuge of their personal judgments. For others, these were the spaces where she and Zella had lived, squeezed and folded in by the theories that explained her fall.

Ouida realized that none of them, save LaRue, would rock her from grief into acceptance. No one else knew the shape of her love. For forty-seven years, she had been exiled by everyone else's theories to untraveled silent space.

For months Ouida woke up calling her name. She opened the door to Zella's closet and smelled her clothes and when she woke in the night she saw into the darkness, as if it clarified, rather than concealed, all that was missing. All that had been lost.

When she slept she dreamed of winding passageways, and fumbling through in darkness for a footing, for a way up and out.

In one long sleepless night she got up and went to find the pictures taken when they had first met that Zella had brought to the hospital. There they were, each one holding the end of that string of fish, and sitting on a lakeside rock, their mouths parted in some kind of anticipation, as if they had had to stop and remember to breathe. She looked at the brown, cracked photograph for hours, trying to remember herself back into the scene she saw and the instant captured. She stared at her image holding those fish and could barely believe it was her, youth and defiance in her face and in her pose, standing without crutches next to Zella.

She went over and over little pieces of the past, wondering about the hidden meanings of conversations and seeing herself with Zella in flashes. Through each thing she did, she wondered what her Z would have said and thought about it, and all the things she wanted to ask her that would now never get said came to her. She punished herself for the things she could have done differently, for the times she wasn't quite listening or didn't extend herself, and she remembered how Zella had wanted so much to go fishing again, and not feeling up to it, she had put it off. Now Ouida wondered how hard would it have been to go, because Zella wanted to, and she said out loud, into the clear and empty night, "How hard . . . how hard would it have been?"

She dreamed of unlit corridors, tunneling up, up, and there she was, climbing. Feeling for each step. Feeling with her hands and with her body in the narrow passageway, the tunnel spiraling like a snake, and Ouida afraid of pushing forward and unable to turn back. Ahead and up the only way through.

The times of grief came gradually further apart, but they still stunned her with their intensity when they arrived. She tried, little by little, to forgive herself for the things she could have done better. But she still found herself lying in bed, bereft at the absence of Zella's breath on the nape of her neck, stopping on her way down the hall or bending to pick something up, shocked at the void and sure that it couldn't, it couldn't be true that she would never again be there.

The pain faded, and then faded some more, until Ouida realized that losing Zella was not going to be the end of her life. Her body was giving in, making it harder and harder to get around on her crutches, but she wasn't finished making memories, she told LaRue. She went through Zella's things, keeping what seemed special and letting go of the rest. She tried to make a home that was hers, one with a place for the parts of her life that were over, and with room for what was to come.

Some things, like playing bridge and eating carrots, she decided she was finished with. She had the house painted in different shades of teal and got rid of the slipcovers they had had for years and began to make new ones. She started plants from cuttings and found new things to be interested in. She learned the new names in baseball and basketball and developed passions for teams she had never liked before. She got another cat and started a kitchen herb garden and tried new recipes. She invited her family to come stay with her, and although December said she would have to plan her visit, Vesta and LaRue came. And despite Vesta's stated disapproval, she and LaRue went out to the back porch in the evening and sneaked a bourbon or two, chuckling about their secret as if they were kids again.

She ordered books from the library, and found that she liked mysteries, which she had never read before. Pulling out sewing scraps from the last decade to start a rag rug for Selena, she decided that she would be the kind of sister to December that she always should have been. She would tell her about Ruby and Polaris and Eula and how they had come to be a family. She would tell her about the times of storytelling at the very least.

In other times of darkness and retreat, she had had LaRue and Zella to pull her back into life. This time Ouida had to do it for herself.

She dreamed of tunnels that shone with little bits of light. She dreamed of passageways and felt her way through.

32

LaRue returned from Detroit overwhelmed, as if from the land of the dead. During his lifetime he had traveled, collecting his people's stories piece by piece. He had wanted to have an expanded understanding of the bloodlines of which he was a part, and to know how to pass his understanding on.

He had wanted to be a doorway, and had spent a lot of time trying to get that right, he thought, to understand what was and wasn't his to do. And now he found himself sitting in his backyard thinking over where he had been. He thought of his family, united at first by descent and flight. Of the ways they had each been marked by the endings and beginnings, inextricable, in which they had all played parts.

There was the generation that had come before, all those dead and gone whom he had seen again on that corner in Detroit. He had set out from the beginning to place himself within the things they had seen and done.

And then he thought about Vesta, taking care, taking care. Holding him in the curve of her body against fists and shattered glass. The sister in whom he could see such pain. And Ouida, who had pulled a blooming cavern from herself and was trying, now, to figure her way alone. And Zella had been family, too, through Ouida's love, and though much had been unspoken between them he had known her as fellow exile and from that first time he met her in Ouida's hospital room, as sister, too.

And Olive, whom he had loved spring into winter, winter into spring. He could picture her sitting on her stoop the very first time he had walked by, her coltish legs tucked beneath her dress. They had had to struggle through lots of hard times and had even had to let go of each other for a while so that she could find her own way. They had come through it, and lately they had even made up a good long tale about LeFoy and Footney pondering how deep down race goes, while making plans to invest in a copper mine. He had had deep love with her, he thought. They had built a house with a big, wide porch.

There was December, who stood at the edge of forging an identity different for herself from what she had ever imagined. He didn't know what she would make of what she had been dealt or what kind of mother she would become to Pearl, but he would try to do his part to help them along, and he wondered how Selena and Pearl would come to place themselves in their lines. They were the next generation, who had never met Ruby and barely knew Polaris and Eula. Selena, whom they had tried so hard and waited so long to have, was off at school now. LaRue considered how she had always liked to create things and though he was trying hard not to interfere in her decisions, he hoped that if she wanted to, she would have the strength to choose a life in art.

What was his role, he wondered, as he sat in the backyard in the declining light. It seemed to him lately that the more he gathered, the less he knew, and he guessed he would be forever figuring out where his own small tale fit into the bigger one he had spent his life piecing together.

As spring arrived, once more, LaRue watched his neighbors begin to plant. Some of them, like Ruby, had only their small front plots from which to conjure flowers and vegetables, and others had large backyards with which to work. He watched bulbs that had been planted the fall before begin to come up, and saw preparations for the season of fullness and ripening. He saw folks clearing the ground of leaves and mulches that had protected roots from the winter freeze, saw them feeding and turning the soil. On his way down the street one day, LaRue saw a man at work in his garden and was overwhelmed with a sense of mystery. He began to stop and talk to the people he saw working outside.

It was as if he had never really noticed the spring-into-summer planting since the times Ruby had knelt out in front of their house. As if he had never really paid attention to it as an option for himself.

He wondered if he might grow a garden, too, and began with a small shiny envelope of seeds in which he didn't completely believe. As he sprinkled them into the small wells he had made in the earth with his fingers he had a hard time trusting that they would turn into plants, and watched anxiously for their sprouting. It was the first thing he thought of when he woke up, and he often crept into the yard barefoot at daybreak to search for bits of green. When he saw the first shoot, finally, pushing through a crack it had forced in the ground, a tiny twin-lipped tip of pale green on a fragile stalk and the whole thing no bigger than his fingernail, he was awed. Down on his hands and knees, he looked for other signs of life and saw the hairline fissures in the ground as other seeds moved to the surface.

He saw a sign of life within one crack and bending to look more closely, found a stalk elbowing its way out, bent double by a piece of soil. He leaned over it, gently, and lifted the bit of dirt off with his fingertip, freeing it so that it could rise.

Once his seeds had sprouted LaRue started to think about what else he would grow. Vesta brought him a thick gardening handbook to help him plan which things to plant and he sat turning the pages, unable to choose from the hundreds of varieties listed and described, or to keep straight all the information on timing, brands of fertilizer, and exposures. He looked at the book for a while and then put it down. "This is no way for me to do this, Sister. I'll never plant a thing this way."

He pulled her out of her lawn chair and drove to the nursery. Walking up and down the aisles, overwhelmed at the variety of colors and shapes, he had come to a stop in front of the dahlias and turned to the young salesman who was following behind him.

"No need to think any further. I have made my selection. I'll take six trays, different colors, of these here. What do you call these beauties?"

"Dahlias. Those are dahlias."

"Daaahhhlias." He stretched the word out and tasted it as he leaned over and touched a silken, vibrant petal. "Well, Sister," he said, turning to Vesta, "looks like I'm about to be a dahlia farmer."

He had started there, and had added things as they caught his attention. Each time he was taken by a new flower he thought of Ouida, and what story she might make up about it. Sometimes his plantings caused him to revisit a tale she had told, and his additions of foxglove and jack-in-the-pulpits brought him unprecedented joy. He kept Ouida apprised of his garden's progress, and when he called her they found themselves lost in conversations that lasted for hours on end.

LaRue was swept up with gardening, and he surprised himself with the care and patience he devoted to the small and precious thing. He liked the heavy smell of life down on the ground and he found that what he did there was a kind of ceremony. When Vesta tried to temper his obsession, he told her he "caught his balance" out there in the yard, where he made up stories, sometimes reciting them aloud, and when they saw him talking to his plants and flowers, his next-door-neighbors called him a "fool."

Whenever he went out back, they leaned forward in their lawn chairs to look over the fence and shook their heads. He had on his gardening pants, trousers cut in big pirate points above the knee, and a wide straw hat. Sometimes he tied a sash around it for élan.

As winter broke he watched for the tiny heads of plants that had seeded themselves and helped free them from the earth with a loving touch. He added used coffee grounds and eggshells, and folded the earth over and over, blending it in as he clipped the dead leaves, and his backyard grew full, with wildflowers and cultivated plants alike. He delighted in plants that sprung up in new places, his "volunteers," he called them, and some of the weeds that had blossoms he kept and even maintained. Vesta had tried to get him to clip the evergreens and pricker bushes into cones and squares, but like Ouida, he laughed and let them grow free.

He planted without a plan, putting things in as he got a notion to.

He planted by feel, and it happened that there was something blooming throughout the summer months. Resisting order, he told Vesta he liked the "thick" feel of his yard.

But his true passion was the dahlia bed, teeming with showy flower heads that escorted him into fall. As the end of the season approached, he began preparing his indoor place for them, and removed each one from the ground carefully for the winter season, cut back their growth as he whispered about the coming frost, and put them to sleep, gently, in their basement crates.

Unable to bear the idea of leaving her home, Ouida arranged to have a young student rent the upstairs from her. She could depend on her for errands and help with the shopping and chores. She was truly housebound and it had been years since she had sewn professionally, but she still knitted sweaters and crocheted afghans and sent them to Selena and Pearl.

After she settled into a routine with her boarder, December came with Pearl to spend the summer, and they played Scrabble and listened to music. Ouida had her renter buy books for Pearl before they came, and she got Pearl started on them as soon as they arrived. December washed and set Ouida's hair while Pearl rubbed her feet, and they sat on the back porch drinking lemonade that was often spiked with rum and watched the birds land at the feeder December and Pearl had brought.

December had questions about the family. She wanted to know about how it was growing up, to know what things Ruby liked and cooked and talked about, and what went on in Black Oak during "those early times." Ouida tried to tell her what she remembered, and they called LaRue and got him to fill in details that Ouida had trouble pinning down. Those phone calls turned into extended conversations with now and then a lie getting told.

Even after she had returned to Detroit, December would call and ask Ouida some question about when or where some family event had taken place. It seemed she wanted to piece together the past while she still could, but she never did ask about Zella, and Ouida guessed that was too much of a stretch for her to make.

Ouida was worn out when she went to bed and her arms and legs felt weak. She had arthritis in her hands that kept her up some nights. It had been good and it had been not good, she thought, scanning the years as she waited for sleep to come, and sometimes, one thing had come right out of another. It had been good and not good. It had been both things. All things. It had been rich.

It took her a while to get up in the mornings, and more and more, her hips and stiffened knees seemed to ache, especially in damp weather. But she still loved the opening up and closing down of each day. Still loved opening her eyes to find herself tiger-striped by the light through the blinds and the smell of coffee brewing. She loved watering her plants and settling down to read, and she bathed at dusk in Zella's name.

Although she got out of bed each morning and dressed, no matter how hard it was, she found that she had to stop sometimes on her way around the house and rest before moving on, and if you had seen her passing down a hallway on her way into evening, you might have found her leaning on her crutches, oddly opening and closing her hands. Gathering the last chinks of day caught in tiny patterns on the wall as they shifted into shadow. Harvesting the light and the dark.

33

It was during one of Vesta's cleaning frenzies that the heart attack knocked her flat. She went down in a cloud of Roman cleanser that dusted her white dress blue. She lay on the kitchen floor for a long time, knowing LaRue was on his way over, but after a while, she began to wonder if she would ever get up.

She tried to prop herself against the wall in a comfortable position, but when she did so, she found she could see underneath the stove and what she saw there appalled her. It was dirty beyond belief. Unable to face it, she slid back down to the floor and waited.

When she looked up she could see one of her cross-stitched samplers hanging on the wall.

Please Keep Us Close Together
And Help Us to Be Good
And Always Love Each Other
The Way a Family Should

She had done a perfect job on that one, she thought, and she remembered that even the back was all neat and tucked, with no loose threads hanging. As she stared at it the words began to blur, and then she started when she heard the mailman push some envelopes through the slot, but she couldn't get it together to call out to him for help. She could hear her neighbors were making lunch in the kitchen on the other side of the wall, their soap opera in the background, and the opening and closing of their cabinet doors. Everything was going on, as usual, outside of her little place.

She lost a sense of when and where she was, and images from her life began to revisit her as she lay on the floor. Some of the memories she tried to stop, but they drifted right up to her anyway. There were rooms and rooms filled with mountains of oranges, and Ruby's face fading in and out. When she saw her she stretched out her arms from the kitchen floor to take a piece of fruit from her hands but there was no one there.

LaRue's face drifted down to her and she could see his eyes sparkling, the light streaming through the wedge in his dark brown iris, and then there was her mother, patting her softly to sleep, and then holding her tight, tight, with a white-gloved hand, her face so close to hers it looked grotesque, whispering, "Look don't touch!"

"Oh God," Vesta said, "no!" but they were coming, the faces she had known in her life. Shag Wilson showed up, a grown man dressed like a little boy, waiting to go to the fair, and looking all ashamed for the way he had made her sit there and wait for him. "No," she cried, "not you! I never invited you!" She was tumbling toward him again, again, into the vortex of loving, loving, loving him, but she closed her eyes for balance, for an end to the spinning past that was as vivid as if it were happening now. It flowed to her anyway.

Her visitors were jumbled now, overlapping like a collage. Faces from the neighborhood and from her job. Faces from church. There were some she recognized and some she couldn't place, and then a parade of white faces she had known. Women for whom she had altered bras and girdles, and people with whom she had worked for forty years who had never said hello. Those of "The Other Side." Elevator faces, and faces at the traffic light. She had never really gotten to know a white person, for she was sure they couldn't be trusted and had wanted as little as possible to do with them, but here they were, in her life anyway. Suddenly a pale gray face came into focus, the face of the woman who had closed her door to them as they had run bleeding in that night so long ago that she felt, sometimes, had never given way to dawn.

Vesta shut her eyes against the people who rose up to remind her, to remind her of all she had tried to forget, but there was someone else coming, there was that little dark-skinned girl from sixth grade arithmetic, taunting her, shutting her out. "You!" Vesta yelled. "You're as black as sin, just like me!"

The little girl faded and she saw Polaris, chuckling to himself about stewed rabbit, and the tenderness welled up inside of her as she waited for his words about the gravy. And there was Dessie . . . what a perfect child she had been, graduated college and a teacher and all, but she couldn't bear to think of how Emeritus had taken her away. He had seemed such a good bet, and look how it had turned out. All had seemed to be well, their new house and reupholstering and the brand-new cars, but that one time she had called her and poured it all out, and Vesta hadn't known what to say, except "Stand by him and try to work it out." Somehow, Dessie had left him, and was making her way alone.

Vesta closed her eyes against Emeritus and saw LaRue again, smiling this time and trying to convince her to go out for ice cream, and then there was a parade of hats, all colors and styles, and Ouida laughing in delight. Ouida, she thought with a mixture of anger and love, who had had everything and thrown it all carelessly away. Ouida, who stood before her, leaning on her crutches, offering an arthritic hand.

Vesta blinked hard as she saw Ouida drift into a young girl, and there she was with LaRue, making up some foolish tale. "Liar!" she muttered at her brother as he told a story. "A purple-spotted snake!"

There was Ruby and Polaris and Eula, sitting together in the evening light, and all of a sudden she saw her father, defeated and absurd, wings spread open, falling through the sky amid a swirl of flying buttons, wailing "Green . . . Green . . .Green."

She tried to look away from Ontario Smalls and noticed that the front of her dress was stained with blue. Thinking it was butter and strawberry jam, she rubbed and rubbed at it fiercely and when it didn't come off she got panicky and tried licking her fingers and scrubbing the stain, which only made it worse, and she began to sob, and the next thing she knew everyone who had showed up was filing past a finger-smudged casket and she got in line, too, and leaning over the edge, her hands locked behind her back, she saw herself, ironed and stretched out in her white dress, stained with big blue splotches across the front. She let go of the tears now in a torrent of grief, and when she was done weeping, she lay flat on her back, her breast heaving, asking, "Where *is* LaRue? Late, as usual, that trifling, dreaming boy."

There were the faces of the dying, over whom she had leaned with the help of comforting words, with final ceremonies delivered to those who remained strangers to her, in the hour of release.

She looked up at the ceiling, wondering if there would be help for her, someone to come ease her into death. She turned away when she saw cobwebs she had missed clinging to the corner, and leaned her head on its side. "Why?" she asked herself. "Why this?" She tried to think of what had been grand, to make a Good List of her own, and she thought of how she had taken care of her mother, and taken care of LaRue . . . and then she had turned around and raised Dessie, damn near herself, and in . . . in the end it had been only her and Polaris. She had been good to her family, of that she was sure.

"And me?" she thought. "What has there been for me?"

There had been shelter and, except for a few rough spots, plenty of food, and "Lord knows, I've had my health." She had handled things for everyone . . . cooking and cleaning and arranging . . .and it had not been easy, not at all. She had been a good worker, never late or absent a single day, and when she left there had been a party and a watch. "I've had all of those things," she said, touching the gold watch whose elasticized band was pinching her now. She checked them off aloud now, all those things she had had, and yet, what she couldn't turn away from was everything there hadn't been.

She had never traveled, or made up a story. She had never flown a kite. And there was no perfect moment, no stewed rabbit, that she could return to, again and again. As she realized she had never climbed a tree she again began to cry.

Except for Shag, she had kept everyone away. Only family had gotten close, and even there, she had drawn her lines. Except by Shag, she had never been touched, and she had never been able to touch herself in the place she couldn't name.

She racked her brain for the heights. "There must have been some," she cried. "There *must* have been." She thought of Wishbone, and the way he had done the cake walk that day, when he wished for the world, and she was glad she had been able to share, sometimes, in his joy . . . and not so very long ago they had been shopping for dahlias.

With Ouida she had had dandelion-ringed oaths and Ouida's late night dreams, and all the reckless choices it had been hard to keep track of. But the tears slipped down Vesta's face when she thought how she had never unlocked herself in those soundless girlhood nights to make that crossing she longed for, to say that thing to Ouida, and she didn't even know, if she could have, what she would have said.

If she got the chance she could fix it, she thought, she could find that doorway and a way to tell Ouida what that something was. "I'll tell her when this is over," she said. "I'll tell her this time."

She was quiet for a while, and she knew she had wanted it all straight and even, like the spines of the books on her shelves. And even it had been. She admitted to herself that she never would climb a tree. She probably never would.

She felt as though she could reach out and touch the sides of her life.

Lying helpless in her soiled white dress, she waited for help to come.

LaRue visited her at the hospital every day and sat with her quietly or told her a story. He figured if his outrageous tales made her mad, it was a sign that she was still fighting. He started in on a tale about LeFoy and Footney applying for jobs.

When he finished, Vesta squeezed his hand, and smiled a little, but she didn't seem to really be there with him. He slipped off his shoes to ease the throbbing in his feet and looked at his sister's blank face for hints of what was underneath.

She stared straight ahead at nothing, and seemed to move in and out of clarity. The nurses said she had been an uncooperative patient, trying to walk to the bathroom when she wasn't strong enough and refusing to do things differently from the way she always had. Vesta was unsure of how old she was and Ouida had told LaRue that when she visited Vesta had seemed confused about where she was.

LaRue could see past the skin of her bitterness to the yearning underneath. She had given him what she knew how to give, and he felt for her now and wished he could make it different from the way it was.

He took her hand, with which she seemed to be trying to scrub at the front of her hospital gown. "You know what I was thinking about, Vesta? I was thinking about the time Papa caught us sneaking around in the night, you and Ouida and me, remember? Remember the look on his face?"

She looked at him fleetingly, and he continued. "And remember the time with the wishbone?" He touched her arm to try to connect, but she wasn't really there. "And Leverett Winters being suffonsified? Now that's just something I heard about over the years, but it seems like a memory of my own.

". . . and remember, remember oranges, Sister, and Mama Ruby and sitting by the stove rocking . . . and stewed rabbit? That stewed rabbit, that wasn't so long ago . . .

"I know what, Sister, remember this . . . how that woman fainted at Ouida's wedding . . . Rhea Winters and the funeral home fans . . . omens we should have paid attention to . . ." He wanted to mention the cake, but thought he'd better not. " . . . and the time, let's see, when was it, that Ouida came home late from school with all those flowers in her sweater, and grass and petals in her hair?

"All the stories on the stoop, when Tennessee Jones and Miss Snake paid us visits . . . and the fixes they got into in those days . . . fried fish and Mr. and Mrs. Ike's . . ."

LaRue was offering himself as a doorway. To the things that had happened before, to the things that happened between them. To their history. He squeezed her hand and tried to rouse her by looking straight into her eyes. "Remember, Vesta? Remember those times?"

She smiled faintly and drifted off to sleep, and while she napped he put his feet up, leaned back, and thought over some more of those rich times in Black Oak. She woke a little later and, turning to him, she whispered, "Bone?"

"Yes, Sister," he answered, putting his feet down and leaning over the bed so his face was close to hers.

"Wishbone?" she said, looking him directly in the eye that held the wedge of light. He took her hand and she looked at him with terror and squeezed his fingers. "Wishbone," she said, "how do I get home from here?"

34

LaRue let the screen door go as he went outside, his trowel and gardening gloves in one hand, and a bourbon and soda in the other.

He had recently started drinking his bourbon with soda instead of water because of the bubbles, which he thought were like celebrations, and he liked to put his face up close to the glass so he could feel them tickle his face.

Tossing his tools down next to the rectangle of old carpet that he used for kneeling on the ground, he addressed his dahlias. "And a good morning to all of you. Each and every one of you women is a stunning delight . . . It is such a profound relief that I shall never be forced to choose between you . . . Now don't you all worry, 'cause I'll be right back."

He went over to the patio to get the little wrought-iron table that he had painted "Sea-crest Green" the week before. That summer he had been intoxicated with Sea-crest Green. After happening upon it at the hardware store, he had painted everything in his path the light green color with a touch of blue: the metal patio chairs and table, ashtrays, and even the chain-link fence, "to soften it up a bit."

Olive had come home when he was finished with the furniture and fence, and found him sitting on the concrete driveway cross-legged, paint all over his arms and face, transforming the stones that he had placed around the edges of the flower beds. The streetlights were on and there was barely any daylight left and he sat there, a man almost seventy, painting rocks.

Olive came through the house and stood at the back door, smiling as she looked around the yard. "LaRue, what on earth is going on?"

He had looked up from under his sun hat, graced this day with a blue batik. "Isn't it marvelous, 'Live. They call it Sea-crest Green." He had chuckled as he put some finishing touches on the last rock, while she had stood looking around, shaking her head.

"I brought you some seedlings," she said. "Selena gave them to me for you, from her little garden . . . said she didn't think you had any of these . . . they're cosmos, she said, the deep purple kind."

He took them from her, kissed her, and said, "I'm cooking your favorite, Wind Pudding and Walk-away Bread."

"I'll be back the twelfth of Nevuary." She laughed. "That always was your best dish."

They hugged and after she went into the house he carried the table across the concrete and grass to where his tools were and put his drink down on a Sea-crest Green coaster. And then he got slowly down on his knees, wincing at the arthritis that Vesta told him over and over was aggravated by the damp earth where he spent hours kneeling with his flowers.

After planting Selena's seeds and pulling away the yellowed and dry brown leaves, he stood up and leaned against the Sea-crest Green fence, and addressed a striking magenta flower. "Do you have any aches and pains this day . . . I sure hope not, cause 'Arthur' has been visiting me plenty for the both of us . . ."

When he got tired he brought the table and chair over to the flower bed and sat with his feet up. He slipped off the tennis shoes without laces that he wore for gardening. He liked the feeling of the sun on this toes. "And you, my scarlet dream, what do you know good?" he said to a flower as he raised his drink to his lips. "I must tell you some time of a distinguished gentleman acquaintance of my youth by the name of Tennessee Coal & Iron Company Jones . . .

". . . It was on his first journey west, I believe, that he met his first black cowboy. Yes, I believe it was his first trip, and it happened like this . . ."

He got up and passed back and forth among the flowers with aching knees. Still telling of places traveled and imagined. Still telling his lies.

The couple next door muttered "Old fool" as they watched him walk back and forth among his flowers, bourbon in hand, his story growing more and more fantastic, talking to his precious dahlias. Serenading them into the late afternoon.

LaRue stretched out in his chaise longue as the day settled down to dusk and a breeze blew the smell of honeysuckle his way.

"Oh my," he said, as he turned toward the vine he had trained to go up the back of the house, "that smells like so long ago . . . a lifetime it must have been." The neighbors shook their heads at how he was talking to himself again.

He chuckled about why Ouida had said vines climb, and closed his eyes, remembering his first trip south after Ruby died. He recalled the kinds of trains where Polaris had spent most of his life, which were now things of the past. His legs had ached from sitting cramped when he finally got off, and he had been excited and terrified at what he would discover. He still felt that way much of the time. Then, it was an age of radios and streetcars, when they still delivered milk in bottles and a Pullman porter gig was a good job. When cotton was still picked by hand, and stained with blood. "My God," LaRue said, "was I ever that young?"

There were so many things he had seen and smelled and heard on that trip away from home, things he had touched and tasted for the very first time. No trip since had compared, he thought. "It was the first." He remembered his initiation into making love, and the woods, and that hidden snake, and he thought of the honking sound those majestic pine trees made as the wind stirred them to dance.

And the people he had met. The sharecropping family that had shared their floor, and the night showing through their walls papered with urgent headlines . . . he still had that piece of cotton he had brought back with him, and those three stones, too . . . he thought they were in a box upstairs. He remembered the lying contests he had heard, some of the best in his life, and the night his wallet had been his entrance fee. "I could never, never have been so young," he said, laughing to himself. He had met so many who were planning their moves North, headed for work in meat-packing plants and lamp factories, for grinding metal and cleaning up, propelled by the promise of better jobs, better schools. The freedom to walk the streets.

They didn't know, they didn't know, how they would be owned next by the company towns they had staked everything they had to reach. They didn't know, like Emeritus, how they would be captive to their shame, for the places they were born, and their drive to "succeed," by the white-walled offices that had them dressing and looking and thinking alike.

LaRue leaned back and looked at his garden, wedged between the garage and the side wall. "Indentured again," he thought, "and we didn't even know."

They had been trapped by the brick and concrete that would shut out the sun, and the crowded rooms and the noise, and the soot, and the rats that would gnaw at the future with their sharp infected teeth. By the cities, where things don't grow tall enough to bend.

He leaned back and looked up at the tree in his own yard, and at the lush wild growth of his garden, closing his eyes to inhale the smell of lemon balm and honeysuckle, started from a shoot Ouida had given him and now overtaking the fence. He decided it was time to praise the gifts, and said out loud, "At the very top of the Good List . . . that's where this moment goes."

He took it in, the decline of the day's light, the leaves that grew pale and dried, falling to decay, and the rising up of the things he had planted. And he did not feel separate. He did not feel separate at all.

Vesta had been in the hospital for weeks, neither progressing nor deteriorating, and after going to see her one day, LaRue changed into his pirate pants and went outside to work in the yard.

Deciding that his dahlias needed stakes, he began rummaging around in the garage for pieces of leftover wood, and as he sorted through the things out there, he came across the rocking chair that Vesta had brought him years ago.

He stood looking at it silently, flushed with a warm feeling. "Yes, Sister, I remember it," he said, barely aloud, "I remember this chair." He moved an old crate aside and lifted out the little chair.

Chipped places in its white paint revealed layers of yellow, maroon, and green. The seat was gone, and only a ragged edge of caning joined to the wood of the frame remained, blackened with grime. He couldn't exactly remember when the seat had broken . . . in fact, he remembered it whole.

He ran his fingers along the carved back, its outlines indistinct beneath layers of paint. "Thank you, Sister," he mumbled as he took the chair out to the patio. After rummaging around in the chaos of his garage for paint stripper, scrapers, and steel wool, LaRue spread a square of newspaper out along the concrete, put his thick canvas gloves on, applied the stripper, and began to scrape.

The yellow layer began to wrinkle and break. It curled up as he scraped along the curved wood of the arm and, freeing itself, the chair began to speak to him of its lives.

"Who painted it yellow?" he thought as he stopped and put the scraper down. "Who was it . . . was it me?" He pushed the arm with his forefinger and the chair began to rock, and then he saw a little girl sitting in it, the heels of her feet lifting off the floor as she rocked.

As he reached out to still the chair, Selena looked over at him and he was flooded with a memory that, somehow, was happening again. He placed his palm gently on her back, which was not much wider than his hand, and rubbed her lightly as she tried to get her breath.

LaRue could feel her chest rising and falling as she struggled with the cold that kept her inside for days and focused on quiet games, and he wanted to ease it somehow, to draw the discomfort out of her back with his love. He knelt next to her chair and told her a calm, quiet tale. Her hair was mussed from lying down, soft and fuzzy and coming unplaited in places, and he had wrapped her in the soft blanket that was her favorite. Her tiny hands held on to the arms of the rocking chair.

He was rubbing Selena's back in soft circles as he looked at the yellow arm of the chair and saw a spot revealing other colors below.

The image of his daughter dissolved slowly into another place and time, until it was no longer she who sat rocking in the chair. He saw himself before the stove in that kitchen with its stamped-tin ceiling and its red and yellow flowered linoleum and Ruby cooking at his side, and returned to a moment which had become both past and present.

The arms of the chair had shifted from yellow to a deep forest green, and he could smell camphor and feel the stove's warmth, and through the window he could see a winter afternoon coming to a close. And there was Ruby's firm but tender hand, easing his coughing, moving softly round and round his back.

And it was happening again, the past, layered, but coming to him at once, reaching him across the years. It was with him now, his daughter's childhood and his own. For an instant, as he knelt by the chair on the concrete patio with his paint scraper in his hand, he was reliving those moments of comforting that he had both given and received. He was connected, father and son.

He looked from the paint scraper to the chair and kept going, breaking through yellow to the layers below.

Yes, he had painted it yellow, yellow for the child who was now a woman and had moved away. He had painted it yellow to make it hers, and he remembered the first time she had sat in it, a smile exploding across her face as she discovered the feel of rocking.

When she was born, he recalled, he had wanted to give her everything but, short of money, as usual, he had gone rummaging in Ruby's attic for something that could be recycled for her. He had come upon the rocking chair and several toys, and set to fixing and painting them. Yellow had seemed fresh, hers.

Alternating between the scraper and the steel wool, he rubbed the four curved pieces that made the border for the seat, and as he reached the layer of maroon, another image came to him: December rocking with her dolls. By now it was Vesta at the stove and LaRue helping with the evening meal while December rocked, whispering to her dolls the confidences that she would never share with them.

LaRue watched her rocking for a while, the person who had only recently opened to him. December, who had loved all the things girls were supposed to love. December, who had been embarrassed by her name and by their makeshift family with its unconventional and foolish ways, who had, until recently, pursued whatever was the opposite with demure tenacity.

He picked up the scraper, and as he returned to the green that showed in spots below the maroon paint, they came to him, the afternoons of his childhood, spent in the kitchen with Ruby, and the smell of her iron as it met damp cloth and mingled with the aromas from the stove, as she listened earnestly to his tales, asking questions to help him flesh out the details of character and plot. He remembered a parrot who talked to flowers, and a chartreuse snake.

Beneath the dark green paint he found the natural wood, and stopped to imagine who had sat in it before him. As he looked at the traces of different colored paint that remained deep in the lines of the wood, he stopped scraping and imagined a child.

He thought of Lilly, the daughter of slaves he and Ruby had invented, and of the father who had built her the chair, sanding the legs and the dowels that made up the back until they were smooth and round, carving the alphabet entwined with flowers along the back. Polishing and oiling the wood until it shone. Thinking of Bertha Crosby and the people he had met in his travels, LaRue saw the chair take shape by candlelight, carved out bits falling to the floor. Mounds of wood dust building and the little seat coming into being slowly, as strong dark fingers braided cane after hours.

LaRue sat back on the concrete and saw a girl rocking in the chair. He thought of a father who sneaked, each night, from field to field to learn to read, and brought back what he mastered for his child, and saw the child's mother sharing the consonants and vowels that he figured were worth his life. LaRue could see the child in the chair, receiving the precious letter gifts, an "A" or a "W," stolen and passed down.

"Yes," he thought, "I believe that's who sat here rocking . . . I believe, Mama Ruby, that it was she."

He worked on the chair every afternoon for a week, scraping and rubbing away the old paint to get to the golden oak underneath, returning to all of the memories of which its colored skins spoke, returning to the girl whose cherished alphabet grew by risk and stealth.

Watching her. Talking her into being. Coming to know her. Each day he was closer to the child he imagined sitting there before him, and he began to store away her tale for passing on.

He took his gloves off now and then to feel the grain of the naked wood that showed through the layers of paint, raised in places and streaked with smooth lines and dark, unpredictable swirls. He polished it with fine steel wool and sandpaper until it was, he felt, as it had been. With a sharp pointed tool he lifted the paint out of the crevices of the alphabet carved into the back, and rubbed the paint from the spools and spokes with a toothbrush. He oiled the wood and watched its rich natural tones emerge.

When he had started stripping the chair, he had meant to remove every trace of paint and make it just how it first was. But in the end, he surrendered to the bits of color that clung to its bends and corners, deciding that they had become a part of the whole. And although he had at first intended to have the seat recaned, he decided to leave it open, after all.